Praise for *Little Stalker*

"It's the story of a thirty-three-year-old one-hit-wonder novelist who's working as a receptionist at her father's medical office, stealing money from him, discovering secrets about her family's dark past, befriending the elderly, dementia-stricken Mrs. Williams, falling in love with a paparazzo while dodging a sociopathic gossip columnist, and spying on her celebrity obsession, neurotic, nebbishy, scandalously kinky New York film director 'Arthur Weeman.' All this energy makes [*Little Stalker*] compulsively readable." —Salon.com

"Hilarious and poignant. . . . This protagonist is an endearing figure."
—*The Seattle Times*

"A smart and hilarious read; you'll fall in love with Belle's neurotic heroine Rebekah Kettle as she struggles to make ends meet, unearth her father's secrets, find love, and manage a bizarre obsession with a movie director." —*People Style Watch*

"There are only so many good novels about single women living the big-city life, and Jennifer Belle's novels are among the best, the most human and genuine. Her first-person narrators are solitary female *flanuers* in continual drift through the pretty and gruesome parts of New York, and it's always a treat to be in on their streaming monologues as they . . . generally afflict their humanity on an otherwise indifferent world." —*Venus*

"Deliciously sardonic . . . You have to admire a writer who can create a character who is monumentally neurotic, yet oddly appealing nevertheless. Jennifer Belle has brilliantly done so with the protagonist—no, let's call her the heroine, because she's earned it—of *Little Stalker*." —*The Hartford Courant*

"'A lighthearted romp through New York' [is] precisely what Belle delivers. That it comes with a skewering as well makes it just that much more fun." —*New York Daily News*

"Will keep you hooked to the last page." —*Cosmopolitan*

"Belle suffuses this story with genuine sweetness."
—*The Indianapolis Star*

continued . . .

"Just buy the damn book." —*The New York Observer*

"Belle has created another unforgettable narrator—funny, self-absorbed, a little damaged." —*Kirkus Reviews*

"Sharp, incisive, and laugh-out-loud funny." —*The Baltimore Sun*

"Hugely funny." —*New York Daily News*

"Liv's wackiness gives this unruly novel moments of great humor, but in the end the book is as much about the peculiar landscape of the New York housing market—the snooty upper-class clients and the real estate agents who kowtow to them—as it is about a young woman finding her own independence." —*The Washington Post Book World*

"Belle deftly mines real estate as a metaphor, especially in Liv's affair with an impulsive architect, and her clients and fellow brokers are both terrifying and hilarious by turns." —*Entertainment Weekly*

"In this latest New York romp . . . Belle draws both Liv and the idiosyncrasies of the Manhattan real estate market so well that one can't help wondering just what is fiction (Belle did a stint as a broker herself) and what may be biography. . . . Belle's skewed take on life in the big city keeps the smirk-per-page ratio high . . . offbeat observations . . . hilarity and pathos." —*The Denver Post*

"[An] amusing . . . humorous real-estate romp with Manhattan views." —*US Weekly*

"If you think the Hub housing market is tough, take a look at this tale of high-stakes real estate—and sexual—wheeling and dealing. Belle knows the world she depicts." —*Boston Herald*

"Like a hot fudge sundae . . . delicious. Gutter-mouthed, smart-ass Liv, she's a Becky Sharp for our time." —*Gotham*

"You'll feel right at home with Belle's . . . follow-up to her racy debut, *Going Down*." —*Glamour*

continued . . .

Also by Jennifer Belle

Going Down

High Maintenance

FOR CHILDREN:

Animal Stackers
(illustrated by David McPhail)

Little Stalker

Jennifer Belle

Riverhead Books

New York

RIVERHEAD BOOKS
Published by the Penguin Group
Penguin Group (USA) Inc.
375 Hudson Street, New York, New York 10014, USA
Penguin Group (Canada), 90 Eglinton Avenue East, Suite 700, Toronto, Ontario M4P 2Y3,
Canada (a division of Pearson Penguin Canada Inc.) • Penguin Books Ltd., 80 Strand, Lon-
don WC2R 0RL, England • Penguin Group Ireland, 25 St. Stephen's Green, Dublin 2, Ireland
(a division of Penguin Books Ltd.) • Penguin Group (Australia), 250 Camberwell Road,
Camberwell, Victoria 3124, Australia (a division of Pearson Australia Group Pty. Ltd.) •
Penguin Books India Pvt. Ltd., 11 Community Centre, Panchsheel Park, New Delhi—110 017,
India • Penguin Group (NZ), 67 Apollo Drive, Rosedale, North Shore 0632, New Zealand (a
division of Pearson New Zealand Ltd.) • Penguin Books (South Africa) (Pty.) Ltd., 24
Sturdee Avenue, Rosebank, Johannesburg 1296, South Africa

Penguin Books Ltd., Registered Offices: 80 Strand, London WC2R 0RL, England

This is a work of fiction. Names, characters, places, and incidents either are the product of the
author's imagination or are used fictitiously, and any resemblance to actual persons, living or
dead, business establishments, events, or locales is entirely coincidental. The publisher does not
have any control over and does not assume any responsibility for author or third-party web-
sites or their content.

First Riverhead hardcover edition: May 2007
First Riverhead trade paperback edition: May 2008
Riverhead trade paperback ISBN: 978-1-59448-292-2

The Library of Congress has catalogued the Riverhead hardcover edition as follows:

Belle, Jennifer, date.
Little stalker / Jennifer Belle.
    p.   cm.
ISBN 978-1-59448-946-4
1. Single women—Fiction. 2. New York (N.Y.)—Fiction. 3. Dating (Social customs)—
Fiction. 4. Stalking—Fiction. 5. Stalkers—Fiction. I. Title.
PS3552.E53337L58   2007   2007001594
813'.54—dc22

PRINTED IN THE UNITED STATES OF AMERICA

10 9 8 7 6 5 4 3 2 1

For my father

Jenny kiss'd me when we met,
   Jumping from the chair she sat in;
Time, you thief, who love to get
   Sweets into your list, put that in!
Say I'm weary, say I'm sad,
   Say that health and wealth have miss'd me,
Say I'm growing old, but add,
   Jenny kiss'd me!

—James Leigh Hunt

1.

*November 19, 1937, her idol, the great
filmmaker Arthur Weeman, is born in Brooklyn,
New York, to parents Otto and Ethel Hamburger*

All day long I called Mr. Moviefone. *Arthur Weeman's* Swan Song *is playing exclusively at the Ziegfeld Theater, Fifty-fourth Street and Sixth Avenue. Today's remaining showtimes are 10, 12, 2, 4, 6, 8, 10, and 12.* And every two hours, at 10, 12, 2, 4, and 6, I imagined it starting without me. It was the first time in my whole life that I hadn't gone to the first showing of the new Arthur Weeman movie, but I had promised I would go to the eight o'clock with Derek Hassler.

Finally at six-thirty I called him to see if we were meeting at the theater.

"Hi," I said.

"Who's this?" he asked.

"It's me—Rebekah," I said.

"Rebekah who?" he asked. I paused. Was he kidding? Rebekah of Sunnybrook Fucking Farm. How many Rebekahs did he know? We had been dating for almost a month, a great first date followed by four mediocre ones but still, it had potential. Until that moment it hadn't occurred to me that he was dating Rebekahs all over town. After almost a month, I hadn't expected the question "Will you marry me?" but I didn't expect the question "Rebekah who?"

"This is Rebekah from the Bible," I said. "God commanded me to call you and tell you you're a jerk."

"Oh, Rebekah *Kettle*," he said. "I'm sorry, I just happen to know two Rebekahs. I'm glad you called, you know there's been something I've been meaning to talk to you about."

"Okay," I said.

"I really like you, Rebekah."

"I like you too, Derek." I actually hadn't been sure if I liked him until that moment when he said he liked me.

"And I'd really like to have sex with you but . . ."

"But?" I asked.

"But I don't want to have to call you."

"I don't understand," I said.

"I want to have sex, I just don't want to have the responsibility of feeling like I have to call you."

I paused for a moment. "If you don't call me, how am I going to know when we're going to have the sex?" I asked.

He didn't say anything.

"Are we just going to hope to bump into each other on the street?" I asked.

Not only would not speaking on the phone make having sex difficult, it would probably make having children an impossibility.

"I just don't want to feel obliged to call you. Like Thanksgiving. I know you wanted to meet my parents but now I'm not even sure I'm going. We'll already be closing the Valentine's issue and tonight I know we were supposed to have a date but I have to stay at the office," he said. "I have to cancel."

I'd had a feeling that Thanksgiving wasn't going to work out. It was three weeks away, which was like three years in early dating time. But I wasn't upset about that. What I was upset about was the movie. "When were you planning to let me know that? It's already six-thirty," I said. "I don't understand how you can do that."

"Sometimes I cancel," he said.

It was a statement of such simplicity and honesty that, as furious as I was, and as much as I hated him at that moment, I almost had to respect him for it. Sometimes I cancel. Sometimes, I cancel. The words lowered themselves slowly through me from my brain to my chest, like the chandeliers at the Metropolitan Opera House, indicating that the show was over.

There was nothing else to say after that. Sometimes he cancels.

Sometimes I hang up.

I sat quietly on my bed waiting for the blow from the breakup to set in. I steeled myself. I was a protester handcuffed to a condemned building waiting for the wrecking ball. I was Anne Boleyn walking to the chopping block, ready to forgive my executioner. But, strangely, I didn't feel the blow at all. That was the worst part, the realization that at thirty-three I could break up with people left and right and not even cause the tiniest spike on an EKG machine. My heart barely looked up from its television, just smiled and gave me the thumbs-up sign.

Ten years ago I would have wailed on the subway. I would have cried myself into a bout of vomiting that resulted in being hospitalized with an IV drip. I would have called Derek Hassler back and begged.

Instead, all I could feel was excitement that in less than an hour and a half I would be sitting in a red velvet chair at the Ziegfeld. I certainly wasn't going to let Derek Hassler ruin that. And I was glad to go alone and not have to hear his opinion of the film after in his gumbo-thick Southern accent.

Thank God for Arthur Weeman.

There are only so many things you can count on in this world. I know that every winter I can find a great vintage coat and that every spring it will fall apart. I know that every summer I can get perfectly sliced watermelon strips that taste faintly of cigarettes, jammed into round plastic containers at the Korean market. And I know that every fall there will be a new Arthur Weeman movie and that a deep depression will overcome me as soon as the closing credits start to roll. Because then I know that it will be a whole year until the next Arthur Weeman movie.

When I left my apartment, on Lafayette, across from the Public Theater, and walked toward the N/R, I saw one of those dirty street book-selling people standing in front of a long table of paperbacks.

I couldn't help but stop for one second and scan the covers for my own. I moved slowly from one end of the table to the other, seeing covers with all kinds of legs on them—legs crossed at the knee, at the ankle, in black stockings, in high-heeled boots—but not my cover's legs with their slender ankles and athletic knees, chiseled and airbrushed and tanned like no other's.

Then I saw it in a cardboard box on the sidewalk he hadn't even bothered to unpack. I picked it up. "How much is this?" I asked the book bum.

"Three dollars," he said. "You want it?" He grabbed a wrinkled plastic bag out of a bigger bag.

My first impulse was to rescue it and bring it home, but then I thought better of it. "No. But I could sign it for you and then you could get more for it." I smiled at him generously.

"You wrote this?" he asked, taking it from me.

"Yes, I did."

"How do I know it's you?" He looked down at my legs to see if they matched the cover.

"My picture's on the back," I said.

"Alright." He turned the book over and scrutinized the tiny photo. He seemed very unappreciative and I was starting to regret the whole thing but I felt it was too late to walk away. I pulled a pen out of my purse and signed my name on the title page. He watched me suspiciously. "Alright, we'll see if that works," was all he said.

Shockingly, the Ziegfeld wasn't that full. I had gotten there very early so I could sit in the fourth row, first seat on the left side of the left aisle, but even when the previews started the place hadn't filled up. I turned in my seat and surveyed the audience. If I had come with someone like Derek Hassler, I would have probably been forced to sit in the center, toward the back, and I glanced in that direction, thinking maybe he had changed his mind and come.

My other thought was that the new Arthur Weeman movie was the obvious place for me to meet my future husband. It almost seemed like the only place I could meet him. The only people who went to the new Arthur Weeman opening night at the

Ziegfeld were true Arthur Weeman fans. And the ones there alone were even bigger and better fans. But his biggest and best fans were the ones like me who not only went alone, and not only went to the Ziegfeld, but went to the first showing on the first day, which is what I would have done if it hadn't been for Derek Hassler forcing me to wait until the eight o'clock. But maybe he had done me a favor and maybe the reason I had never met my future husband at an Arthur Weeman movie before was because what kind of man went to the movies at ten a.m. on a weekday? Not a good kind.

The lights went down and I turned back around to face the screen. There were only two heads in the whole theater obstructing my view, a man and woman sitting in the third row, middle aisle. The woman had little side braids like Laura Ingalls Wilder, and I thought maybe I would try that, although I would probably end up looking more like Pocahontas than Laura Ingalls due to my thick, raincoat-black hair. She took off her shoes and put her feet up on the seat in front of her. I hated when people did that. Her feet were bare even though it was almost Thanksgiving, and her toes looked terrible, spread out and bulbous. The man she was with didn't seem to mind, but I considered moving so I wouldn't have to watch the movie through the skyline of her toes. But then the music started and my heart quickened. Nothing could ruin this. This was my New Year's Eve. This was my ball dropping. This was my favorite holiday.

And there was Arthur Weeman on the screen, wearing red satin boxer shorts and jumping around a punching bag with his dukes up. His legs were incredibly puny and covered in bruises. Already it was funny and I let out a strange lone laugh. He was coaching someone, saying, "You have to be tough, come on you gotta be tougher than that. Try to think like a lesbian," and then we saw that it was a six-year-old girl he was boxing with. The camera closed in on his face. He was a year older, and the skin under his eyes was vast and white, like tiny down comforters. Every year his signature silver egg-shaped glasses looked even bigger on him. The little girl in her big boxing gloves accidentally stepped on his toe and he hopped around in pain, holding his foot and eventually falling to the mat. And then, what always happened happened, tears started pouring down my face. The funnier the movie got, the more I cried. I cried because I was in the presence of genius.

The movie was about a punch-drunk boxer named Icharus Miller, a has-been with amnesia, and it was perhaps his greatest. Especially the scene where he finally gets to go on a date with a nurse he has been in love with for years and, much to the woman's horror, his prosthetic wax ear (his real ear was bitten off by another child boxing student) melts down the side of his face in the hot sun at the Central Park Zoo.

In one scene he fashions a second ear from a piece of prosciutto.

In one scene his dead father comes back to him and they box in his bedroom until his father knocks him out.

And in another scene Icharus sits in bed, weeping. It was hysterically funny and heart-wrenchingly sad and he was braver, more vulnerable and funnier than he had ever been.

When it ended I applauded, something I only did at Arthur Weeman movies, and so did maybe three other people. I noticed that the man in the third row, sitting next to the girl with the annoying feet, clapped.

I sat there for a minute unable to move. Then I felt a tap on my shoulder.

I turned around, thinking whoever this was he could be my

future husband. I was very surprised to see that it was my father.

"Hi, Toots," he said. "I've been sitting behind you the whole time."

"Please don't call me 'Toots,' " I said.

"I don't see what's wrong with Toots."

"What are you doing here?" I asked.

"You know, I was actually hoping to run into you," he said. "I remembered how we used to always catch the new Arthur Weeman flick the day it opened and I'd take you out of school and cancel my morning patients, and we'd have lunch at the Carnegie. I tried to come to the first show but I kept getting swamped. I can't believe I actually found you here. You haven't been here since this morning have you?"

It was true—it was the one thing we did together. An image came to my mind of us sitting at a table, next to framed photos of celebrities I had never heard of, the big brown paper bag of popcorn my father had brought from home to save money, sitting on the chair next to me.

"What'd you think of the movie? I was disappointed. It wasn't very good."

"I thought it was great," I said.

"Really? I thought it was pretty sophomoric stuff. I missed the first third but that didn't seem to matter."

"How can you call the greatest filmmaker of all times sophomoric? The whole world happens to disagree with you on this one." I made a sweeping gesture around the almost completely empty movie theater.

"If I were him I wouldn't have called it *Swan Song*. The press is going to get a kick out of that one."

"That's precisely why he called it that," I said. "He wants the press to have a field day. He doesn't care."

"How's your writing coming?" my father asked. "Are you making progress? Are you in touch at all with your editor?"

"No," I said. I couldn't believe he had the nerve to bring up my editor. "She's still recovering."

"From what?"

"From the conversation she had with you seven years ago at my book party."

"What? Why?"

And then I told him why I, Toots, was so angry at him. "Because you said bad things about my book at my book party."

He was completely shocked by my accusation. "What? I didn't say anything bad about your book."

"You told my editor that I wouldn't be a real writer until I wrote in the third person. She told me you said that."

"I just said that when you stop writing in the first person your work will finally cease to be autobiographical. And when you learn to write in the third person you will have grown as a writer."

"But, Dad," I said. "That doesn't make any sense. There are great autobiographical novels that are written in the third person and great completely fictional books that are written in the first person." My father was an idiot. I knew what I had said was true but I suddenly couldn't think of a single book I had ever read.

"That may be the case," my father said, "but all I said was that your book was an hors d'oeuvre."

"What?"

"I said your book was an hors d'oeuvre."

"Dad, it's not nice to say that something I worked on for five years is an hors d'oeuvre."

"I disagree," my father said. "It just says that the main course is yet to come. That this book is nothing compared to what's to come. I'm enormously proud of what's to come."

I couldn't fight him anymore. He didn't respect me. He didn't think I was a real writer. I imagined my book on a Ritz cracker served with a dollop of crème fraîche and a tiny fold of salmon. If you went to your local library and looked up my book in the Dewey decimal system, the librarian would bring it to you on the end of a toothpick, served on a large tray with a cocktail napkin.

I noticed that the woman with the hideous feet from the third row was turned around in her seat, staring at us. I glanced at the man she was with who had gotten up and was about to walk up the aisle. I almost did a double take because he looked so much like Arthur Weeman. For an instant, I thought it was him, but this guy was young and of course Arthur Weeman would never show up at his own movie. The man smiled at me and continued up the aisle and his date just kept staring at me. Then she stood up and walked over to me.

"Excuse me," she said. "Are you Rebekah Kettle?"

"Yes," I said.

"I loved your novel *The Hard Part,*" she said.

"Thank you!" I said, searching my father's face for a reaction to my great fame.

"I loved it," she said. "I read it in one day."

Everybody always made a point of telling me that they had read my book in one day—which in the past had really offended me but now I was used to it.

"It took me five years to write," I said, sounding a little too angry.

"Oh," she said. "I just meant . . . I mean, I really loved it. The whole older man thing. I'm a novelist too. My first novel is being published next fall. I hope it's a fraction as good as yours." She put out her hand and my father shook it.

"I hope it's better than a fraction of an hors d'oeuvre," I said.

"What?" she asked.

"Nothing," I said.

I tried to figure out where I had seen her before. She was the kind of girl I had always envied, a kelly green–wearing natural redhead with pale white skin and mood-ring eyes that I assumed would change obediently to match her shoes and purse. Her lashes glowed as if they were somehow backlit. She had an innocent expression, wide-open eyes, and squirmy lips that slid all over the place like a child's. Actually, what I figured out about her was her top lip was bigger than her bottom lip so when she smiled it had an upside-down effect of looking like a little girl doing a handstand.

"Is this your boyfriend?"

"Father," I said, horrified.

"Oh, it's so nice to meet you," she said, staring at my father who had risen when she approached as if we were at a fancy restaurant instead of a movie theater.

"That's not my boyfriend either," she said, pointing to the empty seats that she and the man had occupied. "Actually, I think he just developed a little bit of a crush on you, Rebekah." She sounded almost surprised by this. "He wanted to meet you but he's on a deadline so he had to run out of here."

I had no idea what to say.

"Isn't that nice!" my father said.

I really wasn't interested, if he was friends with this crazy girl.

"I was wondering if you would give me a blurb for my book," she said to me. "It's called *Daddy, May I?*"

"Terrific!" my father said.

"I'd love to send it to you. I was actually hoping you'd be

here," she said. "I had such a strong feeling I'd run into you, I almost brought it with me."

"What do you mean? Do I know you?" I asked.

"I'm sorry, my name is Ivy Vohl. I'm the editor of the gossip pages at *The New York Quille*."

"Oh right, I've seen you on TV," I said.

"Yes, well, that goes with the job. I'm a talking head, a celebrity pundit. Admittedly the first one at the opening of an envelope."

First one at the opening of a cliché, I thought. I still hadn't gotten over the fact that she had referred to herself as a novelist, and now she was already on to pundit.

"Oh yes, I'm familiar with your work," my father said.

I remembered that I had a friend whose roommate had gone on a date with her and she had taken off her clothes in the cab.

"I'm sorry, how did you know I'd be here?"

"You're a Weemanologist, aren't you?" she said. "You mentioned him in several interviews."

"What's your book about?" my father asked.

"It's chick lit, like yours, Rebekah," Ivy Vohl said. "I think you'll like it. When I read your book I slept with it under my pillow for weeks."

"My book isn't chick lit," I said. " 'Chick lit' is a derisive term invented by a frustrated magazine hack who probably wished like hell that she could write a novel, but knew she never could. That phrase brought female writers back two hundred years. If it continues, we'll be forced to write under male pseudonyms again."

"Rebekah . . ." my father said.

I looked up at the ceiling of the Ziegfeld, trying to calm myself by its splendor.

"Sorry," Ivy Vohl said. "I love chick lit. You have to admit it's a big trend in publishing."

"Well, we have to go," I said. I tugged on my father's sleeve like a little girl.

"You know all those items that ran about you in the *Quille* years ago? I wrote them," Ivy said, as if she wanted to collect a debt, as if she was handing me an item-ized bill.

"Thank you," I said, in spite of myself. I remembered for a moment what it felt like to have an item in the *Quille*, the waiters at the café seeing it, my father's patients, my friends, ex-friends, ex-boyfriends.

"It was very nice to meet you," my father said.

"The pleasure was mine," Ivy Vohl said, "but I didn't get your name."

"Dr. Frederick Kettle," he said.

"Oh, a doctor! But wasn't the character of the father in your novel a law professor?" she asked, accusingly, as if she had caught me in a lie.

"That's because it was a novel," I said.

"Wow. I consider myself to be somewhat of a Kettleologist, but I guess there's a lot about you I don't know. I know you went to the Gardener School because I had a friend who knew you there, and I know the building you live in on Lafayette, and you're dating an editor at *Maxim,* aren't you?"

"No, actually I'm not," I said. I suddenly felt very shaken up.

"I'm not scaring you, am I? It must be weird to meet your fans. I had a torrid affair once with a famous director who said, 'What is a fan? A fan is a stranger in love.' I've always remembered that. Anyway, even though your book came out, what, seven years ago and you've sort of disappeared, I'd still love to have a piece of your fame on my book jacket."

I didn't know what to say. If I had disappeared, then why did I have the misfortune to be here and to be seen by her? I wondered why I was even having this conversation. The way she talked about my fame, there didn't seem to be enough of it for me to be just giving away pieces. My fame felt very far away, like it had moved to L.A. without me, lost a lot of weight, gotten work done, and was now unrecognizable.

"Are you a physician?" Ivy asked my father.

"Yes, I am," my father said. Then he took out his tattered brown leather wallet and handed her his business card. The back of the card said YOUR APPOINTMENT IS_____DAY,_____ AT_____O'CLOCK.

"I'm actually looking for a new doctor," Ivy Vohl said.

"Why don't you call the office and Irmabelle will give you an appointment," my father said.

"Irmabelle—what a sexy name," Ivy Vohl said. I couldn't believe someone would say something like that to somebody's father.

My father blushed. Even in the red glow from the EXIT sign, I could see him blush.

"Why do you think it is that most doctors have affairs with their nurses?"

"Uh, I don't know anything about that," my father said.

"Sorry, it's just the journalist in me."

"Of course," my father said, as if anything in the *Quille* was journalism.

"So, what did you think of the movie? I wasn't too impressed."

"I completely agree," my father said.

She had gone to the bathroom twice during the film and practically missed the whole thing. A true Arthur Weeman fan knows not to eat or drink anything for several hours before showtime.

"I thought it was fantastic," I said.

Meanwhile, the place had completely emptied out of men, including the man who liked me, and it was Ivy Vohl's voice I heard inside my head, and not Arthur Weeman's.

2.

At 33, she meets her future husband,
the great writer Hugh Nickelby

Another good thing about breaking up with Derek Hassler was that I didn't have to take him to the Hugh Nickelby book party and I knew how much he had been looking forward to it.

On a date, a couple of weeks before, Derek had said that Hugh Nickelby was his favorite contemporary writer and *Thank You for Not Writing* was his favorite contemporary book. As a contemporary writer of a contemporary book myself, I couldn't help but feel a little bit insulted. I was used to it, however, because people were constantly telling me that *Thank You for Not Writing* was their favorite book and quoting long passages of it to me.

"Hugh Nickelby's a really good friend of mine," I had said.

"You're kidding," Derek Hassler had said.

I wasn't so much kidding as lying. I had never met Hugh Nickelby, but I had gotten an invitation to a book party that his American publisher was throwing for him. I had blurbed a book for the editor four years before and she had faithfully invited me to book parties ever since. Hugh Nickelby was going to be in New York on his book tour. "I'm actually having dinner with Hugh when he comes to New York in a couple of weeks. If you want, I can get you a signed copy of his book," I had said.

I had never been so happy to be a writer, than at that moment, just to be able to pretend that I knew Hugh Nickelby.

I searched through the piles of papers in my apartment, stacks of paper everywhere like bales of hay, for the book-party invitation. My apartment, a co-op I had bought with my movie-deal money, was completely empty because I never found any furniture I liked. All furniture seemed ugly to me for some reason, especially coffee tables. It was ugly in stores and ugly in other people's apartments. The only thing I had managed to buy was a mattress and box spring. I just told anyone who came over that I had moved in the day before. I had one friend in London, a girl named Sheba in Hempstead Heath, who had nice things, a headboard painted with swans and a gilt mirror in her kitchen reflecting beautiful china on an old wood table, but until I found things as nice as that, I felt better off with nothing.

I hadn't committed to a garbage can yet either, so Ivy Vohl's manuscript that she'd had promptly messengered to me, with its big-fonted cover page, sat in a plastic bag on a hook near the door, ready to be taken out to its smelly grave. Ivy Vohl, I'd noticed, was very big-fonted.

I couldn't find the invitation but I remembered it was at The Spotted Pig and I'd remembered the date because it was a Sunday which was an unusual night for a book party. I got ready and went at seven. When I got there, I pushed over to the bar and got a martini. I noticed that there were a few of each of Hugh Nickelby's books that were supposed to be for display purposes only, but I had an idea that I could have Hugh Nickelby sign one and send it to Derek Hassler to prove that Hugh and I were friends. I grabbed a paperback copy of *Thank You for Not Writing* and approached Hugh Nickelby. I told him how much I loved his books, and he incredibly nicely told me that he had loved *my* book. "I read it in two nights," he said in his heavy English accent. "I couldn't put it down."

"That means I'd have to write over a hundred and seventy-five books just to keep you entertained for one year," I said, which was extremely flirtatious for me. I was quickly falling for Hugh Nickelby. And why not? I thought. We were both writers, and I loved the way he looked—sort of shy and English and miserable to be in the middle of a crowd at his own book party. The place was totally packed.

"I wish you would write that many," he said. "After I read it I talked about you on the BBC. I must admit I have a bit of a soft spot for strong American female voices."

I had never been so happy to be a strong American female voice.

"Do you get to London? You should call me if you're there. You can get my number from Charles."

"I will!" I said. I didn't know who Charles was but I would certainly make it my business to find out. The moment felt so auspicious that I thought he might be referring to Charles Dickens himself and it seemed almost logical that Dickens would be the one to set us up.

"You *are* writing another book, aren't you? I'm looking forward to it."

It was the nicest thing anybody had ever said to me. I had thought of reasons I should write another book—it would be good for my career; I needed the money; I was under contract and if I didn't write another book, I'd eventually have to give the money back, money long since spent—but I had never thought about someone looking forward to reading my next book. It made me want to race home and get into bed with my laptop. Hugh Nickelby was looking forward to my next book. "Don't take too long with it. Although maybe I shouldn't put pressure on you. A watched kettle never boils and all that."

He was referring to my name!

"I boil," I said.

"I'm sure you do."

My cheeks were boiling that was certain. I had to change the subject. "Would you sign this?" I asked him, handing him his book. "Make it out to Derek Hassler."

"Sure," Hugh said, looking a little hurt that it wasn't for me. "Who's Derek Hassler?" he asked.

"He's just a friend of mine. But he's a big fan of yours. He wants me to tell you that he disagrees with your taste in music." I wished more than anything that I hadn't mentioned Derek Hassler. "Just write—'To Derek Hassler, too bad you cancel.'"

Hugh Nickelby opened his book and wrote, *To Hassler, You have terrible taste,* and signed his name. Hugh Nickelby was so sweet and humble that he hadn't even had a pen at his own book party—I'd had to give him one. At my book party I had practically worn a tool belt of them.

"Can I get you a drink from the bar?" I asked. He was surrounded by hundreds of people, signing his books for them, and nobody had bothered to ask him if he wanted a drink.

"Oh, that would be great," he said. "I would really appreciate that. I'll have a Grolsch."

"A what?" I asked.

"A Grolsch."

"I'm sorry, a what?" I asked. I was really struggling to hear him in the noisy bar and I really had no idea what he was saying. It was like no word I had ever heard before.

"A Grolsch," Hugh Nickelby said.

"I'm sorry, a what?"

"A Grolsch."

"A what?" My whole face was screwed up in concentration. Each time he said "Grolsch" it sounded like a different word, the vowels, if there were any, and the consonants rolling differently. I was starting to panic. My feet wouldn't move. I couldn't bring myself to just go to the bar and say the word to the bartender and see if he could make it out. I just kept thinking I would somehow understand it if he would just say it one more time. "A grog?" I said.

"Grolsch." He was so nice and patient each time, repeating that crazy word.

"I'm sorry, I'm having trouble hearing in here, what drink do you want?"

He looked dismayed. "A Grolsch," he said.

I smiled at him, completely bewildered.

"I know they have it here. I had one before," he said.

I was sweating through my Betsey Johnson book-party dress.

"A Grolsch," he said.

I shrugged.

Then his editor came over and whisked him away. "Hugh, I want to introduce you to Leonard Lopate," she said. She handed Hugh a Grolsch, which turned out to be a simple beer in a bottle with a green and white label.

I watched my relationship with Hugh Nickelby crumble in front of me. I didn't know what had happened. I had been able to understand English people in the past, but this strange word "Grolsch" had ruined everything. I certainly couldn't call him when I went to London if, when he answered the phone, I couldn't even understand what he was saying. What if he told me to meet him at the corner of Grolsch and Grolsch in West Grolschglouster Grolschinshire at Grolsch o'clock. If we couldn't even communicate about a simple drink order, we didn't exactly have a future together, sitting side by side at one of those long desks built for two, typing in tandem and bringing each other coffee and Grolsches in between lovemaking sessions. I watched Hugh Nickelby treading water away from me in an Atlantic Ocean's worth of fans.

I tried to remind myself of my theory that writers shouldn't be with writers—we were better paired with movie stars—but I felt miserable.

I had blown it.

The next morning I brought the autographed book to Derek Hassler's office at *Maxim* magazine and left it with the receptionist.

Without my asking, she hit speakerphone and punched in an extension.

"Y'ello," Derek said.

"You have a messenger here," she said.

Now I was a messenger.

"Please, leave me to my work, woman," Derek Hassler said. He was so weird. Editing *Maxim* magazine wasn't exactly work.

I waited in view of the receptionist for the elevator and then when I got on and the doors closed, I realized I was going up instead of down. The doors opened a couple of flights up and I got out, deciding I would wait for one going down. As I waited, a plaque next to the door of an office near the elevator caught my eye. JASON LISCH, PSYCHOTHERAPIST. Then the elevator doors opened, and I was just about to get back on, when I stopped and let them close and went back to the plaque. Jason Lisch. That was the name of the boy I was in love with in Hebrew School when I was in the seventh grade. When I was twelve. Jason Lisch was the first boy I ever kissed, half-sitting on a twin-hydrant on Ninety-third and West End.

I wondered if I should go into the office and see if it was the same Jason Lisch. But I didn't know if I looked good enough. I couldn't really tell in the brass elevator doors. If I didn't lose some weight by summer I wouldn't deserve to wear a sundress, I thought. But then I told myself not to be so hard on myself. Even the fattest person in the world *deserved* to wear a sundress.

I walked boldly up to the door and looked at the plaque. JASON LISCH, PSYCHOTHERAPIST. So he was a shrinker. The plaque looked expensive and had unusual lettering and an interesting design of two sort of African-looking heads. The plaque was so nice it made me wonder if Jason Lisch had turned out to be gay.

I had been determined to knock on the door, but now I couldn't. If he was a shrinker he could be in the middle of a session with someone and he'd be furious if I knocked.

I stood outside the door for a while, hoping someone would walk out of the office, maybe even Jason himself. I wondered if he would remember me. When we were friends I had worked on a project for Social Studies. My topic was Paul Revere, and Jason had helped me invent a board game called *One If By Land, Two If By Sea* that incorporated the events of Paul Revere's life with little plastic horses as game pieces. We worked on it a few times after Hebrew School in my bedroom—a trail from Beacon Hill to Lexington, with funny stops along the way like Ye Olde McDonald's. You had to draw cards and answer questions about Paul Revere and the Revolutionary War.

I remembered the time line I had made. In 1734, he is born. At

12, he apprentices as a silversmith and earns extra money as a bell ringer at the Old North Church. At 22, he marries Sarah Orne. One year later, he becomes a master goldsmith and his first child is born. At 35, he buys the house that can still be visited today in Boston. At 38, his wife dies during the birth of their eighth child. At 39, he participates in the Boston Tea Party. At 40, he rides to Lexington with warnings that the British are coming. This will forever be remembered as the midnight ride of Paul Revere. At 52, his sixteenth child is born to his second wife. He does many other things, including working as a dentist, and at 83, he dies.

He could lie in bed at night, a lantern flickering on his bedside table, and hear the sound of his bells chiming all over Boston. He would drift off happily to sleep, thinking about the Stamp Act or something important, not have to take two Excedrin PM like I did every night.

I wondered what it would be like to date a great man like Paul Revere. I dated men like Derek Hassler who, by age 37 shared a one-bedroom apartment on the Upper West Side and worked as an editor at *Maxim* magazine. In three hundred years you probably wouldn't find too many kids making a board game out of the life of Derek Hassler.

If Jason opened the door, I was prepared to recite the entire life of Paul Revere but what would I say about myself, I wondered. I thought of my time line turned into a game, sprawled across an oaktag gameboard, with little Excedrin bottles as game pieces. At 22, I graduate from Bennington, where I have spent the better part of four years taking the bus home to New York. At 26, I publish my novel, *The Hard Part,* which becomes a critical and commercial success, and I sign a contract for a second book. At 28, I fail to hand in any pages and I am in default of my contract. In 2001 the World Trade Center is destroyed by terrorists.

The last thing on my time line—the World Trade Center attacks—hadn't really happened to me, I realized, it had happened to New York, so it didn't really count.

There had to be more. I'd made a lot of friends, but one by one they had all moved to L.A. to become either studio executives or marry them, coming home every few months at first and taking in great swallows of the New York air, but eventually coming back in lighter and lighter jackets and finally never darkening New York's door again with all their sunshine. So I had become strangely friendless. There were, I counted on my fingers, nine serious long-term relationships, if I counted Richard De La Croix twice, but those didn't seem at this moment exactly like accomplishments. My mind went blank. And then, oh, yes. I realized I had skipped something.

At almost 13, I am sent to Florida by myself to visit relatives I have never met before during Easter break. There is an air of urgency and panic surrounding the trip and I'm not exactly sure why I'm going. I miss my flight because my father gets confused and drives me to JFK instead of Newark, and as we sit in the airport waiting for the next flight out, my father tells me that he has a headache. The reason I remember this so clearly is that my father, a doctor, has never been sick or had anything wrong with him in his entire life. He sends me to the airport store to buy an individual pack of ibuprofen and a cup of black coffee. Caffeine, he explains, helps a headache, it's a *stimulant*, the medicine moves more quickly through the bloodstream. Strangely, I am intrigued by this conversation, this rare father-daughter talk. I get the feeling it is in lieu of the birds-and-bees lecture I have been half-expecting. He has taught me something valuable that I can take with me. I watch in amazement as he swallows pills I have never seen him take. When he hugs me at the gate, I feel that something has changed. I have not been allowed to drink coffee up to this point, but now I feel that I have been given the go-ahead and choose it for my beverage on the plane.

When I get there, there is nothing to do. They don't seem to really want me there, and I am forced to sleep on what they call the daybed—a hard wooden bench in the sewing room. For two weeks I swim in the pool that belongs to their complex, all day every day, coming back to their house only to eat meals of eggs and cheese and milk, like Heidi, and sleep on the wooden bench. I drink a lot of coffee with milk and sugar in it. The day before I am to return home, they take me to Disney World early in the morning and we decide, since we are interested in different things, to meet at "It's a Small World" at a certain time.

In the ladies' room, I don't even recognize myself. I look taller and I have lost a lot of weight. My face is thin and my skin is dark brown. I am an entirely different person, thin and grown-up. I had waited on a couple of lines to go on a couple of rides but who knew that the line for the ladies' room was the line for the most magical attraction of all? Maybe it came with the price of admission, the Disney hall of mirrors, you get to look like a completely new person. You get to like what you see.

That afternoon, the man who runs the "Pirates of the Caribbean" makes eye contact with me when I slide into the seat and snap the safety bar into place. When it's over, he follows me and says it's his break time and how would I like a behind-the-scenes tour of the place?

Finally this trip is getting interesting. If he had been a boy my age, I would have figured there was no way he liked me and I would have made a sarcastic comment and walked away. I would have been too shy to be myself. But because he is old, twenty-three he tells me, I look him right in the eyes (he has taken off his pirate patch at this point) and go with him, babbling something about how I have a lot of pirate experience myself because I had been in the chorus of a production of *The Pirates of Penzance* in sixth grade. I make sixth grade sound like it's way in my past, and in a way it is, a whole year in the past.

Because he is not my age I suddenly realize the power I possess over him. I wear my mouse ears like heart-shaped glasses. I can't help myself. It's just how I am. At least now that I have seen myself in the enchanted mirror. I'm beautiful now, so I'm irresistible to this man, and I'm from New York, so I'm tough.

We have sex in the employees-only lounge. It feels like nothing. Like a small mistake or a slip of the tongue. Or at worst, like something I shouldn't be doing like buying potato chips after school.

I fly home, determined not to tell anyone my secret. It doesn't matter, I decide, it's just something I tried once. Big whoop. But I am pregnant. My period, which I have had eleven times already, doesn't come.

The realization hits me in Ms. Gorney's hygiene class as she is showing us a plastic model of a vagina. I have no uncertainty like girls have in young-adult books or in the movies. I simply *know*.

For one month I scramble to come up with a plan, but I can't. My parents won't let me have a dog so I'm pretty sure they won't let me have a baby. I feel almost tough enough to go ahead and have it, and one day, when my parents and I are having dinner at Hunan Balcony, I secretly look up on the paper place mat that it will be born in the Chinese Year of the Dragon—which is compatible with me, a monkey—and name it Joshua if it is a boy, but in the end I tell my mother and have an abortion instead. My mother wants to know what boy got me pregnant and I tell her it was just a boy my own age I went on a couple of dates with in

Florida. I base the character of the boy who got me pregnant on a boy I had seen at the pool who wore bathing trunks with sailboats on them and had smiled at me one time.

I lie on a table in a doctor's office staring in disbelief at a poster that has been taped to the ceiling. I find it very ironic because not only is it strange to tape a poster to the ceiling but it is a poster of a smiling, blond-haired blue-eyed baby wearing a diaper and the words EVERYTHING'S GONNA BE ALRIGHT printed over his head. I ask the nurse if it's supposed to be a sick joke and she says she doesn't know what I am talking about.

The doctor turns off his vacuum machines and tells me it's over and for a single moment I cannot distinguish between myself and it, I think I must be gone too, but then I realize I am alive and I think the terrible thought that the unborn are not as important as the already born. That I care more about myself being alive than anything.

My mother says this can be our secret; we don't have to tell my father. She doesn't give the doctor my real name in case the doctor knows my father. But there is a girl, another girl in the waiting room with me. She is wearing roller skates and she is getting an abortion too. However, when hers is over she roller skates out of there, her blond ponytail swinging, as if nothing at all has just happened to her, while I, on the other hand, am bent over, hobbling. The procedure didn't go so well for me and I get an infection and end up missing the whole rest of the school year, so in the end, my father knows, but he doesn't say anything. I don't see much of him because he moves out and they get a divorce.

And it is that year, I think, that I merge with Arthur Weeman. I am too old for Paul Revere and Sir Francis Drake and *Little House,* but behind the red-velvet curtain at the Ziegfeld is *Adopting Alice,* is Arthur Weeman under the spell of a thirteen-year-old girl, and I think finally here is someone who understands me. I see it seventeen times and replay key scenes in my mind when I am lying in bed at night. I imagine that I'm in the movie, and my Disney World and abortion experiences are hilarious and yet moving scenes that he and I have improvised together.

Something in the way he looks at Alice with so much attention and interest and respect makes me see how much deeper he is than all other men. He even makes New York seem different, the place where I have lived my entire life. Here was the real adult New York, where a girl not unlike myself, could step from the playground where she did not belong, into a penthouse where she clearly did. It is then I follow Arthur Weeman up that spiral staircase and make my escape to him. I do not become a woman by having sex in Disney World. I become one by seeing *Adopting Alice.* I go to the box office at the Ziegfeld and say, "One child's ticket please," and when I come out at the end of the movie, my ticket stub reads FULL-PRICED ADULT.

The door next to Jason Lisch's office opened, startling me. A man walked out, looked at me quickly, and then turned away politely, probably figuring I was a nutjob waiting for the shrink.

That was it. The key events in my life. That was all I had accomplished in my thirty-three years.

I couldn't believe how little I had achieved and how little I was probably gonna.

The thought reminded me of the dream I had the night before that I was supposed to meet someone at a movie theater on - Thirty-third Street, and I accidentally walked all the way to Eighty-third Street without realizing it. In the dream I stood looking up at the street sign, 83RD ST, bewildered. I suddenly realized what it meant. I was thirty-three years old, supposed to *meet someone,* a man maybe, on Thirty-third Street, but instead go alone all the way to Eighty-third—the age a psychic once told me I would die. The age Paul Revere died. It was one of those dreams that flattened me all day. My life was rolled out into a New York City street map. Flat like a board game. Engraved like a plaque.

Jason Lisch, I thought, must be a really great shrink if just standing outside his office door made me think about my life like that and analyze my own street sign dream.

It had been a long time since I had thought about my abortion. I had never really thought about it at all actually. The memory had just floated mute in its airtight jar of formaldehyde.

I leaned against the wall with my head on the plaque, exhausted. Then my mouth opened up wide and I started to cry silently. My mouth stretched open wider and wider.

At thirty-three, I date some guy named Derek Hassler. I meet and almost marry the writer Hugh Nickelby, but that doesn't work out. I stand outside Jason Lisch's office door, who may or may not be the same Jason Lisch I went to Hebrew School with, and even if it is, what good will it do and what exactly do I expect will be accomplished by talking to Jason Lisch and reminiscing about Paul Revere and all that one if by land two if by sea nonsense, and I bawl my eyes out, crying harder than I have ever cried.

Paul Revere was in the past. He was dead to me now.

I pressed for the elevator and got on, still unable to completely stop crying. Unfortunately there was a pregnant woman already in it. She was the stylish type of pregnant woman who looked like she probably worked energetically at her office until the very last second, her water breaking all over her oxblood shoes, calling her secretary with instructions up until she crowned. After a few floors she said, "Are you okay?" The last thing you expect when you are crying in a New York City office building is to be confronted with it. I was so surprised by her question that I answered it.

"I was pregnant," I told her. It felt strange to say the words out loud.

"Oh no," she said.

I wiped my eyes dry on my sleeve. I looked up into her eyes and just nodded my head.

"I'm so sorry," she said. Then she hugged me. She put her arms around me and her big round stomach pressed into my chest because she was so much taller. I felt my heart beating against her stomach. If the baby kicked at that moment it would kick me in the heart, I thought. She rubbed my back in little circles. "You must feel so empty." I nodded, my head against her breasts. "But that feeling will go away. I know it will," she said.

"Thank you," I said.

"Your hormones are probably doing a number on you. You should drink a lot of chamomile tea. You know, you should go to my psychic kinesthesiologist, she can help you with all that. Her name is Anita Stefano. She's in the book. You'll get pregnant again in no time."

She said it with so much force I thought maybe I would. We got off the elevator and stood on the mosaic floor of the lobby. "When's your due date?" I asked.

"April eighteenth."

"That's the date of the midnight ride of Paul Revere," I recited. "April eighteen, seventeen seventy-five."

"Really!" she said, sounding thrilled and lighting up like a copper lantern. "Thank you so much for telling me that."

They say that when one door closes, or stays closed as in the case of Jason Lisch's office door, another door opens. And when I got home that night there was a strange message from the girl I had met a few days before, my annoying fan from the Ziegfeld, Ivy Vohl, saying that the man she'd been there with really wanted to meet me.

I thought of him walking up the aisle and smiling at me.

I called her back. "How'd you get my number?" I asked.

"Your father gave it to me," she said. "I called him at his office and asked him if you were dating anyone and he said no."

"Well I am dating someone," I said. "Quite seriously. My father doesn't know about it because he lives in England."

"Great, then you can go out with my friend, and the English guy will never know," she said.

"Why couldn't your friend come over and talk to me himself?" I said.

"Well that's really my fault. I forced him to go because I wanted to talk to you alone."

"What does he do?" I asked. He was probably a hot-dog guy or something.

"He's a photographer. He works for me at the *Quille*."

"What's his time line?" I asked.

"His what?"

"His time line."

"What's a time line?" she asked. "You mean his schedule?"

"No, his history." Ivy Vohl and I had nothing in common.

"I don't know, he's from New York. He's Jewish."

"What's wrong with him?" I asked.

"Nothing really," she said. "He's great."

Still, I didn't trust her. She didn't know me, we had only had one horrible ten-minute conversation, and she would have no way of knowing what I looked for in a guy, especially since I didn't even know.

"I don't think so," I said.

"Even though he looks like a young Arthur Weeman? Don't worry, I didn't tell him you're obsessed with Arthur Weeman."

"I'm not obsessed with Arthur Weeman," I said.

"Yes you are. You even defended his terrible movie."

"That's because he's the greatest filmmaker of all time."

"I really think you should go out with him, Rebekah. He said he was going to go out and buy your book. That's already going to more effort than ninety-nine percent of men would go to."

"What's his name?" I asked.

"Isaac Myman."

She gave me his number which I wrote down even though I had no intention of calling him.

"So are you reading my manuscript?" she asked. "I could really use that blurb. I'm such a big fan of yours, it would really mean a lot."

"I have a lot of things on my desk," I said, looking around my deskless apartment. Arthur Weeman wrote on a legal pad sprawled out on a queen-sized bed in his office. That was the kind of office I would like.

I got off the phone and went back downstairs to buy some chamomile tea. Even though my abortion had happened twenty years before, I thought I should take the pregnant woman's advice and try to balance my hormones. The elevator stopped on the second floor and two men got on wheeling a gurney. "Watch your back," one of them said to me. I moved into the far corner of the elevator and they wheeled the thing in at an angle. That's when I realized that on the gurney, was a corpse fully encased in a gray body bag.

"Oh my God," I said. "Who is it?"

"Old woman in 2B," the man said. In one day I had ridden in

elevators with a pregnant woman and a dead one. They wheeled her off the elevator and I followed behind them, horrified to be so close to death. Death had been in my building and I had been home at the time.

If souls rise, hers had risen through my floor and ceiling. Or it had blown past my window if souls leave through the window like they did in the early film versions of *Little Women* and *Wuthering Heights.*

"This is the last time I open the door for *you,* Mrs. Davis," the doorman said sarcastically.

The men wheeling the gurney laughed.

At the end of my time line, when I was wheeled out of my building in a body bag, I didn't expect a big procession like Evita, or paparazzi like Jackie O, but I did hope for more than just a nasty remark from the moronic part-time doorman. All night I thought I smelled death. I had one of my recurring movie-theater dreams, but in this one the movie theater was outside in some kind of tropical paradise. The screen was suspended in midair and there were rows of spouting fountains on each side of the seats, and I was there with someone. When I woke up I realized the movie theater in my dream was heaven and I was there with Arthur Weeman. Then I thought, no, maybe it was that man, Isaac Myman, I was with.

I got out of bed and walked into the kitchen, trying to shake it off. Anyone who associated with Ivy Vohl wasn't the man for me. I looked down at the Sweet 'N Low packet I had written his name and number on. Isaac Myman. I ripped it open, emptied its precious contents into my coffee, and threw it away.

Then I guiltily turned on my laptop and Googled him just to be thorough and a girl of my time but all that came up were religion sites and Bible quotes.

Rebekah consented to marry **Isaac** even before she
ever met him.

And it came to pass, when he had been there a long
time, that Abimelech King of the Philistines looked
out a window, and saw, and, behold, **Isaac** was sporting with Rebekah his wife.

Rebekah lifted up her eyes, and when she saw **Isaac**
she dismounted from the camel.

I had noticed him at the Ziegfeld, his Bob Dylan hair and uncanny resemblance to Arthur Weeman, but I wouldn't exactly
have gotten off my camel if I'd been on one, married him, and
gone around sporting in windows.

I had forgotten Isaac was the name of the character Rebekah
married in the Bible.

It was never a good idea to start Googling. It was the most
lonely and desperate thing a person could do and I clicked on my
"history" and cleared it, noticing that the last person I had
Googled had been Derek Hassler. I wondered if Isaac Myman
had Googled me.

Then I did what I did every morning from nine to eleven. I
watched two back-to-back episodes of *Little House on the Prairie.*
Since neither of my parents had believed in God while I was
growing up, aside from a very brief stint at Hebrew School, *Little
House* was my only real religious training. I was as much a sheep
in Reverend Alden's flock as the Ingalls, the Olesons, and Doc
Baker. Because of *Little House,* I considered myself to be a deeply
spiritual person. It was my church, even if I attended naked
in bed.

Moments after it started I knew Mary was going to go blind again today. Doc Baker would come to the house and say it was because of a bout of scarlet fever she'd had as a young child. Pa would take her to Mankato. Mary would sit in a chair feeling sorry for herself. She wouldn't let Laura brush her hair. Ma would give her a talking to.

I pulled the covers up to my neck. Mary pulled the lantern closer and closer to the book she was trying to read, and squinted up at Pa behind her little round glasses and already my eyes filled with tears.

The phone rang and I answered it even though it was my father. "I have to talk to you about something, Toots," he said.

"Don't call me 'Toots.' "

"What do you want me to call you?" he asked.

"How about Half-Pint?" I said.

"Huh? As in a half pint of beer?"

"Never mind," I said. I had to end this conversation before the commercial break ended. "I can't really talk now."

"You're not watching that child's program, are you?" my father asked.

"It's not a child's program." My ex-shrink had said that I wasn't alone. Many of her adult women patients watched it from nine to eleven every morning. Women everywhere were secretly doing it. That was one thing I really missed about her, she knew all kinds of facts about *Little House on the Prairie* and about Michael Landon, the actor who played Pa. Ivy Vohl might have called her a Prairieologist. She was also a huge Arthur Weeman buff.

"I'd like you to come into the office today," my father said. When you are a writer everyone assumes you have nothing better to do all day than go to their offices, or even worse, sit in the playground with them and their toddlers. There was no way I was going to interrupt one minute of Mary going blind. He even had the nerve to give me an appointment. "My ten-fifteen is open," he said. I could hear other lines ringing. "Oh Jesus," he said.

"Where's Irmabelle?" I asked.

"Oh Jesus, what button? Hold on," he said and hung up.

I tried calling back but the phone just rang and rang. Then, as Mary had her eyes examined in Mankato, I started wondering what my father wanted to talk to me about. I had borrowed two thousand dollars from him about twelve years before, but he had never mentioned it, so I didn't think that was it. So then I thought maybe he was sick.

I grudgingly took a shower and got dressed.

I stopped at the deli to get a chamomile tea for my hormones and then took the subway for what I decided would be the last time. I would never take the subway again, I decided, under any circumstances. I couldn't stand to see everyone reading other people's books. The woman across from me was completely immersed in a certain paperback I was particularly jealous of. It was my own personal anthrax attack. At least with anthrax you could wear one of those hundred-dollar gas masks, but with everyone reading other people's books, you were totally defenseless.

I changed seats and found a nice-looking man to sit across from who was reading *The New York Times*. The girl I had just moved away from laughed out loud but I forced myself not to look. I just stared straight ahead.

That's when I noticed the name Arthur Weeman in big letters on the back of the man's paper. I leaned forward to get a better look.

Arthur Weeman was having a sale. All of the props and furniture that had appeared in three decades of his films were being sold. He had been storing them all in a huge warehouse in New Jersey, near the Hermit Films studio. It was a four-day sale starting Saturday and now it was Tuesday. Today was the last day. It had been going on this whole time and I hadn't known about it. I had been lying around doing nothing while the most precious objects in the world were being sold across the river. I memorized the address of the warehouse and ran out of the subway.

I called Tel-Aviv car service and ordered a minivan and driver for the day and told them to pick me up at my father's office. Then, as soon as I got there, I told my father I had to leave.

"I was hoping you could help me out today," he said.

"What!" I said, horrified. I was getting one of my headaches. It was like Paul Revere was riding his stallion through my brain yelling, "A headache is coming, a headache is coming."

"I have a headache," I said.

"Again?"

"Yes, again," I said.

"Agh, I think it's all in your head," he said.

"Yes, Dad, my headache is in my head."

The phones were ringing off the hook and he was just sitting hunched at his desk, obsessively shuffling a deck of cards.

"Where's Irmabelle?" I asked.

"She had an emergency," he said.

My cell phone rang indicating that Tel-Aviv car service was outside. "Just stay until four," my father said.

"Sorry, Dad. I can't." There was no way I was going to miss the Arthur Weeman sale. "I have to go to a college in New Jersey to give a lecture on writing."

"What college?" my father asked.

I suddenly couldn't remember a single college in New Jersey.

I was about to just make up a name when he said, "Princeton?" and I said, "Yes, they sent a car for me."

"At least pull the charts," he said.

That had been my job when I was a little girl, pulling all the charts of patients whose last names began with O through Z because A through N were too high up for me to reach.

I looked at the appointment book and pulled the files for his third, fourth, and fifth patients because the first two were scheduled by him and I didn't have time to decipher his handwriting. Then I grabbed a blank check from the office checkbook in case I didn't have enough in my own account, and ran out of the office and slid into the back of the van.

3.

At 33, she tends to her father in his time of need

As we drove through the Holland Tunnel, I tried not to think about terrorism, and by the time we got to the warehouse I was shaking with excitement. My headache had retreated like the English. I told the driver to wait for me.

"How long?" he asked.

"I'm not sure, five or six hours should do it," I said.

The warehouse didn't open until eleven and it was about five till. A line had formed and I got on the end of it, scanning it quickly to see if I knew anyone and could therefore get closer to the door. I counted sixty people ahead of me. I sized up my competition. I was relieved to see that they seemed like a pretty grungy bunch. They didn't look so much like fans as scary New Jersey flea-market people. The warehouse was surrounded by nothing but concrete. Fort Lee and Leonia had been a film capital at the turn of the century, but now Hermit Films Studio and this warehouse were the only remnants.

The girl who was first on line pivoted around and smiled condescendingly at the crowd behind her and that's when I saw that it was my fan from the Ziegfeld, Ivy Vohl. I shifted quickly so she wouldn't see me. Even though talking to her might have meant moving up to the front of the line, talking to her wasn't worth even that.

When the doors finally opened, I pushed my way in as fast as I could but I had to wait a minute for my eyes to adjust to the dark. Kids who must have been interns stood around the perimeter of the huge room.

I walked up to one of them. He was very short and fat, the kind of boy I had always liked since elementary school. "How are things arranged?" I asked.

"What do you mean?" he said, looking at me as if I were a lunatic.

"By film? By genre? In chronological order? Are comedies and dramas separate?" I was trying to get the lay of the land so I could come up with a game plan. I wanted to start with my favorites of his comedies, *Adopting Alice* and *The Dim Sum of All Parts*, and then go for his less popular works, where I would have a better chance of getting the good stuff. Since this was the last day of the sale I was sure there would be nothing left from *Take My Life, Please*, *The Carlyle Capers*, and *The Analyst*.

"There's no particular order, ma'am," the intern said. I couldn't help but notice the word "ma'am," but I didn't have time to confront him about it. "Furniture and props are on the first two floors and costumes are on the third."

"Is Arthur Weeman going to be here?"

"Oh yeah," the intern said. "He's here. He just finished cleaning the men's room and now he's manning register number three."

The guy obviously thought I was an idiot.

I turned and walked away but I heard him say, "Arthur Weeman fans are fucking nuts."

But I didn't care. I walked over to two gondolas leaning against the wall, replete with red velvet cushions. A manila tag on the stern said LIFE IN VENICE on one side and $200 on the other. I tried to think of what I could do with two gondolas. Pretty much nothing. I decided to only take one of them. Next to it was a round black art deco end table with a tag that said THE MERMAID PARADE and was only fifty dollars. *The Mermaid Parade* was the second Arthur Weeman movie I had ever seen. I picked up the table and looked around for some kind of a cash register, but I couldn't see anything. Besides the interns, a few people were milling around, but Ivy Vohl had disappeared.

I marched back over to the intern, carrying my new *Mermaid Parade* end table. "I want this," I said. "And I want a lot of other things." He wrote out some kind of a receipt on a waiter pad and put a red dot on the table.

"You get a sales slip from me for everything you want, and then you take the slips to the cash register there, all the way in the back."

I grilled him on the system for a while and when I was sure my end table was safe from other fans I temporarily abandoned it and ran over to the bed that I immediately recognized from *Take My Life, Please*. It was the very bed that Arthur Weeman and Lauren Bacall had made love on in the last scene. It was two thousand dollars. Next to it was the oxygen tank from *The Tumorist*. Behind that was the scale that they weighed the tumor on, and the chandelier from *Fortune and Fame*. And the actual bottle from *Genius in a Bottle*. I waved wildly to the intern who walked slowly over to me. "I want all of this," I said, pointing to dozens of things. He filled out slips and put red dots on everything. I couldn't believe Ivy Vohl was so stupid as to have skipped over these things.

"Do you mind if I ask what you're going to do with an oxygen tank?" the intern asked.

"My father's a doctor," I said, as if that were the most obvious thing in the world.

"And let me guess, your mother's a gondolier," he said.

I bought chairs and lamps and rugs with the original ketchup bloodstains. I bought art, the giant plastic hot dog from the roller-coaster scene at Coney Island, and a wooden file cabinet that had been used in several movies. I paused over the desk from *Adopting Alice,* where Arthur Weeman as Mitch Eichman had written his failed novel. I had never owned a desk before—I'd only written in cafés or in bed—but this was too irresistible to pass up.

On the third floor, I thought I would swoon. I was in a frenzy. One woman held up a private-school girl's uniform from *Adopting Alice.*

"I'm taking that," I said, grabbing the costume. I was afraid to put down the Underwood typewriter from *Literary Suicide* that I had lugged up from the second floor after wresting it from the arms of what looked like a cab driver. I didn't even bother to look at tags anymore. I just grabbed anything that looked like it would fit. I put a triumphant red dot on a wedding gown, a forties suit, a floppy hat, and a fringed suede vest.

A few minutes before they closed, I paid for everything. It all came to just under twenty-two thousand dollars. I gasped at the amount. But then I thought it was only one thousand for each of Arthur Weeman's films. Plus it would furnish my entire empty apartment. You would pay that much for a few ugly things at a horrible store like Crate & Barrel. All of this was an incredible bargain. I filled out my father's check, making it payable to Hermit Films, and signed his name with my usual expertise, making the letters small and tense and look like they spelled the words "Mad Kill" instead of "Frederick Kettle."

The kid behind the cash register looked at the check.

"Uh, are you Dr. Frederick Kettle?" he asked.

"Yes, I am," I said. "My friends call me Ricki. Dr. Ricki."

"Uh, do you have any I.D.?"

"No, I don't," I said, sounding as annoyed as possible. "I came here straight from my rounds. One moment, please, my beeper just went off." I pulled out my cell phone and dialed my father's office. "Dr. Kettle," my father answered. "It's Dr. Ricki. Is everything okay?" I said. "Dr. Who? Rebekah?" he asked. "Are there a lot of patients for me tomorrow?" I asked. "What? Does that mean you're coming in tomorrow?" my father said. His other line was ringing and he sounded desperate. "Yes," I said, "it sounds urgent. I'll be there, stat." I hung up and the boy just stood there looking at me.

"Wait here," he said, and carried the check away to show it to someone. A few minutes later he returned. "I can't find anyone to approve this," he said. "Just write your phone number on it." I wondered for a moment if I had made a mistake to buy so much when I was running out of money, when I saw the old-fashioned liver-pink shrink's couch from *The Analyst* leaning against the counter. I couldn't believe it hadn't been sold.

"I want this," I screamed at the intern.

"The sale's over," he said. "It's six o'clock. The cash registers are closed."

"I have to have this one last thing," I said. I was also regretting not having bought the second gondola.

"The sale is over, ma'am," he said.

I had arranged for delivery for the bed and the gondola and some of the bigger pieces of furniture I had bought, but I was planning to load the end table and some of the smaller things in the minivan. As soon as the intern turned away, I started to pull the shrink's couch out of the warehouse doors.

The Tel-Aviv driver saw me and got out of the car to help me. The shrink's couch wouldn't fit into the back of the van.

"Please," I said, "you have to help me."

"We can tie to roof," he said.

I helped him hoist it up onto the roof of the van and he got a bungee cord from the front seat and started to tie the V-shaped wooden legs of the couch to the handles on the doors. I went back in to get the rest of the things I had bought.

When I approached the van again, I saw someone talking to the driver. The driver was yelling something. I walked as quickly as I could, wheeling the baby carriage from *Adopting Alice,* and I saw that the person the driver was talking to was Ivy Vohl and she was trying to remove the bungee cord and pull down my therapy couch.

"Oh, hi," she said. "What are you doing here?"

I looked at her in disbelief. What would I not be doing here? I had never hated anyone more than at that moment. How could she have known about this sale and not told me about it on the phone the night before? "When did you find out about this sale?" I asked.

"I was the one who first *announced* it in my column. I would have thought you would have been the first one here on Monday."

"Why are you stealing my therapist's couch?" I asked.

"I bought it," she said. She waved the receipt in my face and bore her finger into the red dot on the fake leather surface that I hadn't noticed.

"There must be some mistake," I said. I had to have this couch. *The Analyst* was Arthur Weeman's most beloved movie, and he had lain on that couch in at least six scenes.

"I'm sorry, Rebekah, but the couch is mine," she said.

"What should I do?" the driver asked, looking miserable.

"Since it's already up there, we might as well just make two stops," Ivy said, getting into the back of the van and slamming the door closed. I got in on the other side. She told the driver her address in Brooklyn. "I hope you won't let my getting the best thing at the sale interfere with your giving me a blurb." She looked at me, smiling.

"Ivy, I would love to blurb your book, I'm sure it's great, it's just that I have a strict policy of reading everything I blurb and I'm just not sure I can get to it in time."

"Oh, there's plenty of time. I gave myself a whole year to get blurbs."

"Great, then there's no rush."

"What if I gave you the couch? No, that would be insulting your integrity."

I had to be careful because I wasn't sure if she was really offering me a deal, and, as much as I wanted the couch, I knew I couldn't blurb a book its own author had referred to as chick lit. I felt for my prized possession in my pocket to give me strength. It was one of the wax prosthetic ears from *Swan Song*. It had been spirit-gummed to Arthur Weeman's head, next to his beautiful brain, and now it was in my pocket. He had Q-tipped it and my laughter had filled the Ziegfeld.

"Look what I have," I said, showing her my treasure.

"Ewww," she said.

Perhaps that could be the blurb I gave her. I could write it on my letterhead and mail it to her publisher. *"Ewww."—Rebekah Kettle.*

My headache clomped back in on its heavy hooves.

We pulled up in front of Ivy Vohl's building on Henry Street and I sulked in the car while the driver got the couch down.

"Do you want to come up and see how it looks in my apartment?" she asked.

I shook my head no.

"Are you okay?" she asked, peering at me.

"Do you have any painkillers?" I asked. I thought about telling her that I'd had an abortion and my hormones weren't balanced yet, but I decided against it. "I have a headache," I said.

"I have Lodine, Tylenol with codeine, and Vicodin—is that good?"

Maybe we could be friends after all.

The driver helped Ivy carry Arthur Weeman's therapist's couch up the stairs to her apartment and I followed after it, wishing I was lying on it the whole time. He promised to wait for me and went back down to the van.

Ivy's apartment was long and thin with one austere brick wall. I noticed my book on her bookshelf. Her bedroom was all the way in the back, dark and windowless. I remembered something Derek Hassler had said to me once, that he knew I wasn't the girl for him because there were too many windows in my bedroom and he liked to sleep in pitch blackness like a bat.

I lay on Arthur Weeman's couch and waited for Ivy Vohl to bring me a Vicodin.

It had been a long time since I had lain on a therapist's couch. I thought of something my ex-shrink had said to me at our final session, that my problem was I was a slave to symbolism. I had imagined symbolism spanking me with a paddle. "That's the reason you live in an apartment without any furniture. The reason you can't choose a couch, for instance," she had said, "is that you want the couch to represent something else. Sometimes it's okay for a couch to just be a couch. You never buy anything unless it reminds you of something. What color nail polish are you wearing?"

I had to admit I had chosen Prairie Dust because of the name and not the dull beige color. I could practically feel her sitting in her ugly brown leather chair behind me. "But unfortunately, we have to stop now," I could hear her say.

I sat up obediently and washed the pill down with a Diet Coke.

I could feel the horse chomp on it like an apple and settle down.

"I have to get going," I said to Ivy.

"So, who's your boyfriend?"

"What boyfriend?"

"The guy you're dating in England," Ivy Vohl said, peering at me again. Her question startled me. She had a certain way of startling you with questions and then peering at you until you answered them.

"Just a guy," I peered back.

"How did you meet him?"

"Our friend Charles set us up."

"What's his name?"

"His name is Hugh."

"It's not Hugh Nickelby, is it?"

Her guess made me wince. "Why do you think that?"

"Just curious," she said.

I hadn't heard the words, "just curious," said quite like that since high school and I was suddenly filled with paranoia, the intense paranoia that came with a hopelessly unrealistic crush. It was always the girls who said "just curious" in just the right way in high school who grew up to be famous gossip columnists. All you said was his name is Hugh, I told myself. But I also said he lived in England. I had merely *based* my imaginary boyfriend character on Hugh Nickelby, I hadn't used the real-life person. I tried to think of another Englishman I could base my boyfriend on, but all I could see were Buckingham Palace guards, Beefeaters and double-decker-bus ticket sellers, a barkeep in a pub, and Hugh Nickelby drinking his damned Grolsch. I had been to London a million times and I couldn't think of a single eligible man I had ever seen there.

"He lives in London but he's Australian," I said, hearing the accent change in my head. I felt dizzy from the pill. I was convinced that this was somehow going to get back to Hugh.

"Did you call Isaac Myman?"

"No," I said.

"I'm telling you, Rebekah, he's perfect for you. If I called him, I bet he'd come over right now. It's so funny because he was going to come with me to the sale but he got a lead so he decided not to. You two keep missing each other. If you got married I'd automatically go to Jewish heaven because you're both Jewish and I'm the one setting you up. I'm the *shadchan*. What's your bra size?" she asked.

Maybe this was how the Internet generation spoke to each other, I thought. Talking to Ivy Vohl felt like some kind of dirty email exchange. Perhaps she thought she was instant-messaging me instead of talking to me face to face.

"Uh, 34C," I said.

"Really? I'm surprised. I'm a 34DD and I was pretty sure we were the same size. Where do you get your bras? I can never find a place that carries my size. All of mine are kind of old lady." She pulled her sweater up to her chin to show me. I looked at her chest in disbelief. Her bra was white and shiny like the satin edging of an electric blanket, but it wasn't so much that it was old lady as her breasts themselves, freckled and shapeless. "Maybe we could go bra shopping together."

"Sure," I said, standing up and walking to the door. That was one thing I was sure would never happen—bra shopping with Ivy Vohl.

"I'm sorry about the couch. I know you understand."

"Sure," I said. I didn't even want it anymore after seeing it in her apartment, pushed up against the brick wall. I felt a little disappointed that Arthur Weeman would just sell his things to anyone.

"Do you want to see where I do all my writing?" she asked. She peered at me expectantly. I laughed but then I realized she was serious. She actually thought I wanted to see where she wrote, as if we were in the historic house of Keats or Balzac or Shakespeare or Dante, instead of in the house of Vohl.

"I really have to go," I said, and got out of there as fast as I could.

After I got home and unloaded all of my Arthur Weeman things, and paid the driver for eight hours—over five hundred dollars plus tip, which Ivy Vohl hadn't thought to contribute to— I took a shower. And that's when I had one of the strangest experiences of my life. Strange, to say the least. Looking down at my breasts, I noticed a milky substance pooling around my nipples. It looked like I was leaking milk. As if tears had started streaming down the face of Mary in a painting in a church somewhere, I had started spontaneously lactating. I had no idea how it could be happening. I knew I wasn't pregnant.

I looked at my nipples in amazement. I hadn't thought of them like this before, as deep and important as eyes. They had always just been decoration.

I didn't know what to do or who to call. I couldn't quite imagine going to the emergency room and explaining to the doctor about my possible Immaculate Conception.

I walked into the bedroom and did the only thing I could think of, I picked up the phone and dialed the number of my ex-shrink. Of course she didn't answer, but as soon as I heard her voice on her answering machine, I started to cry. I could barely speak. "This is Rebekah Kettle. I'm breast-feeding," I said. "I mean, I think I'm lactating. I don't know why this is happening. Maybe it's because of the abortion I had when I was almost thirteen, but why would I just start lactating now?"

I guess this news flash was too juicy for her to ignore, because she picked up the phone. "You're lactating?" she asked. I didn't say anything. "Why do you think you're suddenly lactating?" I stayed silent. Obviously, I had no idea or I wouldn't have called her. Then I remembered the dream I had the night before. I was in a bookstore looking for a book on Cervantes. I was desperate to read Cervantes because I was going to be meeting him. Cervantes had written me a letter telling me that I would be the most creative person he knew if I wasn't so hysterical. I told my ex-shrink the dream.

"The word 'Cervantes' is very close to the word 'cervix,'" she said. "And 'hysteria' and 'hysterectomy' come from the Greek word 'hystera,' which means 'womb.' If you think about it, the womb is the center of creation. It's where the ultimate creativity or creation occurs, right? Having a baby is the ultimate creation. A baby enters the world through the cervix. In your dream, your cervix was the one who wrote you the letter."

I pictured my cervix lying on a white sand beach in sunny Hawaii, and writing me a postcard. *Aloha, wish you were here.*

Meanwhile, I could now fulfill my lifelong goal of being an Elizabethan wet nurse.

"Have you ever heard of someone having an hysterical pregnancy?" my shrink asked.

"Just Queen Isabella of Spain," I said. I wished more than anything I hadn't called her. Soon I would be shopping for a maternity bra with Ivy Vohl.

"You know, I'm not a medical doctor, Rebekah, but I think you're producing milk to feed the child you lost. I think you're having an hysterical pregnancy to replace the baby. The mind is a very powerful thing."

When she said the words "producing milk," I almost threw up.

"That's crazy," I said.

"I know you're not going to want to, but I think you should go to a doctor," she said. I hated doctors and actually never went to one without discussing it with her first for several sessions.

"I wish I could go to Doc Baker," I said.

"Yes," she said sincerely. "Wouldn't that be nice? Many of my patients would love to go to Doc Baker and be driven home by Pa in a horse-drawn wagon. I think you should resume treatment. We have to unravel this."

I told her I would think about it and got off the phone, feeling strangely better. I remembered the name of the psychic kinesthesiologist, Anita Stefano, who the pregnant woman in the elevator had told me about. I got the number from information and called.

Anita Stefano answered in her heavy Spanish accent, and we made an appointment for the next day. She told me not to eat or drink anything on the day of the appointment. "Do you have metal fillings?" she asked.

"No," I said.

"Good. I'll see you tomorrow."

I didn't tell her about the lactating.

Then I went out to get dinner because I was suddenly starving.

I put on my bra, tucking little wads of toilet paper in the cups, put on the biggest sweater I could find, and headed toward the East Village. My cell phone rang. It was my father asking if I wanted to have dinner with him. We hadn't had dinner together in a long time. For a second I wondered if my shrink had called him about my medical problem, and then I wondered if the bank had called him about the check for twenty-two thousand.

"Sure," I said. Then I felt relieved that he had called. Maybe when he saw me he would know right away that something was physically wrong, and he would know what to do about it. He could give me one of those little computerized referral slips, even though I didn't have insurance. "Great timing. I was just about to eat."

"Okay," he said. "I'm uptown at the office and I'll jump on the subway. I can meet you downtown in an hour. How does Mc-Bell's sound?"

"McBell's closed eight years ago," I said.

"Oh," he said, trying to register that he would never again have a beer at McBell's. "Hell, what's there now?" He sounded wounded.

"Some kind of fast-food wrap place," I said.

"I don't like rap music," he said.

"Not the music. A wrap, like the food."

"What's a wrap?"

He actually had a point there. "I'm not sure, I think it's some kind of thing from California with avocado in it."

"Oh yes, pita bread."

"Maybe I should come uptown. Or we could meet in the middle," I said, feeling hopeful. My father really came to life at a place like Joe Allen. I loved when he whispered something like, *Don't turn around now, but I believe that's Barbara Walters.* My father hadn't wanted to spend this much time with me since I was twelve.

"No, I feel like coming downtown to the old Village. How about the Second Avenue Deli?" he asked.

"That closed too," I said.

"How about a Polish joint? Teresa's?" he asked, defeatedly.

"Fine," I said. "I'll see you there in half an hour."

"Great, I'm on Eighty-sixth Street, I'm just going to jump on the subway right now. The number 6."

As I talked to him I started to walk slowly up St. Marks's toward Second Avenue. That's when I saw him. He was wearing his hopeless green sports jacket. He was standing in front of a little kiosk where an African man sold giant batiked pants with animal prints on them, mostly elephants and giraffes. He was talking on a cell phone.

"Where did you say you were, Dad?" I asked.

"I'm on Eighty-sixth Street and Lex, right at the subway stop," he said. "A half hour should do it."

"Oh, okay, bye," I said. And I hung up. I must have been wrong, I thought. There were plenty of people with gray hair and green jackets, carrying an old-fashioned doctor's bag. I walked toward the man who looked like my father, and then I saw that it actually was my father.

"Hi, Dad," I said.

"Oh, uh, hi," he said.

We just stood there staring at each other. It was so awkward, that for a moment I considered trying to pretend I wasn't me, just someone who looked like me, but I had already called him Dad.

"I guess you caught me lying to you," he said.

"I guess so."

I couldn't believe this was happening. And I couldn't imagine why he had lied to me. This made my writing the check for a very good reason seem like nothing compared to his lying to me for no reason whatsoever.

I couldn't think of any reason for my father to be standing there at that moment. I thought it was unlikely that he had come to the Village to buy a pair of African elephant pants. I couldn't imagine what my father was doing that he had to lie about.

Maybe he had a girlfriend, or maybe he was seeing a hooker, or maybe he was pursuing some secret dream and was taking improv classes at HB Studios or something. Maybe he was going to join an improv group and give up being a doctor and he thought I'd try to discourage him. I thought of Arthur Weeman's film, *Literary Suicide,* in which a popular author of spy novels writes a book about a gay recluse living in North Dakota. There's a scene in which his daughter tries to convince him to stop writing something that will never sell.

Or maybe he had Alzheimer's. He hadn't remembered that McBell's was closed even though I had told him that before. Maybe he really did think he was on Eighty-sixth Street and Lexington.

Somehow the fact that I was lactating put this in perspective. I was calm and docile as a cow. I was strong and solid, like an old tree leaking sap. I felt motherly.

He looked nervous and sheepish. "I lied to you, because I just needed some time to make a few phone calls."

Phone calls?

I shrugged it off. "Oh, okay," I said. I smiled a little too brightly at him. It was strangely freeing. He was the one who had lied to me. I, for once, wasn't the one who had lied to him. This one incident, this one bizarre lie he had committed, wiped out every bad thing I had ever done. The thousands of lies I had told, the money I had stolen from his wallet, the semester of college he paid for in which I didn't attend a single class, the constant forgeries of his name on his prescription pads. The twenty-two thousand dollars I had just spent from his checking account at the Arthur Weeman sale.

"So, I'll see you in half an hour," I said, releasing him the way he had once let me release a fish, as I stood crying in waders up to my chest.

"Come on, let's go to Teresa's now," he said, stammering a little, glancing at his watch. I knew we would never speak of his lie again.

"No, Dad, that's okay. *You do what you have to do,* and I'll see you in half an hour."

I turned and walked away, leaving him standing there in a miserable stupor. I heard him call a feeble "Toots" but I just kept going. Fathers were like men. You couldn't spend your whole life trying to figure them out. Although it did occur to me to crouch behind a car and follow him, but I resisted.

I also resisted the urge to call my mother who loved to hear about things like this.

A half hour later he sauntered in to Teresa's.

"I have to ask a favor of you," he said.

"Sure, Dad," I lied. I had done favors for people my whole life and that was going to change right now. Something about a person's father lying to them for no reason caused them to reevaluate things.

"Irmabelle seems to have quit."

"Why?" I asked, with a voice filled with accusation like a kid who blames her father for her parents' divorce.

"I don't know," my father said. "People quit." He said it simply, like *Sometimes I cancel.*

People borrow twenty-two thousand dollars, I almost said.

"You know your generation turned out to be a particularly demanding species."

"What are you talking about?" I asked.

"Health insurance. Aetna U.S. Healthcare. Oxford. Young people your age calling at all hours, demanding conferences. All for two dollars. And I'll tell you something, if you want a conference with a doctor, at least be on time. Don't be forty-five minutes late. And don't come in there demanding a diagnosis so you can get a refund from a travel agent, or ask me to write a phony letter to your employer and have the insurance company pay for it. All the paperwork, all the forms. She said it was either Aetna or her. So I pulled out of the insurance companies, but she left anyway. That's why I called you."

"To tell me Irmabelle quit."

"To tell you I need you to come work with me for a few weeks until I can train someone else. I can't manage by myself. Or would I be tearing you away from the boob tube? It wouldn't hurt you to be a little productive."

"I'm extremely productive," I said. I'm producing enough milk to feed Christian Children's Fund, I wanted to say. "She'll come back," I said.

"Of course I'll pay you a fair salary."

If he paid one thousand dollars a day I could pay off the twenty-two thousand dollars in twenty-two days. It also occurred to me that the job would include going through my father's mail and therefore intercepting the Citibank statements.

"I don't know," I said. "I'm thinking about moving to L.A. and trying to write for television."

"You certainly watch enough of it," he said.

It's amazing that you can still have the same argument with your father that you've been having since you were three.

"How was the lecture?" he asked.

"What lecture?"

"The lecture. The talk you gave at Princeton."

"Oh, the talk. It was fine. I didn't know what you meant by 'lecture,' I don't go around lecturing people."

He took out a deck of cards. "How about this?" he said. "Pick a card, any card, and don't show it to me. If I guess what it is, you start working for me tomorrow, and if I don't, you get a job writing for the boob tube."

"I can't tomorrow," I said, thinking of my appointment with Anita Stefano, which I certainly had no intention of telling my father about.

"Okay, if I guess correctly, you start the day after tomorrow. Would you like to examine the deck?"

I examined it and found that it was marked as always.

The next day, after Ma and Pa forced Mary to go away to the blind school where she meets Adam Kendall, her teacher and the man she will one day marry, I went to see Anita Stefano all the way up near the George Washington Bridge.

The office was filled with crystals and big chunks of fuzzy amethyst and photographs of a donkey and a monastery. She told me to sit on a couch and close my eyes while she did a meditation to surround me in an egg of light and diamonds.

I watched her while she did it. She was around fifty, thin and curvy, with long fine black hair coiled on top of her head with a million pins. She would have been very pretty except for a terrible red rash covering her entire face. I wanted to tell her to use a little hydrocortisone cream, but I didn't think that would be appropriate. Still, it was better than going to a regular doctor.

She was really playing it safe, I noticed. There were angels and crosses, a Star of David, Ganeshes and Buddhas, and a Muslim half-moon. But no magazines or candy. In my father's waiting room there was usually toffee.

When I'd been sufficiently surrounded by diamonds she handed me a small plastic specimen cup and told me to give her five cc's of saliva. "Spit in the cup," she said. I sat on the couch, spitting and spitting until it was filled about halfway.

Then she took the cup and held a small silver pendulum over it. She asked the saliva a series of questions and the pendulum apparently answered yes or no. After about half an hour she said, "You have two souls attached to you. Have you ever had an abortion or a miscarriage?"

"Yes," I said. I had been almost asleep and her question sent a jolt through me. I wondered how she knew about my abortion. I hadn't told her anything on the phone, and I didn't think the pregnant woman in the elevator would have told her about me.

"The soul of that child is still attached to you. But what about the other one? Did you lose two babies?"

"No," I said.

"Did you ever lose a brother or a sister?"

"No, I'm an only child," I said.

"I don't think so," she said.

She asked my saliva if I was an only child and my saliva said no. My saliva said I was one of three. First my cervix was writing me letters and now my saliva was having conversations about me behind my back. "Miscarriages and abortions count. Perhaps your mother had a miscarriage or an abortion?"

"No," I said.

"Well, there are two souls attached to you, draining you,

taking your nutrients. You are not getting enough potassium!" She made me lie on a massage table while she released my two extra souls into the light. "Now your daughter and your little sister are gone. It's much better this way."

She placed a Tinker toy–like pyramid on my chest. I tried to close my eyes and say good-bye to my baby and the mystery soul, but I was having trouble concentrating because I hadn't had anything to eat or drink and I wondered how long until pizza.

"What do you do?" she asked.

"I'm a writer," I said.

"Really? That surprises me because your throat chakra is completely blocked. The throat chakra is the chakra of expression. You don't feel blocked in this area?"

I felt like I was wearing a thousand turtlenecks.

"When you are ready, you may sit up."

I was pretty much ready, so I sat up and went back to the couch. She had a beautiful view of the Hudson River. It was almost worth the forty-dollar taxi ride.

"It's nice here," I said.

"I used to be right next to the World Trade Center until September eleventh. Now I will go through the endocrine system." I sat back down on the couch, and she went back to my saliva and the pendulum and then turned to me and said, "You have an obstruction in your brain."

"Okay, release it," I said, lying back down on the massage table. This woman was really crazy, but I was kind of enjoying being there. I put the pyramid on my chest.

"No, you do not understand what I am saying. You have some kind of blood clot or brain tumor. You could have an aneurysm. You could go blind, die, anything. You have to go to a doctor immediately."

"No, I'm just having an hysterical pregnancy," I assured her. I noticed a brain-shaped ball of coral on the windowsill.

"That's ridiculous," she said. "What kind of lunatic told you that? You're not having an hysterical pregnancy, you have something wrong with your brain. Promise me you will see a doctor, Rebekah!" She was practically screaming at me, and I felt touched by her concern and by the way she said my name, Rebekah, rolling the R and coming to a full stop on the K before saying the ah like a sigh.

I paid her three hundred dollars, promised I would see a doctor, and left with the phone number of a psychic priest, one Father Louis O'Mally, who she was sure could help me.

As I traipsed toward the A train, I called my mother at the inn she owned in Woodstock. The whole time I lived with her she never cleaned or cooked a single meal, but as soon as I moved out she bought an inn and practically turned into Caroline Ingalls. She baked little muffins and left them in baskets for her guests. "Did you ever have a miscarriage?" I asked.

"No," she said. "Of course not."

"Have you ever had an abortion?"

"Rebekah, why are you asking me this?"

"Just curious," I said, using Ivy Vohl's method.

"Well, I did. Yes," she said.

I stopped walking, completely shocked that my saliva had been right.

"When?"

"I had an abortion right before your father and I decided to get divorced. I certainly did not want to have another child with that horrible man."

"Well, I've had the baby's soul attached to me for all these years, and I haven't even absorbed my nutrients," I yelled. "And thanks to you I had to pay five hundred dollars to have it re-moved."

"What are you talking about?" my mother said.

"I had to pay to have the soul of *your* child sent back into the light."

"Rebekah, that's insane."

"I think it's insane that things happen in this family that I don't find out about until I am completely drained of my nutri-ents."

"I thought you recently told me you wanted to lose weight," my mother said.

I was too infuriated to speak. "Nutrients!" I screamed. "Not everything is about weight. What else is going on in this family that I don't know about?"

"What exactly is bothering you, Rebekah?"

"I'll tell you what's bothering me. I'm lactating and I could have an aneurysm at any minute and I don't have a single speck of potassium left in me."

"What? Who told you that? I think you should come stay here for a while. It would be good for you to get out of the city. The leaves are just . . ."

"Since when do I care about leaves!" I yelled. "In my whole life when have I even noticed a single leaf? If you think I give a shit about leaves then you have no idea who I am!"

"I know who you are, Rebekah. You're a wonderful, talented girl. You should come up here and write and I'll cook for you."

I explained to her that I would never be able to write in the country, and all the baskets of muffins and gazebos and swim holes in the world wouldn't change that. "You can't even see the new Arthur Weeman there," I said.

"Yes, you can. It's playing at the Tinker Street Theater."

"Did you see it?"

"No, his movies are vile. He likes to have sex with prostitutes."

"That was a scene in one movie. His movies are the only thing worth watching today. Grandma liked Arthur Weeman," I said.

"Yes," my mother admitted. "She always said he was the eighth wonder of the universe."

I told my mother I had broken up with Derek Hassler.

"You'll meet someone better," my mother said. The man from the Ziegfeld, Isaac Myman, popped into my mind and I almost told her about him, but then thought better of it. I suddenly felt too sad to talk, and I got off the phone. I felt incredibly lonely without my souls attached.

4.

At 33, she rediscovers her love of literature

When I got home, there was a moving truck outside my building and a disgruntled mover who had apparently been standing around waiting for fifteen minutes. I grandly offered him and his smaller assistant a glass of water and when they accepted, I guiltily gave it to them from the tap because I didn't have any bottled in the house. They carried the gondola up first, and while they brought the bed and all the other things up in the freight elevator, I sat in my gondola and listened to my messages.

"Hello, uh, is that Rebekah? It's Hugh Nickelby calling."

I couldn't believe it. After the Grolsch incident I hadn't thought I would ever hear from him again. The message said that he was still in town and did I want to have a coffee with him the next day at four at the Bowery Bar because he was having a meeting near there.

A coffee with Hugh Nickelby sounded a lot better than going to work for my father. And I would definitely need the whole day off. It would take all morning to get ready and then all afternoon to go over the date in my mind. Plus I was still recovering from the lie my father had told me for no reason. It would take a lot longer than one day to get over something like that. I decided not to mention the incident to Hugh under any circumstances.

I called Hugh back and left a message on his hotel voice mail that I would meet him tomorrow at four, and then I left a message with my father's service that I wouldn't be coming in.

The next day, at four o'clock, I walked into the Bowery Bar and looked for Hugh, but he wasn't there yet. I sat at a table outside in the garden next to a blooming wisteria branch.

For the hundredth time that day, I thought of the sentence he had written in *Thank You for Not Writing,* when the main character takes a girl out for a slice of pizza and then thinks it's pathetic that she's all dressed up and acting so datelike. I had gone to great lengths that morning to look like I didn't care that I was getting together with him. After Mary and Adam got married with Ma, Pa, Laura, and Hester Sue in attendance, and Pa hocked his fiddle to buy Mary a hat for her wedding and Mary made Ma return her hat because all she wanted on her wedding day was to hear Pa's fiddle, I had gone to the hairdresser to have her blow-dry my hair straight and dressed carefully in jeans, an embroidered top, and high-heeled boots, casual and very American.

Hugh walked into the garden and saw me. I tried to wave in as un-datelike a manner as possible.

He came over and I stood up and he sort of touched my arm and we sat down at the table. I had been prepared for the single- or double-cheeked kiss but this seemed fine too.

"I thought you were going back to London," I said. I sounded suspicious. Thanks to my father, now I was starting dates off in an antagonistic manner.

"It wasn't a lie, I just decided to stay in New York for a few more days."

"Sorry, I'm a little on edge. The strangest thing happened to me yesterday. My father told me he was on Eighty-sixth Street and Lexington Avenue and I ran right into him on St. Mark's Place."

I tried to explain the story to Hugh but he seemed really confused by it. "Why do you think he did that?" he asked.

"I don't know."

"That's very disturbing, isn't it?"

We sat sort of grinning and shrugging at each other. The waitress came over and I ordered the all-American drink, a Diet Coke. He ordered a Grolsch and she instantly knew what he was talking about and hopped off to get it for him. I noticed she had been wearing a ring I had seen before, a shiny wide silver band that every single waitress who had waited on me lately was wearing. I had seen at least seven waitresses wearing that ring for some reason. It was the most boring chain mail–type thing, and I couldn't figure out why I was seeing it all over the place. When she came back I said, "I like your ring."

"Thanks!" she said. "It's from Tiffany's!" She said the word with as much pride as if she were saying, "My degree came from Harvard." "When I saw it I was just like I just have to have it so I bought it for *myself*." She stressed myself, while looking at Hugh, to let him know that she didn't have a boyfriend buying her things from Tiffany. I instantly regretted this entire conversation. Hugh had a fake interested smile on his face, like he'd rather be writing than talking about this. I wanted to seem American, but I had gone too far. The whole thing had blown up in my face; my inner Jap had made a surprise attack on my inner Pearl Harbor.

When she walked away I tried to clear things up. "I was just curious about that ring because I've seen so many people wearing it lately and it's so hideous," I said. As soon as I said it I realized that all I had accomplished was to make myself look like a horrible person. Talking about rings was pretty much the worst thing you could possibly do on a first date.

Hugh shrugged politely. "It did seem a bit big, didn't it?" he said.

"I don't like jewelry," I said. What a bizarre lie that was.

But he smiled at me then as if he was having a nice time.

Unfortunately all he wanted to talk about was books. He asked me what I had read that I liked lately. Suddenly I panicked, I couldn't remember reading anything at all except for a biography of Arthur Weeman.

"I've been reading biographies mostly," I said. "I read the new Arthur Weeman biography, and Charlie Chaplin's autobiography." I threw that one in even though it had been at least ten years since I had read it.

"Arthur Weeman?" he asked. "The director?"

I smiled and nodded enthusiastically.

"He's a pretty big deal in New York, isn't he?"

"Around the world!" I said.

"Somehow I don't think he's such a deal in parts of Africa and Asia," Hugh said.

"They paid him a million dollars to make a commercial in Japan!" I argued heatedly.

He put his forearm on the table, his hand relaxed and rested very close to my side of the table. The hand he wrote with. He leaned in toward me.

"What novels have you liked lately?" he asked.

Besides his, I couldn't think of a single one. I could suddenly only remember books I had read in high school, and those only vaguely. Interviewers had asked me that question a thousand times, and I'd never had trouble thinking of grown-up books, but he was looking at me so intently. I liked him so much, I just couldn't think.

"*Julius Caesar,*" I said. I put my hand on the table close to his and was appalled to see that I had twisted the wrapper from my straw into a ring and knotted it around my finger without realizing it.

"Well, that's not quite a novel, is it?" he said.

"No," I said, dismayed. "You know, I was a literature major at Bennington. *Of Mice and Men, Call of the Wild, To Kill a Mockingbird,*" I blurted out. "I'm a big Cervantes fan."

"It's funny you should mention *To Kill a Mockingbird,*" he said. "I was just thinking about *To Kill a Mockingbird* in relation to you."

I couldn't believe that Hugh Nickelby had been thinking about me at all, let alone in relation to anything else, let alone in relation to a book like *To Kill a Mockingbird*—a book that, at that moment, I desperately wished I had actually read. *Try to think,* I told myself. The cover was red. Gregory Peck played a lawyer in it, I was almost certain.

"Harper Lee had one of the hugest best sellers in history on her hands," he said, as if it were blood, "and she never again wrote another book. Talk about world-renowned, it was the biggest best seller in something like forty languages."

I had no idea what to say. For one thing, it had never occurred to me that Harper Lee was a woman.

"Don't you think that it's a shame she never wrote another book? I believe she's now a little old lady living in a town house near Central Park," Hugh said. "I almost feel she had a *responsibility* to write another book. I don't mean to sound like your mum, but you really should write another book."

"I don't think you're my mum," I said, sort of slyly.

He smiled and looked down at his hands. "I'm sure you're perfectly aware how many writers would kill to be in your position. You shouldn't just throw it away, Rebekah. Your first book was so good, and what if your next book is just as good or even better and it just remains unwritten? Okay, let me put it this way. Who's your favorite living writer?" he asked.

"You are," I said.

Embarrassed, he became even more English. "Aside from myself, of course," he stammered. "Whom else do you admire?"

"Arthur Weeman," I said.

"Right, back to him. Okay. How would you feel if he never made another film?"

"I would feel terrible," I said. In my darkest moments, I had let morbid thoughts of Arthur Weeman's retirement, and even death, seep into my consciousness. I dreaded the death of Arthur Weeman. "In fact, I hope I die before Arthur Weeman does."

"But he's in his seventies," Hugh said.

"He's only sixty-nine," I said.

"Well, that makes it perfectly acceptable, then." We leaned back in our chairs away from each other.

"Anyway I'm deep in the middle of my second novel," I lied, trying to save myself. "And I lecture from time to time at Princeton."

"That's wonderful!" Thankfully he brought up a more uplifting subject. Right before his book tour, he had gone to the actor Colin Firth's wedding in Umbria.

"I'd been carrying around a roll of film from the wedding, and I only now just had it developed," he said. He tapped his jacket pocket.

"Can I see the pictures?" I asked. Finally I could try to flirt a little and not feel like I was talking to my tenth-grade English teacher.

Hugh shyly handed me the envelope of pictures, and I looked through them with the utmost interest.

"I'm afraid I'm not very photogenic, am I?" Hugh said. He playfully tried to grab the picture from me, but I held firmly on.

"Oh, I think you are!" I said. "You look great in this one." I held up one in which Hugh was smiling on some sort of cliff in Umbria. The scenery was magnificent, lush and green, making the cement garden we were sitting in, with its single wisteria vine, look like what it was—a converted parking garage. I wished I could be in the photo with Hugh, holding his hand in Umbria, bringing him Grolsches at Colin Firth's wedding.

I just kept staring down at that picture.

"Not too interesting, is it?" Hugh said.

"Oh, it is!" I said. "I love this photo of you." I could have looked into his kind, squinting eyes all day.

"Can I have this?" I asked.

Hugh looked startled. He was too polite to ask why but I felt an explanation was warranted. I couldn't say that I was afraid I would never see him again, and I wanted this as some kind of pathetic souvenir of what my life should have been. I couldn't say that having this picture of him was enough to make me happy for the rest of my life. It was enough of a relationship substitute to make me feel that he was my boyfriend, and we were in a long-distance relationship. I could marry the photograph and make reduced-sized color Xeroxes for children.

"I'd love to have this picture to put on my desk," I said. I thought of Arthur Weeman's desk in my apartment with nothing in it except for Ivy Vohl's manuscript, which I'd been too lazy to throw away and had shoved in one of the drawers.

He shrugged and nodded, politely mumbling his surprised consent, and as I slipped the photo in my pocketbook, I realized that I really wasn't a writer anymore. Hugh Nickelby was a writer. Hugh Nickelby read books. I was a complete fraud from the blow-dry-straight hair on my head to the Queen's Guard Red polish on my toes. I was just a girl who worked in her father's office and was one step away from buying the Tiffany Waitress Ring. In true American-girl style, I insisted on paying for our drinks, kissed him good-bye on both of his beautiful, kind, talented, English cheeks, and left feeling like a complete arse.

When I got home I opened my mailbox to find a fan letter from some girl in Cincinnati, forwarded by my publisher. It was pretty much the usual thing, but the end really got my attention.

> *Your book is the first book I have ever read that I didn't have to and it has greatly inspired me to read more books which I have now done but I still like yours more . . .*

I laughed out loud. But then, when I looked at the letter again, something about the ellipses at the end touched me. The three dots seemed to have been written with extra determination, as if she were willing me to write another book, perhaps even a trilogy. The fan had borne her blue rollerball into the loose-leaf page with such force that the three dots had made tiny holes in it.

I felt so much love in that ellipsis that I suddenly felt an incredible amount of compassion toward myself. For a moment, I wondered if I might be my own favorite living writer.

I opened the door to my apartment and went straight to Arthur Weeman's desk and placed my Hugh Nickelby photograph on it. I looked at Hugh Nickelby in Umbria, wearing a burgundy dress shirt and a blue sports coat with no tie.

When I had first bought my apartment, after breaking up with Nathan who I had been living with for five years, I had been lonely. I had yelled and screamed in my shrink's office that she was married and didn't know loneliness the way I knew loneliness. Loneliness knew my middle name and social-security number. Loneliness was my personal trainer. I was sick from it. And one night I remember I was so lonely, I crouched in the corner of my bedroom and stayed that way for hours.

But now I was different. I knew how to handle it. I learned how to almost enjoy it. All I needed was the right cappuccino or martini or big plate of spaghetti. All I had to do was watch *Iris, Isabel, and Isolde,* or *Adopting Alice,* or *The Analyst.* I was conquering loneliness and rising through its ranks and now I was a lieutenant and it was saluting me. I rode through the streets yelling, *Loneliness is coming, loneliness is coming!* until I single-handedly won my own revolution.

5.

At 33, she makes the acquaintance of Ida
Williams, lifelong friend and mentor

As soon as I got to my father's office for my first day of "work" my father took me behind the reception counter and said, "This is your desk."

There were piles all over it of horrible insurance-type forms and about twenty Rolodexes.

"No, Dad, this is Irmabelle's desk."

"It's your desk now," he said.

I noticed a *Chicken Soup for the Soul* calendar and two little furry mouse dolls dressed as a nurse and a doctor. And an official-looking document titled CORONER'S REPORT. My father picked it up. "Milton Milton. His parents must have been sadists. Came in for a flu vaccine last year on 11/8. Ceased 11/12." My father always said ceased instead of died. "Married sixty-two years. Size of a walrus."

Thank God it was Friday.

"This is definitely not my desk. For one thing, my desk would have a computer on it."

"We don't need a computer," my father said. "Computers are always going down."

"What do you mean they're going down?" I asked.

"You know what I mean, downloading."

"Computers are always downloading," I repeated.

"Yes." He abruptly walked into his office and shut the door. Then he opened it again and came back to Irmabelle's desk. "We got a computer and it never worked. That thing caused us more problems . . ." He pointed to a word processor that must have been from the early eighties. Irmabelle even had one of those tiny koala bears from the eighties clipped to the cord.

The phone on Irmabelle's desk rang and my father answered it. "Dr. Kettle," he said. The phone kept ringing. Then he pressed a button. "Dr. Kettle." He pressed a few more buttons. "Dr. Kettle. Dr. Kettle." Finally he hit the right one and had a brief conversation with someone.

He looked down at the green-ruled appointment book and scrawled a name in between all the other names that had previously been written by Irmabelle in perfect schoolteacher script. He hung up. "Life goes on," he said.

I unloaded the six cans of Diet Pepsi I had brought to get me through the day.

The doorbell rang. "Get the door," he said, and disappeared into his office like an actor, in his case vaudevillian, waiting in the wings as the house filled. I went to the door to rip the tickets.

A tiny old man stood in the lobby.

"Well, hello," he said to me. "Where's Irmabelle?"

"She's not in today," I said.

"Isn't today Friday?"

God forbid his exciting routine be interrupted.

I turned and walked toward the waiting room and told him to have a seat. Then I went to Irmabelle's desk and looked at the appointment book to see who he was.

Morris, Casper. F.S. Almost all the appointments in the book had the letters F.S. next to their names, which meant flu shot, which meant they were old.

His chart was already on my father's desk so I got his index card from Irmabelle's little tin file box. Morris, Casper. Medicaid. Age: 87. Marital status: other (widowed).

I walked back into the waiting room. "You can go in now," I said.

"What's that?" he asked, pointing behind me.

"What?" I asked, turning around. "What is what?"

"Nothing, I just wanted to get a look at your caboose."

I turned back to face him. "You can go in now," I said.

He shuffled into my father's office. "Have you got a card trick for me today, Doctor?" he asked. A few minutes later they both came shuffling out again.

"Will you help me with my zipper?" he asked.

I assessed the situation. It was his jacket zipper. His fingers were knotted like nautical rope. One of his fingernails was purple. But the zipper of his jacket was at eye level with his *other* zipper. His nether zipper. I put my hands up in front of me like a surgeon entering the O.R. after scrubbing. I approached the patient, bent my knees, and was just about to pull up the zipper, when he put both his hands on top of my head and pushed my face into his crotch. I stumbled down to my knees, surprised by the force of it, the round hard tips of his fingers in my thick hair, my face against his pilling old-man pants.

"Whoops," I said, managing to get free and stand up again. I noticed that "whoops" was something I had been saying a lot lately. If someone's child fell on the street, I said "whoops." If I was raped in an alley somewhere, I would probably say a polite "whoops."

"Will you be here next week?" the old man asked.

"No," I said.

"If you're here next week, I'd like another appointment."

"That won't be necessary," I said. I decided not to bother with the twenty-five dollars now, I could always bill him. I just wanted him out of the office.

I ignored him as he left and picked up the phone to call my machine in case Hugh Nickelby had called. He hadn't.

The phone rang and I answered it. "Dr. Kettle's office," I said. It was my father calling from the other room.

I walked into his office and he told me to sit in the patient chair. "How's it going?" he asked.

"I was just practically raped by your disgusting patient," I said.

"Rape is nothing to joke about, Rebekah. I don't think a real victim of rape would appreciate your remark. I couldn't give him a Viagra prescription big enough to facilitate that."

"Maybe Irmabelle knew how to handle having her face shoved in a man's crotch but I don't."

"Oh, come on, he's just a lonely old man. Now, aside from that, how are you enjoying your job?"

"It's not my job, Dad. I'm just helping you out for a few days." I'd just wait until I could intercept his bank statement and then help him find someone else.

"It's not a bad profession. Medical assistant. When there's downtime, in between patients, you can do some writing at your desk," he offered. I imagined myself hard at work under the little plaque Irmabelle had nailed to the wall that said: EVERYONE

BRINGS JOY TO THIS OFFICE—SOME WHEN THEY ENTER AND
OTHERS WHEN THEY LEAVE.

We just stared at each other. My head started to pound.

"Do you have any vitamins here?" I asked. "I don't think
I'm absorbing enough nutrients."

"That's ridiculous," my father said. "What quack did you go
to this time?"

"I happen to know for a fact that I'm lacking potassium."

"So, let's draw your blood and if that happens to be the case,
I'll give you a prescription for a potassium supplement."

"I don't need bloodwork."

"Yes you do," my father said. "In this office, we draw blood.
We don't hit a gong, or throw tea leaves, read palms, or stand on
our heads, or chant, or stick needles all over ourselves, or pray to
Allah for a diagnosis. We draw blood and then we analyze the results. I'm sorry if that's too old-fashioned for you. If you would
like to join me in the examining room, I would be happy to do a
complete work up. And if you like you're welcome to ring a little
bell and light a candle while I'm doing it or meditate or call your
psychologist or anything else that makes you feel more comfortable. Come on, why not humor your old dad? Afterwards you
can go get Ralphed or have your tongue read . . ."

"It's not 'Ralphed,' it's 'Rolfed.' "

I remembered the milk pooling at my nipples and Anita Stefano yelling about the obstruction in my brain, and I thought
maybe I should let him do it.

I sulked while he pushed up my sleeve and tied a rubber
band around my arm, unwrapped a needle and took vial after
vial of blood. I looked away, which disgusted him. When it was
over, he hit my knees with his little hammer. "This is so stupid," I
said.

"Yes, medical science, what a scam. Now, take off your shoes and stand on the scale."

"You've got to be kidding."

"I want to make a note of your weight in your chart," he said, as if every girl just allowed her father to weigh her.

"No," I said.

"Then come into the kitchen and I'll show you how to work the centrifuge. You put in the counterweight and then set the dial for twenty minutes."

Luckily the doorbell rang so I didn't have to learn that. I went to answer the door. It was a skinny Hispanic girl, definitely under thirty, standing behind an old woman sitting in a wheelchair. "This is Mrs. Williams to see Dr. Kettle," the girl said.

I ushered them into the waiting room and the girl stood at the counter limply holding some sort of insurance card. I took the card as if I had taken hundreds of cards before that one. It said Medicaid Blue-Cross BlueShield, the only insurance my father still took. I unclipped the koala from the word processor cord and put the Medicaid card between its tiny claws and stood it up on the desk.

The girl sat down as far away as possible from where she had parked the old woman, I noticed, and picked up a copy of *Oprah Magazine*. My father had only had *Time* and *The New Yorker* in his office for years, so the *Oprah Magazine* surprised me. It must have been one of Irmabelle's modest demands.

My father poked his head out of his office and said, "Mrs. Williams."

The girl and I both just sat there. I thought it was pretty much beyond the call of duty for me to have to wheel her in there. But the girl didn't make a move. She tapped her fake nails, painted blue-white with pale pink stripes, on the arm of her chair. Finally I said, "You can take your grandmother in now."

"She's not my grandmother," the girl said. "I'm her home health aide."

Mrs. Williams herself just sat and stared straight ahead.

My father came out again, this time all the way into the waiting room, said hello to the home health aide, and then pushed the old woman into his office and shut the door.

The girl pulled out her cell phone and made a call. It was worse than being in an elevator with someone. I was trapped there having to hear her side of an inane conversation. "So what if I took her? I didn't take her nowhere bad. I think it's good for her to see other places. She liked going to Brooklyn. She's never left Manhattan." She pronounced Manhattan like Manha—an, whizzing through the word like a taxi going through the Brooklyn Battery Tunnel. I found a PROZAC FLUOXETINE HYDROCHLORIDE pad in Irmabelle's drawer, ripped off a piece of paper, and drafted a sign.

Please refrain from cell phone usage due to interference with medical equipment. Thank you.—Dr. Kettle

I was pretty pleased with the sign. I felt I had really captured my father's voice.

"I'm not taking no food," the girl said into the phone. "It's not my fault she wants to eat all that cereal."

While she wasn't looking I quickly reached over and taped the sign to the side of the reception counter that faced the waiting room.

When she looked up I tapped it with my pen.

"I have to go," she said into the phone. She hung up and picked up the *Oprah Magazine*.

The sign was so effective, I thought I would try to come up with some more signs.

Then my cell phone rang and I didn't know what to do. I really wanted to answer it in case it was Hugh Nickelby.

It was Ivy Vohl trying to get me to give her the blurb. "Ivy," I said, "can I call you back later? I'm actually at my father's office right now. I have to go run the centrifuge." The home health aide was staring at me. "I'll call you back," I said.

"Actually I'd like to make an appointment to see him. Does he take insurance?"

"No," I said. "Look, I've really got to go."

"How's Monday at three?"

I looked at Monday in the appointment book. "Three's taken," I said.

I told her we were booked for months and then finally gave her a ten-thirty appointment so I wouldn't be in the office.

"Maybe I'll bring Isaac with me."

"Who?"

"Isaac Myman, the man who wants to meet you. He bought your book."

"Oh, well, I won't be here. I'm just helping my father out for a few days." I made a mental note to convince my father to get caller I.D.

"I thought you weren't allowed to talk on no cell phones," the home health aide said.

"I have a special medical cell phone," I said.

"I'm going to go outside for a minute," the girl said. "But I'll be right back."

About ten minutes later my father wheeled Mrs. Williams out of his office. He pushed her into the waiting room. "Where's the woman who was with her?" my father asked.

"She said she'd be right back."

For the rest of the day, Mrs. Williams sat in the waiting room.

She didn't move except when I brought back a pizza from Mimi's, and she ate three slices, taking tiny bites.

She refused to speak.

"Where do you live?" I asked her. But she just stared straight ahead as usual. "I'm sure that girl will be back soon."

I studied her silvery white hair cut into a pageboy around her square face. She had wide fleshy cheeks and jowls but her body was thin.

"I guess we're both stuck here," I said. It was like an omen for me, to see her sitting there like a zombie. That was what I would become if I stayed with my father for even another hour at this "profession" as he had called it. It was as uncomfortable as having a houseguest. I felt guilty for not trying harder to entertain her, but she was so quiet that I went for long stretches completely forgetting she was there and just sat in my own wheelchair—Irmabelle's chair had wheels too—loudly sighing for no reason when my father disappeared into the bathroom for an hour after lunch.

If I hadn't come up with the no cell phone rule, her home health aide might not have left.

I looked through her chart—four thick folders rubber-banded together—but there was no emergency contact information.

My father finished his last appointment and stood at Irmabelle's desk. "I'm going to go see a patient in the hospital, and then I'm going home from there," he said. "There's no time for our Friday ritual."

I felt enormously relieved. I had no idea what our Friday ritual was but I had a feeling it was Satanic and involved vacuuming.

"Mrs. Williams is still here," I reminded him. "And by the

way, how does she go to the bathroom, because she's been sitting there for five hours."

"Depends," he said.

"On what?"

"It's the name of an adult undergarment."

Talking to my father was always like who's on first.

"She's perfectly capable of going to the bathroom by herself if she wants to. Look, Toots, would you mind taking her home? Her address is on her chart. She lives on Eighty-sixth Street, right around the corner from your alma mater. The doorman will let her in," my father said. He wrote down her address on an IM-ITREX SUMATRIPTAN SUCCINATE pad and handed it to me. "Leave a note asking the aide to call us, and if we don't hear from someone by tomorrow, we'll have to call Bellevue. I'll have the service page me if anyone calls. So that's it, you're done."

Except for wheeling this old wagon all the way to her apartment, I thought.

This seemed like very bad luck for my first day. I thought of how my ex-shrink used to tell me that Rabbi Hillel said if you're not on your own side who will be. I looked at Mrs. Williams staring blankly through her large glasses. "I don't think I can do that," I said. As soon as I said it, I thought I saw a glimmer of something ripple in her watery old-lady eyes. I wondered if I had hurt her feelings.

"Alright, then just stay until Carlos comes to pick up the bloods and then you can go. Don't forget to switch the phones over to the service before you leave."

"What are we going to do with Mrs. Williams?" I asked.

"Leave her there and I'll come back to deal with her later tonight." He walked over to the corner of the waiting room and turned on an old wooden standing lamp. "Shut off the rest of the lights when you go. We'll leave this one on for her. There might be a radio in your room you can turn on for her."

My room was what the X-ray room used to be when we lived there before it became my father's office. It had been our apartment until I was twelve.

When I came back into the waiting room with the radio, my father had left and Mrs. Williams was still just sitting there. Carlos came and left with my blood. I plugged in the radio on the floor next to the lamp and tuned it to WQXR.

"The doctor will be back for you in an hour," I said. I shut the door behind me and stood in the lobby unable to move for a minute. I was remembering something.

The summer I was twelve, when my father's office was still our apartment, I went to a theater camp called French Woods. When I came home, I whipped out my key and opened our front door. The place was completely empty. No furniture, pictures—there was absolutely nothing in any of the rooms. I stood in my parents' empty bedroom in shock. They had moved out. They hadn't told me. They didn't want me to know. I was completely alone.

I didn't know what to do. I only had eight dollars left, after the cab I'd had to take home when my parents forgot to pick me up at the bus. I figured I would sleep on the floor in my empty bedroom that night and then figure out where to go from there. Or maybe I would live there for a while. I could babysit for money and food, you could always eat when you babysat, even if it was just peanut butter. I wondered how long it would be until the new owners took over our place.

My father had always said if I got lost, I should stay put and he would find me, so in case it had all been a mistake, I spent the next three nights lying on the floor in the living room. I had decided against my bedroom because it was too dark, and the living room faced the street where there were lampposts or whatever those things were called. For three nights I cried that I was alone and not back in my bunk with Catherine, Melissa M., Melissa P., Lena, Jenny T., and Jenny R. in their beds around me, breathing in the seeped-into-the-woodwork smell of Fabergé, Nair, and Off. But I was determined to make it on my own. I could have called my Uncle Russell, but I was just too mad and I didn't feel like explaining that my parents had left and stolen all of my stuff.

I listened to *Guys and Dolls,* the play I had starred in, on my Walkman and tried to think about what I had thought about all summer: It is the last day of camp and Nester Perez kisses me before I get on the bus, and he tells me he will call me when we're back in the city. Only it was a lot harder to imagine because the last day of camp was over and Nester Perez hadn't kissed me, and now I was lying on the floor and there wasn't even a phone anymore.

I am Anne Frank, I thought. I am Jo March when she goes off to work, before she meets Professor Bhaer. I am Laura Ingalls in the episode where she runs away up the mountain. But I hadn't run away—my family had run away from me.

I subsisted on Mimi's and bagels and tap water, only allowing myself to splurge on one Tab a day which I savored on a bench in the park, and waited until Saturday when my babysitting job for the Rands would start up again.

On the fourth morning I awoke to see my father standing over me with two strange men carrying his examining table.

"What are you doing here, Toots?" he asked.

"I thought we lived here," I said, burning with anger. "I've been here alone for a week!"

"What!" he said, in total disbelief, as if he had no idea how this had gotten past him. "We thought you were coming home on the fifteenth. Why didn't you come upstairs? Didn't your mother call you at camp? We moved into 14D."

That was the summer before they got divorced and sold 14D and my father moved to the West Side and my mother moved to SoHo and went to Woodstock on the weekends.

I couldn't leave Mrs. Williams alone in my father's office with nothing but WQXR and ghoulish classical music and commercials for Calvary Hospice in the Bronx and a treatment center for wounds that wouldn't heal and insurance that covered one's final costs.

This was why I could never have a dog. I was too good a person, much too caring, to have a dog. I couldn't leave it alone for one minute, couldn't relax, or go on dates, or eat in restaurants, or get any writing done. I couldn't just leave and forget about her.

As I wheeled her to her building, I thought how natural it felt to be walking like that with someone, but then I realized that it should really be a baby in a stroller I was pushing, not an old lady I had never met before.

People we passed smiled at me. I had that good-deed look about me. I hated that.

What a nice young lady. Many girls her age would be getting fucked on a Friday night, not taking their old grandmother out for a walk.

As soon as we wheeled into her lobby, Mrs. Williams suddenly stood up out of the wheelchair, walked over to the elevators, and pressed the button. I had assumed she couldn't walk. The doorman laughed when he saw the look on my face.

"It took me by surprise the first time I saw it too," he said. "Nothing's wrong with her legs, she just refuses to walk outside. She'll walk right up to the edge of that marble there. And she also refuses to talk as soon as she's outside. Come on, I'll take you up. Always nice to meet the new home-care worker."

"No, I'm a . . . writer," I said.

"We don't need you to take us up. We're not children," Mrs. Williams said.

The doorman took us up anyway and let us in. "Buzz down if you need anything." He left, shutting the door behind him.

I was about to follow right behind him when it occurred to me that even though she had eaten three slices of pizza, I should make sure she had something to eat for later. I went to her kitchen and opened the refrigerator, thinking there would be what my grandmother always had, a cantaloupe and a container of cottage cheese, but there was just an old bag of onions and a bottle of Sprite. I opened her pantry but there was nothing, not even a can of Bumble Bee tuna. My grandmother wouldn't have been caught dead without plenty of walnuts and raisins and, of course, fresh-ground sweet paprika in case someone wanted a little goulash. An old glass Tropicana grapefruit juice bottle filled with homemade applesauce. Pineapple was a very big thing.

Mrs. Williams reminded me a little of my grandmother. At least her apartment did. It had that same smell of Fracas perfume and stale olive oil. And it was filled with old spindly-looking Chinese furniture and green Chinese rugs. Everywhere you looked there were depictions of some kind of long-necked swallow-type bird. In the forties, you just must not have been a woman if you didn't have swallows in your house, in rugs, carved in wood, inlaid in lacquer, engraved on silver ice buckets. Except for the lack of food, the kitchen was also like my grandmother's, with its tin daisy chandelier hanging low over the table. The black and white tiles practically forced me to take off my shoes. This kitchen floor was old New York. Most people think that the heart of New York is concrete and asphalt but it's not. It's seventy-five square feet of black-and-white tile, a tiny splendid ballroom. I pressed my bare feet into it.

I heard screams coming from outside so I went to the kitchen window. It was just kids running around in the Gardener School courtyard. The same courtyard where I had spent almost half my life.

A girl about thirteen was sitting on the concrete bench, and I suddenly saw myself there practicing my Queen Margaret monologue from *Henry the Sixth, Part III.* Saying the word "entrails" over and over and letting a handkerchief float to the ground to signify someone's—the Duke of York's?—decapitated head. I wondered where that girl was who had ordered that guy's head cut off with so much glee and gusto. What the hell had happened to me? I had sat on that bench and dreamed of being an actress. I was going to be a stewardess or a stripper while waiting for my big break. But I had let my dreams of acting and stripping completely die. I didn't have the balls for either one of them. Instead, I was doing someone else's job. I was in someone else's apartment, with someone else's grandmother, watching someone else sit on my old concrete bench probably playing my Queen Margaret.

"What's your name, dear?" Mrs. Williams asked. She was standing behind me.

"Rebekah Kettle," I told her, without turning around. She stood next to me so she could look out the window too.

"Where have I heard that name Kettle before?"

"I'm Dr. Kettle's daughter."

"Who?"

"I used to go to that school," I said, still looking down at the courtyard. "I wish I could talk to that girl." I pointed to the girl on the bench. "I want to find out who she is and tell her she should be a stripper if she wants to."

"That sounds like very sensible advice," Mrs. Williams said.

She shifted her gaze to the building facing us on the other side of the courtyard. "Oh, there's that pervert again," she said.

"What pervert?"

She was talking about a man who was standing at his window, looking down at the girls kicking a soccer ball. He was in a kitchen too, with black-and-white tile and fancy copper pots hanging behind him.

"You know, the motion-picture actor. Arthur Weeman," she said. "I usually keep those blinds closed."

I got so excited I banged my nose against the glass because the window was closed. My face was tingling.

Everyone I knew had had an Arthur Weeman sighting at one time or another. On a movie set, getting out of a town car, in Central Park. But I never had. I had never in my whole life laid eyes on him in person before.

"He's certainly a no-talent," Mrs. Williams continued. "Putz."

Suddenly it occurred to me that she was a senile old woman and she was wrong. It wasn't him. I was a fool to think that it was. "That's not Arthur Weeman," I said. "Arthur Weeman lives on Sixty-_. . ._" But then I remembered that he had moved to a town house overlooking the Gardener School. I had read it on Page Six. It was him. It was definitely him.

I was seeing _him_.

I couldn't believe I was watching Arthur Weeman watching the girl I would have been if I was thirteen years old again.

"Rebekah, would you care to study Latin?" Mrs. Williams asked. I turned away from the window to see her sitting at the kitchen table with a text book. When I turned back, Arthur Weeman was gone.

I went to the table and sat next to Mrs. Williams. The wrought-iron metal of the café-style chair dug into my back.

I needed a moment to calm myself down and figure out how to see Arthur Weeman again.

"Why do you say he's a pervert?" I asked.

"Who?"

"Arthur Weeman," I said.

"He likes little girls."

"He likes women of all ages. What about the sex scenes with Lauren Bacall in *Take My Life, Please?*"

"What about the one where he kidnaps the little girl?"

"It's fiction," I said. "And he doesn't kidnap her."

"It's disgusting," she said. "And he spends enough time staring at them *down there.*"

"*Down there?*" I asked. But she pointed down toward the playground.

"He stands there at his window just looking at them. Sicko. *Vir parvam puellam cotidie spectat.* Can you translate?" She waited expectantly and for some reason I couldn't stand the fact that I was going to disappoint her.

"*Spectat.* To watch," I guessed.

"Very good. The man watches the little girl every day. *Specto, spectas, spectat, spectamus, spectatis, spectant.*"

My mind conjugated what I had just seen in a kaleidoscope. *Artho, Arthas, Arthat, Weemanamus, Weemantis, Weemanant.*

"Oh, you're very good. If you like we can read *The Metamorphosis* by Ovid."

I didn't care what we did as long as I was near that window. I kept looking toward it the way, since September eleventh, I compulsively stared at the Empire State Building, afraid that one time it wouldn't be there.

Finally I went downstairs to the D'Agostino's and bought Mrs. Williams some tuna, mayonnaise, a cantaloupe, cottage cheese, tea, milk, applesauce, and a pound of Genoa salami. I bought ten cans of pineapple rings, pineapple chunks, and crushed pineapple, and peaches in heavy syrup, and then I remembered frozen blintzes and a container of sour cream. I grabbed a big box of Depends and put it in my cart. This seemed to be a message to a man who had been smiling at me, because he turned quickly away.

Mrs. Williams cried when I unpacked the groceries. "The other girl starved me," she said. She ate the entire pound of salami, and then went into her bedroom and passed out on her bed. I took off her shoes but that was as far as I was going to go. That was as far, I was sure, as Rabbi Hillel would have gone. I was quickly realizing that my new job involved dressing and undressing old people.

I went back to the kitchen, took one last look at Arthur Weeman's dark window, and tried to decide what to do. With all the food in the house, she'd be fine until Monday, my father was right about that. And I could call her. I jotted down her number which was printed on the phone with the old-fashioned exchange, Yorkville 6. I could see her, and with any luck Arthur Weeman, again on Monday.

"It's still here," the bum said as I passed his book table on the way to my apartment.

My book was in a precarious standing position, facing out toward the street like a prostitute in Amsterdam.

"One person almost bought it," he said. "She looked at it any-way. I told her, hey it's signed by the author that wrote it."

"Well, that's all you can do," I said, trying to sound cheerful.

"She didn't take it."

"I see that."

"It's still here." He looked angry, as if I should be providing rent. "I sold *Three Plays by Chekhov* a little while ago."

"Well, Chekhov's a better writer than I am." What was it Chekhov said? I thought. Houseguests, fish, and autographed books start to stink after three days? Something really did smell rotten at that moment, the compelling, musty-chocolate smell of decaying mice, and I brought my book slowly up to my nose. But it wasn't my book, it was the man and the tree's piss puddle he was standing in front of. Everyone in New York knows never to stand anywhere near a tree for any reason.

I thought about buying my book but I just couldn't bring myself to do it. When you write a book you have to let it go after a certain point. You can't hand-place every single copy like little refugees. Buying it wouldn't have solved anything. It would be on my bookshelf, but at the same time it would still be there, on that table, in spirit.

Sometimes something has a life of its own, its destiny so stubborn there is nothing you can do to change its course. When I was younger, nineteen to be exact, I met Nathan, the man I thought I would marry. It's really what my novel was about: this much older man, this five-year relationship, this brokenhearted crying girl. And even though now I was completely over him and relieved that it hadn't worked out, in fact thankful to God that I wasn't still with him, a part of me *was* still with him. Even though we never married, and broke up, a part of me had con-tinued life with him, was married to him, and living in Oregon with him, while the rest of me was simultaneously living my real life in New York.

"I'm not gonna give up on you," the man said.

Funny, that's what my editor told me when my deadline had come and gone. Funny, you never feel more given up on than when someone tells you something like that.

6.

At 33, she is diagnosed with a life-threatening
illness and bravely carries on

When I got to work on Monday, my father asked me to come into his office and sit in the patient chair. He was looking through someone's chart with a concerned look on his face. I didn't think he could have gotten the canceled twenty-two thousand dollar check from the bank so quickly.

"I've been looking at the lab reports," he said, holding up a computer printout. "Prolactin level is elevated. Now prolactin levels are controlled by the pituitary gland."

"Do you want me to get someone on the phone?" I asked.

"You mean an endocrinologist?"

I had no idea what he was talking about. Hearing the word gland first thing in the morning was enough to make me want to throw up. I had already started the day by sobbing my eyes out as Mary, Adam, Joe, and Hester Sue all traveled to open a new blind school in Walnut Grove. All the little blind children followed the wagon on foot, holding on to a giant rope. They walked for days and days, blind, and unsure of what lay ahead, and I had taken a taxi to work, too lazy to take the subway.

"I don't know. Someone. The patient." I stood up and pointed to the chart in front of him on his desk. "Do you want me to get the patient on the phone?"

"You're the patient," he said.

I sat back down.

"It's nothing to be too concerned about."

I stood back up.

"My guess is you have a pituitary tumor."

I sat back down.

I wasn't going to feel sorry for myself with those blind children holding on to a rope like that. "As long as I don't go blind," I said, knowing my father valued humor in the face of adversity above all other qualities. If a patient made a joke right before he died, my father thought he was the greatest man on earth.

"Only about five percent of people with this sort of tumor lose their vision," my father said, sort of surprising me. He got up and stood behind my chair. He held two fingers up near my right ear.

"Now, without moving your head. How many fingers am I holding up?" he asked.

I slid my eyes over like an Egyptian.

"My vision is fine," I said.

He walked back around so he was facing me. "Follow my finger," he said, slowly dragging his finger through the air, about three inches from my nose.

"Is your finger the most advanced medical technology we have?" I asked.

"I'm testing your peripheral vision."

"My peripheral vision is fine. I live in New York. If there's something wrong with my peripheral vision I'll know about it without your finger."

"We must monitor it. Brain tumors often affect vision and reflexes," he said.

"Brain tumor!" I said. "Who said anything about a brain tumor?"

"That's where the pituitary gland is located. Jesus. Fifteen thousand dollars a year to that damned private school. That biology teacher you had was a moron. Have you had any symptoms?" my father asked. "Any headaches, dizziness, even lactation?"

I looked at him in disbelief. "Lactation? No! You said my headaches were psychosomatic," I yelled.

"That's because you're a real faker. You're always crying wolf. Didn't *New York* magazine call you the Queen of Hyperbole?"

"No," I said. "They called me the Queen of Hilarity."

My conversations with my father always had this same unhappy rhythm. Even with a brain tumor that would most probably make me go blind I couldn't win. And I would be willing to go blind if there was an Adam Kendall in my future. But there wasn't, I was sure. I would go blind and spend my life feeling around my father's office and zipping old men's zippers.

"I was able to get you scheduled for an MRI at Beth Israel hospital in an hour," he said proudly, as if he had gotten me front-row tickets to Ringling Brothers.

"I'll go another time," I said.

"This is serious, Rebekah. You could have an aneurysm. We have to get a picture of your brain and then put you on medication."

"I think I could cure this with pomegranate juice."

I said this just to annoy him.

A white plastic catcher-style mask was lowered over my face and I was slid backward into the MRI tunnel for my brain scan. "Who am I, Hannibal Lecter?" I asked, but they didn't hear me. They didn't even speak English there at Beth Israel for some reason. All the signs were in Chinese. The Jews and the Chinese were becoming interchangeable. The last time I had been to a Jewish cemetery, when an aunt of my mother's had died, I noticed a lot of Chinese headstones, with elaborate dragons and things, had popped up all over the place. Of course that made sense because Jews couldn't face eternity without Chinese food.

"You have firring?" the medical technician asked.

"Furring? I'm sorry, I'm not very medical. I don't know about furring." It was bad enough having a possible tumor in my brain, but if the tumor had fur on it I wasn't sure I could handle it.

"You have metar firring in teeth?" the technician said.

"I don't know what that is."

"You have healing aid, firring, eyeyoudee, or any metar device in body? Any pin in regs?"

"Pinninregs? I don't know."

He handed me ugly spongy earplugs, which I reluctantly put in my ears.

"Ray stirr. No movie."

A tiny angled mirror on the ceiling of the tube made it possible for me to see the technician looking at the computer screen. The machine clanged loudly.

I could not relax my legs. They were sticking out of the tube into the freezing room. The technician frowned. His lips were moving. He was talking to someone I couldn't see. I didn't want anyone else looking at my brain, although I had a lot of confidence that it was even more beautiful than the woman's before mine, like the inside of a genie's bottle.

I tried to think nice thoughts, but all I came up with was

being buried alive and several Holocaust images. Osama bin Laden in a bunker somewhere. The movie *Coma*.

I thought about Isaac Myman. Even though I had no intention of calling him, it was sort of nice knowing he was out there somewhere. The promise of a date was usually so much better than the date itself. I could keep him as a sort of insurance policy or savings account—if there was absolutely no one else, I could date him.

I couldn't see anything in the mirror anymore. The technician didn't seem to be there. Then the clanging and vibrating finally stopped and I was slid back out of the oven. "Did you see anything?" I asked.

"You not finished yet. You get injection and go back in. Injection to right up pituitary." That didn't sound good. He stuck a needle in the top of my hand.

"But did you see anything so far? Anything wrong with my noodle?" The technician didn't seem to understand. "My lo mein?"

"You have to go back in." He lowered the plastic cage and slid me back in again.

This is what I got for always saying my life was an Arthur Weeman movie. Arthur Weeman was worried that he had a brain tumor in at least three of his films. There was nothing more Arthur Weeman than that.

Lying in an MRI tunnel was so Arthur Weeman I practically expected to find him in there with me.

I could almost see his next movie projected on the top of the tube, a close-up of his magnificent brain, the brain of a genius gently pulsating on the screen. The credits roll, and then we see his feet sticking out of an MRI machine, surprisingly big considering his less than average height, wearing big black shoes.

Then we see two male Chinese medical technicians playing mah-jongg, pointing at the brain on the screen. "Look. Big tumor size of pork bun," one of the medical technicians says. Then we cut to Arthur Weeman eating alone in a Chinese restaurant. "I don't know why, I just had this incredible craving for wonton soup all of a sudden. . . . I don't know I. . . ." He becomes too wrapped up in slurping his soup to finish.

I stared up at the white rounded ceiling of the tube through the white bars of the mask covering my face. I thought about Arthur Weeman standing in the window looking down at the Gardener School playground and I wondered what it was he was looking for. It wasn't enough to have seen him, as I always thought it would be. I wanted to talk to him. And that's when I got the idea that I should write him a letter.

7.

At 33, she begins correspondence with
filmmaker Arthur Weeman

When I left the hospital and burst out onto Union Square across from the Virgin Megastore, I felt extremely sorry for myself. My possible tumor pulsed in my brain like a second heart. I was sure my brain was big and it was already a pretty tight fit in my skull, so everything was shifting in there to make room for it. I tried to embrace it, welcome it in, make pleasant introductions, "Tumor, Brain. Brain, Tumor." It was strange knowing it might be in there. It was hard to wrap my brain around it. I certainly had no intention of going back to my father's office for the rest of the day.

When I got home I sat in my gondola and picked up the phone. I desperately wanted to call someone, but I couldn't think of any friends who didn't have babies and would want to drink martinis at the Algon-quin for a while.

I thought about calling Isaac Myman, since I could be going blind and this might be my last sighted date, but then I remembered that I'd thrown out his number and calling him would involve calling Ivy Vohl, and I'd already been through enough for one day.

I felt different. Not so much transformed, as transported. I felt like I had been in a time machine instead of in an MRI. I had gone from child to old woman in one shot. Or maybe I had gone from old to young. I wanted to call a friend but I really didn't have any friends. I had a lot of friends but no one you would want to call. I had a lot of male writing buddies, Omar, Nick, Pat, but whenever we got together all they did was rant about how their careers were in the shitter and did I see this one's author photo and that one's review in the *Times*. I remembered once I had complained to my ex-shrink about not having a real girlfriend anymore and she had asked me to invent my perfect best friend and I had thought my perfect friend would be exactly like me in every way but a little more exotic, probably English or Japanese.

I ordered from Suzie's, I was starving for Chinese food, and watched TV while I still had the eyes to watch it. I could have an aneurysm at any moment and die. I thought about the possibility of dying. It would put an end to my problems. But no, I thought, death would just present you with a different set of problems.

Then I lugged the typewriter from *Literary Suicide* over to the desk from the same film, and put a piece of paper in it. I placed my fingers on the keys that Arthur Weeman had placed his fingers on before me. I typed the words "Dear Mr. Weeman" on the top of the page. I liked the typewriter. It was sort of nice to begin a letter without an animated paperclip with eyeballs popping up and asking if I wanted help.

Dear Mr. Weeman,

    My name is Rebekah Kettle and I am the author of The Hard Part, a novel. I have never written a fan letter before but

I ripped the page out, put another in, and tried again.

Dear Arthur Weeman,

Thank you for your movies. I know you have animosity for your
fans, but

I couldn't type another word. This was impossible. If he ever
even received and read a letter as stupid as this one, he would
have nothing but disdain for the idiot who would write, "Thank
you for your movies."

I didn't know what I really wanted to say to him anyway. Just
that in a world where people do nothing but disappoint each
other, he had never disappointed me.

Again I tore the paper out of the typewriter—it made a re-
warding sound—crumpled it and threw it away. It was almost
midnight, way too late to visit Mrs. Williams. I had been so
wrapped up with my possible brain tumor, I hadn't even given
her a thought all day. She had probably gone to bed hungry, having gone through every scrap of food I had put in her refrigerator. I felt worried about her. Annoyed, but worried. I wondered if
checking on her even this late would be better than not checking
on her. The doorman could let me in and I could fill her fridge
with food for tomorrow's breakfast. Arthur Weeman was known
to stay up late at night and write. I could just go quickly and see if
his kitchen light was on.

I dressed nicely and warmly in case I had an aneurysm and
ended up lying on the sidewalk for any length of time, and
headed uptown to Mrs. Williams'.

Just before we approached Thirty-fourth Street, the cab took a
wide U-turn and I instinctively started yelling at the guy.

"We can't go this way," he said.

"Why not?" I asked. There usually wasn't much traffic this time of night.

"You no see nothing unusual?" he said, completely exasperated.

"No," I said, glancing out my window.

"You no see no elephants?"

I turned around and looked at what turned out to be the most incredible thing I had ever seen. It was the type of experience that you usually had to go to Africa or India for, not Thirty-fourth Street. Until that moment my favorite sight in New York, the most beautiful thing in New York so far, had been the giant sparkling sombrero sign hanging outside the Mexican restaurant Gonzalez y Gonzalez on lower Broadway. Whenever I went downtown I always made the cabdriver go down Broadway so I could see that sombrero, all multicolored glitter. The second most beautiful thing in New York was the wisteria tree climbing up someone's town house on Tenth Street between Fifth and Sixth, but only for about two weeks in May. And the third most beautiful thing was snow, freshly fallen. But now all that had changed because now we had elephants.

The cabdriver started backing up away from them. "Stop," I said. "I have to get out."

I followed the elephants and watched them descend into the Midtown Tunnel. I got snippets of information along the way: they were leaving the Ringling Bros. and Barnum & Bailey Circus, and the only way they could leave Manhattan was to walk.

Everyone was acting nonchalant, but my heart spun around like a red souvenir flashlight at the end of a plastic cord.

I tried to go right down in the tunnel with them, but a policeman stopped me. "I'm a reporter for *Maxim* magazine," I told him.

"I don't care if you're a reporter for my dick," he said.

"Where are they going?"

"I don't know, maybe Philly," he said.

It wasn't every day wild animals, however tamed, were in the streets! The biggest animals in New York up until now were rats and the occasional horse clomping around under some fat cop. The closest we had come to having giant animals were those hideous cow statues that inexplicably popped up all over town for a while and tried to turn New York into a country quilt. It occurred to me that my brain was like New York, the West Side and the East Side, uptown and down, and my possible tumor was like one of those cows.

But if you thought about it, there was nothing more New York than elephants, gray and smart, weathered but resistant. With a giant trunk that throws dirt at people.

I hailed another cab and got in. "Can you take me to Philadelphia?" I asked.

The driver turned around and looked at me. "Oh good, for a minute I was worried you were going to say Brooklyn. Sorry, Baby, that only happens in the movies."

"How much would it—" but I stopped myself. I couldn't just follow elephants like a groupie. And I couldn't spend two hours in a cab with a driver who called me Baby.

I got out of the cab on Mrs. Williams' corner and stopped into the twenty-four-hour deli to buy some more provisions and carried two shopping bags to Mrs. Williams' building. The doorman buzzed but she didn't answer. I was sure she was dead. The doorman let me in and I walked cautiously through the house. I found her in her bed under a hundred afghans. I went to her bedside but there was no breath and no movement. The doorman was waiting in the hall. "Mrs. Williams," I said, loudly, shaking the pile of covers. "Mrs. Williams," I shouted. She sat up completely alarmed and screamed.

After I straightened her out and calmed her down and apologized, I told the doorman I was going to stay with her for a while and he left.

I brought her a glass of water in bed and she propped herself up on pillows and just breathed noisily with her hand on her chest. I sat on a kitchen stool she had by her bed, which she probably used to help herself get in and out.

"I haven't been that scared since I was a schoolgirl," she said. "When I was a schoolgirl, we went camping in Central Park."

"No wonder you were scared," I said.

"Oh, it was so much fun. It was wilderness then. Our entire class would go and pitch our tents and make a fire and sleep in sleeping bags. The chaperones scared us to death with ghost stories. I'd love to do that again some time. We swam in the lake in our bathing suits. I was the bravest one."

She closed her eyes and turned on to her side, and in that moment she wasn't old anymore. She was a young girl on a camping trip and her skin was glowing, not in the light from the hall bathroom, but in the light from a roaring fire.

I walked into the kitchen. For a long time I just stood at the window expecting Arthur Weeman's kitchen light to turn on at any moment. But it didn't.

If I were twelve again, and sitting in that playground, I would know what to say to him, I thought. I would know how to reach him. Now I really had no right to write to him, but my old self, the girl who used to see all his movies at the Thalia movie theater on Ninety-sixth Street before it closed, *she* could have gotten his attention.

There was nothing more selfish than a fan letter. People who wrote fan letters were delusional and grandiose and didn't really care about the person they were writing to. A fan letter should be like a gift, and if you couldn't give the recipient something pleasurable, it shouldn't be given at all.

If a child wrote a letter, though, that was different. That wasn't selfish. Words from a child could inspire men to greatness, make them hit home runs out of the park and things like that.

I picked up a notepad from the counter and the AMBIEN pen I had taken from Irmabelle's desk, and brought them over to the window seat. I tore off a sheet of paper and started a letter.

November 13

Dear

I paused for a moment before coming up with what to call him. . . .

November 13

Dear Awful Writer,

I happen to know that you hate your fans and think they're idiots so I've decided to call you Awful Writer instead of Arthur Weeman so you will know that this is not a fan letter and I am not a fan. I am just a girl who has seen all your movies and has certain strong opinions about them but I won't tell you what they are.

My name is Thalia and I am *almost* thirteen.

I am writing to ask you a question. Q:How do you describe the most beautiful thing you have ever seen? Now

I know why you want to make movies instead of write books so you can just show the most beautiful thing in the world without clumsily taking up page after page.

Last night I was in a cab at midnight heading from Tribeca to the Upper East because I was supposed to sleepover at my friend L.E.'s loft, but I had to leave in the middle for certain reasons pertaining to L.E.. Anyway, when we got to 34th St. you would not believe what I saw.

Elephants! Real ones. At least a dozen of them. They were walking East on Thirty-fourth street, actually trunk to tail. Slowly trudging right down the center of the street like a river. There were police cars and everything was gray on gray and trunks and tails and a strange blue smokey light pouring down from somewhere like it was a Bergman film.

The best thing about it is that it wasn't even a movie. It was real life. Those poor lucky elephants were leaving the circus for Christ sake. Poor because they're in the circus. And lucky because they got to walk down the streets of New York which none of their friends in India will ever get to do. Apparently they leave Madison Square Garden and walk to Queens where they take a train somewhere. I don't know what the blue lights are for. Maybe it soothes them.

When I saw it I thought I was going to have a heart attack. But there were hardly any people around. I guess nobody cares about a beautiful stream of elephants. People in New York will stop to look at almost anything, any homeless person going to the bathroom on the street or fistfight is more interesting apparently than elephants. It was like a ghost town but with Elephants instead of blowing tumbleweed.

It also reminded me of the play "The Rhinoscerous" by Ionesco which I loved.

That's why I am writing to you. You would be crazy not to open your next movie with elephants walking down the street at midnight.

1. Ext. Thirty-fourth Street. Night.
Twelve sad, beautiful, real ELEPHANTS walk
trunk to tail while various random NEW YORK-
ERS mill about, oblivious.

I know, I know, you're probably saying I should stick to writing crazy letters and you'll take care of the screenwriting. Don't worry, my Uncle is an Intelectual Property Attorney and I am officially signing the above screenplay beginning to you.

I am reading *How to Write a Screenplay* by Robert McKee which I think is ridiculous, don't you? He says that the flashback is the sign of a true amateur. I happen to know that isn't true and *Iris, Isabel, and Isolde* is proof of that, not to mention *Literary Suicide.* I don't want to write a screenplay, I was just interested in reading about them.

All Best,

Thalia

P.S. Please let me know if you disagree with me about Robert McKee or any of the above.

I folded the letter and tucked it into my pocket. I felt like I had opened a time capsule. I went into Mrs. Williams' maid's room, right off the kitchen, and lay down on its narrow cot.

When I woke up in the morning Mrs. Williams and I watched *Little House on the Prairie.* Reverend Alden was thinking about leaving Walnut Grove, but I could hardly concentrate. I was thinking about the letter and wondering if I was really going to mail it or not. If I left Mrs. Williams' building and turned two corners, I was sure I could figure out his address.

I didn't have a change of clothes, but I washed up in the maid's bathroom and was about to leave for my father's office when I saw Mrs. Williams just standing in her foyer staring at me. "Nice having company," she said.

I always felt terrible when old people said things like that. "I'll check in on you later."

"Don't worry about me," she said, petulantly. "I'll call the agency and have them send over another girl. I prefer one from the islands."

I suddenly didn't want a girl from the islands there puttering around the kitchen, sitting in my window seat. "I'm taking you with me," I said.

8

At 33, in a futile attempt to escape her critics,
she adopts a nom de plume

As soon as we came down in the elevator and crossed the threshold of her lobby, Mrs. Williams stopped moving and speaking. I almost admired her for it. Most people turned into someone else when they left the house, but she just shut down and didn't bother.

She didn't say a word as I pushed her up Arthur Weeman's block while I found his address. It was a beautiful red brick town house, with wooden shutters painted cinnamon. Like a sound track, you could hear the screams and laughter from the Gardener schoolyard behind it.

We walked to the little copy shop on the block of my father's office and I bought an envelope and paid two dollars for a thirty-nine-cent stamp. In New York the only people who go to the post office are old people, foreigners, and personal assistants.

I put the letter in the envelope, wrote Arthur Weeman's name and address on it, stamped it, drew a little rainbow on it, and put it in the mailbox on the corner. It felt somber with Mrs. Williams as silent witness.

I wheeled Mrs. Williams into my father's office and parked her in the waiting room. Then I pulled all the charts for the day's appointments without even thinking how boring it was.

I brought them into my father's office and put them on his desk.

"I have the results from the MRI, honey. It's exactly what I thought. A pituitary tumor," my father said.

"So it's official?"

"Yes, the tests were positive. I have the pictures here. But it's fairly unimpressive."

My brain was on his desk, spread out like a centerfold. "Unimpressive?" I asked, the insult hitting me. "My brain?"

"No, the tumor." Even my tumor was unimpressive. An hors d'oeuvre. "It's micro not macro. That's a good thing." That was the looking-glass world of doctor talk. Unimpressive was good. Negative was good. Positive was bad. "You have to take a medication called Parlodel, which is a brand name for bromocriptine mesylate. Two point five milligrams, twice a day. With food. I filled the prescription for you because frankly I didn't trust you to fill it yourself."

He handed me the amber bottle and I studied it. I always thought it was funny that the international symbol for "Take with food or milk" was a picture of a hamburger.

"You will experience severe nausea in the beginning, but that should subside in a matter of weeks."

He stood up, left the room for a moment, and brought back a little paper cup of tap water from the bathroom sink. He handed me a tiny white pill. "Swallow this."

"I don't drink tap water," I said. "My homeopath says it's filled with wigworms. And before I take the pill I should probably go to her and build up my system with Arnica or something first."

"Why don't I go out and buy you some aloe vera juice to take it with," my father said.

"Okay," I said.

Apparently he was just kidding. "Swallow the pill, Rebekah." As weak and pathetic as Dr. Kettle thought sick people were, he thought sick people who didn't take their medicine were the lowest of the low. I swallowed the pill dramatically, needing several sips of the wigworm water to get it down. The days of children's cherry Triaminic served to me in a special spoon with a gentle, steady hand were over. St. Joseph's was a thing of the past. "Did you eat breakfast?"

I nodded. Mrs. Williams and I had eaten another pound of salami during *Little House.*

"Maybe you should eat some crackers. There are some over the stove. I'm proud of you for taking it so well."

Not showing emotion was the only thing that impressed my father.

"So what happens now? I just take this medication for the rest of my life?"

"Yes," my father said.

"I don't understand, does it shrink the tumor?"

"No, it has nothing to do with the tumor, there's nothing we can do about the tumor. The medication helps regulate your pituitary gland, which isn't functioning properly because of the position of the tumor."

"Am I going to have brain surgery?" I looked terrible with short hair, let alone no hair. I became instantly terrified. This was really serious. "Why did I get this! Is it from Sweet 'N Low?"

"Honey, no. Tumors aren't caused by anything, or, I should say, no one knows what causes them. And you're not having surgery. Surgeons stopped operating on pituitary tumors years ago because the vast majority of the tumors were benign, and because the pituitary gland is located in the center of the brain, behind the eyes, it is an enormously difficult operation. A large number of patients couldn't be closed up properly."

"So what happened?"

"They had to wear a helmet for the rest of their lives."

"A helmet!" If I ever married, how would I attach a veil to my helmet? I'd have to have one of those terrible theme weddings, outside on a bicycle. I had to think about something else.

"I saw the most incredible thing last night," I said.

"Oh?"

"I saw the elephants leaving the circus. They were walking right up Thirty-fourth Street."

"You've seen that before," he said.

"No I haven't."

"You don't remember?"

"I have never seen elephants roaming around New York before."

"Sure you have. You and I saw them together. I took you to see them when you were ten. It was in the newspaper. . . ." He stopped and looked at me.

I searched the savanna of my brain, standing in the center of it like a hunter with binoculars held up to his eyes, one foot hiked up on my tumor, but I couldn't see any elephants.

"Oh, right, right, right, right, right," my father said. "I was going to take you but I never did." His phone rang and he answered it correctly. "Dr. Kettle. Did you try an antihistamine? Alright, monitor it closely and call me if . . . Well, you should come in. I happen to be an excellent diagnostician, but I can't do it based on your description. Unless you come in, I'm afraid all I can prescribe is chicken soup. . . ." I stood there for a moment longer and then went back to Irmabelle's desk.

I sat for a while eating saltines and trying to figure out why my father had thought that I had seen the elephants. I was the one who had a tumor and yet it was my father, I thought, who might be dying. Alzheimer's. It was the only explanation. Maybe that was why Irmabelle had left. She couldn't stand to see him unraveling. Maybe she believed it was my job as his only daughter to help him make the transition to dementia. In his mind he had taken me to see the elephants and it was in the newspaper. There were elephants on his desk. He had given me bad news. His wires had gotten crossed.

Mrs. Williams was dozing in her wheelchair in the corner. My father's twelve o'clock was late. I thought of the letter I had sent to Arthur Weeman. Maybe Thalia could write letters to my father too, and he would think they were from me when I was younger. With fog in his brain, and a tumor in mine, we could start again. Get off on the right foot. *Dear Dad, My name is Thalia. I am your daughter and I am almost thirteen.*

The doorbell rang and I answered it. It was the enormous black woman who delivered my father's mail. I took the little pile from her and thanked her, sifting through the envelopes for something from the bank.

I wondered if my letter to Arthur was in her pouch. I wondered if he would get the letter and read it. But of course I would never know. Even if Arthur Weeman happened to read the letter, he wouldn't write back, and I hadn't included a return address in any event. My throat chakra was tighter than ever, and I wrote the words *Dear Awful Writer* on top of one of Irmabelle's big index cards because it was the only paper I could find, besides my father's letterhead stationery or prescription pads.

November 14

Dear Awful Writer,

The reason I am writing to you on index cards is because I'm in science and we're supposed to be making flashcards for a test we're having on the endocrine system. If you see the word "pituitary gland" written on top of this card, its because my teacher Mr. Melzer has walked over to my desk.

I just wanted to tell you that my friend L.E. apologized for acting so imature at our sleepover and I forgave her because her mother died and she's anorexic and cuts herself. I myself have a very healthy appetit but I'm naturally thin. By the way I don't have any wierd piercings or tattoos, accept of course piecred ears.

I am so bored! For me there is no difference between a doctor's waiting room and this class room. All I do is wait to get out of here. If you saw my notebook you would think I was crazy because I count down all the minutes of each class from 40 to 1 in the margins like a lunatic.

Last night, after I wrote to you, I had a dream about elephants. I was in an airplane and I could see them from the window walking thousands of miles below me across the earth. It had a very biblical feeling to it now that I think about it.

This might sound strange, but I dream about *you* quite a lot actually. I've had at least 7 Arthur Weeman dreams. I also have reccuring movie theater dreams in which I am always sitting in a strange movie theater and the screen is at a strange angle. I think it's because

I feel like a spectator in life, waiting here in this ugly green classroom when I long to be a part of things, not just sitting in the audience. Anyway I don't even know why I'm telling you this because I hate it when people bore you with there dreams.

I wonder if you happened to notice that I didn't give you a return address on my letter to you. I have decided to give you my grandmother's address because my parents are unbelievably controlling and if you ever wrote me a letter *which I know you never would* they would probably ask a lot of nozy questions. Plus I think my father is going senile. He is a physician but he has been very strange and confused lately and when I told my school's occupational therapist she said she thinks he might be in the early stages of Alzheimer's disease which I think is true. (This might be the beginning of an interesting plot.)

The reason I am giving you my grandmother's address is I go to her house almost every day after school and she always asks me to bring up her mail because she is so old and short that she actually can't reach her mailbox! For some reason I think that is hilarious. She has to stand on the hotel cart and sometimes it rolls around while she's still on it and she gets hurt. Luckily I'm pretty tall. The bell just rang. Thank God.

I hope you aren't laughing at me.

Your devoted,

Thalia

PS (written later at home) I have decided to enclose an x-ray of my brain because I thought you might be

interested in just what kind of a brain a girl who would
write you letters might have. I had to have an MRI because my father is a doctor and I get a lot of headaches
but it just turned out I need to wear my glasses more
often, however that won't be a problem since I plan on
being given contact lenses for my birthday. My father is
really quite overly protective. When he found out my
headaches weren't anything serious like a brain tumor
or something he actually cried. Some fans probably
send you pictures of their naked bodies but I thought I
would go one step further and send you a picture of my
naked mind.

I leaned back in Irmabelle's chair feeling excited by what I
had just done. I had given Arthur Weeman an address!

The letter had taken up eight index cards and I numbered
and paperclipped them. I waited awhile for my father to go into
the bathroom and then I went into his office, grabbed my chart,
and held my brain up in front of me. It was too cumbersome to
send so I took a pair of Toradol oral 10 mg tablets (ketorolac
tromethamine) scissors from a cup on Irmabelle's desk and cut
the films into a heart shape. I slid it into a manila envelope, along
with the index cards, stamped and addressed it, wrote Mrs.
Williams' return address, and drew another rainbow. I dashed
out to the lobby to mail it and when I got back to Irmabelle's desk
a wave of nausea hit me, a tornado sending cars and houses and
cows flying around my stomach.

"I've been poisoned," I told my father. I sat in the chair facing
his desk and then suddenly felt too high up and curled up on the
floor. I needed him to rub my back.

"You're experiencing nausea from the Parlodel."

"I'm so nauseous," I said.

"No. You're so *nauseated*. Nauseous is incorrect."

"I'm so nauseous," I said. "How can you correct my grammar when I'm laying here dying."

"You're lying here dying," my father said. "Give it a couple of weeks. You've always had a weak stomach. The nausea will subside."

"Don't say subside," I said. The word subside made me even sicker. It sounded like submarine and submerge and made me think of surf and seas. "I'm not going to take the medicine."

"Oh yes you are," my father said. "We'll keep you on two pills for a while and if your body doesn't adjust, we'll bring you down to one."

One if by land, two if by sea.

"I have to go home," I moaned.

After I lay on the Persian carpet in his office for a while, I wheeled Mrs. Williams home and lay on what she liked to call the sectional.

"I don't know what to do. Should I get a girl?" she said.

"Just bring me some tea," I said. She brought me peppermint tea and unwound the long white cord from a heating pad, plugged it in, and placed it on my stomach. I was too sick to even walk into the kitchen to see if Arthur Weeman was home.

"Think about something pleasant," Mrs. Williams said.

I tried to grasp on to last night's elephants, as if I were walking with them, holding on to the tail in front of me. Elephants were tough. They didn't have weak stomachs. They could survive the circus, whips and electroshock and tranquilizers. I tried to think about my letter being dutifully carried to Arthur Weeman.

I imagined I wasn't myself at all, but Thalia, sitting in the schoolyard downstairs. As Thalia, I felt lighter, longer, my thighs and knees cold beneath my skirt and above my navy socks. "What do you want for dinner?" Mrs. Williams asked.

I moaned at the mention of food.

"You have to eat something so you can take your second pill. Why don't you order us a pizza pie?"

"I can't."

I heard her in the kitchen ordering a pizza in some sort of accent from the golden age of Hollywood. "Yes, I would like to have a pizza pie sent here directly via courier," she said. When she hung up she said, "Now that's something I've never done and I'm going to do it again."

She brought me a slice and we ate and took our medications together. The nausea increased and the sectional spun. She took my hand and helped me into the maid's room, lent me a nightgown with roses on it and a B ALTMAN label, and tucked me into bed.

Her warm hand on my forehead comforted me. "You're going to feel better soon." She stroked the bridge of my nose until my eyes closed.

"My pa was here this morning," she said.

"Your pa?" I whispered. The youngest he could be was ninety-five.

"My darling, handsome pa."

She then went on to tell me that early that morning her pa had taken her to town in his covered wagon and the nice man at the mercantile had allowed her to select a peppermint stick from a tall glass canister.

The next day I managed to make it to my father's office, despite the nausea. Mrs. Williams sat in her chair, parked in front of the fireplace like a ceramic Chinese dog.

My father came into the reception area. "Hello, Toots." He noticed Mrs. Williams in the waiting room. "Can I speak to you for a moment?" he asked.

I followed him into his office, steadying myself on his desk.

"Does Mrs. Williams have an appointment today?" he asked.

"No."

"What is she doing here?"

"She's waiting for someone," I said.

"Her home healthcare worker?"

"Yes," I said. "Someone's taking care of her."

"You don't look too good."

"Is that your professional diagnosis?" I asked. I was using his desk as a sort of a lifeboat, bravely riding the waves.

"It's good you're here. It'll help you keep your mind on something. I promise you'll adjust to the medication in a day or so. Why don't you sit on the couch and read or try to relax. I have to use the toilet and then I have to leave the office. I have a funeral."

I went out into the waiting room and picked up a *New Yorker*, and flipped through it to the only part of the magazine I liked, the ads in the back. I loved the odd assortment of offerings, a lilliputian sterling silver swan, a customized ketubah, teak Adirondack chairs.

One ad was for an international adoption agency. A very blond Connecticut-type woman who looks like she has never eaten an egg roll let alone known any people with black hair, is ecstatically holding a little Chinese baby. I suddenly got very excited about the idea. I could go to China and bring home a little Chinese girl, go off my medication so I could continue lactating, and breast-feed her. The baby would actually look a lot like me because I considered myself to be very Chinese-looking.

If I could handle taking care of Mrs. Williams, I could handle a little baby.

I rushed over to Irmabelle's desk and called the number. I left a message that I was extremely interested in adopting a Chinese baby and to send me the application and information as soon as possible.

But as I was giving my name and address I noticed another ad under it, for a guided tour of the Galápagos Islands with a picture of a baby bird, open-beaked, head upturned. Again I got very excited and I tried to decide which I would rather do, adopt a Chinese baby or go to the Galápagos Islands with an experienced tour guide. A guided tour was a very tacky and unadventurous thing to do but I secretly liked the idea. When I went to new cities, I always broke away from whomever I was with and secretly took a bus tour. Both the Chinese baby and the Galápagos Islands seemed equally good. I couldn't just sit in my father's waiting room forever like a patient. Life was short. I was thirty-three without a husband or a baby. I had to make some kind of move, and both the Chinese adoption and the Galápagos Islands would get the ball rolling—give me a baby or at least kick-start fertility. I was pretty sure the Galápagos Islands was the place where Darwin came up with the theory of evolution, for whatever that was worth.

I called the Galápagos Islands number and left a message that I was extremely interested and to send me the application and information as soon as possible.

"Okay, bye," my father said. "Just stay until five to answer the phones and then you can go. And I need you to order one box of fourteen-by-seventeen films from DNA, and one box of electrode alligator clips."

I wasn't sure if he said stay until five or stay for five minutes. I waited five minutes and then took Mrs. Williams to her apartment.

When we got there, Mrs. Williams wanted to watch the Home Shopping Network and I went to the window seat in the kitchen to wait for Arthur Weeman. I willed him to enter into view, as if my brain tumor was a TiVo and could start playing an Arthur Weeman movie on demand.

I reached into the back pocket of my jeans to see how much cash I had to buy yet more food for Mrs. Williams and pulled out the piece of paper Anita Stefano, the psychic kinesthesiologist, had given me with the number for the psychic priest. Father Louis O'Mally.

I dialed the Florida number on my cell phone and a nice-sounding man with a Southern accent answered.

"Hello, Father O'Mally? My name is Rebekah Kettle. Anita Stefano told me to call you?" I sort of asked. I didn't know how this worked. I wondered if I should give him my credit-card number.

"She's a nice gal," he said. I hated when people used the word "gal." "Yes, yes, I'm getting a reading on you. Okay, now tell me what's bothering you."

"I'm not sure," I said. "She told me to call you."

"I think you're fragmented," he said. "You've given away parts of yourself and that's why your back hurts."

"My back doesn't hurt," I said.

"It does, you're just so used to it you don't even realize it. Your soul is outside of yourself which is causing pain in your chest. I see good things happening for you at work. There's a powerful woman looking at you."

"A powerful woman?" I didn't think he meant Mrs. Williams dozing on the sectional. Maybe he meant my editor. My mind flashed to Ivy Vohl.

"What about men? You don't have a boyfriend." He sounded

kind, and I imagined he was Reverend Alden, with a full head of white hair and a doughy Irish face. It was so nice of him to care if I had a boyfriend. My own father never asked me about that. This was why I preferred a holistic approach to health care. Blood tests didn't hold all the answers, sometimes you also needed the wisdom of a kindly old priest. And I respected this man for considering my loneliness. For treating my loneliness as seriously as if it were a brain tumor and as politely as if it were a person sitting next to me taking up space. It almost made me wonder how I could have felt alone when I had loneliness with me all along. I hated when people tried to ignore it, dipping my loneliness in sticky pink sugar and handing it back to me on a paper cone.

"No, I don't have a boyfriend," I said.

"Well, from the reading I'm getting, that could be because you really look like you could rip the balls right off a man."

For some reason this was not what I had expected to hear from a priest. I was a bit taken aback.

"You intimidate men," he said. "If a man fell out of the sky, I think you would probably grab him by the balls and throw him out the window."

This was especially shocking since I was sitting in the window seat at the time, leaning against the window.

"What should I do?" I asked, and tears started inexplicably pouring down my face.

"I want you to stop wearing makeup. And don't wear power suits."

I listened intently to every word he said, looking down at my jeans and the peach cashmere cardigan I had borrowed from Mrs. Williams. It seemed delicate, with coral beading in the shape of a flower on the breast, but I realized I was wearing it *like* a power suit. I thought of the aggressive jeans and boots I had worn on my date with Hugh Nickelby and cringed remembering the eye shadow. And the top I wore had a pattern of wheat stalks embroidered on it! How powerful and aggressive that wheat must have seemed to Hugh, conjuring in his mind plowing fields and locusts and homesteading together. And now that I thought about it, I was pretty sure it was a fertility symbol too. He probably thought I had been hinting that I wanted to have a baby with him.

"And the next time you meet a man try to be a little nicer. Not such a dragon lady." His warning sent chills up my spine to the root of my cerebellum. I looked down at my hands expecting to see long talons painted red, but my nails were short and painted a pale, sheer pink called Limo-Scene. But they *were* offputtingly shiny. My brain turned soft and receptive like an apple and my tumor woke up and wriggled his wormy head out.

"There is one man," I said, thinking of Isaac Myman.

"Go out with him!" Father O'Mally said urgently. "You're going to be fine, Rebekah. We're going to gather up all the broken pieces of your soul like an eggshell and put them back together. Now find a fixed point in front of you and stare at it softly."

I looked down at the concrete schoolyard below, picturing my messy eggshell. All the king's horses and all the king's men stood on either side of the schoolyard in perfect chess formation, waiting to put me together.

Then I lifted my eyes to Arthur Weeman's window. "Okay," I murmured.

"Open your mouth."

I opened my mouth.

"Wider."

I opened it wide, like I was at the dentist, and kept my eyes on the window. Just then Arthur Weeman appeared in it. He was wearing a tuxedo. Someone else was with him, handing him a mug.

Once I had been at a book party at Elaine's and some editor I was talking to suddenly pointed to the large window. Bret Easton Ellis and Jay McInerney were outside on the street, wearing stylish coats, deep in conversation with each other. "Now *that*'s quite a picture," the editor said, wistfully, with reverential tears in her eyes as if we were in Milan beholding *The Last Supper*. "What we're witnessing right now is literary history."

But this sight, Arthur Weeman in his kitchen, being handed a mug, with my mouth open taking it all in, this was almost too much to handle. He moved his hand as if he were swatting a fly. He pushed his glasses up on his nose. Every gesture was filled with Charlie Chaplin brilliance. My open mouth filled with gratitude for this private Arthur Weeman viewing. An Arthur Weeman silent movie that only I could see.

"Now, concentrate on all the pieces of yourself coming back into you through your mouth."

Arthur Weeman brought the mug to his lips.

"That's it. You're doing great. Now, close your mouth and swallow."

I gulped down the pieces of myself like a protein drink.

"Okay, now you're whole again."

"That's it?" I whispered.

"That's it."

"Thank you, Fa . . ." I didn't know what to call him. It felt strange to call him Father. I didn't even call my own father Father.

"You're quite welcome, young lady. You should send me a picture of yourself before the next time you call me."

"What do I owe you?" I asked.

"You can send a donation if you like. Whatever you feel is appropriate," he said.

Then, when I went out to get groceries, I did an incredibly benevolent thing. I smiled at a pregnant woman. It caused her to wipe the foul expression off her face and smile back. I was overwhelmed with a feeling of religiosity. I really was a truly good person and my good deed filled me with hope.

Since Arthur Weeman had been wearing a tuxedo, I figured he'd be out for the whole evening and I should go home. I wanted to take a shower and think about what Father O'Mally had said. I fed Mrs. Williams and promised I would see her in the morning.

She was watching *The Golden Girls.* "I'm having dinner with my friends tonight, out on the lanai," she said.

I went back to my own apartment, the psychic priest's words ringing in my ears. I should try to be nice. I should be open, less critical, more easygoing. I thought of Isaac Myman going out to buy my book. I could practice being nice on him, I thought. I called information and was relieved he was listed so I didn't have to get his number from Ivy Vohl.

Just do it already, I said to myself.

"Ivy?" he said, instead of hello.

"No," I said. I paused, thinking that might be enough romance for one night, and maybe I would hang up and go to a movie by myself.

"This is Rebekah Kettle, we met at the Arthur Weeman movie. Well, we didn't meet but Ivy . . ."

"The writer," Isaac said.

"Right."

"I bought your book," he said.

"Oh, you didn't have to do that. I would have given you one," I lied. When you wrote a book, people always assumed you had hundreds of free copies of it lying around your house. "So, Ivy said you're a photographer. What do you photograph?"

"People," he said. "Celebrities for magazines and newspapers. That's how I know Ivy, she's my boss at the *Quille*."

"Have you ever photographed Arthur Weeman?" I asked.

"Yeah, a few times," he said.

The idea of meeting Isaac suddenly seemed very appealing. "You sound a little like him," I said.

"Yeah, I get that a lot. That's how I got to shoot him. I called his doctor's office pretending to be him and asked when my appointment was once. I do things like that."

"That sounds great," I said. It already sounded more interesting than talking to Derek Hassler about his strenuous, high-pressure job at *Maxim* magazine.

"Well, I don't want to give the wrong impression. Usually it's just any monkey could do it, but once in a while something interesting happens."

"I love monkeys," I said. I cringed as soon as I said it.

Isaac laughed. "Is that so? Well, how about having dinner with me on Sunday night then? I can't do it Saturday because I have to go to a wedding."

"Okay," I said. "Where?"

"How about the Monkey Bar at eight?" he said, laughing.

When I got off the phone, I was inspired to carry a vase of almost dead Casablanca lilies into the kitchen to change their water. The color rust spread on my fingers from their stamens and I felt suddenly transformed, anointed, as if my skin had been painted with henna, and life was finally rubbing off on me in a good way. I felt like Cleopatra on the Nile, not Rebekah Kettle at her leaky sink.

Then I took a long bath and lay in my new Arthur Weeman bed and watched Debbie Harry singing on TV. She was so fantastic-looking that something about her made my heart swing inside me like a Murano glass chandelier. She had beautiful cupid's bow lips painted purple. And I thought, all you need to get by in this world is the perfect shade of lipstick and a sense of humor. And, at least once in a while, if only a phone-call's worth, love.

Once I had a love and it was a gas . . .

I sang along with her.

9.

At 33, she meets her future husband,
Isaac Myman

When I got to work on Friday, I was completely exhausted. Working for my father was killing me. It was so boring and tedious. The kitchen smelled bad because no one had taken out the garbage. My father didn't seem to have a cleaning lady. That couldn't possibly be my job.

Just then he called which surprised me because I had assumed he was at his desk with the door closed. I was over an hour late, I had just parked Mrs. Williams in the waiting room and taken off all of her layers—her scarf, wheelchair blanket, hat, and down jacket, which she called her "car coat"—and hadn't even sat down in Irmabelle's chair yet. I had to say she looked quite attractive. She had started dressing up to come to work with me.

"Where have you been? I've been calling," my father said.

"What do you mean? I've been right here for over an hour," I said.

"That's strange."

"Weird."

"Anyway, I'm not coming in til the afternoon. I'm at the hospital visiting a patient. But we'll celebrate at the end of the day."

"What are you talking about?" I asked.

"Champagne Fridays," he said. "Irmabelle and I always had champagne on Fridays to celebrate the week being over."

This was a very strange image, my father and Irmabelle, arms pretzeled, sipping champagne from crystal flutes.

"Dad," I said, "I'm not sure how much longer I can work here." I couldn't just keep coming to this office day after day after day like that. I realized that at first I had thought of it as a sort of joke, something I would do for a week or two to help out the old man, but now it was getting serious. I was really here. That morning, Laura had started teaching at the school in Walnut Grove. Not so long ago she was a student herself, reciting her essay by heart for Ms. Beadle. Life was moving on without me.

As soon as I hung up with my father, the phone rang again and I answered, "Dr. Kettle's office."

There was silence and then the person hung up.

I looked at the new caller ID. BRANCH, IRMAB. It took me a second to figure out it was Irmabelle. I had never known her last name, I realized. I put the receiver down.

About fifteen minutes later the phone rang and BRANCH, IRMAB came up on the caller ID again.

"Dr. Kettle's office," I said.

"Yes, hello, I'd like to make an appointment with the doctor," Irmabelle said in her unmistakable Haitian accent, or wherever she was from.

"Okay," I said. I waited for her to say something. "May I ask who's speaking?"

"Uh, my name is Maryanne."

"Have you been here before?" I asked.

"No, I'm a new patient. Have you been working for the doctor for a long time?" I almost laughed. She really didn't think I knew it was her.

"No," I said. "I'm his daughter and I'm just filling in until his real office manager comes back. Her name is *Irmabelle* and we're just a mess without her. When would you like to see the doctor?"

"Oh, well, I'll call you back," Irmabelle said, and hung up.

Half an hour later the phone rang again. It was Irmabelle. "Dr. Kettle's office," I said.

"Is this Rebekah?" she asked.

"Yes, may I help you?"

"Rebekah, it's Irmabelle," she said.

"Irmabelle!" I said. "When are you coming back? I'm overrun with patients here, and I can't do it without you." I looked out at Mrs. Williams sitting all alone like one of my father's plants. "My father's not in right now, but he'll call you as soon . . ."

"No, I called to talk to you. I want to meet you someplace. Will you meet with me?"

"Sure," I said. "Why don't you come here?" I had absolutely no desire to go to Brooklyn or Queens or wherever she probably lived.

"No, I want to meet you tomorrow afternoon. I want to take you to tea at the Plaza. It's something I've wanted to do for a long time."

"That's silly," I said.

"What's silly about it?" she snapped, obviously insulted.

"Well, the Plaza's closed," I said. I felt like I was talking to my father.

"Oh, no! That's terrible."

"Why do you want to take me to tea at the Plaza?" I asked, but then I looked down at the two little mouse dolls dressed as a doctor and a nurse stuck together in an embrace, and I suddenly knew.

Tea at the Plaza in New York City was a very specific type of ritual that was pretty much the closest thing you could come to family court without having to hire a lawyer and draw up custody papers. It was a place a mother took a daughter. If a woman took someone else's daughter to the Plaza, a goddaughter or a niece or the child of a close friend, it was a kind of staked claim that rivaled the labor and birth itself. It was where, for instance, every single New York stepmother had taken every single New York stepdaughter. There were only two kinds of people who went to tea at the Plaza, tourists and women on a sort of maternal feeding frenzy. Women with motherlust. I had been on both sides of the table many times, both as a child and as an adult taking my friends' children the moment they turned five. It was known among all women in New York to be a solemn bond and, as I was thirty-three years old, being invited to partake of the ceremony now could only mean one thing.

Irmabelle and my father had been having an affair.

Tea at the Plaza. The hugging mice. Champagne Fridays. I suspected it had been a long one.

"Now I don't know what to do," Irmabelle said, miserably.

"There's always the Pierre," I said, to be kind.

"Meet me there tomorrow at four? And don't tell your father," she said.

At the end of the day, I pulled the charts for the appointments on Monday and got ready to leave.

"Wait a minute," my father said, standing in the doorway holding a bottle of Taittinger's. "It's time for our party. Please."

"Oh. Right," I said. I wheeled Mrs. Williams back into the waiting room and stood there awaiting further instructions.

"I'll warm up the quiche in the oven," he said.

"Quiche?"

"I always make a quiche on Fridays. I hope you like broccoli and cheddar."

We sat together on the couch with paper plates of quiche on our laps. Mrs. Williams had already finished hers and was holding the plastic fork up in a somewhat scary pose.

I took a bite. "It's good, Dad," I said.

"Broccoli and cheddar. I hope it's okay."

"I just said, it's delicious."

"Well, the crust is store-bought, but I made the custard from scratch."

He popped the champagne cork and I made a little excited woo sound. He poured champagne into three paper cups from the bathroom, the same cups that were used for urine samples.

"How about a toast?" my father said. "To your tenure here with me. I'm glad you're here. I know it's not what you want to do right now, but I just need you to stick by me a while longer. And to your next book. I expect you to do quite a bit of writing at your desk when there's downtime."

Downtime was certainly a good way to describe it, I thought. This was definitely my downtime. "It's Irmabelle's desk," I said.

We were like Ma and Pa Kettle celebrating a great batch of eggs.

"So you got Elsa off to Forest Hills okay?"

"Forest Hills?"

My father had asked me to call a car service to send one of his patients home but I was almost certain the address I'd given the dispatcher was not in Forest Hills. "I didn't send her to Forest Hills, Dad. I sent her to someplace in Brooklyn."

"Why did you do that?" my father asked, getting flustered.

I stood and went to Irmabelle's file. I had referred to the wrong card. Elsa was on her way to someplace called Avenue L, which was nowhere near Forest Hills. My heart was pounding.

"Oh my God," my father said. "She has dementia. If she got out of the car there, she might never get home."

"Dad, I think it's time for you to talk to Irmabelle and tell her to come back." I wanted to tell him about Irmabelle's call, but I couldn't bring myself to do it.

"This isn't the time to discuss that," he said. "I have to call the cab company. Tell me the number." He was holding his cell phone and his hand was shaking. "This is an important job, Rebekah. With responsibility. A mistake could cost someone his life. The phone's busy. Where's redial?" He looked down at his phone in utter bewilderment.

"You have to get Irmabelle back. It's okay, Dad. Whatever happened you can work it out."

He ignored me and just kept dialing the phone. "I just wanted to sit and enjoy my champagne. A patient gave it to me when I saved his life."

I thought about that for a minute. For a minute I understood his disappointment at my not being a doctor. My editor had sent me flowers when I sold the first hundred thousand copies of my book. My agent had sent me a chocolate cake in a wooden box. But I had never saved anyone.

"It's been a very hard week," he said. As much as I hadn't wanted to work here, it had occurred to me that it might be nice to spend some time with my father. But to him I was less important than Irmabelle. I was my father's temp. "The last time we did this, Irmabelle made wonderful pork patties. I'll certainly miss those pork patties," my father said.

. . .

When I got to the Pierre Hotel the next day at four, Irmabelle was already there, sitting at a table in the Rotunda, looking nervously from side to side. She had lost a little weight and her hair was the way I liked it, in a big puffy pom-pom on the back of her head. She had the kind of body type that was sort of round on top with skinny legs so she always looked a little pregnant. She had deep, dark circles under her eyes. When I was a teenager I thought that dark grooves under your eyes was the most attractive attribute a person could possess. I used to wear no makeup, except for half-moons of plum eyeshadow under my eyes. I told people I had insomnia, even though I slept at least ten or twelve hours a day.

I sat in the chair facing her and looked at the fresco—clouds and a pointy-titted statue and a bare-chested man in a tree. I remembered my old shrink had once said, when I was ready, there'd be men falling from trees.

"Thank you for coming here," Irmabelle said. "I know this is going to sound a little strange to you, but I have always wanted to take you for tea since you were a very little girl. Remember, you used to wear that long calico dress all the time."

I wondered if she was disappointed that I wasn't wearing it now. I was wearing a white Debra Rodman dress and white high-heeled boots with rhinestone Pilgrim buckles.

"How's your father?" she asked. She was sweating in her flowered rayon blouse and black dress pants.

"The same. But he wishes you would come back."

"Did he say that?" she asked.

"I can tell," I said. "He still has champagne on Fridays."

"Yes, he always liked to do that." She looked angry.

The waiter came by and I picked up my menu, sticky from

some other child's jam. I had to say it was almost worth forty-two dollars each for a tea bag and three tiny plastic-tasting sandwiches to sit there and watch people walk by with their Hermès luggage, unfolding their accordion maps. Around us in the oval room, at almost every table, sat a woman and a little girl ranging in age from three to eleven, unless you included me and then the range was three to thirty-three.

When our disappointing, paltry, two-tiered tea tray came, Irmabelle brightened. "It's nice," she said. "I almost got the Royal Rotunda tea but I'm glad I stuck with the Peaches and Ginger. What did you get?"

"When are you coming back to work?" I answered.

"I'm not," she said. "I was wondering if you would do something for me."

"Sure," I said. No can do, I thought.

"I have a photograph that I want your father to have and I didn't want to put it in the mail. It's of the two of us. Remember when your father took me to New Orleans for that medical convention?" She said medical convention as if it was in quotes.

"No."

She took a photo out of her fake Louis Vuitton purse and handed it to me. It was one of those old-fashioned photographs, set in an oval mat, from one of those places where you dress up in a silly costume. Under the photo, *New Orleans, Louisiana* was printed in corny Gold Rush lettering.

It was of my father and Irmabelle in ridiculous costumes, standing under a street-sign prop that said BOURBON STREET. The sepia made their skin seem almost the same color. My father was wearing little gold spectacles, funny baggy wool britches and a long wool coat and fedora, and holding a tall rifle. Irmabelle was wearing a white lace wedding gown, off the shoulder, with her breasts pushed up under the cameo worn on a ribbon around her neck. She had on a Juliet cap with a chapel-length veil spread out on the floor next to her. They both looked somber and cold. My father had his arm stiffly around Irmabelle's ample waist, and Irmabelle held in her arms a life-like doll wrapped in a blanket, wearing a white lace bonnet.

It looked realistic. My father looked quite handsome for him, but Irmabelle looked fat and awkward, her chin up in the air, the camera having caught her in between expressions.

The picture had to be one of the strangest things I had ever seen in my life, and it was impossible to imagine my father slapping down the ten or twenty bucks a photo like that would cost, and yet it somehow seemed like the most natural thing in the world. The weirdest thing about it was the doll Irmabelle was cradling. I wondered if it was supposed to represent me.

I wasn't sure what surprised me more, the fact that my father and Irmabelle had been having an affair or the fact that my father had put on that costume.

"Your father loved that picture, but he wouldn't let me hang it in the office. I thought he might like to have it now."

Once I had drawn a picture of my father and Irmabelle, using a half-empty box of crayons at my father's office. I had colored him in peach and her, black, and she had said, "Is that what you think my skin looks like?" holding her brown hairless arm up to the drawing.

"Your father and I were very close," Irmabelle said. "I worked for him for thirty years."

"What does a-bop-ted mean?" a little Chinese girl asked a gray-haired woman at the table next to us.

If we were at the Plaza there would have been a harp.

Suddenly I felt eyes on me and I saw a camera flash over

Irmabelle's shoulder. A man was standing on the golden sweeping stairway that led to the grand ballroom, taking pictures with an enormous camera, three gowned women on a balcony painted above his head. I looked behind me to see what celebrity was there but, unless the little girl sliding off her chair under the table was a movie star, there was no one. I turned back around, and even though I was now looking right at him, he kept shooting. He was shooting me, now I was sure. He was wearing a sleazy-looking long trenchcoat and a fedora, a look which was way too old for him and not unlike my father's outfit in the photo. He put his camera down and checked something, a beeper or a phone, I couldn't tell which. He walked quickly away.

I hadn't been photographed like that in a long time and I wondered if I was being followed, and if Ivy Vohl was behind this.

For some reason I was furious at being photographed just as I was looking at this photograph of my father and Irmabelle. The moment would be captured forever. I wanted to get up and follow him and grab the camera away from him, but I just sat in my chair and couldn't feel the floor under my feet, as if my white high-heeled boots had changed to Mary Janes.

"Irmabelle, I don't think I can give this to my father," I said, handing the picture back to her. I didn't want to look at it anymore. "You should give it to him yourself." I couldn't really imagine sliding it in between his lab reports and putting it on his desk. He liked things placed on his desk in a certain way: lab reports on the near right-hand corner, the day's charts on the near left-hand corner, the charts of patients who wanted to talk to him on the phone on the far left-hand corner, and mail in the exact center, under the celadon elephant paperweight. He hadn't told me where old-fashioned photos of him and his mistress went.

The waiter brought our enormous check and Irmabelle

grabbed it. "I've always wanted to do this," she said. I felt like an old file she was making her notations on—bill paid, no further examination necessary. I didn't know what she wanted from me but I knew I hadn't given it to her.

"I know my father would like you to come back," I said.

A bride walked by us with a veil covering her face, and we paused to respectfully envy her. The Grand Ballroom at the Pierre was the closest we came to the Taj Mahal in this country.

"Thank you," Irmabelle said. "I'm going to leave now." She stood up and walked away, stopping for a moment to steady herself on the table in the center of the Rotunda.

She had left the photo.

I couldn't just leave it there on the table, so I slipped it in my bag and stood up, trying to think of what to do next. The Café Pierre bar for a martini seemed like a good idea. I definitely didn't want to go home. Then I saw the bride again, with a man I assumed was her father, heading toward the red-carpeted stairs. I suddenly had the urge to go to her wedding. I had to go somewhere to think about everything that had just happened, and the wedding seemed like as good a place as any.

I suddenly felt that she was my best friend and I absolutely could not miss her wedding. She seemed so pure and innocent, and normal. This bride, walking with her father, had probably never had a horrifying tea experience like the one I had just had. She didn't notice that I was following close behind her like a bridesmaid.

For one thing, I wondered why my father wanted Irmabelle when I'd had a perfectly good mother at home. Although my parents hated each other, and had been divorced since I was thirteen, I still couldn't imagine how my father could choose Irmabelle over her.

A string quartet played "Here Comes the Bride" as she walked down the aisle with her father. I waited for a moment and then slipped into a seat in the back row that was covered in white gauze. Everything was beautiful. The bride and groom stood facing each other. Potted topiary marked the altar.

Everything was perfect except for the wedding photographer who was crouched in the aisle, which was extremely tacky. It was distracting to have someone taking pictures like that in such a holy place. Then, as if he had read my mind, he moved to the side of the room and that's when I saw that it was the same guy who had taken my picture in the Rotunda. I hadn't recognized him right away because he had taken off his hat and coat.

He turned his head and saw me. And then he pointed his camera at me and started shooting, rapid-fire. I sat frozen in my seat, unsure of what to do. The rings were exchanged and he almost missed it, he was so busy shooting me. The photo of their first kiss as man and wife was of me, a total stranger, grimacing uncomfortably. I had to get out of there.

I got up just before they marched back up the aisle, and ran down the stairs, through the Rotunda and the Café Pierre, and out the doors onto the sidewalk. I ran, dodging traffic, diagonally across the street and stopped in front of an enormous gold statue I'd never noticed before of a man on a horse, and tried to catch my breath. I read the plaque—GENERAL WILLIAM TECUMSEH SHERMAN, BORN FEB. 8, 1820 AND DIED FEB. 14, 1891—and that's when I saw the photographer running toward me. I felt like Cinderella being chased by the prince, or rather, stalked by the paparazzi surrounding the Palace.

Cinderella, Cinderella, how do you feel out here alone in the street? Aren't you too old for this? Any comment on your father's affair?

The photographer walked right up to me. He had a plodding gait and his camera was bouncing on a strap around his neck.

"Rebekah Kettle," he said.

"Yes?" I said, in the same trapped-bear tone I used with American Express when I accidentally answered the phone. I didn't get recognized very often but I had to admit it was a huge thrill when I was.

"It's me, Isaac Myman—Ivy's friend. We have a date tomorrow night. I didn't mean to scare you."

"I'm not scared," I said, but I was. I didn't exactly enjoy being chased. "You should have put on your coat before you came outside. It's cold out."

"I'm not cold," he said. I liked a guy once who played basketball at the West Fourth Street courts and I was always finding good reasons to walk right by there and look at him through the diamonds of the chain-link fence. I ruined that relationship by one day telling him he shouldn't be wearing shorts because it was too cold. I had a problem being too maternal when it came to good-looking men. "I guess you didn't recognize me. I mean, I guess I didn't expect you to recognize me from the Ziegfeld."

"I'm sorry, you were taking my picture and . . ."

"You know the photo on your book doesn't really look like you. I figured you could use something more recent."

I was slightly insulted and I thought of a line in the song "Black Diamond Bay" by Bob Dylan:

She looks a–nothing like that

Then I was annoyed to hear music in my head at a time like this.

"Anyway, it's a nice surprise running into you. I'm photographing the wedding for the *Quille*. Of course I've done weddings for friends, but never anything like this. I had to photograph the bride getting ready, you know getting into her . . ."

"Wedding gown?" I said.

"Right. Wedding gown. She insisted I shoot the whole time and I've got three rolls of her wearing nothing but a white lacey thong. The groom's in for trouble."

"It sounds like it's going to be an interesting wedding album," I said, not enjoying this conversation in the least. It was a bad sign that he didn't know the word for "wedding gown" but the word "thong" rolled off his lips effortlessly. I wasn't wearing a thong, and I didn't want to hear about him zooming in on one all afternoon.

"How do you know Wal and Kelly?" he asked.

"Who?"

He gave me a strange look. "The bride and groom."

"Oh," I said, trying to think of something. "Actually, I was at the wrong wedding. The wedding I'm supposed to go to is next week. I made a mistake." I looked down at my white dress. "The wedding I was invited to is one of those all-white weddings."

He was about five-seven or maybe five-eight, with a beer belly, which was my favorite kind of man, unless they were self-conscious about it. I loved men who didn't care that they were fat. It was exactly the kind of man I would be if I could, fat with low riding jeans and a big sloppy untucked shirt, maybe stained with spaghetti sauce, and a copy of *Penthouse* or the *New York Post* under my arm. The way men used to be before they became gay. Before *Maxim* and *Men's Health*, when the only men's magazines were respectable ones like *Penthouse* and *Playboy*. Before *Will & Grace*. If I were a man, I would drink scotch and go to OTB and date either a tall blond knockout or an ill-tempered woman from South America or a Jewish New York intellectual type with frizzy salt-and-pepper hair and John Lennon glasses.

Isaac was wearing Arthur Weeman glasses, which he pushed up on his nose a few times with his middle finger, an unfortunate habit because he looked like he was giving me the finger every time he did it. He carried a tote bag that said CHANNEL THIRTEEN on it, a look I could only call old-lady chic.

"Did you actually donate money to Channel Thirteen or did you mug my grandmother for that?" I asked. I was terrible at dating.

"No, I sent them fifty bucks. I liked that series they did on old New York." His voice was gruff, and he stuttered a little, pushing his cloud of black curls back from his forehead and holding his hair bunched in his fist when he talked.

"What do you have in there? Packets of Sweet 'N Low you stole from a diner?"

"You seem like a pretty tough customer," he said.

"More romantic words were never spoke," I said, nonsensically.

"Is that Shakespeare?" he asked.

I tried to remember to flirt. I hadn't been good at it since high school, when it was good to grab a boy's wallet and look through it or make him let you wear his watch. At Bennington nobody flirted, we just had sex, and I'd been with Nathan the whole time anyway.

I didn't think, at thirty-three, it was a good idea to grab this guy's watch, or his wallet for that matter.

Besides, I really didn't appreciate being stalked at the Pierre Hotel and having my picture taken, although I was wearing great boots and I had bothered to put on two colors of MAC eye shadow called Jest and Hoax, despite Father O'Mally's advice.

"You know, I reread your book this morning and I have to say you're not too good at love scenes," he said, smiling. "Every time she likes a guy, she's nasty to him, and every time you start to have sex with someone, your mind wanders and goes off on all these tangents and then you skip straight to the guy 'collapsing on top of you.'"

"It's not me, it's a character."

"Right. Her. Collapsing on top of *her*. *The character*." He said the words "the character" extremely sarcastically. "I like to get really turned on when I read a sex scene. You leave out all the good stuff."

"Well, I'll try to work on that for the next one," I said.

"I can help you with it."

"Oh, yes I'm sure. *Chapter one: Isaac Myman*," I said, pretending to be reading from an imaginary book.

"I'd rather be in the last chapter than the first," he said. "Also, you always have the characters saying nasty things to each other, followed by 'he said, smiling' or 'she said, smiling.' Like 'You're really not my type, he said, smiling.'"

I wondered why he had chosen "You're really not my type" as an example. I didn't remember that being a sentence in my book, so maybe he was telling me I wasn't his type. And at this point, I really didn't care, considering I didn't appreciate having my book criticized by someone who was basically a sleazoid photographer one step up from porno.

"Well, thank you, I'll keep that in mind. Aren't you the reason Princess Di was killed?" I asked. "I mean, people like you?"

He looked a little taken aback. "I also noticed you didn't have anything good to say about men. All the men in your book are either disfigured with missing limbs or violent or fat and they're all sociopaths. When I met you I thought you might have some guy's testicles pinned to your bonnet."

Now I was taken aback. "My bonnet?" I asked.

"You know, like a fluffy hat." It was said with such force that I could feel the hat on my head bearing such heavy fruit I was practically Carmen Miranda. First Father O'Mally had said I looked like I could rip the balls right off a man, and now I was being accused of using them as accessories.

"I don't wear my testicle bonnet to weddings," I said.

"Anyway, it was good. I read it in two hours."

"It took me five years to write," I said.

Isaac looked at the Pierre. "I should really get back. This wedding's a big deal and if I don't get good pictures, I'll be in a lot of trouble."

I suddenly wasn't ready for the conversation to end. We were standing in one of the most beautiful spots on the face of the earth, in front of this statue, flanked by the Pierre and the Sherry-Netherland, Bergdorf Goodman, Tiffany, the Plaza, and the southeast corner of Central Park. The luminous Mac apple and the scaffolding on the Plaza with its gaudy Eloise-pink sign offering suites starting at $1.5 mil. Horse-drawn carriages lined the street in front of us. The smell of manure was overwhelming, making it hard to be anywhere else but there at that moment. For a moment, I pictured Isaac tossing his gross tote bag onto the velvet seat of one of the carriages and helping me up, like Pa helping Mary when they went to the big city so Pa could attend a meeting about the Grange.

"I love that movie theater," I said, pointing to the Paris. Finally something nice had come out of my mouth, even if it wasn't about him exactly. Once I had seen the movie *Metropolitan* at the Paris, and in the movie there was a scene that took place in front of the Paris. I was in the theater seeing the theater, and at that moment I stepped through the screen like Mia Farrow in *The Purple Rose of Cairo*. For some reason I really loved that.

"Hey, do you want to come with me while I work?" Isaac asked.

And then, as if Cinderella had gone back into the ball after midnight, dressed in rags and holding a pumpkin instead of a pumpkin-shaped Judith Leiber purse, happy to be herself and not caring about what a bunch of strangers thought of her, I followed Isaac back into the Pierre Hotel's grand ballroom. I forgot all about Irmabelle and my father.

When I got home I called Ivy, even though it was after one.

"I met Isaac," I said.

"Ha," she said.

I didn't really know what to say to that.

"I know," she said. "He called me. And?"

"I like him," I said.

"So, you *liked* him?" She said it in a certain way, as if it was inconceivable that I liked him, even though she had been the one to think that I would.

"Where are you going on your *date*?" She said date sarcastically for some reason.

"The Monkey Bar," I said. I had been impressed when Isaac had suggested the Monkey Bar. The Monkey Bar was a far cry from going to some awful sportsbar on the Upper East Side with Derek Hassler while he watched some game and actually took a fork off someone else's table that they were just about to use because he had dropped his. What kind of person would actually reach over and take something off of somebody else's table at a restaurant without asking? The Monkey Bar required a modicum of respect and thoughtfulness. An actual reservation and a jacket and tie, a plan. As far as I was concerned he had me at the Monkey Bar.

"When?" Ivy said, pretending not to be at all impressed.

"Tomorrow at eight," I said.

I couldn't sleep so I sat in my gondola for a while and decided to write a letter to Arthur Weeman on loose-leaf paper I'd picked up in the SCHOOL SUPPLIES aisle of the drugstore. I drew ears and whiskers around the holes in the paper to look like foxes.

November 18

Dear Awful Writer,

There's a new boy in my Hebrew class named Isaac. He goes to Dalton and he seems quite interesting. He wears oval glasses like your's which I find quite attractive. His interests include photography and magic which are somethings I know you were interested in when you were a kid. He does not seem like a big jerk. Yet. I met him at a Bat Mitzvah tonight and we spent the whole time together but it's not the same as a date even though at one point we found ourselves in the same old-fashioned phone booth but that's because we were trying scotch on the rocks. I have only been on one date but that was a whole year ago and it was to the ice skating rink in Central Park and I didn't have an enjoyable time. You're not jealous are you??? Don't be. He's no you. And he's no Almanzo Wilder (the man Laura Ingalls married).

By the way, I think the Good Doctor is having an affair and from what I can tell my mother is completely clueless about it. I think he's doing it with his nurse. She's tall and beautiful with blue eyes and he started making quiches and bringing them to the office on Fridays. I think he is going to take her to New Orleans

for a medical convention. It's such a cliché. I wonder if
my father will marry her and have another family and
forget us. This seems like a lot for me to handle right
now with the short story contest coming up. I have to
go now because I drank two glasses of champange (but
not much scotch on the rocks).

    Goodnight. And . . . HAPPY BIRTHDAY TOMORROW!
    Your,
    Thalia

I folded the letter into a square and put it in a lavender envelope.

Although I tried not to, I pulled my own book off the shelf
and started reading it through Isaac's eyes. I couldn't help myself.
I always did it when someone I liked told me they had read it.

"I just don't want to see you anymore," he said, smiling, gath-
ering his crutches next to him on the bed.

In bed, with my eyes closed, I could still see his flash going
off under my eyelids. An impression had been burned on my ret-
inas.

I woke up the next morning unbelievably excited that it was Sunday and I didn't have to go to my father's office. The only urine I
would have to see for the whole day would be my own. I would
spend the day with Mrs. Williams and hopefully Arthur Weeman, and the evening with Isaac Myman. I felt like I was dating
two men and seeing them both in the same day.

I showered, dressed, and took my Parlodel. It wasn't making
me as sick as it used to. Then I packed a bag with my date clothes,
the next day's clothes, and threw in the bottle of Parlodel, not be-

cause I intended to sleep at Isaac's apartment but because I might want to stay at Mrs. Williams'. On my way out, I grabbed an Arthur Weeman biography and the week's worth of mail from my mailbox and headed toward the subway.

At Astor Place, I picked up the Sunday *Quille*. I couldn't wait to see if Isaac's photos of the wedding were in the paper. Standing on the street, with my big bag on my shoulder, I awkwardly opened the paper and turned the pages until I got to Ivy Vohl's gossip column, "In the Buff."

They were in it all right. There on the page was a big picture of me scowling into the camera, with the caption: *Uninvited guest, author Rebekah Kettle dressed in white, crashes the joyous occasion.*

That was it. I was through with Isaac Myman.

Not only was he a manipulator and a liar, he was a terrible photographer. I had never had a worse picture taken of me in my entire life.

I was much too vulnerable to take the subway so I hailed a cab and sat in the backseat angrily flipping through my mail.

I opened a letter that had been forwarded by my agent.

Dear Ms. Kettle,

    I just wanted to write to tell you how much I enjoyed your book. In fact, I read it in two days. As a dental hygienist, I noticed how many references there are in your novel to dentists and teeth, twelve to be exact! They are:

1. *It looked like one of his teeth was rotting in his mouth.*
2. *I stood over him like a dental hygienist.*
3. *Because of my father I had thought the tooth fairy was cheap, and warned my friends to keep their teeth, not prostitute them for a quarter.*

4. *I used Mentadent, which tasted very faintly of sperm.*

5. *[The dog] was completely covered in black spots, including his tongue and gums.*

6. *I used his toothbrush.*

7. *Jack-o-lantern skyline.*

8. *As painful to watch as a child teething.*

9. *I brushed my teeth.*

10. *The commercial where the good-looking man opens his mouth and has bright yellow teeth.*

11. *The scar on his knee looked like teeth marks.*

12. *No one in New York went to the dentist more than once every five years because it was too expensive and usually meant going to the Upper East Side.*

Could you write back and tell me why you have such an interest in dental hygiene? I edit the Dental Hygienists Association Newsletter and I would like to print your response in the next issue. I'd also like a brief explanation of why you used each of the above references and if you are including teeth in your next novel. Thanks again for the terrific read.

Sincerely,

Phyllis Smiley (my real name!), Sarasota, FL

I looked down at the letter in disbelief. This is what I got for being a writer: any idiot could write me a letter or put a picture of me in the *Quille*. I felt like both my book and my mouth had been raped. I swore if I ever wrote another book I'd be careful not to mention anything to do with teeth. I'd go over the book with a fine-toothed comb to be certain it was as toothless as a hag.

When I got to Mrs. Williams' apartment I rushed to the

kitchen window but Arthur Weeman wasn't there. I was so angry at Isaac that I couldn't do anything but sit on the sectional.

Mrs. Williams turned on the Discovery Channel. A documentary about wolves had just begun and I begged her to change the channel but she became stubborn and refused.

The documentary tracked a pack of wolves in some kind of terrible snowy tundra. I knew I shouldn't watch it, my old shrink had made me promise not to watch programs like that anymore, but I couldn't bring myself to stop.

Just as I was about to force myself to get up and leave the room, one of the wolves was rejected by the pack. At night, in their den, he went to play with the alpha female and she turned her back on him. He tried again, rolling on his back in front of her, but again she said no. He was forced to leave, making his survival near impossible. He stood alone in the snow and howled and howled, hoping a lone female would hear him. Meeting a lone female wolf and starting a pack of his own was his only chance for survival. If he didn't meet a lone female, he would perish.

I would have done anything to save that wolf. I would have lain down before him and let him devour me if he could live another day. I would have sacrificed myself if he could use me as an offering, drag me through the snow to the alpha female.

I couldn't stop crying. Mrs. Williams, I noticed, was crying too.

"What's wrong?" I asked her.

"I lost my dog," she said. "He's out there somewhere all alone."

"It's not your dog, it's a wolf on the television," I cried. She was even crazier than I was.

"My puppy," she cried. "My pup-py."

Finally I went into the kitchen and called my old shrink.

"Hi it's Rebekah," I said to her answering machine. "I just saw a wolf. . . . Wolves . . ." I was crying too hard to speak. I just sobbed into her machine and then hung up.

I lay on the cot in Mrs. Williams' maid's room and imagined the wolf lying on his side facing me, his long nose on my pillow. He would press his nose into my skull because that's where my brain tumor was, and wolves were like dogs and knew when there was something wrong with you.

I was so worn-out that I fell asleep, and when I woke up I realized I was supposed to meet Isaac in an hour at the Monkey Bar, and I hadn't actually called him to cancel. He could just sit there waiting for me all night. Why had he done this, I wondered, humiliate me like that in the *Quille*? Of course I had no intention of going, but then I couldn't stop thinking about that wolf howling alone in the tundra. A female wolf was his only hope for survival. Except for the fact that he carried a tote bag, maybe Isaac was a little like that wolf, I thought, running in a pack of paparazzi and answering to the alpha female, Ivy Vohl.

And then I thought that if I didn't show up he would tell Ivy and she would know I had been upset by the item which was obviously what she wanted. I should go on the date, I decided, if for no other reason than to tell him off.

I got ready by taking two Excedrin Tension Headache tablets and my brain-tumor medicine in case I got too drunk on the date and forgot to take it before I went to bed. I soaked my feet in the water foot spa I had found in Mrs. Williams' linen closet. Sitting on the sectional with my feet soaking in swirling water, I realized that I was like a ninety-year-old woman getting ready for a date. Most girls put on sexy lingerie and maybe took a couple of amphetamines, but I took brain-tumor medication and soaked my dogs.

I had read somewhere that the best way to prepare for a date was to watch CNN and brush up on current events so you could seem intelligent, not watch the Discovery Channel and pass out from crying. To take my mind off the wolf, I sat down for a few minutes and read a time line of Arthur Weeman's life in the old biography I had brought with me. It only went up to age fifty, the age he made the movie *Take My Life, Please*. On the day I was born, he married Shirley Mazurski. He was thirty-five.

Aside from the day they were married, and the day they divorced, there was no other mention of his three wives. His time line went on without them. Same with the time line of Paul Revere. Aside from the day they married and the day they died and the days they bore him a total of sixteen children, there was no mention of the women in Paul Revere's life.

I realized that while men easily fit women in and out of their time lines, I needed a man for my time line to begin. Arthur Weeman's time line said things like: *At 41, he throws a New Year's Eve party—Woody Allen, Johnny Carson, and Arthur Miller are in attendance.* But it didn't say: *At 41, he and Alice Marlow throw a party.* It mentioned an important trip he took to Venice but left out that it was his honeymoon trip with Candace Ann. He was a tree, and Shirley, Alice, and Candace merely squirrels or robins or—he would probably say—woodpeckers, making a brief appearance.

I was nothing like a man, when it came to my own time line. Men bounded up their time lines like mountain climbers on Everest, not caring if their Sherpas fell behind. But my time line was the staircase in a tenement building and I clutched to the banister, watching every little step I took.

As I rubbed orange lotion into my feet that smelled like Creamsicles, I thought of how jealous I was of men. I put on my first-date dress, taking it out of the dry cleaner's plastic with the picture of the covered wagon on it. I grabbed my copy of the *Quille* and left.

10.

At 33, her book is advertised on GoCARDS
in bathrooms all over New York, L.A.,
and the Hamptons

When I got to the Monkey Bar, Isaac was already ordering a drink. I walked over to him and thrust the "In the Buff" column in his face. "What the hell is this?" I asked.

"I didn't have anything to do with that," he said. "I gave Ivy the proofs but I put an X through the ones she couldn't use, and she used this one anyway. I called her when I saw it, but she said it wasn't her fault. The art director insisted." He was wearing his Arthur Weeman glasses. He pushed them up on his long straight nose with his middle finger, so it looked like he was giving me the finger again.

"I can't believe you let this happen," I said, still sounding angry.

"I'm sorry," he said. "It wasn't my fault. Please let me buy you a drink."

I angrily ordered a martini because I was starving and I wanted the olives, hopefully three big ones. The barstools had put me in the mood for them, they were round and covered in green velvet to look like olives, with red velvet circles on top for pimentos.

"A martini?" he said. "You sound like my grandfather. What are you, eighty years old?"

"This is a martini *bar*," I said, even though it wasn't. "After what you did to me I shouldn't even be here," I said, thrusting the paper at him again. "You should have protected me. You should have made sure Ivy didn't get those pictures."

"I told you it wasn't Ivy's fault. She doesn't choose the pictures."

"Oh, really?" I said. "And what about the caption. Who do you think wrote the caption?"

"Well, she did, but it's her job. It sells papers. Look, Rebekah, I'm sorry. I really didn't think it would happen. I had a great time with you last night and couldn't wait to see you. And I brought you a present."

"A present?" I asked, warily. A present was usually a bad thing on a first date. Once I went on a first date with a man who presented me with a single wineglass. He said it was the glass he would break on our wedding day. And once I went out with a man who gave me an enormous sunflower that I had to carry around all night like a staff.

"Here," Isaac said. "I hope you like it."

He handed me a man's white handkerchief that had clearly been well-used. It was stiff and glued together in spots. It looked more like the forensic evidence in a murder trial than a gift you might get on a date. It made the wineglass and the sunflower look good.

"Thank you," I said.

"It's a handkerchief," he said.

"A handkerchief," I said. It was a subtle line with men. You had to show them you were grateful for little things but not give them the impression that it was okay to be cheap all the time.

"I'm sure once I wash and disinfect it, it will be great," I said. I was holding it away from me between my thumb and forefinger and I had no idea what I was supposed to do with it now. I really didn't want to put it in my purse.

"It's Arthur Weeman's," he said. "After I put you in a cab at the Pierre last night I stopped by the Carnegie Deli because I got a lead that he was having a late dinner there. He goes there sometimes, you know."

"I know," I said.

"He left it on his chair. I knew how much you liked him so I picked it up when he went to the men's room. Look, it has his initials on it."

I couldn't believe what I was holding in my hand. It was the most thoughtful thing anyone had ever given me. Arthur Weeman's handkerchief. AW was stitched in the corner with blue thread. There was a small mustard stain in the corner. The time line I had just read had included that *at 13, Arthur Weeman's lifelong battle with allergies begins.* I crumpled it in my hand and then brought it to my nose.

"Don't do that," Isaac said, putting his hand on my arm to stop me. "He had a really bad cold."

"I don't care," I said.

"I know this doesn't make up for what happened with the *Quille.*"

"I really love it," I said. "I don't care about the *Quille.*"

"You should care about the *Quille,*" a voice behind us said. "No publicity is bad publicity, as long as they spell your name right. I was expecting flowers all day or at least some kind of thank-you call."

I spun around on my olive stool to see Ivy Vohl standing there, beaming at us. "Look at you two. I'm so proud. I'm definitely on my way to Jewish heaven for setting you two up."

"What are you doing here?" Isaac asked.

"Rebekah invited me, but I'm just going to join you for a few minutes," Ivy said. "My friend Malixa is meeting me here at the bar in half an hour."

Ivy and Malixa. It sounded like two diseases instead of one.

"Ivy, why did you print this?" I asked. But I suddenly didn't feel that mad at her. She had introduced me to Isaac and he had given me Arthur Weeman's handkerchief.

"Oh, come on, Rebekah. It's not like you're exactly a bold-faced name anymore. I honestly thought you'd be thrilled. Oh, I see you're wearing your red dress," Ivy said. I wondered what she meant by that. She said it as if she had known me for years instead of weeks, and knew my wardrobe inside out. She said it bitterly as if I were an old actress on the Broadway stage and she had been my dresser for fifty years. She said it as if every single time she saw me, I was wearing that dress. "I'll have a cosmopolitan," she told Isaac and he ordered it and paid for it like a dog. Then she grabbed my hand and announced that we were going to the ladies' room.

I liked Isaac so much that I didn't even mind going to the ladies' room with Ivy Vohl. I was suddenly flushed with this great feeling of love for her. I truly appreciated what she had done for me, setting me up with him. I tried to remember exactly why I had hated her in the first place. Her only crime had really been asking me for a blurb. Being a terrible writer didn't necessarily make her a terrible person, I realized.

We walked up the stairs and through a white latticed room and into the fancy bathroom. "I'm really sorry," Ivy said.

"It's okay," I said, "you can stay at the bar with your friend, and Isaac and I can go into the dining room for dinner."

"What are you talking about? I mean, I'm sorry I got you into this." She made a cringing face. "This is really awkward."

"What's awkward?"

"The fact that you don't like him. I feel so bad for him."

"But I do like him."

"You're kidding," she said.

"No, I'm not."

"But you're not acting like you're into him at all. You're acting like you can't stand him."

"I am?" I said. Was I? Did I just simply not know how to go on a date? Father O'Mally, the psychic priest, must have been right.

"Well, I like him."

"I'm stunned. I really didn't see any chemistry happening between you."

"Well, I better get back to Isaac," I said.

I left the bathroom feeling extremely confused and bristled a little as I passed the GoCARD display case. GoCARDS were free postcards that were placed outside of bathrooms in restaurants all over the country and for a few thousand dollars you could have your advertisement on them. I was always angry that my publisher hadn't paid to have a postcard made of my book, and even though I had the fight with her about it seven years before, I still relived the whole conversation every time I walked by the GoCARDS. GoCARDS were becoming the bane of my existence. I knew a lot of people would have been happy just to have been published, but I couldn't be completely happy without my own GoCARD. In fact, now whenever I went to a restaurant and had to use the bathroom, I just tried to hold it in.

One of the GoCARDS caught my eye because it had a picture

of a brain on it. I grabbed it and put it in my purse in case I might want to write a quick note to Arthur Weeman later asking him why women were no more than tiny reproductive engines in the time lines of men.

Ivy Vohl followed after me. "I'm going to call my friend Malixa and tell her we'll be in the dining room."

"We have a reservation for two," I said.

"The place is empty. I'm sure it won't be a problem."

"I don't know, Ivy. I mean, we are on our first official date. I think Isaac and I should be alone."

"I think it will be a lot less awkward if I go with you. It'll seem less like a first date and more like just friends hanging out."

"I don't mind it seeming like a first date."

"Trust me, it will take the pressure off."

When we got back to the bar, Ivy went straight to the maître d' and changed our table to a table for four.

"Ivy wants to have dinner with us," I warned Isaac.

"Well, you invited her," he said. "But that'll be great." And before I could say anything, Ivy was wildly waving to us that our table was ready and Isaac jumped up and followed her into the dining room. Reluctantly, I slid into the banquette next to her.

"I like your outfit," Isaac said to Ivy. "It's very dramatic."

"Thanks!" Ivy said, looking at me. She was wearing a sleeveless blouse with little chiffon wings on her shoulder, even though it was cold out.

I couldn't believe that Isaac could actually like Ivy Vohl, even as a work acquaintance. It made me sure our relationship didn't have a chance. The foundation of a relationship was not sex or love, as some people mistakenly believed, but hate. It was very important that both people in the relationship hated the same people. I knew I couldn't be happy unless I could freely vent my hatred for Ivy Vohl as soon as she left the room. Unless Isaac started hating Ivy pretty damn fast, he and I were doomed.

I had to find a way to tell Isaac that I hadn't invited Ivy Vohl on our date, and I was just about to simply state it right there at the table, when it occurred to me that I could write him a note on the GoCARD with the picture of the brain on it. I pulled it out of my bag and fumbled around until I found a pen, and then without even looking down while I was writing, I wrote, *Can we figure out a way to be alone? She invited HERSELF here.*

The couple at the next table got up, abandoning their tray of petits fours.

I saw Ivy Vohl eyeing them. "Guy-Antoine would love those," she said. "Guy-Antoine's my boyfriend," she said to me, even though I hadn't asked. "He's a sculptor and he's at Yaddo now for two months." Yaddo was an artist colony in Saratoga Springs that was famous for everybody sleeping with everybody else. Sculptors slept with writers who slept with filmmakers who slept with performance artists who slept with dancers who slept with themselves. It was like an orgy, but you had to fill out an application, send a sample of your work, and get prestigious letters of recommendation to participate. "Can you freeze those?" Ivy said, pointing to the tiny macaroons, caramels, meringues, and tartlets.

"I'm sure they'll bring us some at the end of the meal," Isaac said.

"I'm Jewish. I hate to see waste like that," Ivy said. She might hate to see waste like *that,* but she certainly didn't mind throwing her food up in the toilet as soon as she had eaten it, I was pretty sure.

I had no idea how I could pass my note to Isaac without Ivy seeing. But then Ivy reached over to the other table and stole the petits fours, sliding the contents of the tray onto a white cloth napkin and then wrapping them into a bunting and stuffing it into her skinny little evening bag, and I just quickly handed the GoCARD to Isaac.

A waiter stood over our table watching Ivy try to zip her overstuffed bag, trying to make room for the petits fours among the condoms. "Do you mind if we keep this here at the restaurant?" the waiter asked, grabbing the empty silver tray from her lap.

"I know a great guy I could set *you* up with," I said to Ivy, remembering how Derek Hassler had often done disgusting things like that.

"I'm pretty serious with Guy-Antoine," Ivy said. "He's definitely in the Ivy League."

I ignored Ivy's repulsive joke. Isaac was still looking at the front of the GoCARD, the picture of the brain, and hadn't bothered to turn it over yet.

"What's that?" Ivy asked.

"It's a GoCARD," Isaac said.

"Did they do a GoCARD for your book?" Ivy asked me.

Isaac turned the card over and read my note. It looked like he read it a couple of times, but the expression on his face didn't change.

"Can I see it?" Ivy asked.

She reached over the table and tried to grab the card out of Isaac's hands but he pulled it away from her. She reached over and grabbed at it again and this time was able to catch on to a small corner of the card. She wouldn't let go. Finally Isaac wrested it away from her and folded it in half. Ivy got up, slipped her pocketbook over her shoulder and walked behind Isaac. "I'm going to smoke a cigarette," she said. Then she grabbed at the Go-CARD one more time, and got it. She read the note out loud.

"Can we figure out a way to be alone? She invited HERSELF here." Ivy looked furious. "What, are you in the seventh grade?"

"I'm sorry, Ivy, it's just that we're on a date," I said.

"A date I set you up on," she said. "If you didn't want me to be here, you could have just said something." She opened her bag and slammed a twenty-dollar bill down on the table. "This should cover my drink," she said and stormed off.

"That was awful," Isaac said.

"I'm sorry," I said.

"That really wasn't very nice of you, Rebekah," he said. He seemed upset.

"She's the one who wasn't nice," I said.

"I just felt sort of bad for her. She's a really good person."

"I don't like her," I said, putting it on the line. This relationship was over.

"You should give her a chance," he said, smiling at me.

"I hate her," I challenged.

The waiter came over and we ordered. "I'll have another martini," I said.

"I like Ivy Vohl," Isaac said.

It was the least romantic first-date conversation I had ever had.

We ate our meal arguing about Ivy Vohl.

He continued to defend her as we walked all the way home to my apartment from the Monkey Bar.

I remembered a time when I was in a play at Bennington, and I was in love with the lead actor. At the cast party, I was talking to him and another girl who was in the play came over to talk to him too. After a while he turned to me and said that he and this other girl had been waiting to have sex until after the play was over and would I mind leaving them alone.

And I remembered another time when I was at a bar with a

friend of mine and a man had been looking at me all night and
then approached us and we both stood up and he shook his head
at me and said, "No, not you, her."

I was starting to get that old Johnny Johnson feeling. Johnny
Johnson was a boy Laura Ingalls was in love with, but he only liked
Mary. This time, I really wanted to be the girl who was chosen.

As we got closer to my building, it started to rain. I didn't
know if I should invite him up or not. I liked him, I just didn't
like her.

"Shit, it's raining," Isaac said. "My glasses are getting all
fogged up."

I remembered my first date with Derek Hassler. He had taken
me to the MTV Awards and when we kissed in front of the foun-
tain at Lincoln Center, it started to rain and he said, "Darlin', this
rain looks really good on you." I thought that, except for the
"Darlin'," it was the greatest thing I had ever heard. Now I suddenly thought that "Shit, it's raining, and my glasses are getting
all fogged up" was the greatest thing I had ever heard.

While he ran into a deli to get a napkin to wipe off his
glasses, I decided I should definitely invite him up.

He seemed a little surprised by the gondola.

"I guess the handkerchief isn't too impressive with all of
this," he said.

"That's not true!" I said. "It's the only thing of his that I own.
These are all just props."

After a big argument about whether this was technically our
first date, or if the wedding at the Pierre was our first date and
this was our second, I finally said he could sleep in my bed as long
as we didn't have sex. After we had sex I wondered what had
made me want to move so quickly. I waited for him to get up and
leave but he didn't.

"So let's see," he said, smiling. "How much like your character are you? I wonder what you were thinking about before I 'collapsed on top of you.'"

"I was thinking about lotsa things."

"She said, smiling."

"Stop it."

"Okay, like what? What were you thinking about?" he asked.

"There's a wolf all alone in the tundra," I said. *The chances of a lone female finding him are near impossible.*

"Not anymore," he said, gripping on to me. "Ivy said you were a little on the crazy side."

"Ivy Vohl said *I* was crazy? I'm not the crazy one."

My phone rang and I let the machine pick up, which was a really stupid thing to do if you were in bed with a man for the first time. My old shrink's voice floated through the room. "Hello, Rebekah, I wouldn't normally call someone back after midnight but it sounded like the television program about the wolves triggered a full-blown anxiety attack. And I *am* concerned. Please call me back tomorrow so we can talk about resuming your treatment. As you might recall, this has happened before with the whales and the elephant burial ground and the pets of nine eleven." She had the most soothing voice imaginable. She hung up.

"Full-blown anxiety attack? Who was that?" Isaac asked.

"Just a friend of mine," I said. "I might go to the pound and get a dog tomorrow."

He nuzzled his nose into my eye. "I'll be your dog," he said.

"You're already Ivy's dog," I said.

"I'll be both your dogs," he said, smiling.

In the morning, I couldn't stop sneezing. "I warned you," Isaac said.

I sneezed.

"You caught Arthur Weeman's cold."

Except for the fact that my throat felt sore, I was thrilled. I couldn't wait for Isaac to leave so I could write Arthur Weeman a letter about our cold.

"I'd stay and chicken soup you all up but I have to go to Florida today. I'm spending Thanksgiving with my mother."

"That's nice," I said. It was important that a man love his mother.

"No, it's not. I'm dreading every second of it."

"Oh."

"What are you doing for Thanksgiving?"

"My mother cooks," I said. "I'm going to go to her B & B in Woodstock. It's her busiest weekend so she can't come here." Thanksgiving was that Thursday and I was looking forward to it.

"Will you still be here when I get back from the tundra?"

"Florida's not exactly the tundra."

"Believe me, my mother's cold enough to make it feel like the tundra. I'll be home on Friday," he said.

First-date sex wasn't a very big deal, but second and third date sex was. My old shrink had told me that all men will have sex with anyone once, and most men will have sex with anyone twice, but if a man has sex with you three times, it means he probably likes you. I had no choice but to wait and see what happened. There was still the chance that he could evaporate. But no matter what happened, I had Arthur Weeman's cold, and that at least was something.

11.

At 33, she spends Thanksgiving in the
Galápagos Islands with her daughter

The morning before Thanksgiving, my L.A. agent, Randi Apple, called during *Little House* to say that she had good news and bad news. I could see her sitting at her desk, talking into her headset, her diamond ring sparkling under the skylight, waving her yoga arms all around. The good news was the producer who had optioned my book had finally gotten a director attached. It looked like it was going to be made. The bad news was the producer was rewriting the script herself and wanted to meet with me the next day. The meeting was going to take place in her hotel room, which meant there wouldn't even be a meal involved and she'd probably be in her pajamas, high as a kite.

"On Thanksgiving?" I said. My book had been in turnaround for seven years.

"You don't mind, do you, Rebekah? It really looks like it's happening. They have some possible actresses . . ." Randi Apple said. ". . . lett Johansson." There was a long stretch of static. ". . . I'm in my car." So she wasn't at her desk, but I was sure, her diamond ring was still sparkling with the BMW's top down.

When I got to work, I told my father my great news about my movie deal.

"You're kidding," he said. He seemed genuinely impressed. "That's why they called you Rookie of the Year." This was a jab referring to the fact that when my book came out a big magazine had put me in their year-end issue, calling me "Best Rookie Novelist." My father had promptly showed me a book he had of baseball statistics. He opened it to a page listing all the Rookies of the Year. Statistics showed that not one single Rookie of the Year ever went on to be a success.

"Don't get your hopes up about the movie," my father said. "Things are very tough in Hollywood."

He spoke with complete authority as if he had been in the film business his whole life, having worked his way up from key grip to executive producer. As if there were Oscars and Emmys on his desk instead of little elephant statues and polished rocks. As if we were on the Warner Brothers lot at that moment and not his office on the Upper East Side.

The next afternoon, instead of eating my rightful meal which included my grandmother's recipe for Ritz cracker stuffing, I sat on a white couch in the penthouse suite of the Mercer Hotel. My producer, Barbra Shapiro, pronounced Sha-PIE-ro, sat on one of the other couches.

Randi Apple had warned me that Barbra was in New York for a "medical procedure."

A Tibetan woman was in the suite's kitchen pan-roasting a whole fish, and the suite's mahogany dining table that sat twelve, was set very grandly for one. Before joining me on the couches,

Barbra had reminded the cook to steam the kale in Evian that she had gathered in tiny bottles from the minibar.

"The Tibetans are wonderful cooks," Barbra said, swaying slightly as if we were on a boat.

"Did you bring her from L.A.?" I asked.

I was used, at these meetings, to talking about anything but the movie.

"No, I got her here."

"From a catering company?"

"Huh?" She looked at me, helpless, swaying.

"How did you hire her?" I asked slowly and plainly, acting interested, as if I at any moment would be hiring my own Tibetan fish fry.

"No!" Barbra said. "You never do that. I found her in the park. You always just go to a park and look for anyone Asian and ask them to come to your hotel."

I wondered if that was how she had found the new director too.

"Do you have any paper?" she asked.

I handed her the Mercer Hotel leather portfolio from the coffee table, which had stationery in it and a pen. "I was thinking that we could try to get Arthur Weeman to play the part of a law professor, as a cameo." I knew he would never do it, but I felt like saying it anyway.

"Now," she said, ignoring my idea. Her eyes rolled back in her head, and it took her a minute to come back to me. Whatever her medical procedure had been, it seemed to me they had given her crack for it. I had never seen her so high. Her white hotel robe fell open, and now she was naked, her breasts from a past medical procedure, taut and tanned, like separate people, producers in their own right. "Now. How does the father meet Semen?" She droned the question slowly, with long gaps of silence between each word. Her pupils were as painfully pointed as stingers in the center of big green irises.

My mind, in a seven-year turnaround of its own, had to think back to the book. "Semen?" I asked.

"Yes. Semen."

I was fairly certain I did not have a character in my book called Semen. "Do you mean the character of Seamus?"

"Yes. How does the father meet Semen?"

"It's Seamus," I said. "It's pronounced SHAY-mus."

She nodded, struggling to keep her eyes open. "How does the father meet Semen?" she droned again.

"Well, it doesn't really matter how the father meets SHAY-mus but since he's one of the father's law students, it's safe to say they met in class, or maybe in a local bar near campus."

She looked at me, holding the pen upside down, her robe now almost completely off her.

Then after a moment, she said simply, "How does the father meet Semen?"

"I just told you," I said. "They meet in class. He's a bright student who the father takes on as a substitute son."

"How does the father meet Semen?" Barbra droned.

"I think they meet in class," I said.

"How does the father meet Semen?"

"In class."

"How does the father meet Semen?"

"Class."

"How does the father meet Semen?"

I thought of Randi Apple eating her pumpkin pie with her three beautiful children, waiting to hear how my meeting went.

"How does the father meet Semen?"

The Tibetan woman came out of the kitchen with the fish on a large white china platter and placed it on the table.

"How does the father meet Semen?"

The Tibetan woman began to fillet the fish and spooned some on to the plate at the head of the table, on top of a pile of kale.

For one insane moment, I wondered if it was for me. I hadn't been offered so much as a Diet Coke.

"I'm sorry, it's time for my lunch now. Thank you for coming," Barbra said to me. "Sweetie, I think the film's going to be soooo great."

"Yes, I'm very excited that you're writing it," I said.

"It's my baby," she said. Then, though her eyes were open, she seemed to be asleep.

Her baby, which had once been my baby, was as good as shoved in a garbage can in a high school girl's bathroom while the prom was going on in the gym. What kind of mother was I? I'd had other offers and yet I'd chosen her. It always turned out like this and yet I always thought the movie was on the verge of getting made, Barbra ShapIro's legs in stirrups, her cervix, like her eyes, completely dilated, the Tibetan cook telling her to push.

I said good-bye to the cook and took the elevator down to the street. At least I'd had a meeting. Most writers would kill to have a meeting like that. And it certainly hadn't been the worst meeting I'd ever had.

I stopped by my apartment to pick up a few things before heading to Mrs. Williams'. On my way there, Isaac called me on my cell phone. I was sitting in the back of a cab looking through the week's mail.

"I'm looking forward to seeing you again," he said, somewhat presumptuously.

"Me too," I said, smiling.

"What are you thankful for?" he asked. The fact that I didn't have to go to my father's office for four whole days was top on my list. I was also thankful for Arthur Weeman, Mrs. Williams, and him, but I certainly wasn't going to tell him that.

"I don't know," I said. "My apartment. Lotsa stuff. What are you thankful for."

"I don't know," he said. "Martinis, condoms, and Ivy Vohl."

"Why those things?" I asked, bristling at the mention of Ivy.

"Because if it weren't for Ivy, I wouldn't have met you, and if it weren't for martinis and condoms, you probably wouldn't have let me have sex with you."

While he talked I opened an envelope I was holding, and pulled out a folder of information about international adoption. A calendar fell out on my lap. January was a nine-month-old Chinese girl; February, a newborn Russian baby with a full head of black hair; March was a three-month-old Korean boy named Kyle.

I suddenly felt very thankful, but I wasn't sure for what exactly, maybe something in the future. The Thanksgiving after my book came out, I'd gone to Woodstock and my mother had dragged me to some kind of a farm and I'd burned with jealousy at the sight of a pregnant goat. I'd cried bitterly up in my room while my mother did her best to try to calm me, but I couldn't tell her that it was the goat's good fortune that had set me off. I was probably the only published writer in history to be jealous of a goat. Now things seemed so much more promising. New York was crisp and Thanksgiving-empty. Nothing made me feel more lucky than watching tourists walking around in coats.

I said good-bye to Isaac and asked the cab to wait for me at the Edison Café so I could pick up dinner.

The Edison Café was no more than an old run-down diner, but it was the place I always went with my mother and her mother so it was the closest I could come to a family meal. I stood by the cash register under a crepe-paper turkey, and a waiter handed me an enormous plastic menu. A wedding ring sausaged his finger. He looked like the crumbling streets of Jerusalem in an apron.

"Turkey platter?" he asked.

"Yes, I'll take two turkey platters," I said.

All around me tourists and old people ate turkey off oval plates. I couldn't get away from old people.

I usually would have ordered the matzo-ball soup and my mother would have the matzo brei with extra applesauce, and my grandmother would have had cheese blintzes, extra sour cream.

I stopped the waiter before it was too late and changed my order to two matzo-ball soups, two matzo breis, two cheese blintzes, two slices of pumpkin pie, and two Diet Cokes. It made me miss my mother, so I called her to say I was sorry I hadn't come see her.

"It's better I didn't come anyway. I'm sick," I said. "I have a cold."

"Maybe it's allergies."

No matter what I said I had, my mother always accused it of being something else. If I'd said I had allergies, she'd have insisted it was a cold.

"Why didn't you have Thanksgiving with your father?" she asked.

"He said he had other plans," I said. I looked up at the magnificently ornate pink and white ceiling. I didn't want to tell her I was working for him because I knew it would upset her. "You know, the last time I talked to him he said Irmabelle quit."

My mother was silent for a moment. "Well, that certainly doesn't surprise me," she said, sounding surprised. "So Irmabelle finally left him."

The way she said it, it sounded like she knew they had been a couple.

"I'm not sure he's doing so well," I said. "He's acting strange. Sort of forgetful and confused." Maybe a part of me thought she might, in the true spirit of Thanksgiving, go to him if she knew he was in trouble, make like a wild Indian to his uptight Pilgrim.

"Oh, who cares about him," she said.

When I got to Mrs. Williams', I hung the adoption calendar on her refrigerator and opened it to November, a two-year-old girl from Kazakhstan. Mrs. Williams and I sat at the table eating our Thanksgiving feast. I looked across the way for Arthur Weeman, and then down at the deserted playground. Thalia would have just finished dinner, I thought. She would have stuffed herself with apple pie and gone to her room to write Arthur a letter. When Mrs. Williams went to lie down, I took a sheet of Mercer stationery out of my bag and began.

                                                        Turkey Day

Dear Awful Writer,

        Happy Thanksgiving! I am so full. My grandmother
made a delicious sumptuous feast and then my parents
dropped a bombshell and announced that they are
adopting a baby from China. Maybe they're trying to
save there failing marriage. I have to clean my room
because a woman from the adoption agency is coming
to look at it and ask me if I would like to have another

sister. I took the news very well but my older sister Lucy, whose sixteen, ran out of the dining room crying. Did I tell you I have a sister?

I hope you're not too sick to enjoy your turkey. Hmmm . . . how do I know you're sick? you might be asking yourself. Because I have your cold! Isn't that romantic? I happened to be at the Carnegie last week when you were there and you left your handkerchief on your chair and I picked it up and my father got mad at me because you were sneezing and then the next day I was sneezing! I wanted to go up to you and say, "Hi, I'm the girl who keeps writing you dumb letters," but I decided to remain a mystery. Uh oh, I hope you don't feel like I'm stalking you or something now.

Anyway you have to take me seriously because I might very well be your muse. My name Thalia means Muse of Comedy but I know my letters haven't been funny at all. I was named Thalia because I was almost born at the Thalia Movie Theater. My parents were seeing War and Peace and my mother went into laber and she barely made it to the hospital. It's lucky she wasn't at the Lowes or the Ziegfeld or they probably would have named me that.

Get well soon! Drink plenty of honey tea and gingerale and eat a lot of chicken soup. Thanks to you I got to miss school and spend two sensuous days in bed!

Your secret germ sharer,

Thalia

P.S. I have enclosed your handkerchief to prove to you that I am real.

P.P.S I have come up with the solution to my problems. Solution: You kidnap me. I will stay out of your
way when you are writing your awful movies and I
promise you won't get caught. I won't even have to
leave your house, I just need food, Diet Coke, and a TV.
I also need movies but you probably have a screening
room in your townhouse. Please, A.W., I am begging
you, come and get me preferably before my math test
on Tuesday. I WILL DO WHATEVER YOU SAY.

My P.S. was reckless. It was a hard decision to part with the
handkerchief. It was my gift from Isaac and I loved it, but for
Arthur Weeman, it seemed like a small offering. I'd lovingly
taken it to the Koreans to have it washed and pressed, but I put it
to my nose one last time. Then I sealed the envelope with the
handkerchief inside.

As soon as I did that I became instantly jealous of my new
older sister and bitterly regretted her. I imagined her life at sixteen was a lot more interesting than mine at twelve. I agonized
over her for a minute, but there was nothing I could do. It was as
if she now existed. Arthur Weeman, I knew, was fascinated by sisters. He'd had sisters, usually three sisters, in several of his films.
I knew he'd be intrigued by Lucy. I just hoped he wouldn't like
her better than me.

When Isaac got home from Florida, we made a plan to go to dinner in Chinatown. I got off the phone and told Mrs. Williams.
"What should I wear?" I asked her.

She opened the coat closet in the foyer and pulled out dress
after dress from the forties. Black lace with rhinestone buttons on

the sleeves, silk prints, red crepe and velvets. Everything was my size, just an inch or two too long. I put on a black-and-white velvet double-breasted dress with mother-of-pearl square buttons.

Then my phone rang. "I have to cancel," Isaac said. "I'm so sorry."

"How come?" I asked.

"Ivy called and said she wants me to go to L.A. with her, to a premiere at Mann's and a party at the Beverly Hills Hotel. She's thinking of expanding the column to include L.A., so I'm going to have to stay a few days."

"So no Chinatown for me, but Mann's Chinese Theater for you," I said.

"I'm sorry, Rebekah. I'll make it up to you as soon as I get back."

"By the way," I asked, "did Ivy say she wanted you to go to L.A. with her before or after you told her we had a date tonight?"

"Uh, after. Why?"

"*Just curious,*" I said, just like Ivy would have said it.

"So I hope this isn't going to ruin your night. What are you going to do?" he asked.

"Oh, no, it won't ruin my night." Mrs. Williams had put on a flesh-colored organza gown and wanted me to zip her up in the back. "I'm with my friend Mrs. . . ." I stopped myself because it sounded sort of pathetic to have a friend called Mrs. Williams. "Mississa. We'll probably go out and do something."

I couldn't budge the zipper but she kept it on anyway and sat on the sectional in it, with a matching clutch.

"Mississa?" he said. "You're not really going to go out with your English boyfriend, Hugh, are you?"

"What?" I said. I hadn't mentioned Hugh Nickelby to him.

"Ivy told me you had a boyfriend in Eng-land." He said "England" in an annoyed-sounding English accent.

"I don't have a boyfriend in England, Isaac. I just told Ivy that to get her off my back." I wondered why Ivy had bothered setting me up with someone just to do everything possible to break us up.

"But you really do have a friend named Mississa?"

"Why did Ivy tell you that, anyway?" I asked, outraged.

"I think she's just looking out for my best interest," he actually said. "Look, Rebekah, I really like you, but if you're seeing someone you should tell me."

"I'm not seeing anyone," I said, miserably.

The conversation unraveled from there, and I got off the phone Chinese-foodless and unsure of whether I would see him again. Isaac had said that he had to do his work. He'd said it a few times. His work. His *work*. I had to do my work too, I thought. All that seemed to be left of my old self was one paperback copy of my book on the book bum's table on Lafayette. It was still there, as he continually pointed out every time I walked by, braving the late-November weather like a trouper. I wanted to write, but all I could do was write to Arthur Weeman.

November 30

Dear Awful Writer,

Do you want to know what I wish? I wish I could buy you the green cashmere sweater I saw in the window of Barneys and give it to you for Christmas. You would look so good in it, and you never wear any color other than grey and brown. Are you a medium or a large? I would like to go there after school tomorrow and the man behind the counter wouldn't pay any attention to me because he would think I was just a child, but then I would say, "I'll take that sweater in green and gift wrap it please," and he would say "Who is the lucky man?" and I would say "It's for my boyfriend" and I'd march out of there with it.

Unfortunately I don't think I'll be able to afford it on $25 a week allowance, but it's the thought that counts! And I am certainly a very nice muse to give you writing advice *and* fashion advice, don't you think?

Yours very generously,

Thalia

Writing the letter turned me inside out, Peter Panned me right out the window and into the night sky. It didn't just make me feel young, I realized, it made me feel like a writer again.

12.

At 33, she is seen frequenting such literary
hot spots as Michael's and Elaine's

A week later I was at my father's office, taping one lone Christmas card—*Season's Greetings from Pfizer Pharmaceuticals*—to the mantle, when Isaac finally called and announced that he wanted a do-over. "Alone this time. Without Ivy," he said.

Relief burst over me like a parachute. The words "without Ivy" sounded unbelievably good to me. "Okay," I said.

"Great. Where are you?"

"I'm on East Eighty-sixth Street," I said.

"That's perfect! We'll go to Elaine's. Maybe you'll get your first Arthur Weeman sighting there. My source told me he was having an early dinner there. I want to be the one with you when you finally get to see him in person."

It was so thoughtful of Isaac to want to take me to a place where I might have an Arthur Weeman sighting that I didn't tell him I had seen him in his own kitchen.

"So when can you meet me there?" he asked.

I looked across the waiting room at Mrs. Williams.

"I have to drop something off somewhere first," I said.

"I have a date with Isaac," I said, when I got her settled on the sectional. I picked up the phone to order a pizza for her, but the look on her face made me hang the phone back up.

"What's wrong?" I asked.

"Nothing, dear, it sounds divine," she said. "So elegant . . ." Her eyes glazed over and her mouth froze in a terrible frown.

She watched me brush my hair the way I had watched my mother when I was a little girl, turning up the black fox collar of her coat and grabbing the braided leather strap of her Ferragamo pocketbook. Elegant and *divine*.

Mrs. Williams sat on the couch with her hands folded in her lap like she was on a long flight. I hated the way she got stiffer and smaller in the evenings. I hated that when I returned, she would tell me that the man from the eHarmony commercials had been over for tea.

She didn't speak or walk when she left her apartment, so there was really no reason I couldn't bring her with me on my date. I was sure Isaac would understand.

Unfortunately she insisted on changing her clothes and randomly scattered some rhinestone bee clips in her hair, actually doing a pretty good job. By the end of it she looked like she was ready to go to a wedding.

She pushed her own wheelchair down to the lobby and then sat in it. "We're going to Elaine's," she told the doorman. "It's a lovely restau—" She stopped speaking as soon as we crossed the threshold.

When we got to Elaine's, Isaac was already there in the room adjacent to the bar, at a table in the corner. I parked Mrs. Williams next to the bar, and I went to explain to him that we weren't going to be alone.

"Interesting coat," he said.

I was wearing a coat from Mrs. Williams' closet that she said I could have. It was a cloth coat from the sixties, embroidered with brightly colored Liberty Bells and American eagles and drums and crossed swords. Very Paul Revere. I felt ready for battle in it.

"Thank you," I said. "Interesting tote bag."

He kissed me and I got over that awkward feeling of not even being sure I would be able to recognize him, even though we'd had two dates and slept together. I recognized him all right.

"I'm afraid we need a bigger table," I said, nervously.

"Don't tell me you invited Ivy again," he said, looking past me. He seemed almost happy about it.

"No!" I said. "The girl I brought is a much better conversationalist than Ivy Vohl." If we were going to spend another whole date talking about Ivy Vohl, I was pretty sure that was going to be the end of me and Isaac.

"Oh, come on, Ivy's a good conversationalist," Isaac said.

"I'm sorry, I wasn't aware this was an Ivy Vohl love-athon," I said.

"Fine, we'll change the subject. If you keep bringing people on our dates, I'm going to start thinking you don't want to be alone with me. Maybe they can bring over another chair," he said.

"We don't actually need a chair," I said. I left and came back a minute later with Mrs. Williams and pushed her up to the table.

"Isaac, this is Mrs. Williams. Mrs. Williams, this is Isaac."

Isaac tried not to look surprised. "Hi!" he said, putting out his hand. "She's really hot," he whispered to me.

Mrs. Williams just stared straight ahead.

"You see she's a lot less intrusive than Ivy Vohl," I said. "She doesn't speak."

"She eats," Isaac said. Mrs. Williams was quickly polishing off the flat sesame crisps she had already slathered in butter. "It's nice to be on a date with a girl who has a healthy appetite for a change," he said to her. I hated when men said things like that. "Please, sit down," Isaac said. "I thought you'd feel at home here." He pointed to the wall behind me which was papered with pictures of gondolas and Venice canals.

"I do!" I said. "Isaac, thanks for being so understanding about everything." He actually didn't seem too thrilled.

"Oh, I think bringing a chaperone was a very wise idea. You'll help me to behave myself," he said to Mrs. Williams.

The waiter came and I ordered the veal picatta for myself and the chopped salad for Mrs. Williams, because I was sure that was what my grandmother would have ordered. Isaac ordered pasta and a bottle of red wine.

"So," Isaac said.

Something about Mrs. Williams' silence made us silent too. It was horribly awkward. Her silence had made her disappear, and with the glinting metal of her wheelchair and rhinestones of her hair clips, she had started to seem more like part of the restaurant, a centerpiece, champagne bucket or dessert cart, than a person.

"Didn't you have your book party here?" Isaac asked.

"Yes I did."

"I read about it on Page Six."

I remembered myself standing in the rain at the newsstand reading the item. "This is me," I'd said to the Indian newsstand man. "This is you too, yes?" he had asked, opening a porno magazine and pointing to a naked Asian woman.

Isaac looked at his watch. "Arthur Weeman should be here soon. Rebekah, are you blushing?"

I'd forgotten about Arthur Weeman. My cheeks started to

feel like they were burning. Even though I was the youngest one in the restaurant, I was the one having a hot flash. I'm not ready for this, I thought.

"Are you going to take his picture?" I asked, suddenly worried. I didn't want anything to happen that would annoy Arthur Weeman.

"No," he said. "I'm on a date with a, with two, beautiful women. I don't want to spend my time looking at his old, shriveled face."

"He's not shriveled," I said.

"Besides, I couldn't sell it for anything, anyway. His gondola's sort of sailed. He's over."

If he was so over, then why, when he walked into the dining room a moment later, did everyone turn to look at him? I sucked in my breath. He was smaller than he was on the screen, but bigger than he was in his window. His nose was different, less pronounced, more delicate. My heart ached for him. The eighth wonder of the universe. A national treasure. My eyes filled with tears.

Isaac grabbed my hand. "Happy?" he asked.

I nodded.

Isaac took his camera out of his tote bag.

"Isaac, don't," I said. I'd been in a trance, and had started to almost slide under the table, but the camera jolted me back. Arthur was with the actor Philip Seymour Hoffman and another man. "Isaac, please, leave them alone."

"I don't want their photo. I want yours. At this moment."

He called the waiter over and asked like a tourist. "Would you mind taking our picture? Just press that button. Rebekah, slide your chair over." Isaac stood and scrunched down on one side of Mrs. Williams' wheelchair, and directed me over to her other side. He put his arm around both of us, and we all put our heads very close together. *"Bellisimo,"* the waiter said.

For the rest of the meal, I tried to chew my veal and not stare at Arthur Weeman. I felt like I was sitting at his table, laughing gaily with Philip, listening to Arthur describe his next film.

"I have to go to the ladies' room," I whispered. It would involve walking past his table.

"So go," Isaac said. "Mrs. Williams and I have been waiting all night for a chance to finally be alone together."

I stood and steadied myself for a moment before making the journey past him. Then, just as I was steps from his table, Arthur Weeman removed his sports jacket. I was behind him, trying to stare straight ahead, trying not to look at him, but something made it impossible for me not to turn and gape.

It was the sweater from Barneys. The green cashmere sweater Thalia had admonished him to wear in her latest letter to him. He had bought the sweater. He was wearing it. He had listened to Thalia.

"Miss, the ladies' room," the waiter said, touching my shoulder and pointing to the back of the room. "Miss."

Arthur Weeman turned in his chair and looked at me.

"Nice sweater," I said, and rushed into the ladies' room. I had never felt more powerful in my entire life.

When I finally got myself together several minutes later and made it back to our table, Isaac had paid the check.

"Thank you for dinner," I said. I wanted to throw my arms around him. I glanced at Arthur Weeman in his sweater one last time, and we wheeled out of there.

He walked us back toward Mrs. Williams' apartment. "Allow me," he said, gallantly taking over the job of steering. He draped his tote bag over the back of her wheelchair. My head was aching slightly. I was worried about the wine mixing with the Parlodel. And I'd let Mrs. Williams have wine too and she had to take at least nine pills before she went to bed. But I didn't care because I'd never been so happy. Isaac yawned. "I'm tired," he said.

I was pretty sure that was some kind of date language for "I don't like you." Maybe it had been a mistake to bring Mrs. Williams. Why, I wondered, was it impossible for me to have one nice normal date with a man? Why couldn't I wear a skirt and sweater set instead of a coat with eagles and swords on it? Why couldn't I carry a slim Fendi bagette instead of an old bag in a wheelchair?

"But I'm not too tired to come upstairs," he said, as we wheeled up to the iron grillwork doors.

We crossed the threshold into the lobby. "Oh, no," Mrs. Williams said. "We don't allow gentlemen callers."

Isaac laughed. "Don't you think you're being old-fashioned?"

"Did you have a nice evening?" the doorman asked her.

"They didn't even let me have dessert," she said. "Next time I'm going to have a Caesar salad and prime rib."

"It's a date," Isaac said. "Well, I guess this is good night, then." He reached out and took my hand, pulled me to him, and kissed me right in front of Mrs. Williams.

He pressed his mouth to my ear. "From now on, every time I see an old woman in a wheelchair I think I'm going to get an erection," he whispered.

I had to admit it was pretty romantic.

I was too wound up to sleep, so I took out a pad of lined stationery I had bought in a store near my father's office. It had pictures on it of old-fashioned Venice scenes, gondolas passing under bridges, pigeons and cobblestones along the Grand Canal, women strolling with parasols in San Marco Square. I got into bed in Mrs. Williams' maid's room and wrote to Arthur.

December 7

Dear Awful Writer,

I just came home from a rather interesting evening for once. My parents picked me up after Hebrew School and said we were having dinner at Elaine's and that boy I like named Isaac was standing right next to me and I just blurted out that maybe we could invite him to come with us and by some Jewish miracle my parents said okay. It was almost like a date except my parents and grandmother were there and Isaac and I didn't say a word the whole time unless you count having to answer the stupid questions my father asked him like what college he hoped to get in to and what he hoped to major in and what his bar mitzvah speech is going to be about.

I had a secret fantasy that Isaac would hold my hand under the table but he didn't. It would have been a perfect evening if my sister Lucy hadn't been there. She monopolized the conversation talking about her stupid math competition. She has very nice hair and she kept spooling it all around trying to show off. I couldn't tell if Isaac liked her or not because he was sort of quiet.

I got out of bed and walked into the kitchen to look out the window one more time. His light was on but no one seemed to be there. As I stood looking out the window, the sky suddenly lit up with snow. Even though I was thirty-three years old, the first snowfall of the year still excited me. The once-a-yearness of it, like a birthday wish. I put the Paul Revere coat on over Mrs. Williams' B Altman nightgown, opened the window wide, and leaned all the way out.

Then I went back to my letter.

> But anyway the reason I am writing to you is be-
> cause it occurred to me suddenly (in the bathtub) that
> you have never had a scene in any of your movies that
> took place in a snow storm. Is it because it would cost
> too much money or because you don't like to be cold or
> is it a coincidence? I have, as you know by now, seen all
> of your movies and there has never been a trace of
> snow and I think that's a catastrophe. Would you con-
> sider putting a snowstorm in your next film? I can't
> imagine anything better.
> Love,
> Thalia XXXOOO
>
> P.S. the restaurant we went to was Elaine's.

Writing it was different now because of that sweater. I felt almost certain he would read it. In a day or two he would be holding this piece of paper in his hands. Shaking with excitement, I found a red lipstick in my purse and dotted it on my lips in the reflection of the window. I kissed the page tenderly. Then I slid the letter into its matching Venice envelope, got into bed, turned off the lamp, and was finally able to fall asleep.

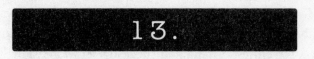

13.

At 33, signed first editions of her novel are sold
for large sums to collectors of rare books

Nine days before Christmas, on Saturday morning, I sat perched at Mrs. Williams' window watching Arthur Weeman. He stood there for a long time staring at the snow fall on the empty playground between us.

When he finally disappeared, I waited for a while for him to come back and was just about to give up, when I saw a very strange thing.

A man wearing dark glasses, a sheepskin coat, and a plaid cap was standing in the middle of the playground videotaping something. He was walking awkwardly, hopping really, and I realized his feet must have been cold because he wasn't wearing snow boots. It seemed creepy for him to be there, almost perverted, a man all alone in the Gardener playground, making big footprints in the virgin snow. I thought about reporting him to someone and I looked up at Arthur Weeman's window to see if he was witnessing this, but he still wasn't there. The man in the playground seemed to be filming his own footprints. He turned the camera up toward the sky and when he tilted his head up, I saw that it was Arthur Weeman.

He was videotaping snow. Then playing it back and watching it on the camera's small screen. He was auditioning the snow, giving it a screen test. Thalia had suggested snow and now he was casting it.

So now *this* was the most beautiful thing I had ever seen. Arthur Weeman was alone in the Secret Garden and I was watching through the shrubbery. In a way, I was his camera. In a way, he was holding me in his hands. In a way, if you thought about it, he was seeing the snow through Thalia's eyes, which were, after all, mine. My voice could be in his head. My letter in his pocket.

This was it. Thalia had affected him. She had contributed to his work, collaborated with him practically. The last letter, the one about snow, had been my golden ticket wrapped up tight in my chocolate bar. And now *my* Willy Wonka, *my* Walt Disney, *my* Arthur Weeman, was twirling in fast circles, filming our snow.

A security guard came out of the building, into the playground and said something to him. Arthur looked annoyed, his concentration broken, and put up a hand to ask for more time. The security guard retreated. Arthur took off one glove and did something to the camera. But he didn't bring the camera back up to his eye.

Go back to work, Arthur Weeman, I whispered, but he seemed to be finished. Worn-out and cold.

I could not bear for this to end. *Make a snow angel, Arthur Weeman, toss a snowball. You know your Thalia would want you to. Do you see her, Arthur Weeman? She's there, alone, sitting on the concrete bench. Talk to her, Arthur Weeman, go to her, she's your biggest fan.*

Arthur Weeman just stood for another minute or two and then, clearly freezing, he left.

I opened the window so I could feel our snow on my face, and I looked down at his footprints and at something brown in the blazing white. It was his glove lying there like the amputated hand of God. It was as if he had been made of snow all along and had melted, leaving only one glove behind. But it was my proof that what I had just seen, the greatest filmmaker who had ever lived, was real. So, I thought, *that's* how the Prince must have felt when he found the glass slipper at midnight.

Mrs. Williams had let me use her opera glasses and I trained them on the glove which was getting heavily dusted with snow and looked as beautiful as a palomino pony. I wanted it. The Prince at least *had* the slipper, he just didn't have the foot. I had to get my hands on that glove. But it was Saturday. There was no way I could get into that playground and if I could get in, what if he, watching from his window, saw me retrieve it.

All I could think of was the glove. I couldn't stand to think of it languishing in a terrible lost-and-found crate next to umbrellas and gym shorts and single socks in the gym teacher's office. The Prince hadn't just kicked the slipper into the bushes. The glove wasn't just any glove, after all. It was the glove of the world's greatest filmmaker.

Then I thought, I had to at least try.

I banged on the big glass doors until the security guard came and opened them. I felt thirteen again.

"Hi," I said.

"If you're looking for Arthur Weeman, he's already gone," he said.

"No." His statement took me by surprise.

"He got into a limo and the papa-rizzo chased after him. He was in-co-nito. Poor guy. Career's over. Hasn't made a funny movie since nineteen sixty-eight."

"Yeah," I said. It was good that he drove off in a car. It meant he wasn't home.

"That one that took place in the movie theater. That movie was terrible."

That movie was magnificent, I wanted to scream. The last thing I wanted to do was discuss the films of Arthur Weeman with an idiot. "Yeah," I said.

"What was it called, *Genie* something?"

"Um, I think it was called *Genius in a Bottle.* Actually, I work for him, and he left something in the schoolyard, so if I could just pop back there. . . ."

"Great, now I'll probably get in trouble. I told him not to leave nothing. . . ."

I walked quickly past him, through the lobby and down the hall to the opposite side of the school, and out into the courtyard. I grabbed the glove, just barely visible, and then looked up nervously at Arthur Weeman's window.

I looked up at Mrs. Williams' kitchen window and was surprised to see that it was the only window looking out at the courtyard. The other apartments had once had windows, but they had been filled in with a different color brick, like eyes shut tight. With the exception of Mrs. Williams' kitchen window, Arthur Weeman had complete privacy.

The playground was a square. On one side of its perimeter was Arthur Weeman's double-wide town house. Facing it on the playground's other side was the back of Mrs. Williams' building. To his right, if you were looking out his window, was a brick wall completely blocking the street from view, along with another brick wall abutting his town house, and to the left was the back of the Gardener School.

With the glove in my pocket, I left as fast as I could, carefully stepping in each of Arthur's footprints.

Out on the street, I examined the glove. It was brown leather, cashmere lined, with a Gucci label. I just hadn't imagined him as a Gucci type. I wondered if the Prince had scrutinized the slipper. Had it surprised him, the whorishness of it? For the first time I wondered if admiring from afar was better. It was so ordinary. His gloves should have been stitched by magic elves in a far-off land. And I felt so ordinary holding it, like a regular *fan*. Thalia was so much more than that. She wasn't the type to run around collecting his used cups and cigarette ashes, although there was his handkerchief, but that had been a gift. In fact I felt even lower than a fan, as if getting his glove had demoted Thalia from muse to stalker.

What other brands did he wear, I wondered, Prada, Church's, Fruit of the Loom? I finally slid the glove on and walked for several blocks hand in hand with Arthur Weeman.

I knew a crazy woman named Ivette once who thought she was destined to be with Bob Dylan. She sold her co-op and moved to Italy so she could be there for his birthday concert, where she was sure she would meet him and he would fall in love with her. Having this glove made me as crazy as she was.

My cell phone rang and I instantly felt better. It was Isaac telling me he'd just gotten a great shot of some rap star and he wanted to go to the movies to celebrate. I thought what a good team we made—the crazy fan and the paparazzo. Only Isaac would understand this glove in my pocket, but I wouldn't show it to him. Ivy Vohl was right, he was perfect for me. I told him I'd meet him at the theater on Twelfth Street and Second Avenue.

"I can't wait to see you," he said.

I got downtown a few minutes early, so I decided, with much

trepidation, to go to the Strand for a while despite how bad it might make me feel.

Going into any bookstore was always a traumatic experience—all those books—but going into the Strand was worse. The Strand was a famous bookstore that sold used books, and even worse, remaindered books. Books in big bins and books shunted out onto the street on shelves marked forty-eight cents.

Inside, old out-of-print books sweated it out on library stacks. I was sure I could hear the sounds of writers crying. Every time I cracked open a book there, I felt its author's tears wet my boots. I heard screams and moans, typewriter keys and quills scratching parchment. Lifetimes of wasted work, bad reviews, blurbs not gotten, royalties not earned, insults, humiliation, and poverty filled the dusty stifling air. Basically it was a poor author's mausoleum, a potter's field, and each book was a tiny, insignificant headstone.

"I'm looking for Proust," I said, when I got to the information desk. I thought maybe Mrs. Williams would enjoy to hear a small passage every night. Being around so many old people had made me think a little bit about dying, and I'd never read Proust.

"I don't know what that is."

This was the kind of help you always got at the Strand.

"Marcel Proust. *Remembrance of Things Past,*" I said.

"Maybe you'll find her in fiction."

The Strand was the great equalizer. The grim reaper. Its bell tolled for us all.

Only at the Strand could you find Proust in fiction on the shelf next to James Patterson, author of *Four Blind Mice.* I wandered around back there for a while determined not to look for my own book.

There was nothing worse than finding a copy of your own

book at the Strand, except for finding an autographed copy of your own book. Especially if it was inscribed with heartfelt words to someone you thought would cherish your book forever, not sell it to the Strand. This had happened to me once with a book I inscribed for my friend Bernadette before she moved to L.A. And what made it worse was that I didn't even find it—Derek Hassler found it and bought it, and called me up laughing hysterically because it said: *To Bernadette, the best friend a girl could ever dream of having in this world. All my love and thanks, Rebekah Kettle.*

I started to get dangerously close to the K's, and one masochistic moment later, I found myself face-to-face with my own book. A first edition hardcover for $2.99. I opened it cautiously and right there on the title page, optimistically round and robust, was my John Hancock.

To My Dad, with all my love. Your daughter, Rebekah Kettle.

To My Dad.

To Dad. It was the book I had given my father. I even remembered ripping open the envelope from my publisher that held the first copy and rushing to his office to give it to him. The very first copy of my book. It was my father's book. My own father's book. My own father had sold my book to the Strand for a quarter.

The sound of authors moaning and weeping sounded louder and louder in my ears. Laura Ingalls Wilder was wailing. She couldn't imagine Pa bringing her first book, *Little House in the Big Woods,* to the mercantile and selling it to Mrs. Oleson for the price of a peppermint stick.

This was the end of me and my father. I was through. With a new sort of determination I walked to the front of the store like I was in a funeral procession and paid for my sad purchases.

I handed the guy behind the cash register my credit card.

Why had my father discarded my book? I wondered. Had he

hated it that much? Why was he so angry at me, that he couldn't even stand to keep my book on his bookshelf next to his precious Stephen Kings? I had no idea just how much my use of the first person had infuriated him.

The guy grabbed a yellow-and-red Strand plastic bag and lowered the Proust into it. Then he picked up my book and did a cartoonish double take at my credit card. "You *wrote* this?" he asked with a voice filled with disdain.

I nodded modestly.

"You have to *buy* your own used book?" he practically screamed.

I autographed my credit card slip and left as fast as I could.

When I hit the street I started to cry. I shook with anger. I didn't know what I had done to make him reject me like this. My ex-shrink was right, it was no wonder I was obsessed with Arthur Weeman. There was no one in this world who needed a father figure more than I did. But to throw away my novel like that. It was the same as throwing me away.

I wrote a letter, standing outside the movie theater.

December 16

Dear Awful Writer,

I am in the Gardener School Playground at this moment, sitting on the freazing cold concrete bench, writing to you. In eight days, two hours and forty-five minutes it will be Christmas vacation. I will miss you. I see you looking down at us sometimes. Do you know which one I am? Do you see me looking back at you? Why do you watch us, Arthur? It makes me happy to see you in your window, but I like to think you have discovered me especially. Anyway, I *want* you to keep watching me, Awful Writer, and whatever Thalia wants Thalia gets!!! I would never tell anyone about my letters to you because they are private.

Today I found a man's brown leather Gucci glove in the playground. I know there is no way that it is yours but I put it in my uniform jacket pocket and I *imagined* it was yours. I will keep it always.

Your beloved,

Thalia

I put the letter in my bag just as Isaac walked up to me. Soon, I thought, we'd be buying popcorn and choosing seats. Soon, I thought, we'd be sitting next to each other, sunk down in our seats, heads touching. Soon, I thought, we'd be at the movies. Thank God for the movies.

On Monday I marched into my father's office, interrupting him on the phone. "I've got Mrs. Katz out there," I said. She'd been trying to hit me up for Seconals. "She thinks she has pneumonia."

"I'm going to have to X-ray her then," my father mumbled. He looked up. "Does she have a cough?"

"Yes."

"Is it productive?"

"In what way?"

"Is it productive? Does it produce phlegm?" My father wanted everything, even your cough, to be productive.

"I got you a present," I said, shoving the Strand bag at him.

"Oh, thank you, I love that place," my father said, looking at the Strand bag I was holding.

"I know," I said.

"I have a set of first-edition Agatha Christies that I got there," he said.

"I know, I bought them for you," I said.

"Oh, right." He stared into space for a minute, trying to remember, and then seemed to give up. "Agatha," he said. "We had that dog we named Agatha Christie. Ceased of distemper. I diagnosed her."

I looked at him as if he were crazy. I was getting angry. "We never had a dog," I said, with my voice raised. "I wasn't allowed to have a dog!"

"What?"

"There was no dog named Agatha Christie."

He sat up in his chair and shook his head. "Oh, right. Sorry, I meant when I was a boy," he said. "In Philly. I think I confused you with my sister."

"You diagnosed your dog's disease when you were a kid?" I said.

"Never mind. I don't know what I'm saying," he said. "I was confusing two things."

"What two things?" I asked.

"What is this, the third degree? Leave me alone, will ya?"

"I just wanted to know why I found this in the Strand," I said, handing him his copy of my book.

"This is your book," he said.

"It's the book I inscribed to you."

He frowned, causing his forehead to look like freshly raked sand. He opened the book to the title page and read the inscription.

"I don't understand," he said. He went to his bookshelf that lined a whole wall of his office and put his fingers in a space on the shelf between *The Botany of Desire* and *Seabiscuit*. It was eye level and centered. I had never remembered the book being in his office, but there was a space there. "It was right here. Someone must have taken it."

"No one's ever in your office when you're not here," I said.

"Not necessarily true. I may have lent it to someone. Yes, I did."

"You lent it to someone? Who?" I wondered why he had the ability to make me feel like I was the crazy one. Had a patient stolen it or had he lent it to someone?

"It's not important. You got it back. There, all set," my father said.

He slid it into the empty space on the bookshelf.

"It is important," I said. And then I did a very unprofessional thing for a medical office assistant. I started to cry like a little girl, complete with chin shake. I just sat in the patient chair crying. I cried for myself and for him and for my book.

He made a sad "oh" sound.

"You never saved anything of mine," I whimpered.

"That's not true." He sounded angry. "I saved all your letters." He was practically yelling.

"What letters?"

He went to a filing cabinet in the corner and handed me a file marked REBEKAH—LETTERS in Irmabelle's neat handwriting.

I wiped my eyes with my sleeves and opened the file. There were two letters. The first one was on beautiful harlequin ballerina stationery.

Dear Dad,

Just a note to tell you I just came from my audition and it went quite well. I mite get the lead part of Adelaide in <u>Guys and Dolls.</u> I absolutely adore French

Woods. It is the best theatre camp on Earth. I have so
many friends and one is a boy named Nedim Seban
from Istambul, Turkey. He pronounces "Friends" like
"Free-onds." There is also a boy named Kenny who does
magic and I told him about your aces trick and he
wants to meet you on visiting day. I think I have an
idea for a novel and I am going to try to write it between the time I get home from camp and school starts.
It's about a girl who is hairy. I can't even believe I
wrote the word school. I don't even want to think about
that again. I had to go to the infirmiry because I am
highly allergic to mosquitoe bights. By the way things
in the canteen are more expensive then you said they
would be and even though I am only having one icecream sandwich and one slushpuppy a day I am already almost out of money so please send more. I don't
think that is spending to much. I hope you have a lot of
sick and dying patients this month because I need a lot
more icecream sandwiches!!! I am not enjoying reading
The Brother's Karamazov AT ALL. It's not very good
AT ALL. I was heartbroken to discover that we don't
have a library here. Please send me something else to
read. I feal like either reading the whole Little House
series again or The Hobbit. One of the councelors is
reading The Valley of the Dolls and that looks quite interesting. The girls in my bunk had a meeting to kick
me out because I am so sloppy. I think their jealous because I'm probably going to get to be Adelaide. But a
girl named Jayne (pronounced like "Jay-knee") said
she would show me how to organize my things on the
shelves. She is very tall and bossy, but nice.

Well, I have to go shave my legs now . . .

Love, your daughter, Rebekah

The second letter in my father's file had been typed on onionskin paper and it wasn't a letter I had written. It was a letter written to me.

Dear Rebekah,

Thank you for your detailed letter of November 1. I think you will be quite pleased with what I brought for you this year. In addition to what you requested, Mrs. Claus and I packed something very special for you. I feel confident you will find that it opens up a world of mystery. Speaking of mystery, I also brought the Nancy Drews you wanted and a book I think you will find quite compelling called <u>Abe Lincoln Grows Up</u>. It was one of my favorites when I was a boy.

Thank you also for the milk and Ibruprofin. One certainly enjoys a change from all those cookies and you were right, I did have a headache. You were a very good girl and I hope you enjoy all your presents. Keep up the good work!

XXX

Santa

"See?" my father said. "I saved the letters you sent me from camp."

"I wrote you a lot of letters at camp. You only saved one. The second letter is from Santa Claus."

He took it from me and read it.

"I wonder what gift it was that would open a whole world of

mystery," my father said, smiling, delighted with the Santa letter he had written. "Oh, I remember, it was a microscope."

"It was the microscope you stole from the hospital," I said, as crushed as if I was right then receiving it again. "And my stocking was stuffed with boxes of slides."

"Ah yes, that was a very powerful microscope. And I didn't steal it. Mandlebaum gave me permission to take it. This is a nice letter. You loved that microscope. I remember that evening we looked at skin and blood cells together."

I wished I hadn't started all of this. I felt so sad for that girl. That girl who wrote the letter to her father, covered in calamine lotion and struggling to read *The Brothers Karamazov* when everyone else was enjoying *Wifey*.

At least I had gotten the part of Adelaide. At least I had that. I had heard that Nedim Seban had gone on to be a big television star in Turkey, but at least I had played Adelaide and only messed up twice.

If only I had written that novel about the hairy girl. I was sure it would have been a triumph. If I could read that novel now, *The Hairy Girl* by Rebekah Kettle, I was sure it would give me back what I had lost. My father would have loved that book. It would have saved us.

But I never wrote it. I read by the lake but never once went in, and wore white satin shoes with florettes on them all summer for some reason. She never wrote it but maybe I still could.

And I thought of myself, the girl I was then, waking up Christmas morning and getting that business letter from Santa Claus. A father and daughter extracting skin and blood from each other's fingers made for strange blood-brothers. An odd Christmas ritual in the Jewish home of the Kettles. A letter written to me that he kept in a slim file of letters from me. The evidence had been misplaced.

"You wrote wonderful letters," my father said. "I always knew you would be a writer. When you were a child, you never stopped reading. You and I used to spend whole days reading together! I was so connected to you. To your *mind*. Your letters were the most important thing in the world to me. I made Humberto buzz me as soon as the mail was in just in case there was a letter from you. I never felt happier or more connected to anyone in my life than you when you were a child. Maybe I've made some mistakes with you but I don't know how you turned out so uptight. I never realized quite how uptight you were until you started working here."

My whole body clenched up with rage. I had no idea what he was talking about. It was like he was confusing me with someone else and didn't know it was me he was talking to.

Once I had watched him make a chicken. His body moved in tense, jolty motions around the kitchen. He made three movements when one would have been sufficient. I realized he made everything more difficult than it had to be. A *production*. After fifteen minutes of watching him get the chicken ready for roasting, I'd had to take a Vicodin. The man in the kitchen doing the crazy chicken-roasting dance was the uptight one. Not me.

I didn't know how to unravel the mystery of my father. Maybe that was why he read so many mystery novels, to try to solve the mystery of me. I was looking right at him but I didn't know what I was seeing. I was Narcissus looking at myself in a cup of urine.

I suddenly wished I could X-ray him. Take a good look at his spine. I had the urge to grab the stethoscope from around his neck and listen for a heartbeat. To dig up my old microscope and see those skin cells again. I wanted an MRI of his brain to clip up on the lightboard next to the one of mine. See if there were any cloudy white areas or suspicious-looking spots.

Instead, I found a cup on the bathroom sink, filled to the brim with Mrs. Katz's urine. No one had asked her to do that. I stared into the urine trying to figure out how I had gotten here. Once I had thrown a coin into the blue-lit Fontana di Trevi in Rome when I was on my Italian book tour. Once I had ridden in a gondola on the Grand Canal and trailed my fingers in the water, swearing to myself that I would one day touch that water again. Now I was staring into a small cup of urine. Now I was wrapping a paper towel around a small cup of urine, and dumping it into the toilet.

14.

At 33, she models for a national
Absolut vodka ad

The next morning I skipped *Little House* because it was the episode where Laura's dog Jack dies after she is mean to him, and I didn't feel like crying my eyes out, so I got to the office early.

As soon as I got there, my father asked me where the pictures of my brain were.

"I don't know," I said. The scraps of the MRI films, left over from my valentine to Arthur Weeman, were still in my unemptied wastepaper basket.

"Did you file them in X-rays?"

"I think so," I said.

"Well, they're not there. I'm going to have you get another MRI soon, and I want to keep close track of the tumor."

"I'm sure they'll turn up," I said. I wondered what Arthur Weeman had done with it. It might be in a pile on his desk touching an early draft of his next screenplay or tossed in the garbage in his kitchen with his tea bags or ... And then I started to panic. What if he had shown them to a doctor? What if my own brain betrayed me? I had just assumed that to Arthur Weeman's untrained eye it would simply look distinctive, like a beauty mark, like the mole above Cindy Crawford's upper lip. But what if someone told him it was a tumor and a tumor in an older brain, and he saw me as some kind of sociopath?

"Uh, Dad," I asked, casually, "does the brain of a thirty-year-old woman look different from the brain of a thirteen-year-old girl?"

"Depends," my father said. "Your brain certainly hasn't developed much beyond a thirteen-year-old's. When you were thirteen all you wanted to do was watch that saccharine television program, *Little Prairie House*. Now, please, look for those films. Maybe they're in my office. This whole place is a pigsty. God, I can't bear it."

I went into his office and sat in his burgundy leather chair. I opened up his desk drawers and pretended to search for my brain, riffling through his files, all labeled in Irmabelle's square handwriting, all letters, even the L's, the exact same height.

The red light of line 2 blinked on the phone, and I heard my father requesting new films. "I need duplicates of a patient's scans. Fine, I'll hold if I must," I heard him say.

I flipped through the files. Dermatologists, DES, Diet Plans, Drug Rehabs, Eisenberg—taxes current, Elephants, Encephalitis . . .

I kept flipping forward but my mind had stopped on Elephants.

I pulled out the file called Elephants, opened it and found a school photo of a little girl, about eight or nine, against an artificial bright blue background. The image was repeated four times, four of the same photo on one sheet, meant to be carefully cut and distributed to grandparents. She was a light-skinned black girl, wearing a pink batik dress with a large butterfly on the front, antennae curling toward the scooped neck. Her hair was in perfect, natural ringlets, like a piece of machinery exploding into a cloud of springs. I figured her parents had given my father the picture because he had helped her and they were grateful. I didn't know what it had to do with elephants.

There was only one other item in the file, a yellowed clipping from *The New York Times*. I was eager to read it because it was probably an article about how my father had saved the little girl.

I turned the clipping over, and there in front of me, was an enormous photo of my father holding the hand of a curly-haired little girl who was pointing up at an elephant. I stared at the photo, and then lowered my eyes to the caption.

The circus comes to town. Dr. Frederick Kettle and his daughter welcome the elephants.

So, he had been right, I thought, I had seen the elephants. I was young in the picture, no more than nine or ten, but it was strange that I didn't remember. I stared at myself in the grainy photo. I was wearing a gray wool princess coat with Persian lamb cuffs, fancy.

"Goddamnit, I've already been on hold a long time," I heard my father say. "Damn Christmas season."

I tried so hard to remember being in that picture that I suddenly could. I could feel my father's hand holding my mittened one, the soft cuffs of the coat against my wrists, the elephant, and the nice man from *The New York Times* asking if he could take our picture. But then I noticed my hair again. It was curly. And my hair had simply never been that curly. But the little black girl wearing the butterfly dress in the other photo, the school photo, her hair was curly.

And then I realized that the date on the newspaper was the

date, twenty years ago, that my father had moved out of our house.

It was a Sunday. My father had gone to see a patient. My mother opened our front door in her nightgown and picked *The New York Times* up off of the doormat. The reason I remembered the date was because it was my best friend Jenny Newman's birthday and she was having a theater party, six girls seeing a matinee on Broadway, front-row center. My father came home and I remember the paper sailing past him, just missing him, the way on a drive in the country once, a wild turkey had flown low across the road, just missing our windshield. It wasn't unusual for my mother to throw something, so I had never connected the newspaper with the reason they divorced.

And then I realized, as the red light on line 2 stopped blinking, that my father had another daughter, and I had a little sister.

My mother knew and had never told me. She had read about it in *The New York Times*. If it was in the *Times* and my mother had seen it, other people must have seen it too. I wondered how many other people knew I had a sister.

You have two sisters, the psychic kinesthesiologist had told me. One was aborted. And the other one wasn't.

I quickly shut the file with the clipping in it and the sheet of photos and shoved it back in its place. I closed the desk drawer and stood up.

"Don't bother looking anymore. I ordered duplicates," he said, wandering into the doorway. "Is something wrong?"

"You ordered duplicates?" I felt dizzy and I steadied myself with my hands on his desk for a minute.

"That's right," my father said. "Are you okay?"

"Duplicates?" My father'd had an affair and it had been *productive.* I managed to get out from around his desk. "It's always good to have two of everything."

"What are you talking about?"

"Nothing," I said.

"You've never been particularly organized."

Was she? I wondered.

"I'm going to go out for a few minutes," I said.

"Okay, Toots." And with total concentration, as if I were walking the highwire and not the familiar worn-out carpet, I made it out of there.

I stood on the sidewalk for several minutes, trying to decide what to do. I'd left my Paul Revere coat in the office closet and I was cold. I thought about taking a cab home but instead I decided to walk for a block or two. As I turned the corner onto Third Avenue, I saw a terrible thing. A dog was running loose in the street. Cars swerved and I stopped, frozen. Other people were standing around too, unable to do anything. The dog ran frantically back and forth. "Please help him," I screamed. I started shaking. "Help him!" The dog stopped for a second and I thought it might come to me. Without thinking, I ran into the middle of the street. But it shot off up the avenue and was gone.

New York suddenly seemed like the most dangerous place on earth, with panicked dogs and elephants everywhere, and stupid people standing around. That's what I got for avoiding that morning's sadness on *Little House*—I had to see this dog and learn that I had a sister. A sister I would have done anything not to have.

When I knew my father was gone for the day, I went back to the office and looked at the wall of charts. I stood in front of the K's. Katz, Kaufman—A, Kaufman—J, Kawalski, Kazinksy, Kellerman, Kelley, Kesterman, Ketch, Kettle—R, Kettle—S.

Kettle—S.

Slowly, I pulled out the chart, which was thick, three times as thick as my own, I noticed.

I sat down at Irmabelle's desk, and, through lab reports and the tight impossible handwriting of our father, got to know my little sister. Her name was Sascha and she was three years younger than me. She'd had the mumps and chicken pox, lice and poison ivy. She was HIV negative. Her bloodtype was A positive, like me, and like me she lacked potassium. She'd had allergies, an ulcer, a lot of diarrhea, the flu every year, constant sore throats. She'd had both her tonsils and appendix out, two surgeries during which, I imagined, my father had visited her in the hospital. She was on the pill—Seasonale, the one that made you miss your periods. On her last visit, just six months before, she'd weighed 140 pounds. I even got to see another picture of her. It was one of those strange photos they used to take of newborns in the hospital, just her head floating on thick white cardstock, with piercing, wide-open eyes glaring at the annoying postnatal paparazzi. There was also a glossy hospital-issue piece of paper with the baby's footprint in blue ink. It listed her date and time of birth, her pounds, ounces, inches, and mother's name: Branch, Irmabelle.

I thought about Irmabelle at the Pierre handing me the old-fashioned photo of my father and her, holding the baby in the white lace bunting. I had thought it was a prop, not my real-live sister.

Our charts were at the same time so similar and so different. At the very back of mine, fastened flat to the folder with bending metal arms, was the medical report of my abortion.

Sibling rivalry had already kicked in. I was jealous of my sister's chart. The year she turned thirteen the worst thing that happened to her was my father proclaiming her to have "weak ankles" after she had a sprain. She succumbed to his physicals every six months, complete with weigh-in and bloodwork. Like a child's height lovingly marked on a kitchen wall, he'd kept a careful record of her time line.

With the exception of my new brain tumor and one or two bouts of bronchitis, my chart pretty much ended after the abortion.

I returned her chart to the place next to mine and went home exhausted to Mrs. Williams' house. We ate dinner together in the kitchen, silently, with me getting up every few minutes to look at Arthur Weeman's darkened window.

I thought of my sister's tiny footprint and the dog running through the streets. And I had a strange sensation of mourning something and celebrating something at the same time, I just wasn't sure what.

I wanted Isaac. But I was too tired to call him and try to explain what had happened to me.

In the morning, I saw Arthur Weeman wave at someone. I was standing at the window, watching Arthur Weeman standing in his green bathrobe and slippers, when I was suddenly startled to see him wave at someone.

It happened so quickly that I thought I must have imagined it, but when I looked down into the playground, I saw a girl with long brown hair wave back and then go over to a group of whispering girls. The girl and her friends couldn't have been older than thirteen because they were wearing the lower-school uniforms under their winter parkas. Once you got to the eighth grade at Gardener, you no longer had to wear a uniform. They were definitely thirteen, or almost thirteen.

I watched the girls for a moment longer and when I looked back up at his window he was gone.

A bell sounded, indicating recess was over, and the playground quickly emptied. I stood there, stunned, for at least an hour, unsure of what I had just seen. I had a terrible feeling, that I realized I'd had for a very long time, that right before my eyes, things were going on behind my back, and I wasn't very happy about it.

"Let me get one thing straight," Isaac said. "I like blow jobs."

"Well that's a problem because my throat chakra is constricted," I said.

We were sitting at a tiny corner table at Pastis and I felt nervous because the writer Jon Kettler was sitting at the next table and he was so tall (and handsome) that our knees were almost touching. We knew each other because our books were always next to each other on bookstore shelves, a fact that made us both a little uncomfortable as if we had slept together or something, and whenever we ran into each other we always made some comment about it. I hoped he wasn't listening.

"How do you know your throat chakra is constricted?"

"A psychic kinesthesiologist told me and she was right about a lot of things."

"Well, how can we unconstrict it?" he said.

"I don't know. I called a psychic priest in Florida and he tried to help me but I think it got constricted again."

"Here's my phone," Isaac said. "Call him again now."

"I'm supposed to send my picture to him before I call."

"We can take care of that," Isaac said. He took his phone back and showed me photo after photo of me on his tiny cell phone screen. "How about one of these?"

"I don't think these would work," I said. I was wearing my favorite dress, a low-cut Issey Miyake, and they were of just my cleavage.

"I think they're perfect. They're of your *throat.* Isn't that where your problem is?"

"These pictures are not of my throat," I said. "I work in a doctor's office so I'm pretty sure my throat is not between my breasts."

"Well, there's nothing wrong with your breast chakra," Isaac said.

Isaac's cell phone rang and he looked at me.

"Let me guess," I said. "It's Ivy."

The phone rang again. "Let me just talk to her for one minute."

"Isaac, this is a fancy restaurant," I said, annoyed. "Can't we have one meal without Ivy?"

The phone stopped ringing. Isaac looked down at his phone as if he expected it to detonate.

"There," I said, "see. You didn't answer and nothing happened."

A moment later the waiter brought a black telephone to our table like in an old movie. "There is a call for Mr. Myman," he said.

"Who are you, Desi Arnaz at the Tropicana?" I asked.

Isaac picked up the phone. "Hi, no, it's fine." He grabbed my hand across the table, as if that romantic gesture compensated for the fact that he was on the phone with Ivy, two steaks with béarnaise sauce between us, as big as her 34DD's.

I noticed a new gold wedding ring had popped up on Jon Kettler's finger. Our books were always together neck and neck, and yet he had gotten ahead of me.

"I'll get you some good shots tonight," Isaac said into the phone. "I promise." I hated his voice just then. Very Willy Loman. "I have some *great* leads. I know I can practically guarantee you

Courtney Love . . . What! How'd he get that? . . . *With* Angelina Jolie. Jesus . . . Sure, no problem, I'll hold."

He took his hand from mine and covered the mouthpiece of the phone. "Sorry, I won't be long. Ivy's got nothing for the column and I have to come up with something by tomorrow. I'm in a little bit of a dry spell."

I thought of Arthur Weeman standing in his green bathrobe, waving to the girl in the schoolyard and the girl waving back. Thinking of the bathrobe made me almost want to cry. I'd thought I was the only one who got to see him in it.

I noticed Jon Kettler talking to his friend about the teaching job he'd just taken. From what I could tell his friend worked in some kind of think tank in Washington. The restaurant was filled with men who probably had nice important jobs doing things other than skulking around New York trying to find Courtney Love. It almost made Derek Hassler's job at *Maxim* magazine seem noble. I tried to think of men I admired. Arthur Weeman, greatest filmmaker of all time. Paul Revere, goldsmith by trade, but also a politician and revolutionary. Charles Ingalls, farmer and homesteader who was also willing to work in a dangerous coal mine, in a mill, and in a noisy big-city hotel to take care of his family. David Letterman, talk-show host. Hugh Nickelby, novelist. Even my father was at least a doctor and a not a celebrity bloodsucking vampire.

Apparently Ivy came back on the phone because Isaac jumped to attention like a newbie at Abu Ghraib. "Yes, I'm still here. Uh, sure, where are you? Where's Guy-Antoine? . . . Oh . . ."

After a few more minutes he finally hung up. "Ivy's broken up with Guy-Antoine," he said. "He met someone at Yaddo."

He said this as if I would actually care.

"That's nice," I said, looking down at my steak.

"I told her I'd go meet her for a drink. You don't mind, do you?"

"Yes, I do," I said.

"I'm her friend, Rebekah. We can still finish dinner and then I'll just go meet her in Brooklyn for a little while. I have to work tonight anyway." I put my napkin on the table and pushed my plate away. "Why don't you come with me? Ivy really likes you. It would really be great if you could be friends with her."

"Why don't you go meet her right now," I said. I told myself not to storm out. I was too old for that kind of thing. Jon Kettler was watching my every move. But I just couldn't stand Ivy Vohl. And I knew myself well enough to know that if he said one more word about her, a wave of adrenaline would carry me out the door past all those better men.

"Ivy told me she would love to go shopping with you some-time."

"What does that mean, go shopping with me? That's crazy. We're not thirteen. What two women go shopping together?"

"What's the big deal? She told me she thinks you have a unique style. It's a compliment. You're not much of a team player, are you?"

I quoted the famous Groucho Marx line: "I wouldn't want to be on any team that would have Ivy Vohl as a member."

"She's trying to be friends with you," Isaac said.

"I just can't take this," I said, standing up and bringing my fingers to my temples like a crazy person. I couldn't believe how loud my voice was. "I am not dating Ivy Vohl. I don't even want to hear her name again. Ivy Vohl! I can't take it! Fuck you and fuck Ivy Vohl."

I stood up and pushed out onto the sidewalk, gasping for the meat-packing district's nice fresh air. At a time like this a girl could really use a sister to talk to.

I walked quickly across Little West 12th Street toward Hudson and stood on the corner, determined not to look behind me, but listening for the sound of running footsteps on the cobblestones, like whoever it was who waited for Paul Revere's lantern to come in the night. I waited tensely for the light to change and was just about to cross the street when I heard him yell, "Rebekah!"

I ignored him and crossed the street. Then he caught up with me. He grabbed my shoulders like a mugger. "Rebekah, what the hell is wrong with you?"

"I think you should finish the evening with Ivy Vohl."

"You're crazy," he said. "We are going to go back to the restaurant now, as humiliating as that may be, so I can pay for our meal. I'm assuming you don't want coffee and dessert."

"That is correct." I shot my arm up in the air and a cab pulled up within seconds. I would die if I lived in a place where you couldn't shoot your arm up in the air and hail a cab like a small God.

"Please, Rebekah, don't get in that cab. I'm sorry. I shouldn't have taken Ivy's call."

"No, you shouldn't've."

The cabdriver rolled down his window and screamed, "Fuck you," before driving off without me.

He took my hand. "I'm sorry," he said again. I didn't say anything for a minute and then let him lead me by the hand back to the restaurant. I was relieved he'd been the one to apologize but I still acted mad and waited for him outside.

When we got home to my apartment, Isaac sat in my gondola drinking a beer he had bought in the deli on Broadway and I sat on my couch from *Literary Suicide.* He patted the red velvet seat next to him and I got up and stepped into the gondola with him. It was held upright on wooden brackets, but I didn't know how steady it would be with both of us in it. Once there, I think we both felt a little awkward until we started kissing.

One thing about Isaac was that he and I had very different kissing styles. I kissed like a normal person and he kissed extra fast, as if we were in the airport and he was about to get on a plane and never see me again.

Kissing like that in the gondola was making me seasick. I'd had three martinis at dinner, my Absolut limit, and I was spinningly drunk.

I pulled away from him. "You and I are very different kissers," I said.

"I think we do all right."

"No, we're fine," I said, "just different."

"Why? How do I kiss and how do you kiss?" he asked, and from the look on his face, I knew I was rowing dangerous waters.

"Well, I kiss sort of regular, and you kiss sort of . . . fast."

"What does that mean, kiss fast?" he asked, defensively.

"I kiss like I'm from New York, and you kiss like you're from Hong Kong."

"I kiss like a Chinese?"

"I kiss like I'm in a Tennessee Williams play, and you kiss like you're in a sitcom on the FOX network."

"Oh, I understand. I kiss like the Concord to Paris, and you kiss like a Greyhound to Atlantic City," he said. "Here, let me try again."

My criticism didn't seem to bother him too much, and we kissed for a little while longer. This time he tried to do it in slow motion, but it felt wrong, like watching an actor in a Japanese karate movie dubbed in English. I started really laughing.

"Should we make out by sea or by land?" Isaac asked.

"Land," I said.

We abandoned the uncomfortable gondola and lay down together on the Persian carpet. I spun my way out of my clothes and so did he.

"Do you have any other helpful observations for me, or was the kissing it?"

"The kissing was it," I said. "Everything else is perfect."

"Good. How's your throat chakra?"

"Constricted," I said.

"Maybe you should try to loosen it."

I thought he was right, I should try, he had given up Ivy Vohl after all, and I kneeled next to him as gracefully as possible. He closed his eyes and ran his fingers over the soft wool of the carpet while I began what I was sure would be the best blow job ever. But as soon as I made contact, the room went from spinning gently like a merry-go-round to reeling joltingly like a Tilt-A-Whirl, and I sort of hung on to his penis with my mouth for dear life. Then, without much warning, I was suddenly like one of those openmouthed clown heads at a fair you squirt water at. He filled my mouth and my cheeks expanded like balloons. That was when I accidentally threw up on him.

I looked down at the Absolut-vomit in total disbelief. It had happened completely silently. His penis stuck straight up like a manatee poking its head out of a murky sea. I had never thrown up on a man before. I tried desperately to decide what to do. Leaving, which would have been my first choice, didn't seem possible because we were in my apartment.

Luckily, he kept his eyes closed and luxuriated on the rug, a wide, warm smile on his face. He started to sit up.

"Don't move," I said, pushing him down.

"Why not?"

"I'm going to get you a hot washcloth."

"Mmmmmmm," he said, totally content for me to serve him like the geisha I was.

I made my way to the bathroom, praying he wouldn't sit up, and soaked half of a huge towel in hot water. I wrung it out, ran back to where Isaac was still lying flat on his back, and gingerly swabbed all the vomit off him with the wet side of the towel and then finished him off with the dry side. The whole procedure took several minutes but he didn't seem to notice because he was almost asleep.

When I was done I carefully carried the towel into the kitchen, put it in a garbage bag, and still naked, hurried it out to the garbage room.

"Where'd you go?" Isaac asked when I came back in and locked the door behind me. He was working his way to standing.

"Nowhere, I'm right here," I said.

"I'm ready to return the favor." He came over to me and hugged me.

"That's okay," I said. "Next time."

"See, why can't you write sex scenes like this? You just gave me a nice normal blow job that we both enjoyed and nobody had to scratch anyone or spit or do anything disgusting. You should try writing from real life. You can leave the gruesome stuff to Stephen King."

I waited patiently for him to finish his writing lecture. "I don't appreciate having my writing criticized."

"I don't appreciate having my kissing criticized."

"I feel like I just gave a blow job to Robert McKee."

"I feel like I just got a blow job from Ebert and Roeper."

"I feel like I just gave a blow job to Gordon Lish."

"I don't know who that is, but I feel like I just got a blow job from my mother."

"I feel like I just gave a blow job to Michiko Kakutani."

Everything was normal. He didn't know I had thrown up on him, and no matter what happened, I would never tell him. I brushed my teeth and we got into my bed, passing a big bottle of Poland Spring back and forth between us.

"Do you have any food?" he asked. "We really didn't get to eat much dinner."

I thought of a woman I knew who made her husband elaborate spaghetti dishes in the middle of the night. And another woman I knew who regularly wore a kimono over her pajamas and carried two wooden sushi blocks to the Japanese restaurant across the street and brought them back to whatever man she happened to be with that night laden with the finest salmon skin, spider, and dragon rolls. And there was my friend who used to make dinners for Bob Dylan after his gigs whenever he was in L.A.

"No," I said. "Isaac, there's something I have to tell you. I threw up on you just now."

"I know."

I was shocked. "You knew?"

"Of course I knew. You do know that the penis is a very sensitive part of the body, don't you? A cock knows."

"I'm really sorry."

"It wasn't your fault. You told me you had a block in your chakra. I should have been more sensitive about it."

He put his arms tightly around me and we stopped talking until he fell asleep. I said my childish prayers. God bless Arthur Weeman, and Isaac, and Dad, and Mom, and Mrs. Williams, I thought. And in a moment of sheer goodness, I even asked God to bless Ivy Vohl and help her to be a better person. I was pretty sure people in the Bible had to deal with a lot bigger obstacles than Ivy Vohl, like floods and locusts and pestilence, whatever that was. Then I remembered my sister and the thought startled me like a looming shadow. God bless Sascha. My time line was shooting up like Jack's beanstalk. Crazy things were happening. I grabbed the bottle of Parlodel from my bedside table and swallowed one like a magic bean.

I tried to think about Isaac, but I couldn't stop thinking about Sascha. Finally I just got out of bed. Quietly, in my gondola, I called information. "In New York, New York for Sascha Kettle."

My hand shook like a teenager's.

"I have a Frederick Kettle, MD, and a Rebekah Kettle, but her number is non-published," the operator said.

"No. Sascha Kettle," I said.

"Oh wait, yes, I have a Sascha Kettle. I'm sorry, that's a non-published number as well," the operator said.

Non-published. Those words reminded me of the novel I was supposed to be writing, and I hung up without saying thank you.

15.

At 33, a suitor rescues her from
a five-alarm fire

Usually when you like a man, you have to endure his parents. I'd been to knitting shops with boyfriends' mothers, nail salons, Broadway shows, and of course the Plaza. I'd had endless lunches and Thanksgiving weekends in terrible states. But with Isaac it became painfully clear that it wasn't his mother I had to accept. It was Ivy.

We stood next to each other in front of the mirror in the only dressing room at La Petite Lolita, topless from the waist up.

"You're not a hundred percent Jewish are you?" Ivy Vohl asked.

I wondered what about my upper body had caused her to ask me that. "Yes I am. Why do you ask?"

"It's just really hard for me to spend ninety-eight dollars on a bra. But I love this embroidery." She stroked the pink and green Aubade bra in her hand.

I put on a black lace one. "I'm going to take this," I said, hoping my decisiveness would help speed us out of there. If I didn't consummate this with a purchase, I was afraid it wouldn't count and I'd have to go shopping with her again.

"Are you going to buy the matching thong?" Ivy asked.

"No."

"Do they let you try on underwear here?"

"I don't think so," I said. There was no way I was going to stand there and try on thongs with Ivy Vohl.

"Are you going to get anything else?" she asked.

"No."

"Do you feel lingerie helps to propagate the objectification of females?"

"No," I said.

"But aren't you buying it to wear for Isaac?"

Ivy asked all her questions with the even intensity of an investigative reporter. It just did not feel like a conversation with a human being. I felt like I was standing half naked on *20/20* next to Barbara Walters.

"No."

The salesgirl opened the door without knocking. "How are you two doing in there?"

She was holding a basket of sachets that smelled of cloves, and an image flashed into my head of me as a young child poking a clove into the hard skin of an orange. I could feel the sharp head of the clove between my tiny fingers, see myself sitting on my father's waiting-room floor, carefully inserting the cloves, and hear someone—Irmabelle it must have been—telling me what a good job I was doing. But there was someone else there too. Another child sitting in Irmabelle's lap. She was younger than I was and I was helping her do it. I couldn't see her face.

"Is everything okay?" the salesgirl asked.

I was gazing into the mirror and Ivy and the salesgirl were staring at me.

"Oh, yeah, I'm fine," I said. "I'm going to take this." I handed the salesgirl the bra I was buying. I *was* buying it to wear for Isaac, although he would probably be on the phone with Ivy Vohl at the time. She took the bra and closed the door behind her.

I got dressed quickly. "I'll wait for you out there," I said.

"Don't you want to help me decide what to get?"

"I think you should get that," I said, pointing to the pink and green. It really did take ten years off her breasts.

"Don't you think it's a little extravagant?"

"It's worth it."

"You're so lucky, Rebekah. You're such a good writer. I was rereading your book the other day. But do you think you use too many adjectives? A writing teacher I had once said it's better to leave them out." Only Ivy could treat writing like the Atkins diet, turning adjectives into carbs. "Speaking of writing. Have you gotten around to my novel yet?"

"I'm working on a blurb without adjectives. What about this bra?" I asked, trying to distract her.

"I already asked, they don't have it in my size."

As I watched her try on a few more bras, she changed her line of questioning.

"Have you ever touched another woman's breasts?" she asked.

"No."

"Aren't you curious to know what it would feel like? I mean, not in a sexual way, just to know what the texture would be?"

"No," I said, firmly.

"I just think it's interesting that our breasts are so different. I mean mine are bigger and sort of longer and yours are rounder like cakes." I had always liked my breasts and now I felt like they might be ruined for me. Every time I looked at them, I'd think of hers next to them. I was glad they were safe in my sweater. I just stared at her with a mute smile on my face, unable to pretend that I liked her any more than I was already pretending. There were some people who just flattened me.

"Do you think Isaac's in love with you?" she asked.

"I don't know," I said. "Maybe." I really didn't want to discuss it with her.

"Do you think you're going to live together?"

"Maybe."

"Do you think you're going to get married? It's just, Rebekah, don't you think that maybe there's something wrong with him?"

I was taken aback, but then laughed, realizing she must be kidding.

"Does that mean you do think there's something wrong with him?" she asked again.

She was serious. "No," I said, decidedly. "I don't."

"You don't think there's anything wrong with him," she stated.

"No?" I asked, wondering for the first time if there was.

"Don't you think he's extremely strange?"

"What do you mean?" I asked.

"Don't you think the only reason you like him is because he looks like a shorter version of Arthur Weeman?"

"He's not much shorter than Arthur Weeman."

"Come on, Rebekah, Isaac Myman is a very short man. I'm only bringing this up because I'm the one who set you up, and I really like and admire you and I don't want to have done anything that might hurt you. I mean, I really like him, don't get me wrong, it's just I know him a lot better than you do, and sometimes I think he's just a little too intense, like in a weird way. Oooh, I like this one." She strapped herself into an aqua bra with pineapples, cherries, apples, and oranges opulently stitched onto the demicups. "It's an Agent Provocateur," she said, missing the irony of its name.

Again, I thought about the cloves. I could see the light brown hands and fingers of the other child, but not her face.

"Just be careful," Ivy warned. Every word she said was like a clove breaking my skin. "He's just so . . ."

"Ivy," I said as calmly as possible, "I really like Isaac. I'm not going to stand here and say bad things about him."

"I'm not saying bad things about him," she said.

"You just said he was extremely strange, and weird and short."

"No, I . . ."

"I'll meet you out there," I said, and left the dressing room. I sat on a pink upholstered puff next to a basket of red velvet thongs trimmed with white fur, and tried to figure out why Ivy was poisoning me against Isaac when she'd been the one, as she liked to point out over and over again, to set us up. Then I went to the sachets and pushed clove after clove into my brain, trying to see the face of the girl in Irmabelle's lap. The wonder I'd felt at those perfectly formed cloves! That was the essence of childhood.

"Would you like one of these?" the salesgirl asked, dangling a sachet by its white satin loop in front of me.

"No, thanks," I said. I was more Jewish than Ivy thought, because while I was willing to pay ninety-eight dollars for a bra, I wasn't going to pay twenty-six dollars for a sachet.

"Um, is something wrong with your friend?"

That's when I noticed the sobbing coming from the dressing room.

"Ivy, what's wrong?" I tried to open the door but she was holding it shut.

"Just leave me alone," she sobbed.

"Ivy." I pushed against the door but I couldn't open it.

"I'm fine," she cried. It was hard to believe that there behind the louvered door, was the menacing gossip columnist for *The New York Quille,* half naked, tears splashing onto the pineapples and other fruit barely covering her breasts.

"Ivy, let me in," I said.

"I'm going to call the manager at our other store," the sales-girl said.

"Please, just go," Ivy choked out.

"Ivy, it's okay," I said. "Just get dressed and we'll get out of here."

"I'm not coming out. I feel terrible about what I said about Isaac," she sobbed. "I don't know why I did that. Why do you think I did that?"

"I don't know, it doesn't matter," I said.

"I think when I set you up with Isaac I didn't really think you would like him." Or that he would like me, I thought. "I've been upset about my break up with Guy-Antoine."

"Open the door, Ivy, okay?" I smiled at the salesgirl, pointed to the dressing-room door, and twirled my finger near my ear so the salesgirl would know I knew Ivy was a complete nutjob.

Ivy opened the door, topless again, with the straps of the pineapple bra dangling loosely around her wrists like handcuffs.

"I'm so embarrassed," she said.

"Come on, get dressed. I'll buy you the bra as a present."

"You would do that?"

"Yes," I said. "To thank you for setting me up with Isaac."

"And you promise you won't tell Isaac what I said about him?"

"I promise," I said. I would tell him as soon as possible so he could finally be done with her.

"Actually, do you have the one she's getting in my size?" she asked the salesgirl. "So we can match. Any celebrities been in lately? Call me if anyone comes in?" She handed over her business card and I handed over my credit card. Ivy seemed cheered up.

We left swinging our tiny pink shopping bags.

I might as well have saved my money because when I pulled off my shirt in front of Isaac and revealed the black lace bra, he barely noticed it.

"Is there an electric socket near the bed?" he asked, glancing around my bedside tables from *Iris, Isabel, and Isolde*. I was a little shocked by his question because I didn't know what he wanted to plug in. I didn't really go in for electronic devices on the fifth date. "Oh, here's one."

He went over to his CHANNEL THIRTEEN tote bag and pulled something with a long cord out of it. When he unfurled it and plugged it in, I realized it was his cell phone charger. God forbid Ivy Vohl couldn't reach him.

After he had taken care of his cell phone, leaving it on, I noticed, he turned his attention to me. We had nice, friendly, almost intimate sex. Almost loving sex. He made me take my bra off in the middle of it.

"Are you hungry?" I asked.

"I love you," he said. He said it passionately, but sleepily, but with total abandon as if it had just spouted out of him. He said it the way I had walked out on him at Pastis, like a reflex action, beyond his control. I had never heard those words before without having to anguish first. "Hel-lo?" he said, obnoxiously. "I believe I just said I *love* you."

"Hel-lo?" I said. And then after a moment I said, "You don't even know me." Then after another moment I said, "I love you too." I decided I would say it now and worry about it later.

"I love you, Rebekah," he said again.

"I love you too," I whispered. But love wasn't really the word for it. More amazement that I liked him so much and that he liked me.

I shouldered into the crook of his arm and remembered how incredibly lonely I had been.

"Ivy said she really likes your father," Isaac said.

"In what way?" I asked.

"I don't know. She said he's fascinating. I'd like to meet him. And your mother."

I had never heard my father described as fascinating before. "Okay," I said, knowing I would put that off for as long as possible. I was so angry at my father that I couldn't even let myself think about him.

"And you don't have any brothers or sisters."

"Who told you that?" I asked.

"I think you did," he said. "Or maybe Ivy. Why? Do you?"

"Let's just sleep," I said, softly. In the past this had always been a question I'd been able to answer easily, without thinking, like most people. Now, I didn't know what to say. I felt like a woman waiting to tell people she's pregnant—should I wait to hear a heartbeat, wait for the doctor's okay before spreading the happy news?

"Rebekah, what's wrong?"

"Nothing," I said. "What about your parents? You haven't told me anything about them."

"My mother lives in Florida and is obsessed with tennis, and my father's dead."

"Oh," I said. I had no idea what to say next. He'd been matter-of-fact about it. "How old were you when it happened?"

"Sixteen. Junior in high school."

"You were so young." The word "young" just sulked there for a minute.

"He was a drunk. He and I went to look at colleges." I braced myself the way I had to for wildlife documentaries, prepared for the worst. "We went to a restaurant for dinner and then he was driving us back to our motel, drunk, and he saw a roadside bar. I remember it was called Snyder's and had Dobermans in a big pen in the front. I said I wouldn't go in there with him, and he said it was his car and he'd do what he wanted with it. So I got out of the car and walked back to the motel, more than ten miles, and he drove frantically up and down the road looking for me and got into an accident and was killed. The car went up in flames."

"My God, that's terrible," I said.

"If I had gone into the bar with him we both would have probably been fine."

"You don't know that," I said.

I thought of Isaac, a teenager, trudging stubbornly along the road. I wrapped my arms around him.

"I'm glad you weren't in the car," I said. He seemed to slip far away from me. I'd said the wrong thing. "Are you sad?" I whispered.

"N' I've made my peace with it. He was a drunk, I was an ass. The worst part is when I got back to the motel I was so angry I sat at the little desk they had and wrote him a very detailed letter telling him how sick and tired I was of his shit, and then there was a knock on the door and it was the police telling me he was dead. So that's my sordid past. I was a real little man back then. Twenty years ago."

"I was a real little man back then too. Twenty years ago," I said. "In my sordid past."

I thought about my father driving me to the airport for my trip to Disney World and how after that, everything'd changed. I'd gone to look at colleges by myself. And I started to cry, but it was the kind of crying I sometimes did where my face remained serene and unmoved, as if my face and body were refusing to acknowledge the fact. Sometimes I stored my tears in my cheeks like a chipmunk, and I'd suddenly turn into Dizzy Gillespie. Isaac didn't know I was crying until tears wet the hair on his chest.

"I don't mind if you feel sorry for me," Isaac said. He held my hand. "Thank you for being so nice to Ivy. You know, I don't have family here, or anywhere really, and she's been like a sister to me. We should take her out to dinner to thank her for setting us up."

"I think we've thanked her enough," I said.

"I don't think so."

"I bought her a . . ." I stopped because I didn't want to say the word "bra" and conjure up an image of Ivy Vohl's enormous breasts. "Lunch," I said.

I fell asleep thinking about the terrible things she had said about him and wondering if I would be doing him a favor to tell him, or if it would just hurt his feelings.

When I woke up in the morning I noticed that the sheets were very damp. Isaac was still sleeping next to me, with his curly hair flattened over his forehead, making him look like a kid. He must have sweated a lot in the night.

He opened his eyes and I switched on *Little House on the Prairie*. Eliza Jane, Almanzo's sister, was coming to town to teach school, which meant that Laura meeting Almanzo was not too far off. Eliza Jane was a wonderful sister to Almanzo; my eyes started to fill with tears.

He threw the covers off him and said, "What's this? Everything's wet."

"You must have sweated a lot," I said.

But then we both noticed that his whole side of the bed was soaked through. The sheets smelled like pee. He had peed in my bed. "Oh my God, Rebekah, I'm so sorry." He had such a surprised and embarrassed expression on his face, I had to stop myself from laughing.

"Do you do this a lot?" I asked.

"No!" he said, mortified. "I mean, I've never done it before. I mean, since I was five."

A man wetting the bed at age thirty-five was definitely a new dating dilemma for me. This made my having thrown up on his penis seem like the most normal thing in the world.

I thought about the other men I'd been with. Nathan, with his tight hamstrings and Pratesi sheets, washed and ironed by his cleaning lady twice a week. If he'd let loose and pissed on them just one time, I might still be with him. When we started dating, he hadn't even let me visit him in the hospital when he'd had his appendix out.

"Do you think it happened because you told me the story about your father dying?" Asking the question like that made me sound like Ivy Vohl.

"No, I think it happened because I dreamt there was a fire and I had to put it out with a long hose," he said. "You should be happy, I saved us with my big hose." He started to laugh.

I was going to point out that he'd said his father's car had gone up in flames, but I thought better of it.

"Too bad you weren't downtown on September eleventh." I quickly stripped my bed and blotted the mattress with sopping wet towels. I couldn't remember much from Hebrew school, but something about the pee felt Biblical. My bed felt like an ark. A man certainly wasn't going to leave a woman after revealing himself like that. He was mine—if I wanted him after this—and it felt like he'd broken a bottle of champagne on our bow.

Two if by sea, I thought.

"I brought the concept of the wet spot to a whole new level," Isaac said. He seemed almost to be enjoying this.

"Maybe you can use some of Mrs. Williams' Depends."

"You won't mention this to Ivy, will you?" he said.

"I wasn't planning to mention it to anyone." I wasn't exactly proud of it. It wasn't the kind of thing I couldn't wait to tell people. *My new boyfriend wets the bed!* But I did embarrassing things too. I lactated, for one thing.

"I'll pay for the laundry," he said.

The fact was, I didn't feel squeamish or disgusted by the pee in my bed the way I was by the cups of it on the bathroom sink in my father's office. It wasn't the pee of old people, it was the pee of Isaac, and therefore it was okay. I had an incredible urge to call my ex-shrink to tell her how far I'd come—I was able to love, to accept a man with all his flaws, to let love leak out the way it wanted to—but school was starting, Miss Wilder was ringing the bell, and the children were filing into the one-room schoolhouse, younger children in front, older students, like Laura and Nellie and Willie Oleson, in the back. "Good morning, children," Miss Wilder said, and even though I already knew, I had to see what was going to happen.

16.

After we showered and got dressed, Isaac went to the *Quille*, carrying the wet sheets and towels in a laundry bag slung over his shoulder to drop off at the Aphrodite cleaners, and I went to a café to sit and think about him. It's the best thing in the world to be alone when you're in love. It's so much more relaxing than being with the person and just waiting for them to do something at any moment to ruin everything.

Nothing could go wrong as long as I was there in that café. I'd had a boyfriend when I'd left the house that morning, and I'd still have one at the end of the day.

I sat in a chair next to the window, watching shopping bags walk by. It was three days before Christmas and the place was filled with gay guys but it didn't matter because I had a boyfriend. We were going to Bret Easton Ellis' Christmas party together that night and Isaac and I were spending Christmas with Mrs. Williams. My L.A. friends—surprise—had decided to stay in L.A. this year. I usually visited my mother in Woodstock, but I couldn't face her now that I knew she had kept Sascha from me.

I wanted to tell someone about Isaac, and, in a burst of enthusiasm, I called my ex-shrink. Her machine picked up and as soon as I heard her voice, I got choked up.

"Hi, this is Rebekah Kettle," I said. I could picture her in her tiny office, hear the white-noise machine whirring on the floor outside the door. "Uh," I said, trying to think what it was I had wanted to tell her. "This is going to sound strange, but I just found out I have a sister. . . ."

I stopped talking because a black girl walked by and even though I hadn't really seen her face, and didn't even know for sure that she was black, I wondered if it was Sascha. I realized I'd been staring very intently at black women ever since finding out about her. The machine cut me off with a long beep.

I sat there for a little while, drinking cappuccinos and looking at black people walk by, trying to decide what to do. And then it occurred to me that maybe I didn't have to do anything. Maybe this was my father's problem, not mine. Maybe when Isaac asked me if I had a sister I could say no, because so far she was just a manila folder, a newspaper clipping, a childhood photo, and a clove-scented memory, and those things didn't add up to much of a sister. Or maybe if he asked me if I had a sister, which I realized he might never ask me again because most people only ask you a question like that once, I could just say, "Yes, but not very much of one."

Maybe I could just forget I'd ever found out about her. She might be crazy. She might be stupid, or worse, successful. Irmabelle, with her teddy bears and Precious Moments figurines, wasn't exactly a genius, but what if Sascha had gotten my father's math and science genes, and was a Westinghouse winner or something? What if she wanted me to fork over some of my grandmother's jewelry, I thought. I instinctively felt for the aquamarine ring I had put on that morning, to make sure it was still there, as if I expected my grandmother to have already snatched it off my finger.

It might all be a trick. Irmabelle might have told my father Sascha was his daughter and he'd been too kind and polite to demand a DNA test. But he was a doctor, I thought. He could collect his own evidence, undiscovered, in the middle of the night, swab the insides of cheeks, pluck hairs from heads, send vials of blood off to a laboratory.

I stood up ready to confront my father, and then sat down again. Maybe he'd just wanted to protect me.

I dialed Isaac on my cell phone and was surprised when my father answered. His voice was harried and upset. "Dr. Kettle."

"Hi," I said. It took me a second to realize I'd dialed my father's office by mistake. It was incredibly creepy to have called my boyfriend and reached my father.

"Rebekah?" he asked.

No, it's Sascha, I felt like saying.

"Rebekah, where the hell are you?"

Three black girls walked down the street, carrying shopping bags and laughing.

"Rebekah?"

"Yeah, Dad," I said. "Sorry, I couldn't come in today. I had a publishing lunch."

"Oh, well, that's nice," he said. "Listen, I'm glad you called. We have to keep tabs on your peripheral vision. There's not much we can do about it, but if your vision starts to drastically decline, I think we should know about it. I want you to have a field-of-vision test to use as a baseline, so we can better monitor that tumor of yours. I arranged for you to have a drop-in appointment with Dr. Max today. I'd like for you to take care of this promptly."

"Fine," I whined, feeling confused because I should have been confronting him, not obeying his medical advice.

"Okay, good," he said. "The other line's ringing. Hold on," he said and hung up.

I paid my check and took a cab uptown to Dr. Max's office.

I had always hated going to Dr. Max's office since I was a kid, waiting for hours, being told your vision is getting worse, leaving with dilated pupils barely able even to hail a cab.

I waited helplessly for my name to be called. The waiting room was filled with old people. The women behind the desk didn't look up when they handed me the clipboard for me to update my information. They were so angry and miserable, I wondered how they had so many Christmas cards taped to their wall. My waiting room only had one old person at a time but this one was chock-full of them.

I tried to turn my attention to the clipboard. I filled in my name and birth date and then stopped for a moment on marital status. They didn't have IN LOVE as a choice, so I circled MARRIED since it felt more right somehow than SINGLE. It felt so good that I decided to answer the other questions as if it were in the future and my life was appropriately improved. I made myself taller and considerably thinner. I gave myself two children, health insurance, and the address of a building I had always wanted to live in, One Fifth Avenue. Although it didn't ask, I wrote in (Three Bedroom Apartment).

All the old people started clucking because a little boy, about five years old, walked into the waiting room. They all stared at him so intently it was as if they thought whomever he turned his gaze on first would instantly become young again. The boy carefully avoided them all, demanded his lollipop in advance, and then sat down next to his mother who had sat down next to me and was trying to sneak a peak at my clipboard. I tilted it subtly in her direction.

"Rebekah Kettle?" she said.

I turned to her. "Candi?" It was Candi Miranda, one of my five best friends in elementary school. Her father had been a famous newscaster. I practically lived at their apartment on Sutton Place.

She turned to the woman sitting on the other side of the little boy. "Mom, you remember Rebekah Kettle."

"Mrs. Miranda! You look great," I said. I had always been so good with my friends' mothers. As if it were yesterday, I remembered us at Serendipity, Candi and I eating our favorite things, vichyssoise and foot-long hot dogs.

"This is Scott. He's getting his first pair of glasses," Candi said, patting her son, who just shrugged and kept his eyes on his little game. "You have children!" she said, pointing to my questionnaire. "That's lucky."

"Why?" I said.

"You know," Candi said, awkwardly, "after what happened."

"What do you mean, what happened?"

"You know, your problem, the abortion," she whispered.

"I can have children," I bristled, defensively.

"I see that," she said.

I had made several attempts to reunite with Candi, and my other friends in the past, but they had ignored me. After the abortion, the infection had caused me to miss the whole end of seventh grade. In that time, while I was recovering from the infection, I was "homeschooled" (i.e., yelled at) by my father, making a few attempts to go back but always ending up at home after half a day. I missed Candi Miranda's East Hampton birthday party and Margaret Eisner and Carly Mandlebaum's bat mitzvahs. My bat mitzvah had been canceled. I had overheard my father and mother having a fight once. In a fit of anger, my father had said that he didn't feel he had to spend ten thousand dollars to make me a woman when I clearly already was one.

I was cliqueless.

"How's L.E.?" I asked.

"She's great. She's married, living in Denver."

"I know, I saw her wedding in the *Times*. I read all about your wedding too," I said. "It looked fantastic." It was a beach wedding, East Hampton, everybody barefoot, all the bridesmaids wore the same color toenail polish called Sugar Daddy.

"Thanks," Candi said. "That's funny that you live at One Fifth Avenue. I remember you always used to say you wanted to live there."

"You remember that?" My eyes instantly welled up with tears because at least she remembered something about me.

"Are you crying?"

"No, that's why I'm here, my eyes keep tearing," I said.

"I have friends who live in One Fifth."

"Really? Who?" I asked, even though I had never even been in the building.

"Drew and Laurie Baum?"

I frowned in mock concentration as if I was really trying to figure out which of my neighbors were Drew and Laurie Baum.

"Do they have a dog?" I asked.

"No, they just had a baby."

"Don't know them," I said.

"I think they're moving," she said. I hoped they moved before they had a chance to tell Candi that I didn't live in their building.

The miserable girl behind the desk called my name.

"Well, Merry Christmas," Candi said, as if that was the end

and we wouldn't see each other again. How could someone not want to be friends with someone they knew when they were twelve? I wondered. To me, Candi looked twelve, and if to her I looked twelve too, that seemed reason enough. And according to my medical questionnaire we had so much in common—I had a son Scott's age, she had friends in my building.

"I'd love to get together sometime," I said.

"Sure," Candi said.

"So much has happened. You know I have a sister now," I said.

"Really? Wow," she said. She made no move to ask for my number or to give me hers. My eyes continued to water. She had an enormous purse probably filled with pens, and the Dr. Max pen fell off my lap when I stood up, but she ignored it. "Maybe I'll leave a note for you with your doorman," she said.

I knew that even if I did live in that building, there would never be a note. "That would be great," I said.

I said good-bye to Candi and her mother and was ushered into a tiny dark office, where a black patch was snapped over my right eye and my face was shoved onto a chin rest and a clicker was pressed into my hand.

"It's like a video game. Click when you think you see a white flash," a woman said. "You know we usually only do field of vision on Tuesdays."

She walked out of the room and slammed the door. For several minutes there were no flashing lights. I clicked the clicker about ten times in case there were lights and I just couldn't see them. Usually if you messed up a video game the most you lost was your quarter, but in this case it was my sight at stake.

I panicked. I couldn't concentrate. I was clickless.

People were laughing right outside the door. Some white

lights flashed, some as bright as opals and some so faint I wasn't sure if I had really seen them. I clicked away like a patient trying to get more morphine drip.

The technician came back in and switched the patch to my left eye.

"This isn't fair!" I said. "I'm not sure what I'm supposed to do. It's too noisy out there, I can't see."

"Just click when you see a white flash," she said and left the room. I spent a few seconds adjusting the eye patch and trying to get comfortable in the chin rest and then clicked several times to catch up. Each flash was a flashback. Andrew Resnick punching me in the upper arm once a week during Hebrew school. The spot was still tender to this day. Vomiting over and over again on a school trip to the Thomas Edison Museum. Telling Candi, Margaret, and Carly, about losing my virginity at Disney World, the looks on their faces.

A flash went off in my head.

Maybe that's why I had lost them: not because of the abortion, but because of the sex itself. I had assumed sex was a good thing, that they'd be impressed. "Were you raped?" L.E. had asked me. "No!" I said. They were so immature. I was adventurous and powerful. Men looked at me when I walked down the street because I was sexy. I was in control. I *wanted* to lose my virginity. I thought everyone did. I had lost my friends, my virginity, my father, my bat mitzvah, half a school year, but I had found Arthur Weeman. Arthur Weeman was the only one who understood someone like me. He introduced me to a whole other New York, the New York I still believed in. New York through Arthur Weeman's eyes was Wonderland. Children could be grown-ups but the best kind of grown-up. You could read *The New York Times* over cappuccinos *and* go to the zoo. You could have sex at Disney

World *and* still go to Serendipity with your friends. You could have an abortion *and* still make it to Carly Mandlebaum's bat mitzvah at the Russian Tea Room.

"Your peripheral vision is within normal range," Dr. Max said, after I had been escorted to his examining room and waited for him in the chair for half an hour. He showed me some computer printouts. Little x's indicated where I had clicked appropriately, but I had no idea what I was looking at. "Now let me check your eyes." He moved his machine toward my face and I stared blankly into it. "And how is Frederick?" he asked.

"Fine."

"Look at my ear." He tapped his ear with his pen to show me where his ear was.

I had hated Dr. Max's ears since I was a little girl.

"Okay, you have blepharitis," Dr. Max said.

"What?"

He said something I couldn't understand but the words "clogging" and "eyelids" jumped out at me. "Blepharitis is usually associated with oily skin and dandruff."

"Dandruff! I haven't had oily skin or dandruff since I was twelve," I said, mortified. With the intensity of a mad scientist, I would empty bottles of Pantene for *normal* hair and fill them with Head & Shoulders so no one would know, if I had a sleepover.

"Yes, it's common in teenagers. Do you use mascara and things of that nature?"

"Of course," I said, as if he were a complete idiot.

"You might want to hold off on all that for a while. You have to use hot compresses and scrub the eye with baby shampoo."

At thirty-three you expect to be buying baby shampoo for your baby, not to scrub your eye dandruff.

No more tears. What a fucking crock.

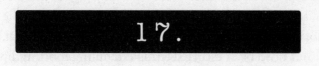

17.

At 33, she attends a private screening

This is my favorite episode," Isaac said. "The one where Albert gets hooked on morphine he steals from Doc Baker." He snuggled into me. It was already the beginning of March, and even though we'd only been dating since November, we were seeing this episode for the second time.

We ordered scrambled eggs and coffees from the diner.

"You're going to work later and later," he said.

"I'm mad at my father."

"How come?"

"Long story," I said.

We kissed good-bye for a long time and I went to Mrs. Williams' to bring her groceries.

When I got there, she was taking a nap so I went straight to the window. I was disappointed to see that Arthur wasn't there. He often wasn't there but I'd just had a feeling that I would see him.

I looked down into the Gardener School playground and saw an interesting sight. A few men were working in it, up on ladders and things, and a woman was carrying boxes in from the school.

Cables for electricity were being pulled along the perimeter, and I realized some of the men were stringing lights, thousands of them, along the walls like spiderwebs. The woman with the boxes was joined by workmen wheeling in topiary and other small lush trees and flowers. It didn't seem like they were setting up for a wedding, or even a party exactly. It must have been some kind of alumni or fundraising event, but I couldn't remember anything like that ever happening on the school's premises before, the invitations I got were always for the Metropolitan or University Clubs, at a museum, or in someone's home.

One square table and two chairs appeared in the middle of everything.

Then, in front of the playground's brick wall, a giant white movie screen was erected, drive-in style, and a movie projector set up on a scaffold facing it. There was going to be a movie!

Eight tall heat lamps, the kind you always saw in L.A. but didn't even exist in New York, were marched in like soldiers and placed around the table and—and this was the final touch—twin red velvet theater seats, that looked like they had been ripped right out of a fancy theater, and were set to perfectly face the screen. I watched in amazement as they were actually jackhammered into the concrete ground.

Mrs. Williams' window must be magic, I decided, a secret portal into my mind, a sort of MRI of my imagination. And, as an old-fashioned popcorn machine was wheeled in—so corny! I thought, delighted—I started to wonder if Isaac was behind this.

He knew how much I loved the movies.

Only love could propel a man to do something like this. I would have been happy with a movie at the Sunshine and dinner at Katz's, but this! It was like my recurring movie-theater dreams.

The last one had been in a sort of symphony hall, a maze of private boxes with seats arranged in circles, so although I was the first to arrive at the theater and had my pick of seats, none seemed to face the screen.

Of course most likely this had nothing to do with me, I knew, but it could, I thought. It could. And if, say, all this really was for me, if Isaac had really set all of this up, a private movie where we couldn't be joined by Ivy Vohl or my father or black sisters or anyone, if all of this really was for me, then I was starting to think that Isaac might be planning to propose with the old diamond ring in the popcorn bucket trick.

Maybe I'd change into the black Oscar de la Renta in Mrs. Williams' closet, I thought.

"What are you doing?" Mrs. Williams asked, coming up behind me.

"Nothing," I said, spinning quickly around. She usually never bothered to look out the window, and I didn't really want her to start now. At least for now, this was mine. The scent from all the flowers was drifting into the kitchen through the open window.

"Mayor Beame was here. You just missed him," she said.

I was pretty sure Mayor Beame was dead. "Are you hungry? What do you want for dinner?"

"Chocolate mousse with loads of whipped cream," she said. I loved when she said things like "loads of whipped cream." When I was old I would eat loads of whipped cream. Loads and loads.

Then Isaac called to cancel.

"Oh," I said, my heart squeezed, like it was in panty hose.

"Ivy's got me working on something, but I promise we'll see a movie tomorrow. Your choice."

"Okay," I said, sincerely. It being my choice counted for a lot.

I was more embarrassed than anything else, that I would have let myself even think all that had been for me.

But I suddenly felt very lucky to have someone to cancel a date with, lucky to be able to make another. You didn't know you were in love until the other person canceled and you didn't get angry. It seemed almost as improbable as seeing a private movie in your old school playground, but that was the nature of love. You turned a corner and there it was.

"What do you mean, 'okay'?"

"I mean it's fine. I understand."

"Don't you want to see me tonight?"

"Yes," I said.

"It doesn't sound like it."

"I'm just saying I understand if you can't make it."

"You certainly don't seem too upset about it. You seem almost glad about it."

"I am upset," I said, smiling. "Very upset."

"Well, maybe I could get away in time for a late dinner. Could we get together at ten instead of eight?"

"Sure," I said, laughing.

"You don't mind not seeing a movie tonight?"

"Not at all," I said, because I was going to see one. I'd have a perfect view of whatever was being shown tonight on that screen. Watching from the window was almost as good as being there. No, it was better.

I thought Mrs. Williams and I weren't so different. She thought Mayor Beame had been to visit and I thought my boyfriend of five months had orchestrated a fairyland proposal for me. She sat around her apartment and took naps and I sat around her apartment and took naps. I was young like her and she was old like me.

. . .

When darkness came, I went to my perch at the window. Below me wasn't the place I had spent so many lonely recesses but a wonderland. Winter had become spring. Night, day. Hard cement, soft with rose petals. I had imagined it this way, sometimes, as I sat on the concrete bench by myself with a book in my lap, willing free-time to be over, that I was in a secret garden, and someone was peering at me through a keyhole in the gate.

Across the way, Arthur Weeman's window was dark, and for the first time I was happy about that so I could open the blinds more freely and focus on what was below. I turned off the kitchen light and like a sea captain, pulled on the blinds' white cords and hoisted the opera glasses to my eyes. Next to me on the window seat was the huge bowl of popcorn I had popped in loads of olive oil on the stove.

Almost immediately, a man dressed in chef's whites entered the schoolyard with a cart on wheels and placed food on the table. Dinner plates under silver domes, rolls and butter, salads containing something dark and red, probably beets. Red wine and water was poured, and in one of the glasses, Diet Coke.

The chef moved the cart off to the side, still laden with a tray of tiny cakes and a bottle of champagne stuck in a bucket. He lit a candle in a glass hurricane lamp and disappeared into the school.

"Dorothy, Rose, and Blanche are coming over and we'd prefer to be left alone," Mrs. Williams said behind me, nutjobbing her way around the kitchen.

"Fine, I'll stay in here," I said.

She left just as the school door opened and a girl came out. And, holding the heavy door open for her awkwardly, was Arthur Weeman.

The young girl and I, at the exact same time, both opened our mouths in amazement. It was the same one with the long brown hair I'd seen him wave to from his window. She twirled around a few times, with her arms outstretched and her head thrown back, which was probably the only logical thing a girl in her situation could do. She was dressed well for twirling, in her school uniform's pleated skirt and riding boots, and a short black puffy jacket. The dress I was wearing would also have been very good for twirling.

Y.G. (Young Girl) skipped all around looking at everything, bent to smell some flowers, and then lifted one of the silver domes an inch and peeked underneath with her cheek on the white tablecloth as if she was expecting to see a trapped gerbil or something. Watching her was so interesting, I almost forgot all about Arthur.

He stood not far from the door with his hands in his pockets, smiling. Arthur Weeman, smiling! My heart throbbed with the sight of it and then clutched with jealousy. He walked to the table and motioned for Y.G. to sit and pulled her chair out for her. She had a sip of her wine and then a sip of Diet Coke.

He sat down and they ate their salads, Y.G. poking at the red things and twirling her lettuce like spaghetti.

When they were done, Arthur Weeman cleaned the plates himself and served the next course, enormous hamburgers on big brioche buns and French fries. Y.G. picked hers up in her greedy mitts and took a bite without even waiting for him to sit back down. She made a face and lifted her knife and dug it into the small silver ketchup dish and slathered it all over her burger and fries. She wiped off her fingers on her white linen napkin, and took sips each of wine and Diet Coke.

She was nothing like me, I thought, disappointed. I would

have twirled, yes, but it would have been a woman's twirl. I would never have worn riding boots, she was clearly the rare type of New York City child who liked horses, and I'd never even been friends with a girl who liked horses. I would have eaten my hamburger carefully, like a grown-up.

Y.G. took another sloppy bite of her burger, but something still seemed to displease her, and after a brief heated negotiation of some kind, they switched plates, and she began the ketchup procedure again, but this time more daintily.

Arthur finished his glass of wine and poured himself another. Again no waiter appeared, and I realized why he had done all this. He wanted to take Y.G. out, on a sort of a date, but he couldn't take her out in public. He must have paid the school a lot of money to arrange it.

By the time he had cut her former hamburger in half and taken a few tentative bites, Y.G. had polished hers off completely and had gotten up to wander all around looking at the lights and flowers. She touched everything—the cakes, the movie screen, and the velvet seats, the popcorn cart and the popcorn in it, and what seemed like every petal of every flower. She was talking but I couldn't hear what she was saying.

Arthur Weeman pushed his plate away. He reached into his pocket for a slim digital camera and started taking photos of her, showering her in tiny flashes.

She ate two cakes.

Arthur directed her to her velvet seat, and while she craned around looking at him, he monkeyed up the scaffold and turned on the projector. He joined her in the velvet seat attached to hers, as *Adopting Alice* began to play.

As a New Yorker, I'd seen only two or three movies outside in my entire life, and only as a child from the backseat of a car or sitting on the grass in some crowded, rat-infested park. I would have to add this to my list of most beautiful sights in New York: *Adopting Alice* in Technicolor lighting up the night sky. Although I'd watched it hundreds of times on video, I hadn't seen it on the big screen since it came out, and every moment of it was like seeing fireworks instead of just remembering them. After this, I worried, movies would be spoiled for me. I'd never be able to enjoy a movie the regular way again.

For the first half hour Arthur Weeman sat rather stiffly while the girl squirmed next to him, looking all around and vying for their shared armrest. At one point she took out some sort of small wireless device and appeared to be texting someone. She seemed entirely uninterested in the film, and, to my astonishment, during one of the best scenes in movie history, when Arthur Weeman and Alice walk through Central Park wheeling the baby carriage, which happened at that moment to be parked in the corner of my bedroom with my dirty laundry in it, Y.G. did a remarkable thing. She simply stood up. She went back to the cart and poked her fingers in the cakes again.

Arthur Weeman gestured to the screen but she wasn't interested. Instead, she took off her puffy jacket and went to stand right in front of him. Facing him, with her back to the screen, Y.G. slowly unbuttoned her uniform blouse, slipped it off her shoulders and arms and let it fall to the ground.

Arthur Weeman clownishly picked up her blouse and tried to cover her with it, with a "What, are you crazy? I could get arrested" kind of a gesture. Y.G. laughed, and pushed him back down in his seat. She reached behind her and unhooked her bra—it was white or maybe the palest pink—and let it fall to the ground with the blouse.

My arm ached in its position, holding up the opera glasses,

and I let it drop to my side. On the screen, Arthur touched Alice's hair and she swatted his hand away.

"Stop it," I said. I sort of whispered it as if we were in a movie theater with other people. "Stop it. Stop it. Stop it." I wasn't talking to Arthur Weeman, or to Y.G. exactly. I was the one who had taken off my own embroidered Mexican blouse and unhooked my own white bra in Disney World. The regular old Disney World, not the one created by Arthur Weeman. I was talking to myself.

Y.G. put her arms up in the air and twirled, this time topless, against the movie backdrop. The movie played on her face and chest. Her breasts were in that impossible stage of development, just after they've appeared out of nowhere and right before you're used to them. I remembered my own at that time, a lot like hers, almost all nipple, as magical as Pez dispensers. As tender and painful as they were, with them came the fortuitous feeling that good things were going to happen, all was as it should be, and life was all up from here. She approached Arthur and, still facing him, tried to climb on his lap, in an awkward half-straddle, because one of her long booted legs was forced to drape over the empty velvet seat. Arthur put his hands on her breasts and she squirmed off of him, grabbing his glasses off his face at the same time.

Without realizing it, I had returned the opera glasses to my eyes.

I'd never seen him without his glasses. He wore them in kissing scenes and sex scenes, shower scenes, rain scenes, and even in the boxing scenes in *Swan Song*. But now she had them and, like a little bully, she took off with his famous signature egg-shaped frames. He got up to chase her, but faltered a little as he passed the food cart, putting his hand out to steady himself. He was off by several inches, clearly disoriented, his peripheral vision failing him.

She came back to him then and sweetly handed them over. He put them on, talking to her heatedly, throwing his hands up and then clutching his heart, which sent her into spasms of laughter. I couldn't help but smile and feel a strange gratitude to her at that moment for her laughter. Without his glasses he had become old, but her laughter had restored him. He grabbed her and pushed her against the cart and spanked her cartoonishly, his hand moving under her uniform skirt, as the movie continued on without them.

She got away from him and smoothed down her skirt. Pouting, she went to where her bra and blouse lay on the ground, and scooped them up, bending at the waist with her legs completely straight.

Arthur Weeman pointed to the screen where he—I knew it so well I didn't even have to look—was about to kiss Alice. Y.G. stopped and watched, cocking her head slightly, and then laughed again. The same laughter that had restored him to greatness a few moments before, now cut him down to size.

She took off again, trotting over to the projector scaffold, threw her blouse and bra over a low bar, and began to climb it like a jungle gym, bending her legs over a high bar and hanging from it upside down, her skirt flopping over to reveal her panties.

Arthur watched from below in a panic, desperately begging her to come down. When she was good and ready, she reached up and grabbed the bar with her hands, pulled herself up, unhitched her legs, and climbed down to the ground. Again he gestured heatedly to the screen, as if he was telling her that if she tried to concentrate on his film for a moment, she might actually like it.

How clever she was to ignore the movie! I could never be that coy. I'd have twirled and eaten my hamburger neatly and sat quietly and watched the movie, weeping in my seat at its greatness.

She had whipped him into a frenzy, and instead of going back to her velvet seat, she moved close to him, stood on her toes, and kissed him hard, with her mouth wide open.

My letters were nothing compared to this.

Then she charmingly dropped to her bare knees and worked to pull down his zipper.

I was startled to my feet by my cell phone ringing. It was Isaac. I was late. He was already waiting. "I'll be right there," I said, "I'm getting into a cab now." I turned my back to the window and got off the phone.

My heart beat as hard as if I was running. She had gone too far. Stupid, stupid. What was wrong with this girl, putting him in jeopardy like this? Even though he had clearly rented out the whole school and playground and probably had the entrance manned with guards, how could he be completely sure he was safe? What about the photos he'd taken and the text message she'd sent?

I knew what it felt like to drop to my knees like that. I could feel the cold rough ground beneath me, feel the power of being both stewardess and pilot of my own magic carpet. She would never be more beautiful and she would never be more ruined. But she won, I thought bitterly. She was smarter than me. She got a hamburger and silken cakes and a velvet seat and a thousand lights, and she twirled like Salome before the adoring eyes of the greatest filmmaker of all time, while I, on the other hand, had gotten myself knocked up by a man dressed as a pirate. She had been chosen by Arthur Weeman and he was willing to destroy himself for her.

At first, I was sure, he must have protested. But then I imagined he had stood still, looking all around at the dark windows of the Gardener School building, the dark windows of his own town house, and the back of Mrs. Williams' building, almost all brick-wall with just the one window exposed. Could he not see from that angle that the blinds that were always drawn were now open? Then, as she pulled out his cock and started sucking it like a little expert, he would look nervously over at the screen, as if he was suddenly afraid his own characters might tell on him.

I sat in Mary's Fish Camp, the tiny, cozy seafood restaurant on the corner of Fourth and Charles with Isaac, rewinding what I had seen in my mind and then fast-forwarding to the part I hadn't. We ate oysters, and lobster rolls, and a hot fudge sundae.

As I talked to Isaac, I knelt at the window and watched Arthur Weeman in the schoolyard.

Although it had been an Arthur Weeman production, it suddenly didn't seem like one anymore. Something this blatantly distasteful would never have happened in his movies. Now it was an X-rated film by Rebekah Kettle, and under the black Oscar de la Renta, my panties were wet, as helplessly gushingly wet as they had been when I was young.

As if he had read my mind, and felt another director edging into the playground, he urged her to stand up. He zipped his pants, and helped her into her blouse and puffy jacket. She shoved her bra in the jacket pocket, and with his arm around her protectively, he led her out of the playground and through the school door, right out of my frame.

When I was Y.G.'s age and I had seen *Adopting Alice,* of course I had identified with Alice, never dreaming there was any other side to things. Then one day, watching it alone in my apartment, I was shocked to discover that I couldn't help but sympathize with Candace Ann! Then, to test this condition again, by way of a second opinion, and third, and fourth, I watched several movies and realized again, to my dismay, that it wasn't the Y.G. I cared about, but the other. It was Diane Keaton who kept me spellbound, while Mariel Hemingway left me cold.

Now, walking casually downstairs to the ladies' room and locking the door behind me, and reaching my fingers inside my panties as if they were someone else's, I was learning the secret that all former Y.G.s are forced to one day learn, a secret that no man, not Arthur Weeman or Lewis Carroll or even Nabokov understood, that in the end we Y.G.s don't grow up to be over-the-hill Lolitas—sexless and worn and fat with child—we simply turn into the very thing that had once lusted after us.

Lolita in the end becomes Humbert Humbert.

And I had turned my back on Alice to find myself seeing things through Arthur Weeman's eyes. I, like all Y.G.s everywhere, had become, to my shock and horror, nothing more than a little dirty old man.

My fingers were cold and sopping as morning grass.

On the screen, playing to the empty schoolyard, Alice ran on Park Avenue, her fingertips skimming along a wrought-iron gate, and Arthur Weeman chased her. On the screen he was young, twenty years younger to be exact. On the screen, he caught her and she pushed him away and grabbed a fistful of tiny green leaves from a potted shrub at the entrance to a building.

18

At 33, she meets a long-lost relative

When I got to work the next day, my father was in his office talking to a patient. He ducked his head out to inform me that he was expecting a new patient who he had neglected to write in the appointment book. I looked down at the day's schedule and noticed that he not only hadn't written in the new patient, he hadn't written in the one he was in with now.

I was early because they had only shown one hour of *Little House*. For some reason the second hour had been preempted by a terrible sitcom called *Mama's Family*. The *Mama's Family* theme music, when I was expecting the soothing *Little House* theme music and Ma and Pa pulling up in their wagon and watching Carrie fall in the grass, had been a complete assault.

The doorbell rang and I got up to let the new patient in. I was dismayed when I opened the door to see Ivy Vohl standing there. She was wearing a vintage halter-top dress which, unfortunately for all of us, didn't allow for a bra. "Hi," she said.

"Ivy, I can't hang out right now. I'm working," I said.

"That's what you wear to work?" she asked. It was actually my favorite thing to wear to work, one of those old skeleton X-ray front and back T-shirts with all the ribs and vertebrae and everything that I'd had since high school. "I'm here to see Dr. Kettle," she said, in a formal tone. "I'm a patient." She looked down at her man's watch that I was sure she wore to go for the For-Esmé-with-Love-and-Squalor look. That was the sure sign of girl with a father-figure complex, a thin-wristed woman wearing a huge old-fashioned man's watch. I would have bet any amount of money she was completely obsessed with Philip Roth. "Oh, I'm early."

That meant she would be sitting in the waiting room trying to talk to me for at least fifteen minutes. I showed her in and handed her the clipboard with the medical questionnaire attached to it and reluctantly wrote her name on a manila folder and put blue V and O stickers on it.

For a brief moment I wondered if Page Six would be interested in publishing the medical questionnaire of its biggest competition.

"I thought I was supposed to be his first patient," she said.

"Well, he's been practicing for forty years."

"I mean today."

"He's *very* busy," I said.

"Well, I really appreciate you setting me up with your father."

"I'm not setting you up with him," I said.

"As a doctor. I really needed a new doctor. My last one and I got into a sort of a weird power struggle. My new shrink said I was in an S and M relationship with him."

"I prefer alternative medicine," I said, trying to knock the image of Ivy whipping some nice old doctor out of my mind.

"Like what?"

"Kinesthesiology, acupuncture, Chinese teas, that sort of thing."

"That's not very Jewish," Ivy said. "What about analysis? You're in analysis, aren't you?"

"I quit, actually," I said.

"I just started with someone new. In fact, guess who my new shrink is?"

"Well, your new doctor's my father, and I don't have any relatives who are shrinks, so I have no idea."

"Come on, guess."

"I have no idea."

"My shrink is Arthur Weeman's shrink," she said.

I turned and pretended to find a chart so she couldn't see whatever look I was sure had registered on my face. "Who is he?" I asked, realizing I didn't know who Arthur Weeman's shrink was. I hated when my knowledge of Arthur Weeman was shown to be incomplete.

"Dr. Ulrich Schneider. He's eighty-four years old. It's really hard to manipulate him. I'm seeing him three times a week because I don't know how much longer he has left."

This is how irrational my jealousy always was. If I found out someone got a forty-thousand-dollar advance for their first book, I got insanely jealous even though I got a five-hundred-thousand-dollar advance for my first book. Somehow, at that moment, in my mind, forty thousand was more than five hundred thousand. And that was how I felt about Ivy Vohl seeing Arthur Weeman's shrink. Even though I, thanks to Mrs. Williams, had a private viewing into Arthur Weeman's kitchen, night and day whenever I wanted it, even though I could see Arthur Weeman himself, and after what I'd seen in the playground might even know more about him than his own shrink, it didn't seem as great as getting to go to his shrink. Ivy Vohl was closer to him.

"Excuse me for a minute, I have to develop some X-rays in

the other room," I said. I went into the examining room and lay on the table for about ten minutes with my eyes closed, trying to relax. Ivy Vohl did not have more than I had. I could call Dr. Schneider and make an appointment with him before he died just as easily as she could. What kind of shrink had a pedophile for a patient? I wondered. But then I thought, what kind of girl had a pedophile for an idol? I wondered if Arthur had told him about Y.G. Or about Thalia. Then I heard the phone on Irmabelle's desk ring and I went back into the reception area to answer it. Ivy Vohl was lounging on the couch in the waiting room, staring at me. She held a book on her lap, her place marked with her finger, and from where I was standing I was pretty sure it was *The Human Stain*.

The call was from my father in his office. "Would you go to Abe's and see if I received a fax?" my father asked.

"Why don't I call over there first?" I said.

"No, I'm sure it's there, please go get it. It's urgent. I also wouldn't mind a bagel. Toasted onion with scallion cream cheese. Light on the cream cheese."

"Okay," I said. Going to the copy shop on the corner and Bagel Time was better than having to talk to Ivy anyway.

My father hung up without saying good-bye as usual.

"Does your father know I'm here?" she asked.

"He's in with another patient. I'm going to pick up a fax," I said, standing up.

"You don't have a fax machine?"

"Nope," I said, enjoying our faxlessness for the first time. I went to the door and opened it to leave, but then I thought better of it, shut the door, and went back to Irmabelle's desk. I didn't like the idea of leaving Ivy Vohl alone in the office. I was sure she would snoop through the files, find mine, and probably my sister's.

The fax could wait. The door to my father's office opened and the patient walked out and went into the bathroom.

Ivy stood up and I signaled to her that she could go right in to my father's office. Before my father had a chance to pop his head out, she sauntered in, proudly carrying her medical questionnaire as if it were the most fascinating document of all time, and shut the door behind her.

I heard the toilet flush and I prayed my father hadn't asked for urine. I was feeling a little too shaky from my encounter with Ivy Vohl first thing in the morning to be pouring urine like a bartender. The patient came out of the bathroom, down the corridor, and stopped when she saw me sitting there.

My father hadn't given me her index card so I didn't know if I was supposed to charge her. She was a pretty black girl with my favorite hairstyle, a big soft Afro. Once I'd tried on an Afro wig just like it and I got a million compliments. It made me look taller and thinner and was the perfect shape for my face.

"I like your hair," I said.

She didn't say anything back, just stared at me. Something about her seemed familiar, but I couldn't think of where I had seen her before.

"Let me just ask the doctor if you owe anything for today," I said.

"I don't," she said. Then she looked down and shook her head and laughed bitterly. "I'm all paid up."

"Okay," I said. I opened the desk drawer and lifted up the metal tray, poking my fingers around the three paltry checks that had been there for a week. "Well, let me just make a note of it. What's your name?"

"Really, I'm all set," she said. "Thank you."

I stood up. "Let me just check with the doctor." I suddenly

felt incredibly nervous about my father examining Ivy Vohl. I knew she wouldn't put on the robe properly and would just be sitting there practically naked when he walked in. I wished I hadn't come in early and that I'd just gone to get the fax and the bagel for my father the way he wanted.

"Fine, you do that," the girl said smugly.

"Is something wrong?" I asked. She was staring at me.

"You're Rebekah Kettle, right?" she asked.

"Yes."

"I'm a big fan," she said.

"Really?" I said, sounding very unsure. "That's great."

She laughed. "You were supposed to go out for a bagel."

"What?" I turned around again, and happened to notice a space in the wall of charts, next to mine. Kettle—S had been removed. And at that moment I realized I had just met Sascha.

I sat down, stunned. I didn't know what to do to keep her from leaving.

"My name's Sascha. Nice to meet ya." She put out her hand and I shook it.

"Nice to meet you," I mumbled.

I tried desperately to think of something to say. So you're Sascha of the New York Kettles. Sascha of the New York elephants. This was all wrong. Nice to meet you wasn't what I had wanted to say. I was stopped cold, but, to use my father's favorite expression, she was cool as a cucumber. This isn't how I had imagined it would be. I had thought our first meeting would be planned. We would meet on elephantback in the desert somewhere, or on some national television morning show, or at my father's untimely funeral. Not trapped and feeling like cheated-on wives. She slung herself into an Il Bisonte bag. My bag also happened to be an Il Bisonte. And she was wearing a top I recognized from a store I loved called Dosa that I had tried on but decided I was too short for. Her hand felt very dry, I realized. She had eczema. She had more of my father in her than I did. But she had green eyes, and my father and Irmabelle both had brown.

I remembered my ex-shrink asking me to describe my perfect friend.

I have a sister, I have a sister! I wanted to scream with joy as if she'd just been born. I wanted to pass out cigars. "Sascha," I said, staying calm. "How did you know my name?"

"I told you, I'm a big fan of your writing."

"So you recognized me from the photo on my book jacket?" I was speaking slowly, trying to piece things together. If she didn't know I was her sister I wasn't sure I wanted to be the one to break it to her. But wait, I thought, panicked. She would have to know. She knew my last name, and my father had been thanked in my acknowledgments.

It should be him sitting here explaining this, I thought. But I had known and hadn't done anything. I should have confronted him, I thought, demanded her address and phone number. "So you know about me," I blurted out.

She looked shocked and one eyebrow rose like mine did. "I've known about you for a long time. Like I said, I'm a fan." From the way she said it I could tell she probably wasn't a fan. "Although I noticed you don't have a single black person in your book. You know there are some black people that live in New York."

More than anything, I hated when people confronted me with this, as if I was a member of the Ku Klux Klan. There was a crazy black girl named Robbie Finch who was always running into me on the street and berating me for that. I didn't want to talk to Sascha about my book. I didn't say anything and she stared at me with a sort of hostile look on her face.

"Look, I want you to know I only just found out about you,"
I said.

"Well, there's been black people in New York for a long time."

"No, I knew about black people, I only just found out you
were my sister." The word sister made us both frown.

"He doesn't know you know?" she asked, losing her cool for
a moment, her voice filled with betrayal. So this is what she had
with him, I thought. What she had and I didn't. A secret. A confidence. The Dad-and-Sascha-don't-tell-Rebekah club. If he knew
I knew we might all be in one club together. I'd had legitimacy
but she'd had him.

I shook my head.

She laughed bitterly again.

"I tried to call you but you weren't listed," I said. In the weeks
since I'd found out about her, I'd also called Irmabelle several times
and hung up, but that didn't seem worth mentioning. I should
have found her, I thought. I should have found her and gone to her.

"You're not listed either," she said. I felt my stomach turn
over with excitement. She had tried to call.

"You have green eyes," I said.

"From Nana." I had to think for a second. Nana was what I
called my grandmother, my father's mother. She had green eyes. I
couldn't believe Nana was both of ours. I couldn't conceive of
anyone else calling her Nana.

"She's dead," I said.

"I never met her."

Sascha had gotten her green eyes while I had gotten her
freakishly short stature. When you go to your father's office, you
don't expect his patient to have your grandmother's eyes. At some
point I had stood up, and now I sat back down. I wished I had
gone for the fax and the bagel.

"Can I ask you a strange question?" I said, suddenly remembering my conversation with my father about his "childhood" dog. "Did you have a dog named Agatha?"

"Yes, she died of distemper. Why?" She seemed irritated. I hadn't imagined she'd be such a bitch. Who the hell wanted this bitch for a sister? I was starting to understand why people always told me how lucky I was to be an only child. "My mother wants her things. Do you mind if I take them for her?"

I pushed myself slightly away from the desk and put my arms up in the air in what was meant to be a be-my-guest gesture but ended up looking like I thought I was getting mugged. She went into the kitchen and opened the cabinet that had all the bags shoved in it and started filling a few with Irmabelle's doctor and nurse mouse dolls, and candy canister, stuffed animals, and plaques. I felt like I was losing my best friend.

"How did you find out about me?" I asked.

"I've always known about you. I knew what camp you went to and what you wanted for your birthday. When you got a TV in your room I wanted a TV in my room. I knew about your abortion and how you had to miss school."

I thought of Y.G. twirling in the playground.

I suddenly felt sick, like I was going to throw up. Sascha had known about me, and I was forced to sit there in a state of shock. "Why didn't I know about you?" I asked.

"I don't know, ask him," she said, pointing to my father's closed door. "At first I think it was to protect your mother. But then I think he was just scared. *Everyone's scared of Rebekah.* When I was a kid I used to watch that show *Wonder Woman* and I always thought that was you. I told my friends that Lynda Carter was my older sister. I figured that's why we couldn't tell people I was your sister, because you were Wonder Woman."

I thought of a photograph I had of myself in high school. I
am sitting on my bed, slightly over five feet tall, and well over one
hundred and seventy pounds. On the wall behind me is a giant
French movie poster of *Adopting Alice,* and there is quite a contrast between the lovely Alice and myself, my face as round and
puffy as a Portuguese sweet bread, my black hair coarse and
winged. Oh, how I longed to be Alice. Oh, how far I was from being Wonder Woman.

I felt like jumping up and spinning around and around, my
gold-banded wrists crossed in front of my creamy corseted
breasts, karate-chopping my father's door open and strangling
him with my magic lasso. But all I could do was propel myself
into a tiny half-spin in Irmabelle's rolling desk chair. How dare
my father be afraid of me! I was lovable. Even in that photo, looking like a public service announcement for teenage suicide, I
looked like a girl who deserved to be loved.

"I wish I had known about you. I would have loved to have
had a sister," I said, choking up slightly.

"Dad didn't want us to say anything."

I couldn't believe that word "Dad" coming out of her mouth
like that. I wondered what happened behind my father's closed
door. I wondered if she came every morning while I was inno-
cently watching *Little House.* What the hell did they have to talk
about for so long in there, I thought, when he and I couldn't come
up with two words to say to each other?

"We could decide to be sisters now," I said.

"Sure," she said. "What should we do first—have a tea party
or play Barbies?"

I laughed and stood up. "We could hug," I said. I had meant
to match her sarcastic tone, but it had somehow come out like a
plea and then in a flash her arms were around me, hugging me,

squeezing the air out of me. The shock of it brought tears to my eyes and I held her, trying not to fall back in Irmabelle's chair. She was sobbing, her face buried in my neck, her hair like black lamb's wool against my eye and cheek. I didn't know what else to do but hang on to her.

"Shit," she said.

"It's okay."

When she finally broke away from me I still felt the wet impression of her face on my neck.

"I'm going to tell him it's all out in the open now," I said.

"No, don't tell Dad," she pleaded, visibly shaken. "Please don't tell."

My father's door swung open and we both froze. I stood up ready to confront him, but it was Ivy Vohl who came bounding out into the reception area.

"Rebekah, your father is so great," she said. She adjusted her top. "Oh, sorry, I didn't know you were with a patient."

"She's not a patient," I said, instantly regretting saying anything.

"Oh?" Ivy asked.

The three of us stood awkwardly in the tiny space. It was clear Ivy was waiting for some kind of introduction. I looked at Sascha for some kind of guidance as to how she wanted me to handle this. Ivy was the last person I would want knowing something like this and I tried to communicate with Sascha telepathically.

"Ivy," I said, "this is Sascha. Sascha, this is Ivy."

"Hi," Ivy said to Sascha.

Sascha just looked at me. She was still trembling. I smiled at her but her expression shifted. She looked hurt. "Alright, I'm gonna get out of here," she said, her voice dripping with disgust.

She grabbed her plastic bags filled with Irmabelle's things and started to leave.

"Wait, Sister." I had said "Sister" when I meant to say Sascha. "Sascha's my sister," I heard myself say to Ivy.

Ivy let out a shriek of laughter. "What did you call her?" she asked.

"My sister," I said, looking her right in the eyes.

"Rebekah," Ivy said jovially, "that's so seventies. Do you realize you're being mildly racially insulting? African-Americans don't all go around calling each other 'sistah' and 'brothah' anymore."

Sascha's eyes dulled and her face became soft and brown like mud. "I think what Rebekah means is that we're *like* sisters," Sascha said, heading toward the door again.

"Sascha, wait, don't go," I said. But she was gone.

"Wow, you really offended her," Ivy said.

"No, I didn't," I said.

"I swear, women are so touchy. That's why I don't have a single female friend," Ivy said.

Yeah, I thought, because women are touchy.

"Let me get your file so I know what to charge you for today," I said.

Ivy looked surprised that there would be a charge, as if I'd invited her home to a family dinner and handed her a check after dessert. The word "charge" sent an electric shock through her. "Can you bill me? I totally forgot to bring my checkbook."

"Sure," I said, glad to speed her exit up as much as possible.

When she left, I sat at Irmabelle's empty desk with my head in my hands. All I could think about was Sascha and how I could see her again. The desk was so bare and cold without Irmabelle's trinkets. They didn't make a Precious Moments doll for this occasion. And if they did, Sascha would have taken it with her.

For the rest of the day, I avoided my father, obeying Sascha's wishes not to tell. He didn't seem to suspect anything had happened, and he never even bothered to ask for the fax he'd used as an excuse to get me out of the office, or the bagel.

I left early and sat on a bench in Central Park for a while under the freezing white winter sun. It was something I almost never did in any weather, because I usually had no desire to see people biking and pushing baby carriages, or, worse than that, reading.

One summer I'd been in a jealous frenzy over a certain book I'd noticed everyone reading. I saw people reading it in the park and on the subway, and even walking down the street, they were so absorbed. The book had a distinctive blue jacket but I could never catch the title, and then finally I discovered that this huge literary sensation I'd been sick with jealousy over, was called *Nuevo York*. I'd been jealous of a guidebook.

I thought about writing a letter to Arthur.

Dear Awful Writer, Sometimes I think my sister Lucy is my only friend in the world!

But my heart wasn't in it. I couldn't think about him right now when I had a real sister to worry about. I had a sister. Sister. The strangest word I had ever known. I felt rich, in love really. I liked her. I loved her. She was mine.

I walked quickly until I was almost running, suddenly excited to tell Isaac all about her.

19.

At 33, a former sweetheart comes crawling back

March 27

Dear Awf,

Just a quick note to say that you may not know
this but you and I have actually kissed. Of course it
was at Madam Tussaud's and you were made out of
wax but I think it was good for both of us. I was very
careful not to knock your glasses off. I know you always like to wear them but I might have stolen them if
the security guard wasn't staring at me. It was very
polite of you not to use any tongue. I wonder if kissing
you in real life is like kissing a giant chapstick. Write
back soon and let me know.

By the way, I did not win the short story competi-
ton. I came in second. In case you're wondering my
story was called "Werner Apple's Brain". It's about an
almost thirteen year old girl who writes letters to the
most famous filmmaker in the world, and in the end

they meet (by accident) at the Alice in Wonderland statue in Central Park. Robert McKee doesn't believe in Deus ex Machina but I think it can sometimes be very fantastic.

A girl named Eve who's father is a math teacher here won. I find it a little suspicious. Her story took place in a deli in Little Italy and had a lot of descriptions of salami and people going in and out. I think I should have had more descriptions. I am very disappointed. But at least I have you.

Yours with no talent,

Thalia

March 28

Dear A.W.,

I won after all! It turned out the girl who won plagerized almost her whole story from some famous writer. Our teacher, Mr. Goff, said that something had been gnawing at him, how the description of the Italian deli was so accurate and then he questioned her and she got caught. I have always been terrified of plagiarism since I read the autobiography of Helen Keller in Second grade. So I am the supreme winner. You should be thrilled that I dain to write you letters now that I am an award winning writer.

Love,

Thalia the Great

I stepped outside Mrs. Williams' apartment door, dropped the letters down the old fashioned glass mail chute, and watched them fall. The elevator door opened and I turned with curiosity because there were two other apartments on our floor and I hadn't met the neighbors.

An old Jewish man came teetering out. He wore baggy, old-man elastic-waisted denim jeans, a denim shirt, and a silver and turquoise bolo tie around his neck. He was in his eighties, or maybe nineties.

"Where's that whore?" he asked. He rattled a plastic Duane Reade bag he was holding.

His voice was thin but determined, and he asked it like he really wanted me to answer. "I don't know," I said. I backed up toward Mrs. Williams' open door.

"Is she in there? Is this where the men line up to make love to her?" He pointed to the wall so convincingly, I almost saw a line of men standing there, but there was really just a narrow, white marble-topped occasional table with a glass fishbowl on it filled with potpourri.

"I don't know what you're talking about," I said. I walked into the apartment and tried to close the door, but he pushed it open. I got scared. I imagined him pulling a gun out of his big pants or his Duane Reade bag and shooting me.

"So, you work for her. What, you bring her the men? Or you just want to get in on the bonanza?"

"I bring her the pizza," I said. I stood in the doorway blocking him.

"Whore, I'm home!" he screamed. "I'm coming into the bedroom now!" He started stamping his cowboy boots on the marble floor, escalating the noise to make it sound like his footsteps were getting closer.

"Howard, what are you doing here?" Mrs. Williams said, coming out of the dining room.

"Hello, whore."

"Howard, how did you get out of Croftville?"

"I'm going to use the bathroom." He pulled a four pack of Charmin toilet paper out of the Duane Reade bag. "I brought my own." He went into the master bathroom.

"That's my husband," Mrs. Williams said. "He has dementia." What a couple, I thought. "He thinks I'm having sex with the doorman and the doorman is using up all our toilet paper." It was strangely romantic. "I told him the doorman's a young boy. I should call the home."

I followed her into the kitchen and while she called Croftville, I went to the window and looked for Arthur Weeman but a shadow passed by his window just as I got there. I had just missed him. If it hadn't been for Howard, I would have had a full-fledged sighting. Then I thought it might not be him, it could be a cleaning lady or someone, because whoever it was had moved so quickly and he usually plodded slowly and contemplatively around his kitchen. I stood waiting expectantly to see if his cleaning lady would be like the ones in his movies, nice clichéd middle-aged ladies in a gray uniform.

In a burst, a figure suddenly appeared filling the entire window frame, surprising the hell out of me. She leaned all the way out the open window, arms dangling down, and it took me a moment, until she lifted her head, to realize that it was Y.G. I looked to see if I could see Arthur Weeman reflected in the Sub-Zero refrigerator, but there wasn't a trace of him.

Y.G., in her Gardener jacket, held a video camera out the window and pointed it at her friends in the schoolyard. She pushed her elbows into the brick windowsill to steady the camera. I held my breath. I couldn't believe she was there, in his apartment, in the middle of a school day after what had happened in the playground.

Her face was long and narrow, but pretty, with an angular jaw. She left the camera, precariously, stupidly on the windowsill, and then disappeared out of my view.

Behind me, Mrs. Williams finished her conversation, assuring the administrator that she would send her husband back there in a car service, and hung up.

"I'm going to stay here today and make sure you're okay with Howard," I said, not taking my eyes off of Arthur's window. Y.G. came back to the window holding a goblet filled with dark liquid. She was definitely pretty, I decided, but she wasn't the prettiest one in the playground.

"No, dear, I think it would be better if you went."

I turned to look at her, trying not to show the panic I was feeling. Arthur had Y.G. in his apartment. But where was he? She didn't seem to be talking to him, in fact she seemed to be entirely alone. I had to stay. I couldn't be turned away now. "I think it would be better if I stayed," I said. "I can call the car service."

"No. I want to be alone with Howard. I know how to call the car. You just dial all sevens."

"I think I should stay," I said, defiantly. "He could get violent."

"This isn't your house, dear," Mrs. Williams said.

"I know," I said, my voice quaking I was so angry. "But I can just stay here in the kitchen and make sure everything's okay."

"This isn't a rental property, dear. You're not invited to stay right now."

"Fine!" I said, infuriated. "If you don't want me here, I'll go!"

I tried desperately to think of a way to stay at the window.

"May I at least please use your telephone to make one important local call?" I said, with sarcastic formality.

"Of course, dear, as long as it's quick." Why don't you looney-toon out of here? I thought.

I grabbed the phone, and stretching the long cord as close to the window as I could, and never once taking my eyes off Y.G., I dialed Mr. Moviefone.

If you know the name of the movie you want to see, press 1.

I couldn't press 1 because Mrs. Williams had a rotary, but it didn't matter because the only movie I wanted to see was the one in Arthur Weeman's window. I wanted to see it more than anything.

I went to Serendipity and sat there for an hour and a half wedged in with a hundred children, fuming at Mrs. Williams, and Arthur Weeman, and my father, and myself. All I did was help other people all day long. I had given myself away like a box of UNICEF pennies. I helped my father, and wrote inspiring letters to Arthur Weeman, and nursed that ungrateful old cunt Mrs. Williams. I was like Paul Revere riding in the night to save a nation, but I wasn't exactly making history. I was making appointments for my father, and salami sandwiches for Mrs. Williams, and wasting all this time. Sitting in the old-fashioned café chair, I prayed for some Freaky Friday magic to take me back down my time line to age thirteen so I could be sitting on the cement bench in the Gardener School playground again and Arthur Weeman could invite me upstairs to sip dark liquid from a goblet, give me his video camera, and turn me into somebody as great as himself.

That night I had a morose date with Isaac. He looked terrible, unshaved, with a strange bleached spot on his jeans right at his crotch. He was wearing his beloved *Quille* baseball cap and I almost wondered if Ivy Vohl had been right about him that day in La Petite Lolita, if maybe he was too intense in a strange way. He was upset about his career. He needed some sort of nasty scoop on some sort of celebrity, the sort of picture that could earn him a hundred thousand from *The National Enquirer.*

I really didn't know what to say to him. Helping Isaac get into *The Enquirer* didn't exactly make me feel like Eleanor Roosevelt helping her husband lead a country out of the Depression.

As we walked home from the restaurant, just as we got to the northwest corner of Washington Square Park, a gust of wind blew his *Quille* cap right off his head and into the sky. It wasn't even a windy night, there was just that one menacing gust. It happened in an instant. The cap was gone.

"My hat!" Isaac shrieked. He looked around wildly and then started running down the street. At the corner, he looked around wildly again and then ran back to me. "We have to find it," he said.

"You can get another one."

"They don't make that one anymore. Goddamnit."

"I'm sure we'll find it," I said.

For the next three hours, we searched the park for Isaac's hat. I opened every gate leading to every town house and searched the bushes and stairs. Isaac stopped and looked up at every tree. We looked behind benches, surveyed the playgrounds, eyed the drug dealers. Finally we just stood in the middle of the putrid deserted dog run. The acrid smell was overwhelming. Behind Isaac was a sign that said DOGS LEFT HERE ALONE WILL BE BROUGHT TO THE ASPCA.

I was really starting to consider leaving Isaac there.

"I just wanted this night to be nice," Isaac said.

"Well, it isn't." I felt my high heels sink further into the piss-soaked gravel.

The terrible smell reminded me of something, but I couldn't think of what it was for a moment. It was something beautiful and exciting like the circus, but I couldn't put my finger on it. Then I realized it was when I had first talked to Isaac, standing next to piles of manure from the horses across from the Pierre.

"What can I do to make it better?" he asked. Something caught his eye behind me, and he rubbernecked around as if he was looking at a half-naked woman, but it was just a black plastic bag he had mistaken for his hat. That was the thing about losing something—you never really stopped looking for it. "Sorry. Please tell me what I can do to save this night?"

A crazy thought came into my head. You can ask me to marry you, I thought. I didn't know why I thought it, it was probably just force of habit because I was tired of all these men never bothering to propose. I barely knew Isaac and I certainly wasn't too impressed with him at this moment. I was thirty-three years old. I'd done nothing with my life, except spend what felt like half of it looking for this man's hat. By thirty-three, Arthur Weeman'd had three wives. By thirty-three, Paul Revere'd had four wives. I'd been pregnant but had no children. I'd lactated but never nursed a baby. My father had two daughters, but I didn't know my sister. It seemed like it was time to get on with it.

"I was wondering if you wanted to marry me," Isaac said. "I was planning something romantic, but then my hat blew away and everything got ruined."

In *Little House,* the book not the movie, *Those Happy Golden Years* to be precise, when Almanzo proposed to Laura, he took her for a ride in a horse-drawn carriage. He said something like, "I was wondering if you would like to have an engagement ring?" and she said, "Well, that would depend on the man giving it to me." Then he said something like, "What if the man was me?" and she said, "Then it would depend on the ring." I read it just once, never going back to read it again in case it would somehow be spoiled, and I don't know if that's exactly what happened word for word, but that's how I remembered it. Reading that was the single most thrilling moment of my entire childhood. No, I would go further than that. Reading that was the single most thrilling moment of my entire life. Until this one.

"Then it would depend on the ring," I said.

"I thought you made it pretty clear that you wanted to choose the ring yourself." I had actually made that clear by cleverly telling a story of my friend who wanted a certain ring and was proposed to with something else, and never liked it, and ended up calling off the wedding. "But I will get down on one knee."

I tried to stop him from kneeling in all that dog piss, but he insisted.

"I love you," he said. "I tried to get you that flower you like but leave it to you to like a flower that doesn't exist."

"What flower?"

"Wisterious."

"Wisteria?" I said. I remembered he'd asked me what my favorite flower was but I hadn't known why. I remembered Almanzo had taken Laura in a horse-drawn carriage to pick wild grapes.

"I've put aside twelve thousand dollars for the ring. Eight to twelve. I don't want you to spend less than eight or more than twelve."

"I don't want to spend less than twelve," I said. I liked being proposed to with a budget like that.

"So whadaya say?"

"I always want to live in New York," I warned. "And I want a dog." I wanted children too, but I didn't want to scare him.

"We'll write it into the ketubah."

The word ketubah reminded me of Ivy Vohl. "One more thing. I don't want to hear the name Ivy Vohl ever again."

"I can't promise that. That's crazy. For one thing, we have to invite her to the wedding."

I pictured Ivy in a tux standing next to Isaac at the altar. "She doesn't even like you, Isaac. She thinks you're strange."

He cocked his head up at me. "She's coming to the wedding."

"We'll see."

"You still haven't said yes."

"Yes," I said. "Wait! I want to go to Venice on our honeymoon."

"You already said yes, all negotiating is over."

He rose and we stood in the dog run and kissed.

We left the park and kissed again on the corner of Fifth. A bus passed us, and when I looked up I noticed ONE IF BY LAND TOURS on its side, written in giant red, white, and blue.

The next morning after Isaac and I watched one of the most suspenseful episodes ever, in which Pa lets Laura adopt a pet raccoon she names Jasper and gets bitten by another raccoon that might have had rabies, but thank God didn't, I went to my father's office.

He was sitting at his desk looking at a chart.

"Dad, something happened last night."

"Oh?"

I sat in the patient chair. "I got engaged."

"Are you pregnant?"

"No," I said, feeling the whole thing dampened. My news was never big enough. Being pregnant would be much better than merely being engaged.

"I didn't even know you were seeing anyone."

I didn't know you had another daughter, I thought. "I wasn't and then I was. It happened quickly."

"What's your man's name?"

"Isaac Myman," I said.

"Well, your man is my man," my father said. He smiled at his own joke. "I think it's wonderful, Toots. As you know, I am a great believer in marriage." I laughed because I thought he was being sarcastic. "I'm serious, I think marriage is the greatest thing in the world. Having someone you can really talk to, to really *talk* to, is the closest thing there is to a heaven."

"You hated being married," I said, shocked.

"No, I didn't. Your mother was impossible but I would have loved being married to the right person." He was being serious. He was talking about Irmabelle. "You've really made my day," my father said.

"Thank you," I said, totally confused by the way this was going. I had expected him to curse and scream and say I wasn't ready. That five months wasn't long enough to date. That I hardly knew this person. That I was a fool. I had expected to call him a coward for keeping my sister from me, defy Sascha's wishes, and finally confront him with it.

"So my daughter's getting married," he said. One of them, I thought.

"Let me know if you want a wedding. I'll give you money for it. I'm very proud of you."

I almost fell out of my chair. I was so surprised, I felt my old love for him. Money! I got a little overexcited until I reminded myself that there was money and then there was my father's idea of money, but still I felt supported by him.

Then I felt a little angry that the only thing I ever did to earn his approval was agree to marry some guy, any guy off the street really, who he hadn't even met yet. He didn't care who Isaac My-man was as long as he was willing to marry me. His approval was giving me cold feet.

"Well," I said, "you might not like him. He's a paparazzo."

"A what?" my father asked.

"He photographs celebrities."

"Ahh, I don't care for all that," my father said.

"He was there that night at the Ziegfeld. At the Arthur Wee-man movie."

"Oh right, I remember," he said.

"And he's very strange." I sounded like Ivy Vohl.

"So are you," my father said, smiling.

I smiled too. It was the single nicest thing he had ever said to me. He meant it lovingly and it was true. Isaac and I were right for each other. My love and sureness about Isaac returned full blast. I was like Marilyn Monroe with wind blowing my skirt up, in love and vulnerable.

"How's your head?" my father asked.

"What do you mean?"

"Your head. Any headaches?"

"No," I said, astonished. I had a strange giddiness from the neck up, a lightness, and it took me a second to realize that's what it was not to have a headache. And now that I thought about it, I hadn't had one in months.

I closed my eyes and tried to remember what they had felt like, the galloping horse, the sides of my skull tightening like a drum, my neck and shoulders turned to stone, the drilling at the very top of my brain, the three tender points on my face like the eyes of a coconut. Without my headaches I was a different person. A part of me was gone.

Once I had answered a personal ad that said *Migraineur Seeks Same*. It sounded so romantic, like a French film, two migraineurs in bed, in a darkened room, moaning with pain. The man called and we made a date, but he canceled at the last minute because he had a headache.

But those days of headaches and personal ads were gone.

"You see what going to a real doctor can do for you, Toots," my father said. "You took the medicine I prescribed and your symptoms subsided."

"We don't know that," I said. "It coulda been a lot of things that cured me." Like knowing the truth about Sascha. Like love. Like Isaac.

That night I lay in bed with my fiancé.

The phone rang and I answered it. "Hello?"

"Hi, Rebekah." It was Derek Hassler. "It's Derek."

I paused. "Derek?" I said. "Derek who?"

"Derek Hassler."

"Oh, hi," I said.

"I was just sitting here sort of thinking about you."

I sank back into my pillows, ready to enjoy the moment. He had called. They always called. You might have to wait a while, but in the end the call always came. Even if they got married right after breaking up with you and had a daughter named Catherine, you could rest assured the call would come. Even if, right after they broke up with you, they became an Orthodox Jew and moved in with a rabbi in Brooklyn, the call would come. Even if they moved to Oregon and you heard they were dating some trashy nurse and were paying for her adopted daughter's karate classes, the call would eventually come. It was one of those moments of pure pleasure that made being single great.

"I'm sorry, what did you say?" I asked.

"I said I was just sitting here thinking about you."

"Oh that's nice. I've thought about you too, Derek. But I thought you didn't want to feel like you had to call me." I let out the carefree laugh of a beautiful single girl.

"Well, I didn't have to call you now, but I wanted to."

"How come?"

"I have two tickets to the Daytime Emmy Awards, and I . . ."

"Oh, I love the Daytime Emmys!" I said, interrupting him.

"Well, I was just remembering what a good time we had when we went to the MTV Awards. You know, our first date."

"Oh, right, that was our first date," I said, as if searching my memory.

"Who's that?" Isaac asked.

"No one," I said.

"Who's that?" Derek asked.

"Actually, Derek, I'm already going to the Daytime Emmys with my *fiancé*. He's photographing the event."

"Oh," Derek said, sounding shocked.

"Yes, Derek, I'm to be married," I said.

He didn't say anything.

"Yes, we're very excited about it," I continued.

"All right, well, I guess that's that then. Bye," he said.

"Bye," I said. And my moment was over.

20.

At 33, she relies on her editor as Steinbeck relied on his during the writing of East of Eden

The next morning, after the schoolchildren helped make a bell for the church, I went to look for my ring. I went straight to Once Upon A Time, the antique jewelry store on Eleventh Street, where I had always known my ring would be waiting for me. I picked out three, like Goldilocks, and chose the right one as soon as it slid onto my finger. Using mental time-lapse photography I watched my hand grow old and knotted and decided the ring would always suit me.

I called Isaac and told him he could come any time and pick it up.

"Wow, that was fast," he said.

It was thirteen thousand and he'd told me to spend no more than twelve, so I was comfortably within my budget.

Making that call, I had never felt so loved in my entire life.

I left Once Upon A Time and walked to SoHo to buy shoes to go with my ring. I stopped into Kelley & Ping and ordered wide sweet and spicy noodles which I ate with enormous chopsticks under the sloping skylight in the back. I'm engaged, I thought.

I'm engaged. Then I started thinking about Thalia. I'd gone off and gotten engaged while she was naively writing letters to Arthur Weeman who was possibly screwing a twelve-year-old. How she would burn if she knew what her awful writer had done behind her back! But then another thought occurred to me. What if his actions with Y.G. were in some way an extension of his feelings for Thalia? What if Thalia had in some way shown him what could be possible, sent Arthur Weeman over the edge, or over the ledge, or over the schoolyard wall? Or had he done this a thousand times before? I wondered.

The truth was, I wasn't angry at Arthur Weeman, and I didn't think Thalia would be either. I almost loved him all the more for it in a terrible way. Thalia and I were like his cheerleaders. Like Val and Gil watching Peter Sellers from behind a rock in *The World of Henry Orient,* we were still his greatest fans.

I took out my CARMOL40 (40% UREA) LOTION pad and began a letter to Arthur Weeman.

                                                            March 30

Dear Awful Writer,

       I was right. My father is having an affair. My mother found out and my father moved to the Upper West Side after doing only three nights of couch time. My friend Jenny said most fathers do a lot more couch time than that before they finally move out. He also didn't have one ounce of therapy. I am taking it quite well. I just hope he doesn't marry his girlfriend because I hate her. My friend Jenny took me to the movies to take my mind off things. See I watch OTHER PEOPLE'S movies too. Jealous?

I feal very angry that this might intefere with my going to French Woods Theater Camp this summer because I'm supposed to spend summers with him now and he's to cheap to send me to camp. I can not imagine spending the whole summer on the Upper West Side. I won't do it.

And now there is a rumor that we are supposed to go to Disneyworld for a family reunion during Easter break which is in only eighteen days. Can you imagine New York City intellectuals going to Disneyworld. All because my cousin whose five wants to go and my aunt had to have all kinds of fertility treatments to get him so they do whatever he wants. I hate Disneyworld. It almost makes you hope for terrorism or something. I refuse to go to Disneyworld. Micky Mouse can kiss my ass.

Here's a little skit I just made up:

"Hey Thalia, your father is having an affair, what are you gonna do next?"

"Go to Disneyworld!"

I'm very good at writing gags. By the way I feal angry at you to because you haven't written me and I'm thinking of giving you an ultamatum. Ultamatum: if you don't give me a sign that your reading these scintalating letters then I'll stop writing them and you'll never hear from your secret un-admirer again and you'll never know what happens to her. For instance will I give in and go to Disneyworld, will Isaac ask me out, will I never see another Arthur Weeman movie again.

Yours quite ambivalently,

Thalia

P.S. I love you

P.P.S. I realize this stationary isn't very sexy but it's all I could find in my father's office.

Then, when I finished the letter, a strange thing happened. I burst into tears. I just sat there sobbing into my touristy noodles, crying for Thalia and everything that was about to happen to her. I wanted to write her a letter telling her none of this mattered and not to worry about any of it, everything would turn out all right. She'd write a book and get engaged. I was crying the way I used to cry the whole time I was writing my novel, without any idea why.

I knew what would happen to her in Disney World and I didn't want it to. I knew she would promise to be at "It's a Small World" in two hours and go off by herself. I knew she would meet the man who ran the "Pirates of the Caribbean" while he was on his break and go off with him to an employees' only building where there were cots. I knew she would boldly take off her Mexican peasant blouse and unzip his zipper. I knew he would say to her, "You're the best ride in this place," and flying home, she would have no idea of everything bad that was about to happen to her.

Then it occurred to me that maybe she didn't have to meet the man at Disney World, and maybe she didn't have to go to Disney World at all. I suddenly remembered something I had bought at Golden's stationery store when I was thirteen. It was a new thing called the erasable pen and I'd thought it was the best invention ever. I could erase that arrow on her time line. Instead of one if by land, I could make it two if by sea. I could press a different button and select a different movie.

Instead of what happened to me, she could refuse to go to Disney World. During spring break, she could just stay in New

York and get ready for her bat mitzvah. Or she could go to East Hampton with her best friend, Candi Miranda, and Candi's father could treat them to lots of dinners at Nick and Toni's and Della Femina's and they could be best friends for the rest of their lives.

At the counter where they sold green tea from giant barrels, they also sold strange Japanese stationery with young geishas on it drinking some sort of soft drink from a can. I purchased several sheets and sat down to write the letter I realized I had wanted to write for a long time. I dated it a month in the future, and nineteen years in the past.

April 30

Dear Awful Writer,

    I'm sorry I haven't written in so long. I was away at Disneyworld and I didn't think a great independent filmmaker like yourself would appreciate getting a postcard with Mickey Mouse on it. I thought about you the whole time however. Well not the whole time . . . Not while I was practically having SEX with a MAN . . .

    NOW THAT I HAVE YOUR ATTENTION . . .

    Here's what happened. My moronic family finally agreed to let me go off by myself for a while. I guess they figured if I can wander around New York City alone and take the subway then I'd be fine at Disneyworld. It's not like I was going to get mugged by Huey, Dewie, and Louie. So I met a MAN who runs the Pirates of the Carribean ride and we made out in the employee rest area and I was wearing a beautiful white Mexican top I bought on Bleecker Street and I took it off and I

let him take off my bra and he pulled down his pants
and sort of pushed my head down towards his huge
hardon and I sucked on it which I have to say came
quite naturally for some reason. He really wanted to do
it and I asked him if he had a condom and he said he
couldn't feel anything through a condom and I said that
was funny because he seemed to have felt plenty
through his big pirate pants and I thought maybe it
would be a good idea just to get it over with so I
wouldn't have to obsess about it anymore but then my
cell phone rang and I looked at my caller ID and it was
my father and I thought I'm not going to do this. I
haven't even been on that many real dates yet. I still
really like that boy Isaac. And did I really want to lose
my virginity in a place like this, a place for *children,*
with a 23-year old man who runs the Pirates of the
Carribean ride for a living. I wish there was a place
called Weemanworld. It's not like I expect to lose my
virginity with you, Awful, but I wanted something better then the pirate. So I jumped up and put on my bra
and my top and he seemed really P.O.'d so I gave him a
hand job and then met my parents.

So here I am back in New York and nothing has
changed. I'm still in tact virginity and all. Tonight my
friend Candi's father is taking us to The Palm which I
love and then we're going to sleep at her mother's
house. Her mother lets us sleep on the giant pull out
couch in the living room so we can watch the Plasma.
Tomorrow I'm seeing Giselle at the Metropolitan Opera
House with Candi, Carly, and Margaret and then having
dinner at O'Neil's Balloon which isn't as good as it used

to be. My father says it used to be good back in the
olden days when the waitresses wore rollerskates. Life
goes on and I have to write a speech for my bat mitzvah. Maybe I'll tell the story of my experience at Disneyworld and shock the hell out of everybody.

    Anyway just because I didn't do it in Disneyworld
doesn't mean I'm not ready to do it any time now but
until then I remain

    Your pure and virginal,

    Thalia

So that was that. Easy peasy lemon squeasy. A do-over. I
brushed imaginary dirt off my hands. Like a great film editor, I
had sliced and spliced and half a year of my life ended up on the
cutting room floor where it belonged.

I sealed the letter in its envelope, addressed it, and drew a small
picture of my brain wearing a pair of Mickey Mouse ears. I put it in
my bag to keep there for a month until it was time to send it.

My cell phone rang. It was Isaac.

"What are you doing?" he asked.

"Writing," I said.

"Writing what?"

"What?" I paused for a second.

"What are you writing?"

"A new novel," I said. And then I realized in a strange way it
might be true.

The hair on the back of my neck prickled. The letters, I
thought, suddenly flooded with excitement. The letters that
Arthur Weeman had probably tossed away were the foundation
for a great little book. The letters were so vivid in my mind, it
would take me no time at all to reconstruct them.

I looked down at my writing, that same sure cursive I'd had since I was ten. "Hey that's great," Isaac said.

I wrote until I had filled almost the whole pad. Then I walked to my apartment to pick up some clean clothes and my laptop before heading uptown to make up with Mrs. Williams. I knew she might not want me to stay there but I thought I'd bring clothes just in case. I was tired of rinsing out my underwear and hanging it to dry next to hers in the shower which I always did after we had our tea and took our medication. My phone rang just as I hoisted my bag on my shoulder and was walking out the door. My machine picked up.

"Is that Rebekah Kettle?" a man said, in a familiar English accent. I froze. "It's Hugh calling, Hugh Nickelby. I'm in London but . . ."

I ran to the phone as fast as I could.

"Hi, Hugh," I said. I couldn't believe it.

"I know this is incredibly last minute, but they're doing a screening of *Thank You for Not Writing* in New York day after tomorrow and I'd really love it if you would come."

"Of course, I would love to come," I said, completely forgetting I was engaged. He gave me the information while my mind whirled like a Jane Austen character at a ball. "Then I was hoping we could have a chat about it." A screening and a chat. With Hugh Nickelby. "Terrific, then your name will be on the list," he said.

I looked at my apartment through Hugh's eyes. My bed was unmade and there were take-out containers on the kitchen counter. I would have to clean it up in case our chat was going to be at my place. Then I remembered the small complication of my engagement. I wasn't sure if I could be engaged to Isaac and date Hugh Nickelby at the same time, but it seemed that since Hugh and I were both writers it would probably be okay. And I wasn't really officially engaged until I was given the ring. Hugh and I probably wouldn't kiss or anything or even hold hands, considering we'd be at a crowded screening with all eyes on him. If he asked me to dinner afterward, which he probably would so we could have our chat, I'd have to play it by ear. I decided not to let something like an alleged engagement get in the way of the most glamorous, exciting date I had ever been asked out on, and I really saw no reason to mention it to Isaac.

The day of my date with Hugh, I went to my friend Cynthia Ree's clothing design studio on Prince Street and let her dress me up in an incredible Asian-looking velvet thing. I was going to show Hugh that we could talk about something other than books. And that I could still be a strong American female voice but with an ever so slight, sexy English accent.

I got out of the cab at the Director's Guild practically expecting a red carpet, but there wasn't one, just scraggily-looking publishing types and some kids who looked like film students.

Hugh hadn't told me exactly where to meet him, so I just went in and gave my name to the boy at the table and entered the auditorium.

I stood in the back and scanned the crowd but I didn't see Hugh so I leaned against a wall and waited, resisting the urge to get a tub of free popcorn. I noticed an empty row of reserved seats, but I wasn't sure if I should sit in one and save one for Hugh or just wait to see what he wanted to do.

Then I saw my editor dressed in plunging red, walking up the aisle toward me. Seeing her was almost as exciting as seeing Hugh. My heart pumped in gratitude to Cynthia for making me dress up like that, and instead of avoiding my editor as I had since my book had been overdue, I suddenly felt ready to face her.

"Hi, Evan," I said, when our eyes met.

"Rebekah Kettle! How are we going to get another novel out of you?" she asked.

"Well, I am actually not too far off from finishing a new novel." The words coming out of my mouth totally shocked me.

"What's it about?" she asked.

I froze for a second and then, to my complete surprise, the answer came pouring out of me as if the whole thing had already been written. "It's about a one-time famous writer who finds herself unable to write. So she starts writing letters to Arthur Weeman, pretending to be a thirteen-year-old-girl and through these letters she deals with something bad that happened to her when she was almost thirteen and . . ."

She was quiet for a minute and I wondered if I had made a mistake to blurt all that out. We had a great relationship. Only once during the publication of my book had we had a problem. It was over the word "come." I had spelled it "come" and she had wanted it to be spelled "cum," and we battled for weeks until my agent convinced me to do it her way.

"Why does she pretend to be a thirteen-year-old girl?" she asked, finally breaking the silence.

"Well, you know, because of the director's movies, he hates his fans but she feels it would make her stand out, that he would like to get letters from a young . . ."

"Yes, and that's disgusting. Rebekah, pedophilia doesn't sell," my editor said. "I don't think you should go anywhere near pedophilia."

"No, it's not really about pedophilia."

"No one wants to read about some old sick man and an underage girl." She sounded hysterical. She had two daughters and she was going through a divorce and custody fight with her husband, so this was probably some kind of sore spot with her.

An obscure little book called *Lolita* by an unknown named Nabokov came to mind, but I decided not to mention it. "I'm just saying it's not really touched on in the novel." Touched on was probably the wrong word.

"Oh," Evan said. "Well, what about the fact that everybody hates Arthur Weeman? I mean, he really hasn't made a good movie since *The Analyst*. I think it might turn off a lot of readers."

"I could change his name," I said.

"Well, how does it end?" she asked.

"She gets married."

"To Arthur Weeman? Don't make me throw up."

"No, to the love interest. In the end she realizes she doesn't need Arthur Weeman anymore."

"Marriage is a very bad idea, Rebekah," she said bitterly. "People pick up a Rebekah Kettle novel to read about sex and the single girl. They want a lighthearted romp through New York. They don't pick up a Rebekah Kettle to read about child molestation and settling down."

While she was telling me why people pick up a Rebekah Kettle, I couldn't help thinking about *Little House on the Prairie*. Something had been bothering me lately, and I suddenly realized what it was. We were back in Season One, having just come to the end of the final season, the one called *Little House: A New Beginning*, and something had happened to Laura. She had lost her spark. Once her braids came out and her hair retreated into a bun like Ma's, she just wasn't that interesting anymore. Pa was still interesting and Almanzo and Adam and even the thin-lipped

Albert, but Laura was stuck teaching in the schoolhouse, making disapproving looks all the time and standing silently next to her husband. She pumped well water and wore eye shadow and had her baby daughter, Rose, constantly glued to her hip, but the girl who had panned for fool's gold, and worked in the circus as a clown, and kissed Mr. Edwards' on the cheek, was gone. When you really thought about it, as soon as she added Wilder to the end of her name, her time line was as good as over. Laura Ingalls was through.

"Maybe she doesn't have to get married," I said.

"I think that would be great!" my editor said.

"I promise you a lighthearted romp through New York," I said, my voice slightly unsure.

"Oh. Well, then, this is wonderful news," Evan said, cumming around. "I'll call Ben and tell him we're all set, and I'll release a check as soon as you turn in pages." We set up a lunch at The Four Seasons like old times. Like old times. I felt like myself again.

I looked around for Hugh.

"Who are you looking for?" Evan asked.

"Well, I was actually invited here by Hugh," I said. "I was supposed to meet him here but I don't see him."

"Hugh Nickelby?" she asked.

"Yes," I said, nonchalantly, smiling. "He personally invited me."

"Hugh's in London," she said. "He personally invited everyone here. Anyway, get me those pages. I think this book is going to be big." She kissed my cheek, but I was too stunned to say anything before she rushed off.

While we had been talking, almost all the seats had filled. I noticed Ivy Vohl in the third row next to an empty seat. It seemed impossible to leave so I slid into a seat in the last row and covered my eyes with my hands. I couldn't focus on one minute of the movie. I just sat there, wondering how I could have been so stupid to think that I had a date with Hugh Nickelby. *Men come and go like pens,* I thought wistfully. But then I remembered that I was engaged, and that made me feel much better. I wished more than anything I had brought Isaac.

21.

At 33, she betrays a sacred trust

The letters poured out of me effortlessly. Thalia completely took over. For all of April and half of May, I sat in my spot at Mrs. Williams' kitchen window, writing on my laptop and crying. I made Sascha a successful publisher. I made Isaac tall, and Ivy ugly.

I was deep in the playground movie scene, when I noticed the light come on in Arthur Weeman's kitchen.

Then my cell phone rang. It was Isaac.

"Do you have my ring?" I asked. He'd taken his time with it.

"Don't worry about that," he said.

"Well, don't you think this whole engagement deal is very oral in nature?"

"Not oral enough," he said. "Guess where I am?"

"I was hoping you'd be at Once Upon A Time on East Eleventh Street between University and Fifth, closer to University, handing your credit card to the woman behind the counter."

"Actually, I'm someplace even better."

"Harry Winston?" I asked. That would be better.

"Arthur Weeman's."

"What!" My eye went to Arthur Weeman's window again as if I expected to see Isaac looking back at me.

"I'm outside his building. Did you know he lives on Eighty-seventh Street in a double town house? Right near Mrs. Williams."

"Oh, yeah, I remember reading that," I said, my voice catching a little. This couldn't be considered cheating on Isaac, I thought, sitting in an old woman's apartment looking into an empty window, but it somehow felt like it was.

"I'm pretty sure I'm going to get him. He had an early reservation at Shun Lee East, so he should be coming home soon."

"That's your big scoop? That he ate fancy Chinese today?" I hoped I respected Isaac enough to become his wife. It was important to respect what your husband did for a living. I thought of Ma standing at the window in a terrible blizzard, waiting for Pa to come home, a giant buck draped over his shoulders followed by a nice Indian whose life he would save at the end of the episode.

"No, it's that he ate fancy Chinese with a thirteen-year-old girl he seems to have taken a fancy to. He's probably there right now teaching her how to fold a moo-shu pancake." He did a bad Arthur Weeman impression. "You take the pancake like this, see, and you wrap it around my old-man dick."

As he was saying something obscene about an egg roll, Arthur Weeman appeared in the window, far back near the sparkling granite island.

"Maybe he's already home," I said.

"No, he's definitely not. I've been standing here for two hours and there's seven other schmucks here with me. There's the *Post,* the *News,* the *Times,* E!, EW, ET, Fox, and me. And some private guy I think Candace Ann might have hired. Oh shit, is it rain-ing?"

Arthur Weeman walked to the open kitchen window and shut it.

"You're just going to stand in the rain and wait for him?" I said.

"I'm a hunter," Isaac said.

"That's ridiculous," I said.

"Why? This is a huge deal. Arthur Weeman is hanging around with a thirteen-year-old. That doesn't bother you?"

"I care about his work, I don't judge what he does in his per-sonal life."

"Yeah, well, everyone else in New York does. This could be the start of a trial. The rumor is her name is Thalia. You would know this, wasn't Thalia the name of one of the Greek muses?"

I tried to say something but I couldn't. The name Thalia coming out of his mouth like that made me speechless. He pro-nounced the *Thal* of Thalia like *thal* in thalamus gland, and in my mind I'd been pronouncing it like *Thay-lia.* I stopped myself from correcting him because it suddenly occurred to me that he knew about my letters. He was teasing me, he had to be. What kind of man would go through a person's things? I wondered. But I almost always mailed the letters as soon as I wrote them so there was really no way he could have seen one lying around. Even if he had found my Arthur Weeman stationery collection—scenes from Venice, Charlie Chaplin, old Hollywood stars, old New York, rainbows, American Girl, Hello Kitty, New Yorker car-toons, Degas ballerinas from the Metropolitan Museum gift shop—he wouldn't have any reason to think anything of it.

So how did this rumor start? I wondered. What hands had my letters fallen into? Maybe he'd thrown them all in the garbage and some deranged fan had gotten them, or maybe some angry, frustrated Bukowski-type mailman had intercepted some of them. I certainly would have if I was a mailman. Or maybe he'd talked about them to someone.

And then the terrible thought occurred to me that maybe I had gotten Arthur Weeman into some kind of trouble.

Then Y.G. appeared. She went to the window and opened it up again and stuck her head and shoulders all the way into the rain. Her hair got wet and she was laughing. Arthur Weeman came up behind her and put his hands tentatively on her shoulders. I could tell he was trying to get her to come back in.

"This must be him now," Isaac said. "There's a limo coming around the corner. I have to get off the phone so I can hold my camera under an umbrella."

"Okay," I said.

"Shit, it wasn't him," Isaac said.

"It was probably him, and he didn't get out when he saw us," I heard someone say.

"That definitely wasn't his limo," Isaac told the guy.

"Arthur Weeman doesn't travel by limo," I said. "He uses a town car."

"He uses a limo too," Isaac said.

"No, he uses a town car. That guy was probably right. You should go."

"I'm not leaving," Isaac said. "This is going to be a great shot. Don't you want me to be successful, Rebekah? I happen to love what I do, not a lot of people can say that. And it's how I make a *living*, Rebekah. It's how I'm going to pay for your ring, for instance."

I didn't want the ring if it was at Arthur Weeman's expense.

"I just think it's a little ridiculous to stand around stalking Arthur Weeman," I said.

"A shot like this could get me a hundred thousand dollars. An exclusive of him in a compromising position could get me a million."

I felt so incredibly guilty with my picture-perfect view of what Isaac so desperately needed.

Through the slats of Mrs. Williams' vertical blinds, Isaac could make a million dollars.

"I don't see what's so ridiculous about it. I'm actually surprised you're not here stalking him with me."

"How do you know Arthur Weeman is with a thirteen-year-old girl named Thalia?" I said. I pronounced Thalia his way.

"Ivy Vohl told me."

"And how does she know?" I asked, trying not to let my voice quaver.

"They go to the same shrink."

My heart started to really pound. "The shrink told her?"

"No—and this is between you and me—she spied on him. She waited outside the shrink's office at all hours until she discovered when his appointment was. Then she managed to be there in the waiting room during his session and she pressed her ear against the door. Apparently there's a white-noise machine in the waiting area and she simply turns it off and then she can hear everything. She has a gift for gossip." He said this with a voice filled with respect.

"That's horrible! Who would spy on a person like that?"

"The public has a right to know if Arthur Weeman is fucking a thirteen-year-old girl."

"That's disgusting," I said. "Just because he's visiting with a thirteen-year-old doesn't mean he's fucking her. Maybe she's an actress. Maybe he's getting material. Maybe he's helping her, tutoring her or something."

"Yeah right," Isaac said. "I'm sure he's in the fucking Big Brother volunteer program and he's just helping her with her algebra. The man's a pervert. He's probably got his hands up her skirt right now. Anyway, where are you?"

"I'm at Mrs. Williams'," I said. I couldn't stand talking about this anymore.

"So we're a block away from each other. When I'm done here I can come over and pick you up and take you to dinner."

I didn't know what to say. Maybe I should just let him come up and get his stupid sleazy picture, I thought. Someone would get the shot sooner or later, why shouldn't it be Isaac? Arthur Weeman was asking for it, letting a little girl take off her clothes in the playground for him. That was the amazing thing about Arthur Weeman, he simply didn't care what anyone thought enough to hide anything for long.

"Okay?" Isaac said.

Arthur Weeman was patting Y.G.'s hair dry with a white towel. She wrapped her hair in the towel like a turban and I was suddenly reminded that there is nothing more glamorous than being thirteen and wrapping your hair in a towel.

I was as torn as when I hadn't wanted to tell Ivy Vohl that Sascha was my sister. Isaac was my future but I had to protect Arthur Weeman, and even more than Arthur, I had to protect Thalia. I had created her, and I couldn't let her end up with Ivy's filthy black inky fingerprints all over her.

"Maybe I'll come meet you," I said, gently.

"Okay. I love you," he said.

"I love you too," I said, and hung up.

Mrs. Williams came into the kitchen and asked me if I would help her take a shower and get ready for bed.

"It's only four o'clock," I said.

"I'm tired," she said.

She sat on the edge of her bed, her feet dangling several inches off the floor. I squatted down and untied her pointy white sneakers and slipped them off her feet. I wondered why she bothered to struggle into them in the first place. I helped her stand and tugged her striped shirt up above her breasts, which were bare and the shape of dill pickles, and slowly eased her wings out of the armholes and over her head. She worked on the elastic waistband of her pants until she had gotten them down to her thighs. I squatted again and pulled her pants down, backed her onto the bed again, and slid them off, and then her white stocking socks. I got a towel from the closet and draped it over her before we headed into the bathroom.

Arthur Weeman was drying the hair of a thirteen-year-old girl and I was going to be drying off Mrs. Williams. But I didn't mind. I had gotten used to her body the way I had gotten used to the hanging skeleton my father had in our living room when I was growing up. There was something about her curved Styrofoam back that gave me comfort, like a favorite Royal Crown Derby teacup. You had to be so delicate with it, it became the most valuable thing in the world to you. Her decaying body was more alive, not less. She was hyper-alive, every breath could be her last, I could break her spine with two fingers. Like a cut flower, her days were numbered.

"Do you want a massage?" I asked.

"No, your father said it makes it worse."

I ran the shower on a low drizzle and helped her in.

When I had dried her and put her in her cotton nightshirt I tucked her into bed. I put a cup of peppermint tea and a plate of Lorna Doones on her bedside table and made sure she hadn't knocked the phone off the hook the way she usually did.

"I'm so excited about tomorrow," she said.

"What's tomorrow?"

"The camping trip!" she said, as if I was completely crazy for forgetting. "It's the spring trip. We made maps and sewed our own sleep sacks. Oh no!" She sat straight up.

"What's wrong?" I asked.

"Mother, the marshmallows. Did you remember to get them?"

I nodded as reassuringly as possible under the circumstances and she settled back down. "Oh, thank goodness!" she said.

She closed her eyes and said, "Goodnight, Mama."

"Goodnight," I said. I paused and then kissed her on the forehead, and left.

I found Isaac and his cohorts still standing in the rain in front of Arthur Weeman's building, and like a doting wife-to-be, I stood under Isaac's umbrella with him staring at Arthur Weeman's door for the next four hours.

One by one, the other paparazzi left and Isaac and I were left alone at Arthur Weeman's mahogany door.

"Well, this seems like a good place to do this," he said, smiling.

He reached deep into his PROTOPIC (TACROLIMUS) OINT-MENT tote bag that I had given him from my father's office and handed me a black film canister.

"What's this?" I asked, thinking maybe it was some shots of Arthur Weeman.

"Open it."

I flipped the lid and poured its contents into my hand. It was my engagement ring.

"Look," Isaac said, pointing to a town house across the street. An old gnarled wisteria vine climbed up it in full bloom, bright purple flowers, like wild grapes, peaking into every window. "Is that it?"

I had almost forgotten it was spring, and as if on cue, I felt the yellow silk lining of my Paul Revere coat start to tear.

We kissed and then hugged, and over Isaac's shoulder I saw the door open and Y.G. slip out and walk quickly down the street, stopping only once to pull up one navy blue kneesock that had slipped down to her calf.

22

At 34, like a plant regenerating its stem cells,
she heals an old wound

Finally I agreed to start seriously planning our wedding. I had never dreamed of my wedding growing up. I had always been more interested in the honeymoon. Eventually my fantasy wedding, the plan that seemed the most romantic to me, was a City Hall affair with just me and my betrothed and our respective shrinks. We'd say our vows, sign the papers, and have separate private therapy sessions before heading off to Italy. Maybe since Isaac didn't have a shrink (yet) we could invite Arthur Weeman's shrink, Dr. Schneider, instead.

My parents hadn't been in the same room together since I was thirteen. It just didn't seem like a wedding at the Pierre with ballroom dancing lessons and flowers and calligraphy seemed like a good idea. My mother wanted us to do it at her inn, but I wanted to smell like jasmine perfume on my wedding day, not Deep Woods OFF!

Isaac said no to the Laura Ingalls Wilder Museum in Walnut Grove, Minnesota, and he said City Hall seemed too cold. For me, Vegas was out of the question. I hated Las Vegas, it was like land of the living dead. I'd rather get married in a cemetery, standing on the site of my own grave.

At Irmabelle's desk, I worked on my novel and made my wedding preparations for a ceremony and reception at a beautiful restaurant in an eighteenth-century carriage house on Barrow Street called One If By Land, Two If By Sea. On June second, my thirty-fourth birthday, Isaac had taken me there, and as soon as we saw it, we put a deposit down.

I sat bent over Irmabelle's desk, looking at the small guest list Isaac and I had come up with. His people consisted of his mother and several unsavory photographer friends. Ivy Vohl was right up at the top. Isaac was also insisting we go to her thirtieth-birthday party the following week. "It's a very big deal. I don't want an argument. We have to go," he had said.

I looked out at the empty waiting room. The modern sleeper sofa and the two antique chairs. The industrial carpeting with the fringed Persian carpet over it. The large square coffee table with the two tiny tot chairs that I had once sat in and that probably hadn't been sat in since. The nonworking fireplace with the seven Christmas cards still taped to it, mostly written to Irmabelle, even though it was the middle of July. My father's three VIP's— very important plants—watered weekly, propped up with bamboo, carefully prodded and poked and cared for, even more than his patients.

I had spent so much time staring at the beige-walled waiting room with the tacky Matisse print, purchased on my parents' honeymoon. The white teddy bear hanging from the ceiling in the corner. It was strange enough that Irmabelle had brought teddy bears into the office of an internist with absolutely no child patients, but the practice of suspending them from the ceiling I found disturbing.

For almost a year I had sat on the outskirts of the waiting room watching people wait, but really I had been the one waiting. I was the one who had been waiting to see my father the whole time.

Then I realized that if I wanted to see the doctor I would have to make an appointment.

I squeezed Kettle, R in the appointment book just above my father's four o'clock and pulled my own chart. The doorbell rang and I explained to the patient, an old woman dressed in sporty white pants and a sleeveless floral sweater like she had just gotten off the bus from Florida, that the doctor was a little backed-up and she would have to wait. Then, when my father's 3:15 left, I buzzed him through the intercom and told him his four o'clock had arrived, and walked into his office. I put my own chart on the center of his desk.

"Where's the patient?" my father asked.

"Right here," I said, sitting in the patient chair. "I'm willing to have a checkup. You said we have to monitor everything."

"I also said you should go to Brown instead of Bennington and major in history," he said, smiling. He picked up my chart. "No one in this country knows anything about history or politics," he muttered comically to himself, perusing my last blood-work lab results.

"I know a little history," I said. I knew about the pioneer days on the prairie. I knew about the Korean War from *M*A*S*H**. I knew about Paul Revere. I knew a little more family history than he thought I knew. "Anyway, I'm ready to have my bloodwork done and take the peripheral vision test or whatever you want to give me." I held my finger in front of my nose and moved it from side to side to remind him.

Suddenly he laughed. "Is this an attempt to extort more money for the wedding?"

I followed him into the examination room and after I refused to get on the scale, he wrapped a tourniquet tightly around my arm.

"Wait a minute, I thought I had Frances Siegal at four," he said.

"She's in the waiting room."

"What! I don't want her in my waiting room unattended."

"Why not?" I asked.

"She's a kleptomaniac and a sociopath."

I couldn't imagine anything in the waiting room that a little old lady would want to steal. "I'm sure she'll be fine," I said.

"There was a prior incident," my father said. "Unfortunately my accusations are well-founded."

I didn't want to spend my appointment talking about Mrs. Siegal.

"Dad, there's something I have to talk to you about. I can't work here anymore," I said. My arm was starting to throb from the tourniquet.

"Oh? I was afraid that was coming," he said.

"I've been writing," I said. "I have to work on the book full-time. I've almost finished a draft, and my editor says if I hand it in now it might be able to be published this fall." I was so used to lying about this, it was hard to believe it was true.

"Okay," my father said. "Well, that's great news. I've liked having you here, Toots. I know I haven't always been such a good Dad . . ." His voice trailed off and I wondered if I was supposed to interrupt him. I wondered if he was going to tell me about Sascha. "I appreciate your helping me out."

"Dad, there's something else I have to tell you. I sort of did something." I wanted to tell him I was sorry for getting pregnant and keeping it from him and making such a mess out of things. "I used one of your checks to buy twenty-two thousand dollars' worth of props from the Arthur Weeman warehouse sale."

"You mean this?" he said, pulling his wallet out of his back pocket and handing me the canceled check. It was like one of his magic card tricks.

"I understand if you don't want to help out with the wedding, and I can pay you back as soon as I get the check from my publisher."

He put up his hand to stop me. "I haven't even been to your apartment yet. It sounds like an interesting place. When I had the check investigated they said something about a gondola. I should stop by."

"I'd like that," I said.

He smiled. "Consider it a bonus for a job well done." He unwrapped a needle and I looked away. "You shouldn't tell a man holding a needle that you stole twenty-two thousand dollars from him." He stuck the needle into me and I grimaced. "See that wasn't so bad."

He was right. I had expected him to blow his lid, demand I keep working to pay him back. Then I was going to tell him I knew about Sascha and suggest we call it even. I was surprised he was just going to let me go.

"Dad," I said. "Twenty-two thousand. It's too much."

"It's okay," he said.

"Thank you," I said, but I was still looking away from the needle so I wasn't sure what his reaction was. "The wedding plans are coming along," I said, stiffly. "Besides Uncle Russell, Aunt Jackie, and Chelsea, was there anybody else you wanted to invite? Mandlebaum or anyone from the hospital?"

"Well, let me think." He mentioned a couple of his doctor friends and an old patient of his who took him to Peter Luger's once a year. "I'm going to wear my tuxedo," he said.

The proud way he said it made me laugh out loud. "It's not that kind of wedding, Dad. It's in a restaurant."

"I don't care if it's in the monkey house at the zoo, I'm the father of the bride and I'm going to wear my tuxedo. Ha." He made a fist and knocked on my head with his knuckles. "Numbskull."

I thought that was a strange thing to say to a bride-to-be with a brain tumor. "Okay, all done," he said, pulling the needle out of my arm, and removing the tourniquet. He put a cotton ball over the healthy droplet of blood that had formed where the needle had been. "Apply good pressure, please."

I handed him an invitation.

He opened it and studied the card. "Wait, it's on a Friday night?" he asked, sounding upset. "Jews can't get married on a Friday night."

I looked at him in disbelief. He hadn't acted Jewish one day in his life.

"Well, the restaurant wanted twice as much for a Saturday night and I just thought any true Jewish God would want us to save money."

I couldn't believe his nerve. If he was such a good Jew then why did he have a mistress and an illegitimate daughter? "I'd like to invite Irmabelle," I said, Ivy Vohling him with my eyes.

"Why not get married on a Tuesday for Christ's sake?"

"So, if it's okay with you, I'm going to invite her."

He turned his back to me and pretended to be busy writing my name on the labels that went on my six vials of blood. "I don't think that's such a good idea," he said.

"Why not?"

"I don't think she'd come." He turned around and pulled a deck of cards from a drawer in the metal cabinet. "Pick a card, any card," he said, fanning them out in front of me.

"Irmabelle should have the option." My throat tightened with frustration like it did when I was little girl and he forced me to play chess in Washington Square Park.

"Rebekah," my father said, putting the cards back in his pocket. "There's something you don't know about Irmabelle. She and I actually . . ."

I sat on the examining table looking up at him, my legs dangling off the edge. I was the patient but he was the one in pain. He rolled his little round stool over to me and sat on it. Then he took my hand in his.

"Irmabelle was more than my employee," he said. "She was . . ." His whole face tightened with pain. "Like my wife."

"I know," I said, and burst into tears. I pressed the cotton ball into the crook of my arm with all my might.

"I'm sorry, honey."

It was like when he took me to Chinatown for dim sum to tell me he wasn't going to be living with us anymore, knowing the news beforehand hadn't helped at all. Every kid I knew was divorced, I was completely prepared, unfazed, relieved even, but somehow I hadn't thought about him actually moving out. He hadn't seemed until that moment to be an integral part of my life, but suddenly it was as if my right arm had announced it was going to another body, or my brain stood at the door with a packed suitcase and said it was leaving but would call me every single night and see me on the weekends. When you are twelve, a goodnight call is nothing like a kiss goodnight.

He stopped squeezing my hand, got up, and tore the wrapper off a Band-Aid, securing my cotton ball in place.

"And there's someone else I want at my wedding, Dad. I want Sascha to be there," I gasped.

I used the folded paper hospital gown to wipe the tears that were pouring out of me.

"I know about her," I said.

"Oh my," he said. He had a wild, trapped look in his eyes that I had seen someplace before, but I couldn't think where. Then I remembered. The wolf alone in the tundra.

He doubled over on his stool and shook with terrible silent sobs. Then he got a hold of himself. That was the difference between the way men and women cried. Men always cried very quickly.

"I want her address."

"She lives on St. Mark's Place over the Porto Rico coffee shop, apartment number two, on the third floor," he said.

So that's what my father had been doing the day he'd lied to me, standing on St. Mark's Place when he was supposed to be on Eighty-sixth Street. He hadn't been buying African elephant pants, he'd been visiting my sister. I had spent so much time wondering where in this big wide city she lived, what borough, what neighborhood, what street, and all along she lived less than five blocks away from me.

"She has to come to the wedding, Dad," I said.

He smiled. "I don't think your mother would like that too much."

I smiled back at him. Then we both just sat there feeling exhausted and exposed, without our secrets to cover us.

"Well, I'll put these in the refrigerator," my father finally said, standing up and leaving the room with my blood.

I sat there for a few minutes too stunned to move and was startled to hear yelling coming from the waiting room.

"How dare you accuse me of stealing," Mrs. Siegal screamed.

"Get out of my office," my father yelled.

I jumped off the table and went to see what was going on.

"She dismembered my nightblooming cereus," my father said. "And you've done it before, you lying, crazy, c—" He stopped himself for a moment. "Oot. That's it, you are no longer a patient here. I'll be happy to refer you to another physician, but I will not examine you again. Good day, Madam."

"I didn't go near your plant," Mrs. Siegal said.

"Oh no?" He grabbed her pocketbook from her shoulder and opened it. The woman screamed. My father pulled out a slender green tentacled stalk in a plastic ShopRite bag. "What do you call this?"

"That is a cutting from my friend's plant."

I noticed a wet patch form at the crotch of her white pants and start to spread down her thighs. She had wet herself, but my father didn't seem to notice.

"I know my nightblooming cereus inside and out. I've raised this plant for twenty-one years," my father said. "This plant is like a child to me."

Suddenly my father had turned into King Lear with three daughters instead of two. One lived in a one-bedroom apartment with furniture bought with money stolen from him; one lived on St. Mark's Place over the Porto Rico coffee shop; and one lived in an Italian ceramica planter in his waiting room. Although she was the least doting, she was also the least competitive, and the least demanding, and so she was his favorite of the three. If Sascha was at my wedding, this plant should really be there too. I suddenly boiled with loyalty for my father.

"Taking a small cutting doesn't hurt the plant," Mrs. Siegal said, calmly. "You obviously don't know anything about it."

Then my father got more upset than I'd ever seen him in my entire life. "I don't know anything about nightblooming cereus, selenicereus grandiflorus, epiphyllum oxypetalum? You, Madam, don't know a thing about horticulture. You are a sociopath and a liar." He was waving my blood at her and his face was red with rage. His whole body was shaking.

"I'm going to report you to the American Medical Association."

"Very well, Madam, you do that. Get out before I wring your neck. Crazy old bitch." He grabbed her coat off the coatrack, opened the front door, and threw the coat and her purse into the lobby. He took her by the top of her arm and pushed her out after them and slammed the door as hard as he could.

I remembered after dim sum, he had dragged me with him to the courthouse so he could get out of jury duty, and when his request was denied, he had screamed and yelled at the stubborn black woman behind the desk until we were thrown out by some kind of bailiff. He had called that woman "Madam" a lot too.

"I'm closing the office for the rest of the day. Call my last three patients and tell them," my father said. "Carlos should be here for the bloods soon, then you can leave."

I pointed to the small pool of urine Mrs. Siegal had left on the Persian carpet. I shrugged. "It's not really my job anymore," I said. "I'm no longer a medical office assistant. I'm a writer." I felt the sad, enormous relief of that.

"Fair enough," my father said. He got a roll of Bounty and a bucket of soapy water from the kitchen, kneeled on the carpet, and started sopping up the piss. I kneeled down too and we worked next to each other, kneading the paper towels into the rich, wet wool.

.   .   .

When I got to the Porto Rico coffee store on St. Mark's Place, I looked up at the third-floor apartment above it. It had a run-down terrace covered in potted plants. I could see where my father would be more at home here with Nightblooming Cereus Jr. than at my place. I couldn't take my eyes off that terrace and I stood Romeoing up at it for so long, I started to get self-conscious. People in Myoptics were staring at me. Finally I decided to see if she was home. The label on the buzzer read KETTLE #2.

Kettle #1 rang Kettle #2 but there was no answer.

I dropped her invitation in the mailbox on her corner, never so excited to mail anything in my whole life.

23.

At 34, in a gruesome Orwellian spectacle,
she is witness to the murder of one of
God's creatures

On the morning of Ivy Vohl's stupid thirtieth-birthday party at the Boathouse in Central Park, Isaac announced that I had to buy her a present. The invitation sat on top of the television facing us.

"Pick out a nice blouse or something," Isaac said.

Sometimes Isaac sounded like an eighty-year-old woman when he said things like "blouse" and "bonnet."

On *Little House,* a newspaper was started in Walnut Grove and Mrs. Oleson volunteered to write a column called "Harriet's Happenings." It turned out to be a nasty hurtful gossip column about her neighbors. Just in case Isaac didn't make the obvious connection, I said, "Harriet Oleson is exactly like Ivy Vohl."

I went to Arthur Weeman's desk from *Literary Suicide,* that I had moved into the kitchen, turned on my computer and got to work.

I noticed I was scratching my hands and looked down to see eczema sprouting up on my fingers. I'd had terrible eczema on my hands when I'd written my first book. I got up from Arthur

Weeman's desk and walked around the apartment for a few minutes, scratching my hands and thinking about my old book. I thought about it sitting by itself on the book bum's table while all the other books were snatched up one by one like children being chosen for a team.

I grabbed my bag and ran downstairs to the street.

I rushed up to his table and noticed my book wasn't shackled in its usual stockade in the center of town. A growing panic overcame me, but I didn't ask the book bum what had happened to it, I just walked slowly back and forth along the table, eyeing each and every book. Its constant companion of the last six months, *Little Dorrit* by Charles Dickens, was still there.

"Are you looking for your book?" the book bum asked, smugly.

"No," I said, picking up *Little Dorrit,* which seemed to flinch at the human touch.

"Don't you wanna know where it is?"

I smiled at him as if I didn't speak the English, and continued to consider *Little Dorrit.*

"Someone finally bought it."

"Well," I said, "congratulations."

"No, I mean this man just walked right up and said he wanted it. Although he tried like hell to Jew me down. I told him I'm not taking less than three dollars for that thing."

My eye fell on a copy of *Memoirs of a Geisha,* and I remembered a line from it that some women sold their virginity for thousands and thousands of yen, and I felt like I had sold mine for three. Still I felt some relief that it had been sold and not sent to whatever the next circle of hell was for books like mine. If it didn't make a book table like this one, it could end up in a cardboard box on the street or worse. Once I had found a copy of my book in a bar with unbelievably filthy pornographic cartoons drawn in the margins of every page.

"I've seen you with him," the book bum said.

"Who?" I asked, feeling almost frightened that I would have been seen by this man with anyone.

"The man who bought your book."

I put *Little Dorrit* back in her cell, leaving her to rot.

"Short guy with wavy hair, glasses. You know who he looked like? A younger Arthur Weeman."

I smiled thinking of Isaac coming along to save me. Slipping me into his raincoat pocket and walking away with me.

"He's my fiancé," I said, proudly.

"You've got to be kidding me! That guy? You could do a hellofa lot better than that jack-me-off. If I'da known you was interested in going out with the scum of the earth I'da asked you myself."

But I wasn't standing there at the book table anymore. And I wasn't me. I was my character writing a letter to the movie director she adored.

When we got to Ivy's party, I had to admit the place was beautiful. There may have been joggers lying in bloody murdered heaps all around us, but here, at the Boathouse, you would think Central Park was the enchanted forest. A buffet was set with lobsters and every kind of shellfish—an odd choice for Ivy, who seemed to practically consider herself a rabbi and was always grilling everyone on how Jewish they were—and enormous trays of some kind of impressive-looking meat. A band was playing "I Could Write a Book," and even though it was so early in the party, people were already dancing and having a good time. Ivy was in the middle of everything in a green satin dress, pointing for people to put their presents on a big table near the bar.

When she saw Isaac, she ran over to us like a fawn in her Marni high heels and gave him a big hug.

"Happy birthday," I managed.

"Thanks!" Ivy said, eyeing the little La Petite Lolita shopping bag I was holding that contained the matching thong to the bra I had gotten her. "Bret Easton Ellis is here! And I really want you to meet my shrink."

"Your shrink is here?" I asked. "My shrink would never come to my birthday party."

"Yup, he goes to all Arthur Weeman's premieres and he's at my party. Speaking of premieres, I thought I'd see you at Hugh's New York premiere."

"Hugh who?" I asked.

"Hugh who? Hugh Nickelby!" Ivy said.

"What premiere?" I asked. I hadn't mentioned to Isaac that I had gone.

"See, Rebekah," Isaac said. "I always tell you, you have to get out more and go to parties."

I bristled, remembering how my mother always called my father a hermit.

"I go to parties. If I don't go to parties then how am I here? And I go to Bret Easton Ellis' Christmas party every year, don't I?"

"I didn't see you there at the last one," Ivy said. The reason she didn't see me there was because Bret's loft was packed with so many supermodels who were all a foot and a half taller than me, so I was forced to move through the crowd like a submarine. People talked over me, and ate over my head, dripping pumpkin soup he'd served in tiny cups on top of my hair, which I didn't notice until I got home. The only person I managed to talk to was

Monica Lewinsky because she was around my height. "So you guys are really engaged?" Ivy said, looking at my ring.

"That's right," I said, matching her dry tone.

"Are you going to move to another apartment or squeeze into your one bedroom?" she asked.

"We're going to squeeze," I said.

"Rebekah has a really big apartment," Isaac said, trying to defend my honor as a woman and a New Yorker.

"Yeah, but it's just a one bedroom, isn't it?" she said.

"One bedroom plus an office," Isaac said, referring, I guessed, to the desk in the kitchen.

"Well, I'm going to be making a little announcement of my own. Oh, I have to say hello to some people, I'll be *right* back." She fawned greedily over to the dance floor.

"Please don't criticize me in front of Ivy, Isaac," I said. I was so annoyed that I was considering braving the muggers and finding my way out of there.

"I didn't criticize you."

"You said I don't go to parties, implying that I'm some kind of hermit or something."

"That's not a bad thing. You're a real writer and real writers are hermits. Come on, let's get in line for a gondola ride."

He took my hand and we made our way through the crowd, out the glass doors to the small dock on the lake. A few people stood before us waiting for one of the two gondolas to return. I leaned over the wooden rail and looked into the soot green water at a giant turtle swimming with its shell just above the surface. It wasn't every day you saw a giant turtle in New York, and I started to feel a little better about being there.

Finally it was our turn and the gondolier, wearing a black-and-white striped costume, held out his hand to help me into the boat. I sat on the frayed velvet bench and the gondolier tried to help Isaac. "That's okay, I think I know my way around one of these things," Isaac said. "We do this all the time at home." He wobbled over and sat next to me with his arm around me.

We crawled along the bank toward the center of the lake, the second gondola passing us, heading back. Of course we had to awkwardly wave at the guests on the other gondola. But then something very strange caught our attention. A sound rang out, a long chilling cry.

And then we saw it: an elephant wading into the middle of the lake, spouting water over its back with its trunk. It was terrifying, and we all froze and watched it. People screamed. It was so huge that the water barely came up to its ankles. It swooshed its trunk violently from side to side.

It was so out of place but, at the same time, it wasn't that surprising. I thought of Sascha suddenly showing up in my father's office, coming out of nowhere. Having every right to be there and yet somehow trespassing. I shrugged off the feeling about Sascha and tried to focus only on this spectacle. I was seeing an elephant on the loose with my fiancé. Nothing better, not even seeing Arthur Weeman, had ever happened to me. For a second, I wondered if Arthur Weeman was part of this. I looked quickly around me but no one seemed to be shooting a movie, it was just there of its own free will. There were no lights, in fact the sun was quickly setting. What was stranger, I wondered, an elephant in the lake in Central Park or a gondola? An elephant flailing his trunk or Isaac gripping me to him, loving me enough to want to marry me?

Everything was silent except the sounds of splashing. It turned its head and looked at me with one eye. It took a step toward us and then spouted water at us. It seemed angry and not at all playful, but I didn't flinch. I just sat there sort of thanking God for everything that had led me to this moment so I could be here to see the elephant.

This elephant was like Arthur Weeman, I thought. Looming large before me with his huge trunk set so high up between his silver-rimmed eyes like a giant Jewish nose. It gave him a funny pinched, nasal look, like Arthur Weeman playing a saxophone in *Adopting Alice.*

Then a terrible thing happened. His knees buckled under him and he crashed in slow motion down into the water. Our gondola rocked and almost capsized. A round of applause broke out on the bank. I thought he was doing some sort of a trick. I turned to see men on the bank, police and others in ranger outfits or something. Then I saw the blood pouring out of a hole in its neck and I realized they had shot him.

My whole life I had been on the lookout for something bad to happen. I always thought it just went along with growing up in New York, you look up and you wait for a body to fall or a plane to crash or two 110-story buildings to collapse. You know something will happen—a bullet or a dirty bomb or just an old-fashioned rape or mugging. But this was not something I had been prepared for.

Isaac on the other hand seemed as prepared as a hunter in the bush. He pulled a camera out of his suit jacket that I didn't even know he had with him and started taking its picture.

"Stop it," I said. It suddenly occurred to me that Ivy had staged this whole thing to get publicity for her birthday party. Or maybe she just wanted the tusks for ivory. "Leave him alone!" I yelled. It seemed the elephant had been shot twice, first by the terrible men and now by Isaac.

The gondolier steered over to the men and asked what was going on.

"He escaped from the children's zoo," a cop said. "He's vicious. He almost trampled a child. You'll read about it in the paper tomorrow."

"We certainly will," Isaac said. "Can you row us back to him, right up to his eye?" He put another roll of film in his camera. "I'd love to get a close-up of that."

"No," I said.

"Yeah, I'm not sure that's a good idea," the gondolier said. "We don't know if it's dead or just stunned or something."

"I'm surprised you don't have a telephoto lens on you, shoved down your pants or something," I said, bitterly.

"I do, but I left it inside," Isaac said. He brought the camera back up to his eye, and I blocked the lens with my hand, a surprisingly violent gesture.

"Rebekah, cut it out." I grabbed for the camera, desperate to get it away from him. "Whoa, Rebekah, sit down. You're gonna tip us over." He tried to restrain me with one hand while still pointing his camera at the elephant in the bloody water.

"If you take one more picture, I'll jump out of this boat right now." I started to sob. Isaac stopped taking pictures and held me, but I couldn't stop crying.

"Rebekah, you're overreacting. She gets like this with animals," he told the gondolier.

"No, I don't. This has nothing to do with animals." He made me sound like some kind of PETA freak. "How could you take pictures of him?" I cried. "How can you sit there, like an innocent bystander, and take those cold-blooded pictures?"

"Because I *am* an innocent bystander. It's just news. I'm serving the public. Raising awareness." He was being condescending. "This is a *camera*. It just takes *pictures*. It's not an evil soul-stealing device. You act like an Aborigine who's never seen one of these newfangled inventions before. Stop judging everybody, Rebekah. Your eyes are more lethal than my camera because I'm just taking pictures, but you sit there judging everything so harshly and permanently recording it in that bear-trap brain of yours. If you'll notice, I'm the only photojournalist here. I have to document this. Please, Rebekah, you have to calm down. I'm sorry. I didn't mean to upset you. Just let me take a few more shots."

His speech shocked me into silence and I stopped crying. I had never thought of my brain as a sleazy paparazzo before. His camera went off like wildfire, the flash turning the lake into Times Square. He shot the elephant with passion, as if it were a beautiful thing, like Richard Avedon shooting a Dior model. Within minutes it was over, and the gondolier turned the boat around and ushered us up onto the dock, where Ivy's guests were gathered along the glass doors, watching.

To my amazement, the band played that awful "In the Jungle Wimoweh" song and the party slowly got back to normal. Isaac had a point about the camera, and I tried very hard to relax but something was really bothering me. I felt so terrible for the elephant, but I also felt terrible for myself. And for Arthur Weeman. And even for Isaac. We were all dancing a sort of cannibalistic dance to the Wimoweh jungle song.

People went on eating shrimp and drinking a terrible green drink the bartender had named "The Ivy," and giving toasts. Then Ivy took the microphone.

"Everyone, I have an announcement to make. Thank you all for coming to my birthday party. I feel like I'm at my bat mitzvah, although that took place at the B'nai Israel Temple on the Upper West Side and no animals were killed." Uproarious laughter poured from the moronic crowd. "I love every single person in this room."

I felt about as loved as the poor waiters stationed behind the buffet. She stood with her back to the glass doors, and behind her an elaborate system of ropes and pulleys was being used to haul the trussed-up elephant out of the water. He was being dragged in slow lurching motions toward the shore. I looked away. I couldn't watch.

"So, I wanted you to be the first to hear the news that someone in this room is engaged."

Isaac and I looked at each other. I had to admit it was nice of Ivy to announce our engagement at her party like that. I tried to smile.

"Mom, Daddy, Dr. Schneider . . ." She turned to an old olive-skinned man sitting in a chair watching the elephant. He was crying. At the sound of his name, he looked up and wiped away his tears with a handkerchief, put his glasses back on, and stuffed the handkerchief in his pocket. Seeing him crying for the elephant made my eyes fill with tears again. "I'm engaged!" Ivy said. "Someone finally roped me in."

I wished it were Ivy roped up in the water like Houdini and the elephant holding the microphone in his trunk.

"I'm sorry my fiancé couldn't be here tonight. He just called and said he couldn't get away from work. Mom, Daddy, I know you're upset that Derek's not Jewish, but I know you're going to get to love him. He's a real Southern gentleman, and I can honestly say that I've finally met a man who treats me the way I deserve to be treated. Everyone, his name is Derek Hassler and he's an *editor* at *Maxim*."

My mouth fell open. It was the most hilarious thing I had ever heard. I remembered that on our second date Derek had stopped me in front of a store window to point out a pair of clear plastic stripper shoes with at least a ten-inch Lucite heel, not exactly the type of glass slipper every young girl dreams of. "I want you to buy those and wear them for me," Derek had said. I couldn't believe that not only did he expect me to wear them, he expected me to buy them too.

"Stop laughing," Isaac said. I hadn't even realized I was.

I took a glass of champagne from a passing tray and drank it down. Ivy's parents were hugging her, and her father said something to the band that immediately started up a moving rendition of "I'll be seeing you in all the old familiar places," and everyone cleared the dance floor so Ivy could dance with her father.

When the song was over, the elephant was gone.

Then Ivy walked over to us. "Isaac, what are you still doing here? If you get that film to the lab by nine we can run it in tomorrow's paper. You've got to get going. You can take the limo out front."

"I'm sorry, Rebekah, Ivy's right. We should really go."

"What a shame," I said.

"You don't feel weird about me and Derek, do you? I know you and Derek used to date," she said.

"I think it's great," I said. "I really think you're perfect for each other."

"I guess you'll have to tell your father I'm no longer single." She winked at Isaac.

"I'll tell him," I said.

We got into the back of the car, and I listened numbly as Isaac made a series of phone calls to every newspaper and TV news station, offering to sell the film. I was shocked.

"I thought this was going to be a *Quille* exclusive," I said.

"I'm loyal to Ivy, but not that loyal," he said. "I'm going to have a wife to support now. I have a honeymoon in Venice to pay for. This will get us enough money for two weeks at the Gritti Palace."

"I can't believe you're going to betray Ivy like that."

I thought about the eye of the elephant, open wide and staring, as beautiful as a peacock feather, as terrifying as an open wound. I just felt that at all costs, I had to protect it.

Isaac was right about celebrities. He wasn't doing anything wrong to photograph them. But exploiting an innocent elephant was different. Arthur Weeman was responsible for his own actions, and he knew what he was doing. He could hide or dart out from between the rocks and rattle the bars of his cage whenever he wanted attention. But this elephant had left the zoo. This elephant had marched past the llamas and the brass rabbit hole and Jonah's whale and took a right at the Delacorte clock. In a way, Arthur Weeman was like the elephant, shot by the very public who had once loved him. I had been protecting and defending him as best I could since I saw *Adopting Alice* so many years ago. But Arthur Weeman could take care of himself. He didn't need my help the way this elephant did.

I thought of Y.G. dropping to her knees on the cement ground of the schoolyard. I thought of Arthur Weeman looming above her, big and mighty.

Why was I protecting *him,* I wondered bitterly, outraged at myself. An elephant was dead, while Arthur Weeman sat up in his town house laughing at having gotten off scot-free.

"Isaac," I said. "What if you didn't give anyone this film? Just pretended you didn't take the photos, or that they got exposed or something."

"Why would I do that? That would be stoo-pid," Isaac said.

"What if I traded you that film for something even better?"

"As much as I love your blow jobs I'm not trading these pictures for one."

"I'm not talking about a blow job. I'm talking about a . . . scoop."

"A *scoop?*" he said, smiling. "Who are you? Nancy Drew, girl detective?"

"Access," I said. "You could call it 'access.' "

"Access? That's probably the sexiest thing anyone's ever said to me. What kind of access. Access to what?"

"Call Ivy and tell her you lost the film," I said.

"Rebekah, please, I don't understand this," Isaac said.

"I don't want those pictures developed. I promise that what I have access to can make you ten times more money. Please tell me you won't publish those pictures."

"Give me the access first," he said.

"How do I know I can trust you not to publish these pictures?" But really I thought, how did I know he would marry me and stay with me and love me?

"Here," he said, handing me the three rolls of film. "I don't want to upset you. You can hold on to these. Rebekah, I love you. If you feel this strongly about it you can have them. Here. Let Babar rest in peace."

"Don't make jokes," I said. And then, even though he had already told me he loved me, and promised to marry me and love me forever, now, with the elephant film in my hands, for the first time I knew unquestioningly that he did. He really, really did. He had given me Arthur Weeman's handkerchief and a ring and this film, and I had been withholding everything. I had poured my heart out to Arthur Weeman, written him love letters, kept his secret, and what had he done for me? He'd never even written me back. Oh what the hell, I thought. I would do this for Isaac. I would do this for us.

I gave the driver Mrs. Williams' address.

"Wait, we're going to Mrs. Williams'? That's your big scoop?" Isaac asked.

"Not exactly," I said.

"Come on, Rebekah. Where are you taking me?"

"Arthur Weeman's kitchen," I said.

His light was on when we approached the window. Isaac stood at it like a temple, as I had done so many times. "How do you know it's his kitchen?" he asked.

I smiled. "You see that coffeemaker?" I asked, pointing to the incredible chrome Taj Mahal–like thing on the counter. "It costs eighteen hundred dollars. It's from Italy. Makes one personalized cup at a time. But Arthur drinks tea."

"That doesn't really prove anything."

"Just watch," I said.

Isaac went into a meditative silence.

Then I saw something on Mrs. Williams' kitchen table and I went to see what it was. It was a large manila envelope. I turned it over and saw that it was addressed to me. Well not to me exactly, it was addressed to Thalia. Quickly I put the envelope back down on the table and looked up to see Isaac staring at me.

"What's that?" he asked.

"Mrs. Williams' mail," I said.

He turned back around to the window.

My heart pounded. Arthur had written Thalia a letter. It was here, right on the table.

I picked it up again and tried to figure out what to do. I couldn't leave it on the table because I couldn't risk Isaac seeing the name Thalia written on the envelope. I thought about bringing it into another room, but Isaac would wonder why I was doing that with Mrs. Williams asleep in her bedroom. There was no way to slip it into my purse because it was too big.

I decided to stand there and open it.

"Oh, my God," Isaac said. Arthur Weeman was in his kitchen. "I have to change lenses." He emptied the contents of his tote bag on the window seat and glanced in my direction. "Why are you opening Mrs. Williams' mail? Isn't reading other people's mail a federal offense?"

"That coming from a man with a long lens pointing into someone's house. She likes me to go through it for her."

I held the contents of the envelope in my hand. It was a large X-ray of some kind.

"What's that?" Isaac asked.

"Some medical records, I guess," I said. The X-ray shook in my hands. "You better hurry if you want to get some photos."

I held the X-ray up to the light and saw that it was of a brain.

Clipped to the X-ray was a hand-written note on an old-fashioned jagged-edged parchment card.

> Dear Thalia,
> This is my brain.
> Your devoted,
> Awful Writer

"Is everything okay?" Isaac asked.

"Yeah," I said. "I guess so. I mean, just because I work in a medical office doesn't make me a doctor."

"I mean, with you. Are you okay? You look . . ."

"I'm fine," I said.

This is my brain. It was like a book I had loved as a child called *This is London.*

I looked at his beautiful brain—his jokes and themes and characters swirling in it. It was like looking into History's brain at

Plato and Aristotle, Shakespeare, Cervantes, Dante, Chekhov. I saw every movie ever made, the first motion picture—*Workers Leaving the Lumière Factory*—and Thomas Edison's *Electrocuting an Elephant.* I saw snow in it, and gondolas, Chaplin and Bergman were there, and center stage in the frontal lobe, was Thalia. I saw her so clearly looking right back at me, brain to brain. The lobes unfurled like film in a projector, and there, in Arthur's magnificent brain, I saw the whole plot of my new book. Beginning to end, it was there like a time line. My book was all right there just waiting for me to finish writing it.

But then, as Isaac started shooting, I held the brain away from me. A feeling of dread shot through me. What had I done? I wondered. Just when he had written to me, said he was devoted, I had ruined everything. Holding his brain, I felt like Queen Margaret in *Henry the Sixth,* holding the Duke of York's head in my hands.

One more letter, I thought. Before it was all over, Thalia could at least thank him.

In Mrs. Williams' kitchen drawer, I'd found an ancient box of yellowing note cards with a drawing of three old people having dinner in their underwear, with the words COME AS YOU ARE printed on the bottom.

I went to the drawer now, slipped a card out of the box, and quietly sat at the table and began to write.

July 23

Dear Awful Writer,

My heart is still pounding from opening your letter. Can someone who is almost thirteen have a heart attack? So you are devoted to me after all. I knew it I knew it I knew it! I will treasure your brain as long as I live. I will kiss it every night before I go to sleep. I'll never let anyone see it. No matter what happens, I promise.

WRITE BACK SOON!

Your very happy,

Thalia

PS something terrible just ocured to me. Why did you get a brain Xray? Was it just a special present for me or is there something wrong with you? Please, Awful, write to me and tell me you're fine.

I went out quietly to the hall to mail the letter, praying silently, my forehead and lips pressed against the brass of the mail chute, that everything would somehow be okay. Dear God, I thought, please let me be forgiven. Please forgive Arthur. And Y.G. And Isaac. I tried to think of the prayer that had to do with forgiving us for trespassing but I couldn't come up with it right then.

Mrs. Williams was very surprised to find us both there in the morning. Isaac had his camera propped up on a stack of cookbooks, aimed at Arthur's window. The Levolor blinds were bent around it. It was sort of cozy, and I was tempted to try to make eggs or something but I didn't want to spoil everybody and have them think it was going to be a regular thing.

Mrs. Williams and I watched *Little House* while Isaac stayed at the window and then, when Mrs. Williams went to take a nap, I set up my laptop on the kitchen table and started to write. And as soon as I started, the same thing that always happens happened: I started to cry, trying to hide my tiny crying sounds.

"What's wrong?" Isaac asked, without turning around. "Did Mary go blind again?"

I stopped crying and smiled. Nothing had happened, I was just writing. "No, Nellie Oleson got engaged to Percival. She fell in love with him, even though he was short and Jewish."

"Mrs. Oleson must not have liked that very much."

"No, she didn't."

"Well, he was the only one who could tame her the same way I tamed you. You ever notice that Michael Landon takes every opportunity to hold other men's hands or hug them or stroke their hair? In every other scene he has his arms around another man."

"Don't say anything bad about Michael Landon. He's the greatest father of all time."

"I'm going to be the greatest father of all time. And I'm not going to have to hug and kiss a lot of men in the process."

While Isaac talked about the two or three little future paparazzi I would bear him, I wrote.

"Holy shit," Isaac said, his camera clicking away. I didn't even look up. Isaac was manning the ship now so I didn't have to. I'd like to think that the first time I saw Arthur Weeman in the window, I had said something more interesting than "Holy shit." Isaac didn't exactly possess the poetry of Ishmael harpooning Moby Dick. "Holy shit, he's touching her."

24.

*In 1826, Joseph Nicéphore Niépce takes the
first recording of a negative image on a light
sensitive material*

Isaac and I rushed his film to a photo lab on Twentieth Street. Usually he dropped off his film at the *Quille* and didn't bother to develop it himself, but for something like this he rented space.

I stood next to him in the tiny darkroom and watched him work with a sort of calm intensity, lovingly handling the paper. My job was to lean against the door, because once he had developed film there and someone had barged in and ruined his pictures. This showed how much Isaac trusted me. I could still go back on our deal. All I had to do was open the darkroom door and Isaac's film would be exposed instead of Arthur Weeman.

"Do you want to see them?" Isaac asked.

"What about the door?"

"We'll switch posts for a minute."

He put his tongs down on a paper towel and we traded places, brushing up against each other in the process. "This is really why I wanted you here," he said. "I love to get a big-titted girl like you into a cramped space."

"I thought you needed me to lean," I said.

"I certainly do. I need you to lean over or bend over or whatever makes you the most uncomfortable," he said, slipping the metal hook into the metal eye on the door to lock it.

I pretended to be annoyed and sidled over to the counter. I peered down into the trays of chemicals and watched in total awe as Arthur Weeman slowly came into view in front of me. It was somehow more real than seeing him in person in his window; it was as if I had invented him myself, starting from the inside out with his brain and now finishing from the outside in with face and body, glasses and rumpled shirt. Watching him emerge atom by atom under the clear glassy liquid made me believe in God, the way a sonogram of a baby, or corny time-lapse photography of a flower blooming, or an Arthur Weeman film did.

I felt like I was hovering overhead, gazing down on Rebekah and Isaac in a strange, tiny temple, Isaac standing behind her with his hands on her breasts, as life was created in the glow of a red lightbulb.

First the outline of his face, long and narrow with its firm jaw, then his slightly egg-shaped glasses, then the deep furrows of his forehead and the creases running down his cheek and jowl. Only one side of his face was visible because he had been shot in profile. He was kissing Y.G. Openmouthed. Passionate. Behind his glasses, his eye was closed tight, swollen and wrinkled, and hers was wide open, alert, aware, and smiling.

"Holy shit," I said.

I wondered if this girl would one day lose her spark. If she would go from that great girl in the picture to some used-up, washed-up, bun-headed wife, never really moving on from the time she was thirteen, experiencing the thrill of womanhood with Arthur Weeman. Would she be as faded as an old Polaroid just ten or fifteen years into her time line?

I had spent my childhood thinking ahead and my adulthood thinking back to my childhood. And it was stupid. There was no reason I would lose my spark if I did fun interesting things, like making love to Isaac in darkrooms.

I turned my back to the photo and kissed Isaac as hard as I could and reached for his belt buckle.

"Better make it quick," Isaac said. "This place is costing me fifteen dollars an hour. I might have a condom in my tote bag."

"Forget that," I said. I didn't want to think about tote bags.

He pushed me against the door and we did it for at least three dollars and seventy-five cents' worth. I felt myself coming back from old-fashioned sepia to vivid Kodachrome.

The next day Isaac's photos were on the front page of the *Post* and the *Daily News* and on every television network. The girl was being called "Thalia" and her parents were suing Arthur Weeman and the Gardener School.

Isaac was moody. He should have been ecstatic but instead his success had made him nervous. Ivy wasn't speaking to him and I wasn't being too sympathetic. I couldn't help but get a little thrill at the idea of Ivy waking up next to Derek Hassler and opening her morning paper to the headline WEEMAN'S MUSE SUES, and the tiny words "photos by Isaac Myman."

When I got to Mrs. Williams' he wasn't there but the papers were spread out across the kitchen table. I put down the two plastic bags of groceries I had brought and looked at the article in the *Times. With just four weeks left to the August 25th release of his new film* . . . it began.

I had been so busy on my book that I had completely forgotten it was almost time for the new Arthur Weeman, and I'd had no idea it was opening on my wedding day.

I said hi to Mrs. Williams who was looking out the kitchen window. She didn't turn around.

I put away most of the groceries. I got her gefilte fish, which I had discovered to be her favorite thing, white horseradish, kugel, applesauce, paper towels. Watermelon for me, a grapefruit for her. I had gotten used to throwing a box of Depends in my cart along with my Tampax, denture glue in with my Herbal Essences.

"What are you looking at? Is he there?"

She didn't say anything, and I wondered for a moment if old people could sometimes die standing up. I got a terrible feeling that something was wrong.

"What is it?" I said, walking up to the window. I stood behind her, looking over the shoulder of her Talbots sweater.

Mrs. Williams pointed out the window. I followed the direction of her finger with my eyes but I wasn't sure what I was looking at. I wasn't looking at anything. It felt like a kind of blindness.

There were no copper pots and pans, no cappuccino maker and blue ceramic mugs on hooks, no granite island, wooden salad bowl, modern pepper mill. My private movie was over. The credits had rolled and the projector had been turned off. His kitchen window was covered—not with a red velvet curtain like at the Ziegfeld that would rise again at the next showing—but with wooden shutters, sealed up tight as coffin lids on every window on the house.

I started to panic the way I had when I came home from school to find that my father moved out, his clothes and books and treadmill gone, his hanging skeleton, his wok and Chinese cookbook, all the plants.

I didn't know which was more shocking, the barricaded windows or the fact that Mrs. Williams had started to sob. I had never seen an old person cry before. I couldn't believe she had that much moisture in her. The tears and mucus slid down her wrinkles and the rims around her eyes turned bright red in stark contrast to her white face. She was bent over and shaking like a palm tree in a tropical storm. I was afraid her back would break or she would have a heart attack. I put my hand on her slight hump, fighting back my own tears.

"But you don't even like him," I said.

"That's true, but I love him."

"You loved Arthur Weeman?"

"No, my husband. Howard. He got out of Croftville again. They called but I didn't know how to answer the phone." She was sobbing too hard to talk. Isaac had insisted on replacing her light blue rotary with a black cordless. A square of brighter yellow wallpaper that had been hidden for at least four decades framed the new smaller phone. "A voice came out of the phone and said Howard was missing. And then he showed up here. I'm not going to make him go back there." She stopped crying, and dried her eyes with the backs of her permanently cupped hands. "I'm going to tough it out with him."

"Where is he?" I asked.

"I thought they were calling to tell me he had passed. I never should have let him go to that place." She started to sob again. "He's taking a nap."

I led her to the sectional and got a roll of toilet paper from the bathroom so she could wipe her eyes and blow her nose. I sat down next to her and held her hand. Even though I had helped her shower and put on her underpants this felt more intimate somehow. I wasn't the kind of girl who was always hugging other women and holding their hands. At Bennington I was one of the few girls who didn't make a point of walking around naked all the time and climbing into every other girl's bed.

"So I suppose you're going to move on now," she said. "You're on to bigger and better things. I don't think I can hold your attention as much as a big-time movie star." She batted her sunken eyelids comically.

I hadn't thought of that before. That, if I were honest, the reason I had been there all this time was for Arthur, not for her. But now I loved her. I couldn't imagine eating pizza without her, or watching *Little House*, or not wheeling her to work with me in the morning or to the hairdresser once a month. I tried to think of what my life was before her. I had a vague memory of life before her, of something a little more glamorous. I know I drank a lot of coffee alone in a lot of cafés.

It wasn't normal for Isaac and me to spend so much time with her. We were going to be newlyweds and the maid's room off her kitchen with its olive carpet and tiny cot, wasn't exactly the honeymoon suite I'd always dreamed of. But Isaac and I could be newlyweds *with* Mrs. Williams, I decided, even if Arthur Weeman was no longer in the picture. I couldn't have stood losing Arthur Weeman and Mrs. Williams in the same day.

"I'm still going to come here to visit you. And you and Howard can go on double dates with us," I said, but I somehow knew they wouldn't be up to it.

"Well, that may or may not be, but we have to get me a new girl," Mrs. Williams said. "A nice black. A live-in."

"Okay," I whispered, feeling as replaced as Irmabelle must have felt. "I'll tell Isaac to come and put your old phone back."

"That's probably not a good idea. It'll upset Howard. He's just never been the same since our son died."

"I didn't know you had a son."

"He died of a brain tumor when he was very young," she said.

I thought of Mrs. Williams burying her small son. "How old was he?" I asked.

"Forty-six. His name was Norman after my father. He was a *doctor*." She said doctor proudly, as if she was trying to set us up.

We were interrupted by a strange heaving sound coming from the bedroom. She looked stricken. "What is that?" I said.

"Oh, no, Howard's found his old harmonica. I thought I'd hidden it sufficiently. You'd better go."

"But you haven't told me about Norman."

"Please, dear, just go."

She didn't get up, just stared straight ahead, as I packed all my things in shopping bags, scooped up the newspapers from the kitchen table, and left.

The next day I printed my manuscript, put two big rubber bands around it, and headed uptown to deliver it to my editor in person.

I wore my long white Morgane Le Fay sleeveless top with tails that fluttered out behind me in the wind and I felt like Jo March sneaking off triumphantly into town to drop off her story and get all her hair chopped off.

"What's that?" someone asked coming up beside me.

I thought it was a short black man, but it was Robbie Finch, the girl who was always giving me a hard time because I didn't have enough black people in my book.

"My new book," I said.

"Oh yeah? I'm working on a screenplay. It's about a girl who's obsessed with Philip Roth."

"I thought you were a lesbian," I said.

"I am but I'd make an exception for Philip Roth. What's it about?" She gestured disdainfully at my manuscript.

"Just a girl in New York," I said. "A lighthearted romp." Where were all the cabs? I wondered, thrusting my arm in the air, like an Olympian.

"Any black people in it?" she asked.

"As a matter of fact there are," I said.

"Really! So, who is it, this alleged black person in your book, a light-skinned maid or a homeless lady or something?"

"No, it's the sister. The girl's sister is black," I said.

"What do you mean the girl's sister is black?"

"The protagonist discovers she has a half sister who's half black."

"That sounds ridiculous," Robbie Finch said.

A cab finally pulled up and I dove in, clutching my manuscript to my chest like a bullet-proof vest. Robbie Finch was filled with rage, but I sort of liked running into her from time to time. It felt like a good omen seeing her on the day I was handing in my book. She was kind of like my muse the way she showed up out of nowhere like that, all four-foot-ten of her, with her scraggily short Afro with the single braid sprouting out the back like a broken dandelion, and tiny square wire-rimmed glasses, and old leather bomber jacket.

"I'm getting married next week," I said.

"Mazel tov."

"Would you like to come?"

"To your wedding?" She looked extremely dubious.

"There'll be other black people there," I said. "Well, two others."

"And what are you having, like four hundred guests?"

"One hundred."

"Alright, I guess I can help you out," she said.

I gave her the info, slammed the cab door, and we took off.

When I got to the publishing house I was treated like a king. A poster of the cover of my book still hung in my editor's office.

"This is going to be big," my editor said, handing my manuscript carefully to her assistant, a girl named Huck, to be Xeroxed. "We're going to speed up publication to capitalize on this whole Arthur Weeman little girl controversy. This just couldn't be better. We already have a designer working on the cover." I started to feel faint with excitement. I couldn't wait to see my new pair of legs.

25.

At 34, she marries

On my last night as a single woman, I wrote one more letter to
Arthur Weeman.

Dear Awful Writer, I wrote.

Then I crossed that out and wrote *Dear Arthur Weeman* because I knew it was my last letter to him.

August 24

Dear Arthur Weeman,

Tomorrow I am a Bat Mitzvah. I didn't send you an
invitation because I didn't think you would come but
now I wish I had just in case you would. My mother is
making this all about HER. They wouldn't let me get
the shoes I wanted because they said I'm still growing
and they'd be too small for me in five minutes, even
though I am sure that my feet are not going to grow. My
grandfather's wife—he's eighty and she's forty—said

that the first thing people notice about a woman is her shoes and her hair, which makes the shoes even more essential. My feet are an adult size six which I think is pretty much the best size you can have. Japanese women *strive* for that. I still haven't written my Bat Mitzvah speech even though it's tommorrow and I might say something about the hippocracy of not being allowed to wear adult women's shoes the day I am supposedly offically an adult.

Instead of getting Bat Mitzvahed tomorrow, I am pretending that I am getting married and tomorrow I will move out of here and start my real life. I am a woman now, Arthur. A breast bearing, menstruating citizen of my community. Maybe I won't even go through with it.

Maybe I just won't show up and no one will notice I'm not there and they'll accidentally bat mitzvah my mother instead.

I sent a picture of myself to the casting director Sylvia Fay. I am thinking maybe I could be in sitcoms.

I'm going to write my Bat Mitzvah speech now.

Instead of working on my Bat Mitzvah speech, I think I will write the beginning of a screenplay.

INT. NEW YORK CITY KITCHEN.   DAY

                                        CLOSE-UP:
The BLACK and WHITE TILES of an expensive KITCHEN FLOOR.

PAN TO:

Expensive COPPER POTS hanging on a POT WRACK

PAN TO:

Famous movie director, ARTHUR WEEMAN, stands reading a LETTER.

ARTHUR WEEMAN
(smiling, sotto)
Thalia.

CUT TO:

INT. GRAMERCY PARK SYNAGOGUE.   DAY
THALIA, a lanky gamine girl with chocolate brown cropped hair stands, next to a RABBI, facing a congregation of FAT OLD JEWISH PEOPLE.

THALIA
(into microphone)
I don't want to be here.

CUT TO:

EXT. GRAMERCY PARK SOUTH.   DAY
Arthur Weeman is frantically running down the street holding the letter and a shopping bag.

CUT TO:

INT. GRAMERCY PARK SYNAGOGUE.   CONTINUOUS
Arthur Weeman bursts into the synagogue, running down the center aisle. He pulls a shoe box out of the

shopping bag and hands Thalia beautiful wooden high
healed sandals with red leather straps.

ARTHUR WEEMAN

Happy Bat Mitzvah. Mozel tav.

He grabs Thalia's hand and they run back up the
aisle.

That's just the beginning but what do you think? I
think it's The Graduate meets Cinderella if you ask me.

Anyway, my Arthur, I am going to write my bat
mitzvah speech about you. I'm going to talk about your
movies and your time line and my true devotion to you.
The truth is I never really thought you were an Awful
Writer. There I said it. I think you're an Awesome Writer.
I think you're the greatest writer who ever lived. Now
you probably won't respect me but I don't care. After tomorrow I'm not a child anymore and the truth has to
come out. I can't keep writing to you forever, you know.
Besides, according to all the newspapers, etc. you are really quite involved with someone! (No comment.) I
wanted to say I love you, and thank you. Thank you for
your movies and your brain and letting me write to you
all year. It turned out to not be as bad a year as I
thought it would be thanks to you. Thank you for everything. Maybe one day I'll let you know how it goes. How
it all goes. But until then, goodbye.

Your,

Thalia

The morning of my wedding I woke up next to my groom-
to-be and did what all brides probably do. I called Mr. Movie-

fone. *Arthur Weeman's* Thalia *is playing exclusively at the Ziegfeld Theater, Fifty-fourth Street and Sixth Avenue. Today's remaining showtimes are 10, 12, 2, 4, 6, 8, 10, and 12.*

I called again. Arthur Weeman's *Thalia. Thalia.* I couldn't believe what I was hearing.

And at ten o'clock I was sitting in the Ziegfeld, fourth row, first seat on the left side of the left aisle, watching it.

The film started with a spectacular shot of elephants, walking trunk to tail. You think they're in India or Africa but then the camera pulls back to show you Thirty-fourth Street. Ace Woods, a famous filmmaker, is watching the elephants leave the circus. He pulls a letter out of his overcoat pocket, and we see it is from someone named Thalia, aged almost thirteen.

Without realizing it, I had risen to my feet. I turned to look up at the projection booth as if I could plead with the ghost of a projectionist to make it stop.

"Hey, lady, sit down," someone said.

I was shaking. But there was nothing I could do. The film just kept rolling. Ace Woods received another letter.

But here was the twist. Thalia wasn't the thirteen-year-old girl she claimed to be in her letters to the director. She was a lonely, repressed thirty-three-year-old woman played by Angelina Jolie who spies on the director from her kitchen window when she's not working as a ninth-grade English teacher at the all-girls Drowler School. And the whole time she thinks she is spying on him, he is really spying on her.

There had been one day I thought our eyes had met. He was eating something at the window that I think the girl had made for him. A kind of soup. She was hovering around him, watching his every bite, and he was eating it animatedly, at first pretending he was afraid it might kill him and slowly bringing the soup spoon

to his lips, screwing up his face, his hand shaking so most of the
soup must have spilled, and then, after much mock surprise, he
gobbled the rest of it up while she did things like hit him and put
her hands on her hips.

I'd even put that scene in my novel.

I thought of my manuscript lying on my editor's desk and
bent over in my seat, certain I was going to throw up. There was
no way my novel could be published now. Now Thalia belonged
to him. I had given him his greatest film, sent it to him on pretty
stationery, with upside-down stamps and lipstick kisses. I had
saved him like Charlotte saved Wilbur, my eight legs curling in
on themselves, shriveling to dust while he rolled in his glorious
mud. My novel was gone. It was done. He had taken it from me.

And he had topped me. Especially the scene where Angelina
Jolie masturbates at her kitchen window while he eats a plate of
runny scrambled eggs at his.

And the scene where she finally gets a man to go out with her
and she pulls a pair of "Ace Woods glasses" out of her purse and
asks him to wear them when they make love.

And the scene where she lifts her skirt for the wax statue of him
at Madame Tussaud's while an amused security guard stands by.

There was the scene where I watched him filming snow in the
playground, the scene where I saw him at Elaine's, the scene
where he sent me his brain.

In the final scene he meets the adult Thalia, whose real name
is Rachael, at the merry-go-round in Central Park. He thanks her
for her letters and explains that the carousel was transplanted in
Central Park from Coney Island at the turn of the century and that
it used to be pulled by blind horses. He tells her he has a brain tumor, he is going blind, and her letters pulled him through to make
one more film—his last. While Angelina Jolie wept on the screen,

I wept in my seat. But this time I didn't weep because I was in the presence of genius. And I didn't weep for Arthur Weeman. I didn't even weep for myself or my ruined novel. What got me when it really came down to it was the thought of those blind horses walking around and around in a circle all day long in the summertime heat of Coney Island. It was too much for me to handle.

When it was over, I applauded.

"Shouldn't you be getting ready for your wedding?" someone asked behind me. I turned to see Ivy Vohl standing in the aisle, looking down at me. "What'd you think of it?"

It was truly uncanny the way she always managed to ask the obvious. What'd she think I thought of it? I had just seen one of the greatest movies ever made and I was sitting there bawling my eyes out in a napkin.

"What did you think about the end?"

"What do you mean?" I asked. "I loved it."

"I was a little disappointed with them meeting in the end. Too predictable." If Ivy had been there when the *Mona Lisa* was painted she would have stood around saying how disappointed she was with the smile.

"That's what's great about it. It's so satisfying. It's what makes Arthur Weeman a genius. He knows just how far he can take it."

"I think it's unsatisfying to have them meet." Ivy Vohl was like some kind of movie nymphomaniac. If this movie didn't satisfy her nothing would.

"I think not having them meet would have been stupid."

I collapsed back in my seat, exhausted. I was furious because a little part of me *was* disappointed that they'd met. Because he'd written that part without me. In my novel—may it rest in peace—I'd not dared to do it.

"Anyway, it doesn't matter. I think it was his best," Ivy said. "It was as good as *Lolita,* the distant love between Arthur Weeman and Thalia. The way they needed each other and used each other and ultimately betrayed each other. I wish my book was a fraction as good as that."

"Thank you," I mumbled under my breath.

"Thank you? Thank you for what?"

"Oh, just thank you, like *thank you,* I agree."

"I'm really worried about my book. It's about to be printed, and the galleys didn't get such a great response."

She looked so genuinely tortured by how great Arthur Weeman was and how untalented she herself was that I couldn't help but feel incredibly sorry for her, the way you feel sorry for someone in the early stages of Alzheimer's, who knows what is to come. She couldn't make herself as good a writer as me, and I couldn't make myself as good a writer as Arthur Weeman. Our creative visions were just carrots on sticks. No matter how hard we tried, we could only write what we could write. All writers were just blind horses walking in the same circle over and over again pulling our crappy books behind us.

"Speaking of which," I said suddenly. "I'm writing a blurb for you. I'm working on something, something like: 'Ivy Vohl is this generation's Philip Roth' or 'Portnoy's real complaint was that he didn't know Vohl,' something like that." I was as stunned by what was coming out of my mouth as she was. It was my wedding day and I was the quintessence of bridal goodness. Beauty, I was sure, was radiating out of me, sparkling on my lapel like a diamond broach. Forgiving those who had trespassed against me was my something new.

"Maybe I'll compare your protagonist to Lolita," I said, with so much charity and goodness boiling inside me it made a soup that could feed every bum on the Bowery.

"But my protagonist is a man."

"Of course, I know that . . . did I say Lolita? I meant Humbert Humbert," I said.

I took a pen out of my pocketbook and wrote the Philip Roth thing and the Humbert Humbert thing on a napkin and signed it as solemnly as if it was a ketubah.

"Really?" Ivy said. She looked down at the napkin in disbelief.

"Sure," I said. "I loved your book." Maybe, I thought, I might even read it on my honeymoon, although it was unlikely. I wasn't a saint. Blurbing it was painful enough, I shouldn't also have to suffer reading it.

An usher cleaning the floor under the seats gave us a dirty look. Ivy tucked the blurb into her bag. "So, I'm looking forward to your wedding later. I'm going solo. Derek had to cancel because they're closing the Thanksgiving issue of *Maxim*." I didn't even know she was coming. I had just assumed she wouldn't be there after Isaac hadn't given her the exclusive Arthur Weeman photos. A few people started to file in for the noon showing, very few I noticed. "You taking a cab downtown?" Ivy asked.

"I'm staying for the twelve o'clock," I said. "I have to see it again."

"I'll see it with you," Ivy said. "May I?" She smiled at me with her upside-down mouth and made her eyes a little less piercing than usual. I tucked my legs to the side and she slid in past me and called her assistant to say she was working from home. Then we sat there next to each other and watched the movie again.

In the middle, I had to leave to go get married. I had to meet my friend Cynthia Ree so she could do my hair and makeup and then take a car service from her studio to the restaurant. I had told Cynthia I wanted to look young and fresh, but now I wanted her to make my eyes smoky and drunk. I wanted to marry as a grown woman with a past, not a young girl with a future. I wanted my wedding to be funereal in nature, and I wished I had chosen to wear black instead of the gown I currently had draped over my arm in its dry cleaner's plastic. All the best weddings were funereal, with people weeping in the pews.

Cynthia helped me struggle into my gown.

"Who's the designer?" she asked.

"I don't know," I said.

"You don't know who made your wedding gown? What was it, your mother's or something?"

"I got it at the Arthur Weeman warehouse sale. Candace Ann wore it in *Adopting Alice.*"

I could tell from the look on Cynthia's face that she didn't really like it too much. Candace Ann, it turned out, was a lot thinner than me in *Adopting Alice,* and the dress was a little tight.

"Are you sure you want to wear that hat with it?"

"She wore the hat," I said. I took a long look at myself in the mirror and tried to adjust the hat a little but the effect suddenly seemed a little mushroomy.

"How about this?" Cynthia said gently, holding up a long, skinny black silk dress. There was nothing mushroomy about it.

"I didn't even like that movie. And Candace Ann was terrible in it."

"She won the Academy Award."

"Yeah, well, she didn't wear *that* to the Oscars," Cynthia said, snatching the hat from my head. And, like Frida Kahlo changing out of her white gown into something else at the last minute before her wedding to Diego, I changed out of mine.

When I burst through the old wooden coach-house doors of One If By Land, Two If By Sea, I suddenly couldn't imagine my wedding any other way. My mother stood talking to Isaac's mother. My father stood talking animatedly to my editor. Mrs. Williams was in her wheelchair, being pushed to the bar by Irmabelle. My L.A. friends were shivering by the fireplace and my writing buddies were gawking at them from the bar and hungrily grabbing hors d'oeuvres as they passed. The only one missing was Sascha. Still, I thought, even if it meant a lifetime of standing on St. Mark's Place and staring up at her terrace and waiting for her, I could find a way to be her sister. I was good at staring at other people's apartments and waiting for them, after all.

But then she walked in. Before I had a chance to go to her, everyone gathered, forming a tiny aisle, and my father walked me to where Isaac and the judge were standing. Just as the judge began to speak, I said, "Wait, stop." The whole room gasped.

I walked back to the doors where Sascha was standing and grabbed her hand.

"What are you doing?" Sascha whispered, pulling her hand away from me.

"This is my sister," I announced loudly. "Sascha, please come with me." I grabbed her hand again, and pulled her up to the makeshift altar with me. "Everyone, this is Sascha Kettle, my father's daughter who he had with Irmabelle. Irmabelle, please come here and stand next to Dad."

Irmabelle froze for a moment and then walked elegantly over to my father. Everyone had turned around to look at her.

"Okay," I said, handing Sascha my four-hundred-dollar bouquet.

"Hi, Toots," my father said to Sascha. He took her head in his hands and kissed her.

"Don't call me 'Toots,' " she said.

"He calls me Toots too. I hate that," I said.

"I love you both so much," he said, kissing my head too.

Then Sascha started crying, and so did Irmabelle, and my mother started wailing, and even Isaac had tears in his eyes. Finally my wedding was just how I wanted it.

After we said our vows, Isaac and I did one of those pathetic kiss/hug combos instead of something a little more passionate and I wished we'd rehearsed that part but other than that I was completely happy.

"Rebekah, when do you get back from Italy? I have to talk to you about your book," my editor said nervously, leaving her beef Wellington to come talk to me.

"You can talk to me now," I said, taking a sip of champagne to ready myself. I was glad I was wearing black.

"This really isn't the right time," she said.

"Evan, I know about the Arthur Weeman movie. I've seen it."

"Well, then I think we both know there's a serious problem here. As you know, we were all very excited about your book in-house. It was the biggest book on our spring list. Oh, Rebekah. We really shouldn't do this now."

"It's okay," I said, looking over at my handsome husband across the room.

"I happened to get invited to a screening of the new Arthur Weeman film. Rebekah, did you plagiarize Arthur Weeman?" my editor asked.

I repeated the word "plagiarize" in disbelief. I knew my book couldn't be published but I hadn't thought I'd be considered a plagiarist.

"Well, then did you 'borrow' Thalia from Arthur Weeman?"

I knew I had forgotten something. My something borrowed. I had my something new: my sister, and, of course, forgiving those who had trespassed against me. And my something old:

myself. Now my something "borrowed": Thalia. And something blue: my mother who was still crying.

"I didn't borrow Thalia from Arthur Weeman. *I* gave her to *him*," I said. I'd have to think about borrowing later when I had more time, maybe look it up in the dictionary or something. Who had borrowed who from whom and is it possible to borrow something that cannot be returned, or for that matter lent in the first place?

"What do you mean?" my editor asked, angrily. "Why would you do that? Do you know him?"

I thought about that for a moment. In a way I knew him better than I knew anyone. "No," I said.

"I mean it's a tragedy really, because I think the book would have been an enormous commercial *and* critical success. I'm sorry, Rebekah. Even if we write this off as an amazing coincidence, great minds thinking alike or something, it's still very embarrassing. I'm sorry to tell you this at your wedding." She let out a nervous laugh. "Anyway, everything's really lovely." I looked over at Sascha deep in conversation with the scowling Robbie Finch. I loved Sascha so much at that moment for being my sister and for showing up, it suddenly seemed like the only important thing. "I know you'll be able to come up with something else for us."

The room was spinning and then I saw Isaac and it stopped.

I kissed my editor on the cheek and thanked her for coming and then went to stand next to my husband.

He was talking to Ivy Vohl.

"I have good news and bad news," Isaac said, taking my hand. "Ivy has forgiven me for not giving the *Quille* the Arthur Weeman exclusive." He didn't specify which one that was, the good news or the bad news.

"Money's money," Ivy said.

"What's the . . . other news?" I asked. From the way Isaac was gripping my hand, I was starting to get worried.

"We're going to have to postpone our trip to Italy."

"It's not a trip, it's a honeymoon," I said.

"Ivy needs me to work. There's a big benefit in New York next week. I have to be the one to photograph it. We can go to the benefit and then leave for Italy right after. Postponing it one week won't matter. Venice will always be there."

I hated when people said things like "Venice will always be there." They were the kind of people who never went to Venice or anywhere.

"Not necessarily," I said. "I've heard it's sinking."

"Oh look, your first fight as man and wife and I'm to blame," Ivy said.

"I'm sorry, honey. We'll just have to put it off a week or two."

"I'm not postponing my honeymoon," I said.

26.

*At 34, she embarks on what will forever be
remembered as 'the midnight ride of
Rebekah Kettle'*

I highly recommend honeymooning alone. Being a bride is
stressful and the last thing you need to have to worry about
right afterward is being married.

First I invited Sascha to go with me, and I could tell she was
considering it, but she said no. I met her at the Veselka, the plane
tickets in my bag, but she couldn't be convinced.

"Why not?" I asked. "Two sisters together."

"I want to," she said. "But I have to work. And I don't even really
know you."

"What do you mean? We're sisters."

"We're strangers," she said, smiling warmly at me. I didn't feel
that we were strangers. "I don't think we're ready for a honeymoon."

"We're friends."

"I don't go to Venice with my friends. I go to the movies with
them, or a bar, or Chumley's for a hamburger, or someplace like
this."

"Maybe we'll go to the movies some time then," I said.

"That sounds nice," she said. "We'll have dinner too, Dad's treat."

I laughed. It was possible that she was prettier than me, I couldn't decide, but I was more successful. She hadn't finished college.

"Maybe we will go to Italy together one day," she said.

"It's a date," I said.

I kept staring at the Star of David she wore on a chain around her neck which was so different from anything I would ever wear. I was still secretly stalking her, looking for clues, even when we were face-to-face.

"My mother's having dinner with Dad tonight," she said. "I think they might get back together. They talked a lot at the wedding."

I felt a pang of jealousy. I couldn't help but wish that "Dad," as she called him, had talked to *my* mother instead. As far as I was concerned, "Dad" belonged with the woman I called "Mom."

When I'd left her on the corner of Ninth and Second, we'd hugged again.

I waited on line for a water taxi. *"Grazie,"* I said to the driver. "Gritti Palace *per favore.*"

"Ah, Americano," he said, smiling at me. "Welcome to Venezia." He put my luggage on the boat and helped me in, taking my delicate bridal hand in his enormous Italian one. I couldn't help notice the difference between him and the average New York City taxi driver. He had beautiful black curly Italian hair and huge sandaled suntanned feet. "What brings you here to Venice?"

"I'm on my honeymoon," I said.

"But you are alone."

"I know," I said happily. In six days I was going to meet Isaac in Capri, but until then I was going to enjoy every minute of my time alone.

We sped through brown water past tall wooden posts, each with its own Italian seagull perched on top.

"Do you want to drive the taxi?" he asked.

"No," I laughed.

"Come on, it is happy." He took my hand again and pulled me toward the steering wheel. Then he took his hands off the wheel and stepped away, and I had no choice but to grab it. I didn't know how to tell him that I'd never even driven a car before and now I was steering his boat toward Venice. "I can show you the sights later."

"I don't think my husband would appreciate that," I said. I had used that line for so many years, it was strange to actually be married and say it.

He took over the driving and we pulled into the tiny dock at the Gritti Palace. He wrote his name, Davide, on a scrap of paper with his phone number and handed it to me. "You call me?"

I shook my head. "I really am married," I said, presenting my sparkling rings.

"But you are not very married. It is not yet a habit."

"I'm married enough," I said.

"*Ciao, Signora,*" he said, climbing back on his boat, and turned to wave at me as he drove off.

I tucked his number carefully into my wallet to keep always. I would put it on my refrigerator at home as a reminder that, married or not, there was always a man named Davide waiting for my call. My honeymoon was off to a fantastic start.

I checked into the Gritti. "I'm in the honeymoon suite," I proudly told the woman behind the desk. It sounded so glamorous.

"Of course, congratulations, Signora," she said. She looked behind me. "And where is your husband?" she asked.

"At home in New York," I said.

The woman made a surprised frown.

"Of course, Signora. At what time is he arriving? I can place an order for a water taxi."

"He's not," I said, cheerfully.

"Do you still require the honeymoon suite, Signora? It is the time of the film festival and we are very full, perhaps you would prefer a single room?"

"No, I'm on my honeymoon," I assured her. "Could you have room service send up a bottle of Dom Pérignon?"

I handed her my credit card.

"Rebekah Kettle," she said. "Are you Rebekah Kettle, the author?"

"Yes," I said.

"I am a big fan of your book *La Sezione Solida*. I read it in just two days."

"*Grazie,*" I said. I didn't know how to make any wisecracks in Italian.

"If you do not already have a reservation for dinner tonight, I'm afraid it will be impossible."

"I have a reservation at Harry's Bar," I said. I started to walk away and then turned back. The lobby was filled with paparazzi taking pictures of everyone who walked in the door in case they were famous. There were celebrities and models everywhere and tourists gawking at them. The Gritti practically had its own red carpet. "Do you know," I asked, "if Arthur Weeman is here in Venice?" Even though it didn't matter, I just had to ask. It was a habit, as Davide would say. Not that I really cared, but if he was here, I knew he'd be at the Gritti.

"I don't know, Signora," the woman said, "but I do know he has just purchased a home here in Venice, just across from us on the other side of the Canale."

My heart started pounding in spite of itself. "Do you know which one?" I asked, trying to act *normale.*

She smiled. "Of course. It is the yellow house just across from this hotel."

As soon as I got to my room I stepped out on the balcony and looked out at the Grande Canale and the magnificent yellow house on the other side. I laughed at myself, thinking how ironic it would be if I spent my entire time in Venice on the balcony trying to catch a glimpse of him.

Then a light came on in one of the windows.

"Don't do this," I said, forcing my eyes closed. I was on my honeymoon, and the last thing I was going to do was waste one minute of it on Arthur Weeman.

Although I was tempted, I did not call Davide and went out by myself that night. I had a romantic dinner alone at Harry's Bar and wrote postcards to Isaac and Mrs. Williams.

Ciao Isaac!

I am really enjoying our honeymoon. I am getting many phone numbers from many Italian men. I'll drink a bellini for you.

Love, Rebekah

Ciao Mrs. Williams!

I am really enjoying my honeymoon. I am getting many phone numbers from many Italian men. I'll drink a bellini for you.

Love, Rebekah

I paid my check with wedding money and was just about to get up, when the waiter brought me a telephone. "You have a man on the line," he said.

"Hello?" I asked, tentatively. It was Isaac.

"I miss you," he said.

"I miss you too," I said.

"Well, you won't miss me for long," he said. "I'm at JFK, about to get on the red-eye. I'll see you in the morning. We have to consummate this thing."

"We already did that," I said.

"That was in New York. We have to consummate in Italy."

"What about Ivy?" I asked, smiling.

"You know what I figured out about Ivy?" he said.

"What?" I asked.

"She's kind of a bitch," Isaac said.

When I left the restaurant, a little before midnight, it started to rain and I bought the same bright-green hooded plastic poncho that everyone was wearing, the Venice equivalent to the New York $3 umbrella. I started back to the hotel but then, I felt so festive in my Venice poncho, so a part of everything and at the same time so exotic and incognito, I thought I would stay out longer and take a romantic walk by myself.

As I walked toward San Marco Square, I became aware that a man was following me. The streets were crowded, so I couldn't be sure, but when I stopped to look at leather books in a shop window, the man stopped suddenly a few feet away. I couldn't see him too well in the dark, foggy night but from his green hooded poncho I figured he was a tourist too. When he saw me looking at him, he turned away and adjusted his hood.

I stopped again in front of a crowded *caffè* and caught another look at him. Under his hood, I saw he wore a baseball cap pulled down all the way to his glasses. I tried to read what his cap said in the moonlight, and finally made out that it was from the Strand bookstore. The last thing I wanted to see in Venice was a baseball cap from the Strand. He was probably one of those middle-aged men who hung around the ninety-eight-cent bins and wore shorts in winter.

But then I noticed a heavy gold watch glinting on his thin wrist, and the glasses. . . . I stopped dead in my cobblestone tracks. I could almost have sworn it was Arthur Weeman. That was crazy, I thought, starting to walk again. I was crazy. It was just some sleazy tourist and I started to get really scared. I picked up my pace, almost running in my red-and-white polka-dot honeymoon shoes.

When I turned a corner, I saw a bridge with a gondola just pulling up beneath it, and I ran down the stone stairs, without stopping to look behind me. A couple paid the gondolier and started up the stairs, and I stepped onto the gondola. The man might not have even seen me duck down the stairs, and if we could pull out quickly, I might actually have gotten rid of him. To be safe, I thought, I'd ask the gondolier to leave me off at another bridge or take me directly to my hotel.

"I'm sorry," the gondolier said, "but it is now midnight and I am out of duty." He stood defiantly on the stone dock and began to rock the gondola menacingly with his oar, as if he was trying to shake me off it like a fly.

"Please," I said, "*per favore,* can you just take me to my . . ."

"Would you mind terribly if we shared the ride?" the man in the green hooded poncho asked, carefully descending the last three stairs and standing next to the gondolier. He put his hand to his chest, trying to catch his breath. "Jesus, you follow me all the way to Venice, and then you run away from me like a cat. You won't be happy until you've killed me."

The gondolier was so surprised he had lifted his oar from the boat and hadn't noticed that I had started drifting away from the dock.

"It is Mr. Wee-a-man, no? It is an honor, Signore. I am a large fan of you," the gondolier said.

"Uh, thank you, but the girl, could you get her back?" Arthur Weeman said, and the gondolier's long oar quickly dragged me back in.

"Please, Mr. Wee-a-man, *prego*, it would be an honor. . . ." The gondolier put out his hand to help Arthur Weeman onto the velvet cushion facing me and then took his position looming high up at the stern, and as we pushed off in the inner canal, I pushed off into the air. I became more and more weightless, separating atom by atom, until I was the fog.

"I wanted to talk to you back at Harry's Bar," Arthur Weeman said, "but there were so many people there."

I didn't say anything because I was fog.

"I'm a big fan of yours," he said.

It was such an absurd thing for him to say to me that I let out a lone American laugh, as if I was watching one of his movies at the Ziegfeld. He took off his hood and smiled. I wanted to reach very slowly and casually over to him and put both my palms on his cheeks.

"So," he said. "Two writers alone in Venice, taking in the sights."

I'm not ready for this, I thought. I cringed, realizing that, at my feet like a dead fish, was my manuscript in a plastic bag. I had lugged it all the way to Venice because I'd had the idea to scatter its pages in the canals, and I was waiting for the right moment, although I knew I probably wouldn't do it at all.

"So, Rebekah Kettle. I, I guess I don't know what to say. Is there anything you want to say to an awful writer like myself?"

"Don't tell me you expect *me* to write the dialogue," I said. "I think I've already written enough."

"Fine, I'll do the talking, but, I hope you won't try to throw me in the water." The way he said it was so funny that I laughed, picturing myself doing it. "First of all, I know everything about you. I had you followed by an agency man."

"What's an agency man?" For a moment I thought he had me followed by someone from William Morris or CAA.

"A private investigator."

"Why?" I asked. It was the craziest thing I had ever heard. I wished I had dressed up a little more over the past few months, taken a little more time to put myself together. I cringed, thinking of my jeans and skeleton T-shirt, no makeup.

"Look, I thought you were a little girl, but, you know, I could get into big trouble with that, so I tried to find you, but when there was no 'Thalia' registered at the Gardener School, I started to get suspicious. Then when you gave me your address, the address of that old lady, I had the building put under surveillance. The agency man saw you walk by my house several times and got a close-up shot of one of your letters while you were mailing it. I even had your brain looked at by a top surgeon in New York. I know your novel, I know you work for your father, I know that dementia case you take care of, and that dick paparazzo you sold my soul to. Is he here? Because I'd really like to punch him in the nose." He looked around and shook his fist in the air a little. "I cast an Academy Award–winning actor—

Philip Seymour Hoffman—in the role of him. I should have saved my money and cast a weasel or a small squirrel or something."

"No, he's not here," I said. "But I did marry him." I showed him my ring.

"I need your binoculars to see that thing, no seriously, it's very tasteful, you know, if you like small diamonds. Jesus, why didn't you tell me? That's terrible, I mean, how wonderful. I have to send a gift. My invitation must have gotten lost in the mail. Seriously, you picked a great man," he said sarcastically.

"And Mrs. Williams isn't a dementia case." I said it as convincingly as possible, but I remembered the last night I had spent with her just a few days before, when she'd begged me not to make her go to bed. "Please let me stay at the party, Mama," she'd said. Maybe she was a dementia case but hadn't I been a dementia case too? In a way, hadn't I too begged to be at a party that didn't exist? Being a fan was a kind of dementia, I realized. You did more than suspend your disbelief, you stabbed your disbelief to death with a machete and left it bleeding on the concrete. What on earth had I been thinking?

"Fine, she's completely lucid," he said, and I laughed out loud in spite of myself.

We entered a narrow canal and another gondola grazed us as it passed. Arthur turned away and put his hood back up.

My poncho was making a rustling sound, and I realized I was shaking with a kind of excitement from head to toe. Endorphins darted like fish in the water all around me.

The rain stopped and his glasses cleared. A plane flew overhead and yet it seemed to be flying under me.

Suddenly I wondered if I was being put on, or filmed, or if I might even be in jeopardy. Maybe he was going to kill me off. For all I knew, I could be riding in my own coffin with my manuscript at my feet. The scenery was so eerily beautiful. Looking up, I saw the crumbling houses, the magnificent windows and wrought-iron balconies, hundreds of years of peeling paint in colors that just didn't exist, laundry hanging from clotheslines. Venice was as impossible as Hollywood.

In lit-up windows I saw two-hundred-year-old beams and Murano chandeliers. Arthur was talking but all I could hear was water splashing on wood and stone.

"I want to thank you. I don't want to give you all the credit, but you're definitely, partially responsible for my comeback. At least that's what the critics are calling it."

"You don't need a comeback. You never left," I said.

"Look, as far as I'm concerned I need a comeback like a hole in the head. But in any case, I want to thank you."

"Don't thank me," I said. The last thing I wanted was to be thanked. "I exposed you."

He laughed. "I don't blame you for that. I opened myself wide up."

He was right. He had given himself away just as I had given away Thalia. He couldn't blame me for taking him and I couldn't blame him for taking her.

"I just want you to know, you, Thalia, *gave* me something. I hadn't felt excited like that since I wrote *Adopting Alice.* It's like you were Alice coming back to me, or my past, my youth, my inspiration . . . something."

Now I had to be my own something, I thought. I could be my own Paul Revere.

"If I was your inspiration shouldn't I have gotten some of the back end?"

"Muses aren't what they used to be. You didn't see the muses in Ovid asking for a cut or a producing credit and running around suing everybody. It's almost not worth having one anymore. You *gave* me the elephants, I have it in writing, so don't try to be a little Indian giver now. Did you see it? How'd you like that opening shot?" The rain started lightly again, and his glasses fogged. "You know, I read your novel. *The Hard Part*—catchy title. I thought it was pretty good. You might have tried it in the third person."

"I liked it in the first person," I said.

"When are you going to write another one?"

"I did," I said. "But you wrote it first. It's dead in the water." I grabbed for my manuscript, like a stowaway, and sort of flung it at him, its rubber bands barely containing it.

"Can I read it?" he said, putting it on the seat next to him and giving it a little pat. It was like a baby had floated up next to us in a Moses basket and he had gathered it up in his arms. The gesture was so tender that it took me completely by surprise, and a sound came out of me, a cry from deep in the back of my throat. I felt like I was drowning, like my chest was filled with sloshing canal water. I doubled over in shaking pitiful sobs. The tears just kept coming, splashing somewhere behind my sternum and spilling out of me. I couldn't stop.

"Jesus, Rebekah, can you cool it?"

"I'm sorry," I sobbed.

He stood very shakily and moved tentatively with arms outspread to sit next to me on my bench. "I hate riding backwards," he said. "It's okay, it's okay. Jesus, sweetheart. Try to take deep breaths." He took a deep breath to demonstrate and then started coughing. "No, don't breathe. There's hundreds of years of mold in this town, one deep breath can kill you." He patted my back tenderly through the wet green plastic and then took my chin in his hand and I opened my eyes and looked at him.

But it didn't feel real. It felt like one of my movie-theater dreams, the angle of my seat was all wrong, and while I knew I was looking at him, I somehow still longed to see him.

I stopped crying, as if the director had yelled cut, and we sat silently for a few minutes, poncho to poncho. I felt filled with fondness for him, like a child.

Then he looked down at my manuscript. "I really would love to read what you wrote," he said. "Is it double-spaced? My eyes aren't what they used to be."

If Arthur Weeman read my book, maybe that was enough, I thought. "You have to get started on another one, right away. I'd love to talk to you about it." He looked so sincere as he said it, like the young Arthur Weeman had in his earliest films. In the moonlight his wrinkles were gone and I hadn't seen him like this in years, vital and happy. I knew that in the end I was supposed to realize that I didn't need Arthur Weeman anymore, and maybe it was true. Maybe I didn't need him, but I still loved him. "What's wrong?" he asked, when I looked away from him.

"I have to say I'm a little disappointed."

He looked hurt. "It's always disappointing when you meet someone you've admired."

"No, not that. I thought Thalia had really gotten you."

"She did. That's why I had her looked into. I have had other little stalkers, you know. But of all of them, Thalia was the one who got me."

The gondola nosed up to the dock and the gondolier pulled us in with his oar.

"We'd like to go around again," Arthur said.

"I'm sorry Signor Wee-a-man, no."

Arthur pulled out his wallet and offered a roll of euros.

"No, Signore. I have a new baby and my wife would, how you say, kill me."

"Jesus, no one in Italy ever wants to make any money. Fine, we'll walk. Is that okay with you?"

I shrugged. "One if by land, two if by sea," I said.

"Well put. Either way, during the film festival, the streets and canals are filled with rats. And then there's also the rodents. I hate getting out of these things." Practically crawling on his hands and knees, he slowly and carefully disembarked and took a long time to get his land legs back.

"So, let's talk about your comeback," he said. He cocked his head toward the bridge. "Shall we?"

We put up our hoods and started off.

"Maybe my next novel should take place in Venice," I said.

"Big mistake. There is almost never any reason to have your characters leave New York."

"Maybe you should stick to the movies, and leave the novel writing to me."

We walked all over Venice, my manuscript, in its I LOVE NEW YORK shopping bag, swinging between us.

ABOUT THE AUTHOR

Jennifer Belle is the author of *Going Down,* for which *Entertainment Weekly* named her best debut novelist of the year; *High Maintenance,* a national bestseller; and *Animal Stackers,* a picture book for children. Her stories and essays have appeared in *The New York Times Magazine, The New York Observer, The Independent Magazine* (London), *Harper's Bazaar, Ms., BlackBook, Mudfish,* and many anthologies. She lives in New York City with her husband, Andrew Krents, and their son, Jasper.

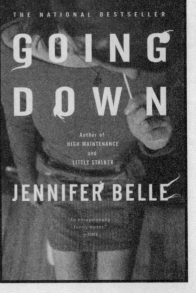